GN00838548

Jennifer Fallon is the author of many bestselling books published in Australia, the US, the UK, and foreign language editions. She has been shortlisted for the Aurealis Awards and the World Fantasy Awards; in the US for the Romantic Times Epic Fantasy Awards and in the UK for the David Gemmell Legend Awards.

Jennifer is a qualified trainer and business consultant with 20 years experience in designing and delivering training courses ranging from basic computer training to advanced project management.

Having lived in the Australian outback for many years, Jennifer recently moved to New Zealand.

To find out more about Jennifer Fallon, her books and her writing, visit her website:
jenniferfallon.com

For all the latest news, visit:
voyagerblog.com.au

Books by Jennifer Fallon

DEMON CHILD TRILOGY
Medalon (1)
Treason Keep (2)
Harshini (3)

SECOND SONS TRILOGY
The Lion of Senet (1)
Eye of the Labyrinth (2)
Lord of the Shadows (3)

THE HYTHRUN CHRONICLES
Wolfblade (1)
Warrior (2)
Warlord (3)

THE TIDE LORDS
The Immortal Prince (1)
The Gods of Amyrantha (2)
The Palace of Impossible Dreams (3)
The Chaos Crystal (4)

THE RIFT RUNNERS
The Undivided (1)

JENNIFER FALLON

THE UNDIVIDED

RIFT RUNNERS
BOOK ONE

HARPER
Voyager

Harper*Voyager*

An imprint of HarperCollins*Publishers*

First published in Australia in 2011
This edition published in 2012
by HarperCollins*Publishers* Australia Pty Limited
ABN 36 009 913 517
harpercollins.com.au

HarperCollins*Publishers*

Level 13, 201 Elizabeth Street, Sydney NSW 2000, Australia
31 View Road, Glenfield, Auckland 0627, New Zealand
A 53, Sector 57, Noida, UP, India
77–85 Fulham Palace Road, London, W6 8JB, United Kingdom
2 Bloor Street East, 20th floor, Toronto, Ontario M4W 1A8, Canada
10 East 53rd Street, New York NY 10022, USA

ISBN 978 0 7322 9087 0 (pbk.)

Cover design by Darren Holt, HarperCollins Design Studio
Cover images by shutterstock.com
Author photograph by Infocus Pty Ltd
Typeset in 10/12pt Sabon by Kirby Jones
Printed and bound in Australia by Griffin Press
50gsm Bulky News used by HarperCollins*Publishers* is a natural,
recyclable product made from wood grown in sustainable forests. The
manufacturing processes conform to the environmental regulations in
the country of origin, New Zealand.

5 4 3 2 1   12 13 14 15

"FOR THE FAVOURITE"

AUTHOR'S NOTE

There are some real places in this story (obviously), including the Castle Golf Club in Dublin. While I'm sure they'll forgive me for carving up their fairways with an imaginary car chase, the stone circle hidden in the rough on the ninth hole does not exist (that I know of), nor does St Christopher's Visual Rehabilitation Centre, something you might have figured out if you realised why I called it St Christopher's.

If my Gaelic is correct, then it is thanks to the awesome talents and advice of the lovely Josephine Walsh. If it's wrong, it's my fault. Thanks also to Gillian Pollack for her advice regarding Druids, bards and ancient Celtic locations, as well as to Lyn Tranter, Mark Timmony, Sharyn Lilley and my daughter TJ, for their incisive advice and proofreading.

As for the Druids and the *Tuatha Dé Danann*, I don't doubt for a moment there are many readers out there who are preparing to email me as we speak, telling me how wrong I got them. Please don't. This is a story of alternate realities and, more importantly, a story about how things are distorted over time. Of course, things have changed over the past 2000 years. Even in a reality where the people cling desperately to the status quo, the very act of clinging will force changes on them they could not anticipate.

If, however, you actually know a genuine member of the *Tuatha Dé Danann*, by all means drop me a line. I'd truly love to meet them.

Jennifer Fallon
Oxford, New Zealand 2010

THE
UNDIVIDED

PROLOGUE

It shouldn't be so easy to take a life.

The assassin pondered that thought as he approached the cradle rocking gently in the centre of the warm, candle-lit chamber. Their mother would have set the cradle in motion to soothe the twins before she left the room, trusting their visitor so profoundly that it would never occur to her the children might be in danger.

He reached the cradle and stopped to study it for a moment. The oak crib was carved with elaborate Celtic knot-work, inlaid with softly glowing mother-of-pearl brought up from the very depths of the ocean by the magical Walrus People, the *marra-warra*. It had been a gift from Queen Orlagh, centuries ago, and had rocked generations of twins to sleep since then.

Generations that would end now. Tonight. By his hand.

He glanced down at the blade he carried. The *airgead sídhe* caught the candlelight in odd places, illuminating the engraving on the blade. He hefted the razor-sharp weapon in his hand. Faerie silver was useless in battle, but for this task, nothing else would suffice.

Warmed by the fire crackling in the fire pit in the centre of the large round chamber, the twins slept peacefully, curled together like soft, precious petals, the left one sucking her thumb, the other making soft suckling motions with her mouth, unconsciously mirroring her sister. The girls were sated and content, blissfully ignorant of their approaching death. Even if they had been awake, it was unlikely they would recognise the danger that hovered over them. The man wielding the blade above their cradle — the man who had come to take their lives — was a friend, a dependable presence they trusted to keep them safe.

'You can't seriously mean to do this.'

He glanced over his shoulder. A figure stood in the shadows by the door, a presence that was both alien and familiar. A presence so like himself it may have been nothing more than a corporeal manifestation of his own conscience.

'It has to be done. You know that.'

The figure by the door shook his head and took a step further into the room. The assassin found himself staring at a mirror image of himself, except the face of his reflection was filled with doubt and anguish, while his own was calm and resigned to what must be done.

'They are innocent,' the anguished manifestation of his guilt announced.

'They are our death.'

'If preventing our death requires the death of innocent children, then perhaps we deserve to die.'

The assassin didn't answer, turning back to stare down at the twin girls he had come to murder. It wasn't *who* they were, but *what*, that made their deaths so necessary.

Why am I the only one who sees that clearly?

His conscience took another step closer. 'I won't let you do it.'

'How will you stop me?' he asked as he raised the blade. One of the girls was stirring — they were too alike to tell which was which. She opened her eyes to smile up at him, her face framed by soft dark curls. Her sister remained asleep, still peacefully sucking her thumb.

Which will be harder? he wondered idly. *Killing the one who is asleep and ignorant of her fate, or the one staring up at me with that sleepy, contented smile?*

'I'll kill *you* if I have to, to stop this.'

The assassin smiled down at the twins, dismissing the empty threat. 'Even if you could get across this room before the deed is done, you can't kill me without killing yourself, which would achieve precisely what I am here to prevent.'

He moved the blade a little, repositioning his grip. The candlelight danced across its engraved surface, mesmerising the baby. He was happy to entertain her with the pretty lights for a few moments. His mission was to kill her and her sister, after all, not to make her suffer.

There was a drawn-out silence as he played the light across the blade. Behind him, the presence that was both his conscience and his other half remained motionless. There was no point in his trying to attack. They were two sides of the same coin. Neither man could so much as form the intent to attack without the other knowing about it.

The girls would be dead before anybody could reach the cradle to stop him.

'There must be another way.' There was a note of defeat in the statement, a glimmer of acceptance.

'I wouldn't be here if there was,' the assassin replied, still staring down at the baby he had come to kill. 'You know that,' he added, glancing over his shoulder. 'You're just not willing to accept the truth of it.'

The other man held out his hand, as if he expected the blade to be handed over, and for this night to be somehow forgotten. Put behind them like a foolish disagreement they'd been wise enough to settle like men. 'They're just babies ...'

'They are our death and the death of much more besides.'

'But they're innocents ...'

The assassin shook his head. 'Only because they lack the capacity yet to act on what they were bred to manifest. Once they are grown ...'

'Dammit ... they're your own flesh and blood!'

The assassin gripped the blade tighter and turned back to the cradle, steeling his resolve with a conscious act of will. It didn't matter who they were. It's *what* they were. That was the important thing.

It was the reason they had to die.

'They are abominations, bred to cause chaos and strife.'

'What we've seen in other realms may not come to pass.'

'Of course it will,' he said, growing impatient with an argument he considered long resolved. He reached into the cradle with his left hand to pull back the furs covering the children. The twin who was awake grabbed his finger. Her blue eyes smiling, she squeezed it gently. Behind him, his other half watched, too appalled to allow this, too afraid to stop it.

'Help me, or leave,' the assassin said, feeling the accusing eyes of his companion boring into his back. 'Just don't stand there feigning disgust, as if you had no part in bringing us to this pass.'

His nemesis wasn't ready to give up just yet. 'Perhaps what we've seen won't happen here ...'

'I'm not prepared to take that risk.'

'But you're prepared to have the blood of innocents on your hands?'

'Better the blood of two children than the blood of the thousands who don't deserve to die.' The assassin was still a little amazed he felt so calm. It was as if all the anguish, all the guilt, all the fear and remorse, all the normal human emotions a man should be battling at a time like this were a burden carried by someone else, leaving him free to act, unhindered by doubt.

If that wasn't a sign of the rightness of this deed, he couldn't think of anything else that might be.

He extracted his finger from the soft, determined grip of the baby girl, her skin so supple and warm, her gaze so trusting and serene it was heartbreaking.

But not heartbreaking enough to stay his hand. He raised the blade, transfixed by the guileless blue eyes staring up at him. And then he brought it down sharply, slicing through the swaddling and her fragile ribs into her tiny heart without remorse or regret.

He was quick and, he hoped, merciful, but the link between the sisters was quicker.

Before he could extract the blade from one tiny heart and plunge it into another, her twin sister jerked with pain and began to scream.

PART ONE

CHAPTER 1

'If we had to take our clothes off, couldn't we have done this indoors?'

Brydie glanced down around the circle of her sisters, cousins and friends, wondering who was brave enough to voice such a sacrilegious thought aloud. It might have been Anwen. Since her betrothal to the queen's only son, Torcán, last *Imbolc*, she'd become full of her own opinions, and with the security of her position of a soon-to-be princess, wasn't afraid of sharing them. Not that Brydie disagreed with her distant cousin, shivering as she stepped out of her shift, leaving it in a puddle of pale linen on the grass behind her, but she would never have dared to say so.

Hugging her arms across her naked body against the chill, Brydie glanced up at the sun, barely visible through the trees. The sun lacked warmth, and what little there was the tall trees stole with their shadows. She shivered again and turned to her companions, noting with concern that the queen seemed to have only called the unmarried women of her court to this gathering in the sacred grove. Looking around at the dozen or so girls undressing around her, Brydie wondered what it meant. Was there a treaty to be sealed with a wedding?

More importantly, would the bride be ordered to the altar by her queen or permitted to volunteer?

Brydie chewed her bottom lip with concern. Queen Álmhath had been talking with quite a few border lords of late, even a couple from across *Muir Éireann*. The man visiting from Albion wasn't anything to boast about, but he seemed a decent enough fellow, the few times Brydie was called to wait on his table these past few weeks. The other man, the Gaul … he was a pig. Brydie fervently hoped if this gathering had been called to select a treaty bride, it wasn't because the queen of the Celts wanted something out of the Gauls.

'Don't slouch!'

Brydie straightened her shoulders, dropped her arms and lifted her chin, despite the bitter wind. One didn't defy Lady Malvina unless one was feeling particularly in need of trouble.

The Druidess stopped beside Brydie but, fortunately, she fixed her attention on the girl beside her. Ethna was a year older than Brydie, but much thinner, her long brown hair tied back in a tight braid. At least Brydie had thought to let her own hair down as she undressed, figuring she might glean a little warmth from the thickness of it. Poor Ethna seemed to be feeling the cold a great deal more than the other girls, and a thin line of blood was trickling down her inner thigh. It was her *mìosach* time. Brydie felt sorry for Ethna and was relieved hers had finished a couple of weeks ago. Poor girl. Brydie might be teased constantly by the men of Álmhath's court about her child-bearing hips, but at least she didn't look as if she was going to snap in the first strong breeze like her companion did. The unfortunate girl was turning blue.

'By *Danú*,' the old Druidess sighed, shaking her head. 'You're a sorry specimen, Ethna Ni'Connell. Did your father never feed you at home?'

Ethna's eyes began to well with unshed tears. Brydie wasn't sure if that was because she was upset or just cold. Her pale, freckled skin was prickled with gooseflesh, and her teeth were actually chattering.

'I ... I ...'

'It's not her fault, *an Bhantiarna*,' Brydie said, taking pity on the girl. They weren't exactly friends, but nobody deserved Malvina's heartless scorn for such an insignificant thing as not having enough meat on their bones. 'Ethna's just naturally thin.'

Malvina turned her pale, watery eyes on Brydie, eyeing her up and down like a farmer calculating the net worth of a freshly slaughtered carcass. 'And what's your excuse for the way you stand there, Brydie Ni'Seanan? You're just naturally built for sin, are you?'

A few of the other girls sniggered. Brydie refused to react to the taunt. It was a tired one, coined a few months ago by some *Ráith* lord, who'd drunkenly tried to petition the queen for a night with her, in honour of *Imbolc*. The queen had refused, of course, loudly telling the lord — and the other three hundred or so inebriated guests in her hall — that her court maidens weren't put on this Earth by the goddess to sate the drunken lust of a man with ten children, and he'd be better served going home to his own wife to make number eleven.

It had all been a bit of good-natured fun, until then. Anwen and Torcán had just announced their betrothal, spirits were high, everyone was drunk and it was part of the sport to try coaxing a court maiden into your bed. It was just as much a part of the fun of being a court maiden to avoid a tryst until the queen gave her permission, and even Álmhath had laughed while she delivered her rebuke. As Brydie walked away from the table, however, the lord had called out to the queen in a plaintive voice that reached every corner of the hall. 'Really? Not even a kiss, my lady? But look at her! She's built for naught *but* sin!'

That had set the revellers rolling in the aisles and Brydie had not been able to shake the description ever since.

Failing to get a rise out of Brydie, Malvina moved on. Ethna smiled timorously at Brydie as the Druidess moved around the circle. 'Thanks, but you didn't have to say anything. It's not that cold.'

'You look like a freshly hooked fish, Ethna,' Brydie said, smiling.

Ethna rubbed her arms for a moment and glanced toward the entrance to the grove. There was no sign of the queen yet. 'Do you think Álmhath is looking for a treaty bride?'

'Probably.'

'Will you stand forth?'

Brydie shook her head. 'With my luck she's done a deal with that Gaulish pig, and he'd beat me every day, feed me nothing but snails and expect me to bear him ten sons who all have manners just as bad as his.'

'I'd go if I was asked,' Ethna said, lowering her voice. 'I'm sick of this place. Sick of Temair.'

She glanced down the line at Malvina's back. The Druidess had stopped to chastise another girl for taking too long to get undressed. 'Sick of the Druids.'

'Then I hope for your sake Álmhath asks for volunteers,' Brydie said. 'You can be sure I won't be fighting you for a seat on any boat crossing *Muir Éireann.*'

They fell silent after that, each girl wrapped in her own thoughts while they waited for the queen, all of them thinking much the same as she and Ethna were thinking, Brydie supposed. Álmhath needed a bride to seal a treaty and, as was the custom, the bride would come from among her court maidens. She cast a furtive glance across the circle at Anwen, wondering what she was doing here. With her betrothal to Torcán, she should be off the market. Had she angered the queen in some way? Had Torcán wearied of her already?

'Kneel for your queen!'

Each of the twelve girls knelt on one knee as Álmhath swept into the grove, wearing a long white cloak. A handsome woman in late middle age, she had an air of timelessness about her that Brydie envied. She hoped she would be as commanding some day.

'You have been called to discharge your sacred duty,' the queen announced with no preamble, as she pushed back the hood of her robe to reveal her thick, braided auburn hair, flecked with more and more silver each year. 'As daughters of *Danú*, you are honoured to do her work, and there is no greater honour than to bring forth the next generation. We are women, blessed by *Danú* with the means to nurture our race and ensure its continuation. As court maidens, you are further

13

blessed with the means to keep our borders safe. To that end, I will be selecting two of you …'

Brydie bit her lip. The queen had said 'selecting'. There was no chance of avoiding a marriage now, if she was one of the chosen.

It wasn't that Brydie was averse to the idea of an arranged marriage, in principle. She just didn't like what was on offer. Brydie wasn't naïve enough to believe in dashing princes and happy-ever-afters, the way the bards went on and on when they told their romances. She clung to the hope, however, that the accident of birth that gave her enough noble blood to secure her place as a court maiden also meant she'd eventually marry someone with a modicum of good manners, at the very least.

'… to take up this blessed duty for your queen, your country and your race. Rise now, so that *Danú* and I may see you as you truly are.'

All of the girls stood a little taller as the queen approached them. Unlike Malvina, Álmhath seemed aware it was cold and knew the girls must be suffering. She made her rounds quickly, examining each girl critically for a moment, asking her when her most recent *mìosach* had finished, before smiling at them briefly and moving on. Every girl got the same attention and the same brief smile, unless like Ethna, there was clear evidence of their menstrual cycle, and the queen had no need to ask. It was impossible to tell what the queen was thinking. Malvina stood at the entrance to the grove, as if to block any girl foolish enough to attempt an escape.

Finally, the queen finished her circle and turned to face them. 'Those blessed by *Danú* this day are Ethna and Morann.'

Beside her, Ethna let out a little squeak of glee. Sighing with relief, Brydie hoped the young woman still felt that way after six months in a Gaulish court. Whatever plans the queen was making, apparently they didn't involve her. Perhaps she'd chosen girls with clear evidence of their fertility, which would make sense if the queen of the Celts was promising these border lords fine healthy sons out of their new brides. Brydie waited, head down, for the queen to leave the grove so she and the others could get dressed and out of this persistent, bitter wind, relieved her cycle had apparently excluded her.

'Brydie Ni'Seanan?'

'*An Bhantiarna*.' She dropped to one knee, her heart in her mouth. *What have I done now?*

'Come with me,' the queen commanded. '*Danú* has work for you, too, my dear.'

CHAPTER 2

'You're wounded, *Leath tiarna*.'

Darragh pulled his linen shirt down over his head, covering the fresh cut on his left side.

'It's nothing. Just a scratch. Alessandro got the better of me.'

Colmán nodded, frowning, but asked for no further details. Darragh was counting on that. After all, he regularly practised swordcraft with the *Ráith's* Roman swordmaster, Alessandro, down in the yards. The true reason for his injury was something he intended to share with no one — a good thing too, as his experiment had apparently achieved nothing more than a nasty slice across his ribs.

'You probably should have healed it magically as soon as it occurred,' the Vate scolded, 'rather than risk an infection that might take you from us.'

'I'm lucky like that, Colmán,' Darragh told the Vate with a shrug, as he tucked the linen shirt into his leather trousers and then pulled his hair out from under the collar, so he could tie it back with a strip of leather. 'I rarely suffer infection.' He was glad that was all Colmán was asking. It had not occurred to the Vate — thank *Danú* — to question why it was he was training with Alessandro and not his Druid bodyguard and mentor, Ciarán. It would be difficult and awkward to explain away Ciarán's absence. And how Alessandro had managed to wound him using a blade forged from *airgead sídhe* when they should have been practicing with wooden blades, or blunted iron at the very least.

Nor had he asked why Darragh hadn't healed the cut even now. That was also a relief, because his reason was one he didn't want to share with anybody. It sounded too insane if he said it aloud.

'*Danú* smiles upon thee, *Leath tiarna*,' the Vate agreed with a low bow. 'We should offer her our gratitude.' He closed his eyes for a moment, clasping his hands in the deep sleeves of his robe. '*Danú* smiles upon Darragh of the Undivided,' he intoned, committing the statement to memory.

Unable to read Latin or any other written language, but able to recall the entire oral history of the Undivided at will, Colmán took his job as court bard and chief custodian of Druid history very seriously. Colmán was a stickler for detail, too. Darragh sometimes feared he might start chronicling what he ate for breakfast each morning, believing such minutiae should be preserved for posterity. Unfortunately, Colmán had a habit of composing his epics as events unfolded around him, rather than waiting until he had the whole story, as Amergin had. The old Vate always found a way to make his chronicles interesting, leaving audiences hanging off his every word, fighting for space at the table when news got about that he was ready to relate another tale.

Darragh finished tying back his hair and studied the new Vate. The Vate opened his eyes and was looking at Darragh expectantly. In the flickering candlelight of his large underground bedchamber, it wasn't easy to tell if the old man was waiting for him to do something worthy of being chronicled, or was simply there to act as an advisor. His role as Vate required him to be both.

Not that Darragh trusted Colmán's advice.

After Amergin's betrayal it was hard to trust anybody.

Even with the ability to see glimpses of the future, Darragh was still not certain his new Vate was really on his side. Not that his gift of prescience was much of a gift, he often mused. His dreams had given him no warning of Amergin's betrayal. These days his dreams focussed on future events involving his long-lost brother — a mixed blessing, given they indicated he would eventually find Rónán — but that they would fall out over the fate of another set of twins Darragh had never been able to identify.

Darragh missed Amergin. The old Druid might have been able to shed some light on his disturbing visions of the future. Odd that he felt that way, given how comprehensively his most trusted advisor had betrayed him, but he was still a lot more fun to be around than Amergin's dour, overly formal replacement. In his whole life, Amergin had not called Darragh '*Leath tiarna*' more than a handful of times. Colmán managed to work it into every other sentence.

'I'm sure the goddess appreciates your devotion, Vate,' Darragh told him, bracing himself for the coming day. He glanced around the stone-walled underground chamber and realised with some relief that it wasn't the one in his dream. Last night had been the clearest vision yet. The chamber of his dreams might not even be in the vast network of Druid halls here in *Sí an Bhrú*. 'Are they on their way yet?'

'The lookouts have not reported any sightings, *Leath tiarna*.'

'That might be because they don't *want* us to see them, Colmán.'

'Aye, *Leath tiarna*,' the Vate agreed, nodding his balding head as he stroked the greased ends of his grey-flecked, forked beard. To Darragh's immense relief, the fashion these days among younger men was to remain clean-shaven. But Colmán was old-fashioned. He didn't just *dislike* change. He actively discouraged it, believing even minor alterations to the way they lived were a direct path to the loss of all their magic. 'The deceitfulness of the *Tuatha* knows no bounds.'

'Probably not wise to mention that while we're dining with them,' Darragh pointed out with a wry smile. It wasn't that he disagreed with the Vate. The *Daoine sídhe* were notoriously untrustworthy and nobody knew that better than Darragh. It was Colmán's intense, implacable hatred of the Faerie that amazed Darragh. Or rather, his suspicion that this most recent Vate of All Eire had been chosen for that quality alone.

There would be no epic poems composed by this bard, repeated with reverence and awe by future generations. No songs, no plays, no grand tales of derring-do. Colmán was unsmiling, unlikable and uninspiring.

But Colmán would never — as Amergin had — allow himself to be seduced by the *Daoine sídhe*.

The Druids had learnt their lesson. There would be no more talk of closer ties with the *Tuatha Dé Danann*. No Vate would ever again stand at his right hand with a *leanan sídhe* for a wife. The music, the songs, the epics and the laughter that came with a bard magically inspired by his Faerie muse were gone from *Sí an Bhrú* and the place felt poorer for it.

On the other hand, there was a chance that someday soon — assuming today's meeting wasn't a plan to unseat him — for the first time in fifteen years, the Undivided might be reunited. Darragh forced that thought away. It was too easy to get excited at the prospect, which more than likely would end in nothing but bitter disappointment once more. The chance of finding one soul among hundreds of millions in an unfamiliar reality ... well, Darragh was many things, but a foolish optimist wasn't one of them.

Guilt and impending death had forced the confession from Amergin about the fate of Darragh's brother. His life force finally drained by his *leanan sídhe* wife, Amergin had gasped the belated admission of his role in Rónán's disappearance with his very last breath.

The revelation had shaken the Druids to their core. Even Darragh — with months to get used to the idea — still wasn't sure how he was supposed to deal with the news that the man he'd considered both a father and a friend — a man he'd trusted with his very life — was the one responsible for taking half of it away.

Amergin's co-conspirator was on his way here now. Marcroy Tarth. The most seductive, the most deceitful of all the *Daoine sídhe*. Darragh knew it was going to be hard to keep a level head. Hard to listen to Marcroy's silver-tongued flattery and not accuse the *sídhe* to his face of being a lying, cheating ghoul with no interest in anything but his own amusement.

Even harder not to ask for news of Trása.

Darragh had tried looking into the future a number of times since they'd sent Trása away, to see if there was any sign of her, but his dreams of her were blurred and unsettled, never stopping long enough for him to form a clear picture of her destiny. Whatever the future held for Trása Ni'Amergin, it was not fixed. That gave Darragh cause for hope. And sometimes despair.

'Did the *Tuatha* indicate how many of them we should expect?' Darragh asked, as he fell into step with Colmán. They headed into the torch-lit passage leading to the cross-shaped chamber where the Undivided usually held court.

Built several thousand years earlier, *Sí an Bhrú* was originally intended as a place to prepare the *Tuatha* dead for their journey to the underworld. The rise of the Druids and the need for a secure home for the Undivided had caused the kidney-shaped stone fort, which covered more than an acre of the rich farmland of the Boyne Valley, to be turned into a thriving community of Druids, bards, magicians, and their families. They'd occupied the site since Boadicea ruled the Celts in Britain, extending it and repairing the quartz-covered exterior walls, so it looked today exactly as it had 3500 years ago, when it was first constructed.

As they left the long passage carved with the tri-spiral triskalion similar to the one magically tattooed on Darragh's right hand, they entered a large round chamber with a steeply corbelled roof rising to an opening some twenty feet above them, which served as a chimney and provided the only source of natural light. Around the walls recesses containing large stone basins — once meant to hold the cremated remains of those being laid to rest — blazed with fires kept burning to provide both light and heat. The hall was filled with servants setting up tables for the evening's feast and the enticing aroma of roasting meat. Darragh's stomach rumbled, reminding him he hadn't broken his fast yet this morning.

'The *sídhe* gave no indication of the size of their party, *Leath tiarna*,' Colmán said. He looked at Darragh anxiously. 'They simply asked to meet with you and Queen Álmhath. Did you hope to limit their numbers for some purpose?'

'Not really,' Darragh said with a shrug, thinking it would pay to eat something before the cooks became so engrossed in the preparations for tonight's feast they forgot to see to any other meals for the residents of *Sí an Bhrú*. 'I just wouldn't put it past Marcroy Tarth to turn up with the entire *Daoine sídhe* host so he can pretend to be wounded by our inhospitable rudeness when we can't accommodate them all.'

'He'd not dare!'

'He'd dare it … and before you know it, we'd find ourselves in his debt for not smiting us where we stand for breaking some long-forgotten clause in the Treaty of *Tír Na nÓg*.'

Colmán looked alarmed, not aware, apparently, that Darragh wasn't serious.

'I shall have the lookouts report on their numbers as soon as the *Daoine sídhe* are in sight,

Leath tiarna, so we may make the appropriate preparations.'

Darragh nodded, thinking Amergin would have known he was joking. And he'd have issued such an order without being asked, too. Just in case.

'Is there anything else I should know before our guests arrive?' Darragh asked, as he glanced around the hall. Like the rest of *Sí an Bhrú*, the stone walls were carved and painted with brightly coloured emblems depicting the Druid castes — the scales of the *Brithem*, the sword of the Warriors, the herbal wreath of the *Deoghbaire* and *Liaig* among the most colourful, and the tri-spiral of the Undivided. Dried flowers and herbs festooned the ceiling corbels, sweetening the air by combating the lingering smell of smoke from the peat fires that warmed the hall in the stone recesses. Wooden tables were being laid out for the occasion, with additional benches brought in to accommodate the expected influx of guests. A special head table had been set up on a raised dais at the far side of the hall, overseeing the rest of the tables, for Darragh and Marcroy, Álmhath, and her son Prince Torcán and his betrothed, Anwen, Colmán, whatever escort Marcroy chose to accompany him, and an empty seat, as always, for Darragh's missing brother, Rónán.

'I wish to renew my objection to this meeting, *Leath tiarna*.' Colmán's whole stance reeked of disapproval. 'Particularly with Ciarán away.'

That made Darragh smile. 'You think they're going to try and murder me over dinner?'

Colmán tugged on his beard again, a sure sign he was worried. 'I'm just saying, *Leath tiarna*, no good will come of letting those unnatural creatures believe they are entitled to be treated like men.'

23

'Not a lot of good has come of treating them any other way,' Darragh pointed out. 'And you must admit that, without them, the Druids would have faded into oblivion a thousand years ago.' Darragh wasn't trying to pick an argument with his Vate. He had no radical reformist agenda, and certainly no time nor sympathy for the growing Partitionist movement who didn't understand the role of the Undivided in maintaining the Druids' magic and wanted the rule of the Undivided — and him along with it — brought down. But there was a certain amount of amusement to be had watching Colmán's face turn purple as he contemplated the idea that Darragh might actually be entertaining a modicum of compassion for the Faerie race. 'Do we know when our beloved queen and her not-so-beloved son will arrive?'

Colmán shook his head. 'We've received no word from her majesty either, *Leath tiarna.*'

'The respect for our order is overwhelming,' Darragh remarked. 'Did the queen of the Celts even bother to let us know if she is planning to attend this summit?'

'She sent a message saying she would try, *Leath tiarna.*'

She'll try. Darragh shook his head. There was a time when the mere prospect of meeting with the Undivided struck fear into the hearts of rulers across the length and breadth of the land. Across the whole world, even. And into the Otherworld, besides. There was a time when oriental emperors, Egyptian pharaohs, Roman consuls and Indian maharajas made the long trek to these emerald shores to pay their respects.

No longer. Not since the Undivided were,

well ... divided. These days, despite the lip service they paid to his rank, Darragh was painfully aware the leaders who once deferred to his position now considered him weak and powerless.

He was Darragh the Divided. They thought him an annoying young man whom tradition forced them to acknowledge, but one increasingly easy to ignore.

They thought of him as nothing but an ineffectual figurehead at the mercy of men like Amergin who — at the behest of a *leanan sídhe* whore — had betrayed his own people in return for his need to be immortalised as a poet.

That would change, of course, if the Undivided were ever reunited.

When we're reunited, Darragh corrected himself silently. Rónán was alive. Darragh knew that. He simply wouldn't be breathing if his brother wasn't — the psychic link between them was too strong to let a small thing like being separated by different realities get in the way.

But finding his twin in that other reality and bringing him home was an entirely different matter.

And something he didn't have time to dwell on now. Darragh closed his eyes for a moment, hoping to glimpse the reason the *Tuatha* had asked for this meeting, but the future was dim. He would just have to trust Ciarán, Brógán and Niamh. His disturbing dreams of infanticide notwithstanding — which came to him unbidden — when Darragh consciously tried to see the future, all he saw were boring, mundane things like snippets of the upcoming feast, even a glimpse of a servant accidentally spilling an amphora of apple wine on one of Álmhath's men-at-arms.

Nothing he could use. No idea what this meeting was about.

No comforting vision of Brógán or Niamh rushing into the hall to inform the entire gathering that Darragh's long-lost brother had been found …

Nothing but a minor fistfight, Marcroy's untrustworthy smile and Torcán's contemptuously curled lip as he sat beside his equally disdainful fiancée, Anwen, on the raised dais, looking down his nose at the other occupants of the Druid hall.

Darragh shook his head to clear the image, certain the last one hadn't been a vision so much as an educated guess that came from knowing the Celtic prince so well.

'Is something the matter, *Leath tiarna*?' Colmán asked anxiously, recognising Darragh's vague expression. 'Have you Seen something? Something we can use?'

'Álmhath will be here by sunset,' he told the Vate. 'And she's bringing Torcán with her.'

The Vate ventured a cautious smile. 'That should please you, *Leath tiarna*?'

'I'm thrilled,' Darragh murmured to himself, knowing if he said it any louder, he'd have to explain his sour tone to Colmán. Amergin would have understood. He had thought Torcán a royal pain, too.

Damn you, Amergin, for being so selfish …

'Pardon, *Leath tiarna*?'

'Nothing, Colmán,' Darragh sighed, wondering if he could escape *Sí an Bhrú* long enough to go for a ride alone to clear his head — and his Sight — before their guests arrived. Unlikely, he knew.

Colmán hated to let Darragh out of his sight for more than a few moments for fear the young man would do something worthy of being recorded for posterity. 'Just ... carry on ...'

'As you wish, *Leath tiarna*,' the Vate said, bowing low. And then he closed his eyes, crossed his hands in his sleeves once more and began to intone his next composition.

'Darragh, the Undivided, waits to meet the Queen of the Celts. *Sí an Bhrú* rings with the sound of many busy ... belts ...'

Darragh sighed. *Amergin, your greatest crime against the Druids wasn't betraying the Undivided*, he lamented silently, as he turned and headed for the long passage leading outside, unable to bear another word of Colmán's recital. *It was naming this fool as your successor ...*

CHAPTER 3

'How long have you been here at Temair now, Brydie?' the queen asked, slipping her arm through Brydie's as they walked back toward *Ráith Righ*. Even with the crisp breeze, it was much warmer out in the bright sunlight, walking the gravelled path that led up the hill toward the castle. The sky was glorious; a pale, cloudless blue canopy. The distant clashes and shouts of men-at-arms training over on the practice field reached them faintly, but the men were out of sight of the path they were taking back to the *Ráith*.

Malvina had hurried on ahead, probably to get ready for her departure later in the day. The whole *Ráith* was in an uproar as the queen prepared to leave, which made this morning's choosing in the sacred grove all the more unusual. These matters were rarely settled so hastily.

The queen's familiarity worried Brydie a little, too. Until that incident in the hall a few months ago, when she acquired the unwanted description of *built for sin*, Brydie had barely spoken ten words to Álmhath since she'd arrived from her father's court in the west. She'd thought she'd remained hidden and anonymous among the scores of court maidens at Temair, some married, some single, and most of them working — as Brydie was — as servants.

'Almost eight months,' she said, wondering why her length of time here was significant.

'Your mother was Mogue Ni'Farrell, was she not?'

'Yes, my lady.'

The queen nodded and smiled. 'I remember her. She too, was built for sin.'

Brydie was beginning to tire of this. 'My lady …'

Álmhath laughed softly and squeezed her arm tighter, cutting off her objection. 'Forgive me, my dear. I am teasing you. Your mother was an extraordinary beauty and a loyal sister. As are you.'

'Thank you, *an Bhantiarna*,' Brydie said, a little warily. Álmhath didn't hand out compliments like that on a whim.

'Do you remember her?' Álmhath asked, her tone softening a little.

'Not really,' Brydie said with a shrug. 'Just what my father has told me about her. I was very little when she died.'

'She was a great loss to us,' Álmhath said, smiling sympathetically. 'Her line was very precious.'

The comment intrigued Brydie. She'd never heard her father claim her mother had any special connection to the queen. 'Was she a court maiden, too?'

'A very special one.'

'Did you arrange her marriage to my father?'

'Of course.'

'Did you *make* her marry him, or did she volunteer?' Brydie had never been sure about that.

Her father spoke well enough of her dead mother whenever Brydie had asked about her, but he didn't seem too broken-hearted by her demise. And he'd replaced Mogue within a year of her death with a new wife, but that could have been practicality, rather than a sign of disregard for Brydie's mother.

The queen stopped walking and turned to look at Brydie, her eyes squinting a little as the rising sun was directly behind Brydie now. 'Do I detect a note of disapproval in your tone, young lady?'

'No, *an Bhantiarna*. Of course not.'

Álmhath raised one eyebrow as she studied Brydie curiously. 'Are you in love?'

'No,' Brydie replied, puzzled by the question. 'Why would you ask that?'

'Because, in my experience, court maidens only question the marriages I arrange for them when they've already gone and done the choosing for themselves.'

Brydie shook her head. 'I swear, *an Bhantiarna*, I have been true to my oath. I will do as you command. Happily. Provided ...' Her voice trailed off, as she realised she may have overstepped the mark.

The older woman smiled knowingly at her. 'I don't normally permit my court maidens to put qualifiers on their oaths, Brydie. I'm in the mood to indulge you, however. Provided *what*?'

Brydie hesitated, and then decided she might as well have her say now. The queen seemed in a remarkably congenial mood. It might be the only chance she was ever offered to have her opinion noted. 'Provided it's not that Gaulish brute you've been entertaining all month.'

Álmhath laughed. 'By *Danú*, as if I'd waste someone of your pedigree on a penniless pretender like Atilis. Rest easy, young Brydie, I have much bigger plans for the daughter of Mogue Ni'Farrell.'

Brydie wasn't sure that sounded any better. What did she mean by *bigger plans*?

Is that what she was talking about when she said Danú *had work for me?*

'Have you been to many formal banquets since you arrived?' Álmhath asked, before Brydie had a chance to inquire.

'I've served at most of them,' Brydie said, frowning. *That's what I get for being assigned to the low tables. The queen doesn't even know I was there.*

'I'm leaving this morning for a meeting at *Sí an Bhrú*,' the queen said, which was no news to Brydie. The meeting had been planned for days. The queen, her son, Torcán, and her large entourage were planning to leave as soon as they got back to the *Ráith*. 'There will be quite a feast in *Sí an Bhrú* tonight.'

Brydie nodded, not sure if the remark required her to respond.

'Have you ever been to *Sí an Bhrú*?'

'No, my lady,' she replied.

'You've never met the Undivided, then?'

Well, that would be a bit of a chore, Brydie was tempted to respond. *One of them is missing.* But she restrained herself and shook her head. 'No, my lady.'

'You've met Marcroy Tarth, though, haven't you?'

She nodded. 'Only recently, my lady. When the *Tuatha* visited last.' Just before riders headed out to *Sí an Bhrú* to arrange today's meeting. She remembered that visit well. Although she had no idea what it was about, the queen had been in a foul temper for days after the *sídhe* lord left Temair. Brydie didn't warm to Marcroy, thinking he looked far too young to be lord of the *Tuatha*. He certainly didn't look thousands of years old. With his fair, flawless skin, his far-too-pretty-to-be-masculine features and his delicately pointed ears, he looked like a youth in the first flush of manhood.

'Did Marcroy say anything to you?'

'He said I reminded him of his niece.'

Álmhath frowned. 'He has thousands of them. Did he say which one?'

'I believe I remind him of Trása.' Brydie remembered the name well because, even in the west, in the relative isolation of her family home on the coast far from court, they'd heard of the traitor Amergin's half-*Beansídhe* daughter.

That made the queen smile, which worried Brydie a great deal, because it was a sly, secretive little smile she had never before seen Álmhath display. 'Did he now? Isn't that interesting?'

'Is it? I thought it was an insult. She's a mongrel.'

'A very enticing mongrel,' the queen informed her, apparently amused by Brydie's indignation. 'Which is why we had her removed from *Sí an Bhrú*.'

'Oh ... I didn't know that.'

'No reason you should, dear.' The queen glanced around. They were still stopped on the path, standing in the open amid a field of emerald clover, kept close-cropped by the sheep herds belonging to the *Ráith*, far from the shadows of the earth abutments that circled the keep.

Brydie realised then why they were talking out here. Only in an open space such as this could Álmhath be certain there were no *Tuatha* spies about trying to listen in on their conversation. She glanced around, wondering what Álmhath feared the Faerie might overhear.

The queen turned back to study Brydie thoughtfully for a moment. 'Are you truly your mother's daughter, Brydie Ni'Seanan?'

'I'm not sure what you mean by that, *an Bhantiarna*,' Brydie said, certain it was a loaded question.

'If I ask you to do something, to make a sacrifice for me, for your people, would you do it?'

Brydie nodded. 'Of course ...'

'Provided it doesn't involve that Gaulish pig?' Álmhath asked, with a raised brow.

'Even if it involved that,' Brydie replied with a sigh, realising now that Álmhath wasn't being friendly, she'd been toying with her. 'I'm sorry, my lady. What you want of me, I will do. I'll marry whoever ... or *whatever* ... you tell me I must.'

Álmhath studied her closely for a moment, as if trying to determine her sincerity, and then nodded. 'Then return to your rooms and pack, my dear. You'll be coming to *Sí an Bhrú* with us. I'll explain what I want of you on the way.'

CHAPTER 4

With a final and eminently satisfying shake of his thick white fur, Marcroy Tarth relinquished his wolven form and changed back into a more human-like appearance as he topped the rise overlooking *Sí an Bhrú*.

The Faerie lord stared across the valley at the sprawling human settlement with mixed feelings. The huge stone complex sat atop an elongated ridge within a large bend in the Boyne River about five miles west of the town of Drogheda, bathed in the setting sun. It was a sacred place, defiled by humans as part of a deal that had gone horribly wrong. Now sheep grazed on its slopes, the trees surrounding it had been murdered for firewood, and smoke curled out of the roofs of the roundhouses clustered at the foot of the hill, and was quickly snatched away by the chilly breeze almost as soon as it escaped confinement.

Sí an Bhrú hadn't always belonged to the Druids. This place had been built by his people, the *Tuatha Dé Danann*. But that was long ago. Now the sacred halls were filled with drunken men-at-arms, talentless bards and sorcerers wielding stolen magic, who plotted and schemed the way humans do, uncaring of the long and hallowed history of the place they now called home.

'It must pain you to see *Sí an Bhrú* still occupied by men,' his companion remarked.

Marcroy turned to the djinni, scowling, as he materialised beside him in a wisp of blue flame that defied the wind by barely moving.

'It would pain me less if you didn't gloat about it, Jamaspa.'

The *Marid* shrugged as his upper body formed a human shape similar to Marcroy's, shimmering a little as he moved. 'If you recall, Marcroy Tarth, I advised against this foolish bargain. Am I not entitled to remind you, now and then, that you should have listened to me? To the Brethren? Had you heeded our advice, we would not be in the position we are in now.'

'You couldn't have known,' Marcroy pointed out, folding his arms across his body. He would have to wait here until the *Leipreachán* charged with bringing his clothes arrived. It would not do to arrive in *Sí an Bhrú* naked.

Jamaspa shrugged, wavering a little in the crisp, cool breeze. 'It should have been obvious, cousin,' he said. 'No matter how you justify the reason, you willingly gave humans access to your magic. You didn't expect them to relinquish it without a fight, did you?'

Marcroy scowled again, not wanting to get into an argument with the *Marid*, a djinni so old and powerful he made Orlagh look like a newling. He was tempted to point out that it had seemed an exceedingly reasonable proposition at the time. The *Tuatha* were under attack and the deal with the Druids had been contingent on finding a set of ludicrously rare psychically linked twins to channel Faerie magic to human sorcerers. There'd only been a handful of such twins ever found. It didn't seem a lingering threat. Who could have anticipated that the humans would keep finding such rare, gifted twins, again and again, for the next sixty generations?

'The harm is done, Jamaspa,' Marcroy said with a shrug. 'All we can do now is mitigate the damage.' Although he couldn't resist adding, 'Assuming your rift runners are not mistaken about the future that awaits us if we do nothing.'

The djinni shook his head, making his whole ephemeral body bob up and down in the air. 'They are not mistaken. The Undivided twins, RónánDarragh, will destroy us — *Tuatha*, Djinni and all the others of our kind. We have seen it in the other realities where they were allowed to rule united. For the sake of all the Faerie races of this realm, we must destroy them first.'

Marcroy wished he was able to voice such a definitive sentiment so readily, but he couldn't. The Treaty of *Tír Na nÓg* was inviolable. He was Faerie and so bound by Faerie law he could barely contemplate endangering the treaty his queen had made on behalf of the *Tuatha*, let alone breaking it. Yet the warning the Brethren had brought him all those years ago — the warning that had prompted him to subvert Amergin and sunder the Undivided — called to another, even more profound oath he was sworn to uphold. The protection of his people.

Marcroy had never before been so conflicted; never had to deal with two binding oaths so at odds with one another.

'I have rift runners combing the other reality,' he assured the djinni. 'They will ensure Rónán stays out of reach until the new Undivided are invested. Once that happens — once the power is transferred — Darragh will be dead and he'll take Rónán with him, wherever he may be. The threat will be gone.'

'But not this cursed treaty of yours.'

Marcroy shook his head. 'Unfortunately, no. The Treaty of *Tír Na nÓg* will remain intact. But then, it must. I have no choice in the matter.'

'Orlagh has much to answer for, binding us to that cursed treaty,' Jamaspa said, his form darkening with anger. 'She had no right to make such a promise. No right to swear a treaty that binds all Faerie into this absurdity. Would it not cause the breaking of the treaty, and the oath she took on our behalf, the Brethren would remove her themselves.'

Although Marcroy had always known of the resentment among the elders of the Faerie races over the arrangement the *Tuatha* queen had made to save her people, he'd never realised just how angry they were.

Perhaps he should warn his queen?

All in good time. After all, if anything happened to Orlagh, he would become king of the *Daoine sídhe*.

'How will they find him?'

'Pardon?' Marcroy had become lost, for a moment, in the enticing prospect of kingship.

'The realm Amergin sent the child to? It's populated by millions, I'm told.'

'Billions,' Marcroy corrected, although the concept was just as hard for him to grasp as it was

37

for Jamaspa. No full-blooded *Tuatha* or Djinni could travel to a world without magic. They were forced to rely on the reports of the half-human rift runners they sent in their stead, for news of what was happening in the other realms.

'How will they find him among billions?'

'I sent someone who knows Darragh by sight. She'll know Rónán when she finds him.'

'Who did you send?'

'My niece, Trása.'

Jamaspa smiled. 'Amergin's mongrel daughter?'

Marcroy nodded.

'You have a wonderful sense of irony, cousin.'

Before he could respond, Guinness McGee, the *Leipreachán* he'd arranged to manage his wardrobe for this all-important meeting in *Sí an Brú*, popped into existence a few feet below him, on the steep slope of the hill. With a squawk, the *Leipreachán* and the bundle of clothes tumbled backward for a short distance, until they came to a halt, tangled in the branches of a small shrub, several yards from where Marcroy and the djinni waited.

Guinness scrambled back up the slope toward them, struggling to keep his hat on, his pipe upright and the bundle off the ground, muttering to himself. Jamaspa shook his head, frowning, and turned to Marcroy. 'Your lesser *sídhe* make the *sílā* seem graceful and intelligent by comparison.'

Watching Guinness stumbling over his own feet as he tried to drag the bundle of Marcroy's precious clothing up the damp, grassy slope, Marcroy was tempted to agree, but he'd had enough of Jamaspa's smug superiority for one day. 'Do you think so, cousin?' he asked curiously. 'I've always considered a lesser *sídhe* who can be trained to fetch and carry, far more useful than one who prefers to inhabit rocks and trees with no other purpose than to leap out and kill things when the mood takes it.' He gave Jamaspa no chance to reply, turning to Guinness. 'You're late, McGee. I said sunset.'

'The sun not be set yet, me lord, so I be here, when and where ye asked me,' the *Leipreachán* exclaimed, looking wounded as he handed the bundle over to Marcroy. 'It not be me fault that ye big blue friend here threw me off course.'

'The bug speaks,' Jamaspa remarked, glaring down at the *Leipreachán*. 'Shall I squash it for you, cousin?'

'If you wish.'

Guinness squawked with fear and took a step backward, which sent him tumbling back down the hill. Marcroy smiled at the sight and then turned to Jamaspa, offering the jewelled brooch holding the bundle together, intended to secure his cloak once he was dressed. 'Here,' he said. 'I'll carry you in this.'

Jamaspa frowned. 'It's very small.'

Marcroy examined the gold filigree and amethyst brooch for a moment and then shrugged. 'I'm sorry, cousin, I assumed a *Marid* of your power could possess any item, no matter how small. A thousand pardons for overestimating your skill.'

The djinni couldn't ignore such a blatant challenge. He glared at Marcroy for a moment and then abruptly turned into a narrow plume of blue smoke, which quickly disappeared into the brooch, darkening the stone to a purple so deep it was almost black.

Marcroy held the brooch up in front of his face to address the jewel's occupant. 'I'll tell you when it's safe to come out, but it won't be until we've left *Sí an Bhrú*. The humans can have no hint of the presence of a djinni in their stronghold, and you know as well as I that, unrestrained, Darragh and probably more than a few Druid sorcerers in *Sí an Bhrú*, will feel your presence. Be patient, cousin.'

The jewel flared in acknowledgement of Marcroy's warning. Satisfied that he would be able to carry his djinni companion into the very heart of the Druid stronghold without them being any the wiser, Marcroy tossed it onto his cloak and began to get dressed. The sun was almost set. They would be waiting for him in the main hall, expecting him to arrive with a huge entourage. Appearing alone would confuse the Druids no end.

As he pulled the silk embroidered shirt over his head, he caught sight of a plume of dust on the road below, heading toward *Sí an Bhrú*.

So Álmhath has arrived, he thought, as he spied her canopied wagon in the centre of the line of armoured, pike-carrying riders. Her response to his news — and the reason for this meeting — had been enthusiastic, but forced. One would think, given she had been living in the shadow of the splintered Undivided for so long, his news would have pleased her. And after she recovered from her initial shock, she seemed keen enough to call this meeting and set the wheels of change in motion. But she wasn't. And that puzzled Marcroy.

Still, it didn't really matter now. The trap was closing. Very soon, the Undivided would be replaced with twins far less dangerous than the divided RónánDarragh. The treaty would remain intact. The fate the Brethren had seen in other realms would not befall them here in this one.

All it needed now was a little time, and for Marcroy's half-human niece, Trása, to prove worthy of his trust by ensuring Rónán of the Undivided never found his way home to this realm.

CHAPTER 5

The only thing that made losing one's magic bearable, Trása thought, as she picked up the remote control, was television. Even after six months in this strange realm with its huge cities, its countless people and its incomprehensible array of gadgets for every purpose — no matter how trivial or inane — the real magic in this world, Trása decided, was television.

She could watch it for hours, and often did, using it as a visual instruction manual on how to exist in this reality. Nothing she'd been told before she left her own realm had prepared her for the sheer enormity of this one.

It was overwhelming, and to make matters worse, her search wasn't so much looking for a needle in a haystack as searching for a single grain of sand on an endless, sparkling beach.

'Can we watch *The Simpsons*?'

Trása started at the unexpected voice and turned to her newly arrived companion with a puzzled look. He had materialised out of thin air and stretched out across the bedspread, his red coat unbuttoned to reveal an orange and green tartan waistcoat underneath. His matching red hat sat at a jaunty angle on his head, forced there by the fact that he was resting his pointy little chin on his left hand.

'How long have *you* been there?' she asked the *Leipreachán*, flicking past the news channels as she turned back to the TV. Trása found television news boring beyond words. The programs — and there seemed to be thousands of them — just repeated the same thing, over and over, never actually adding anything useful to the discussion, more often than not on subjects that made no sense to her at all. She preferred programs that showed real human dramas, true glimpses of life in this strange reality, like *Coronation Street* and *The Bold and the Beautiful*.

'Long enough,' the *Leipreachán* said. 'Ye're up early.'

'So are you,' she replied, stopping when she came to a channel dedicated to her other favourite topic — celebrity gossip. She was fascinated by these golden creatures called celebrities, even though — after nearly six months — she still hadn't figured out what made one human a celebrity over another. 'You haven't been out causing trouble again, have you, Plunkett?'

'Of course I have,' the *Leipreachán* said, looking at her as if it was the most foolish question ever posed. 'This is London.'

'It's nothing like the London I know,' Trása said with a frown, stopping on a channel showing scenes from a movie premiere the night before. Trása had no interest in the film, but she did love the pretty dresses parading down the red carpet. There were so many colours, so many gorgeous fabrics, so many wonderful jewels, all worn by beautiful, elegant women who didn't seem quite real.

'Ye think this place is strange? Wait 'til ye see New York.' Plunkett pulled his pipe from his pocket — already alight — and began to puff on it contentedly, despite the 'no smoking' sign prominently displayed on top of the TV. 'Did ye know New York has a big parade every year for us? On St Patrick's Day?'

'Who's St Patrick?' she asked, only half listening to the little man. His daily escapades were of little concern to Trása. He was here to aid her search for the missing Undivided twin. It was an almost impossible task, made worse because there was so little magic left in this realm, only the smallest of the *Daoine sídhe* could still tap into it. Trouble was, the smaller the Faerie, the more easily they were distracted. The *Leipreachán* were about the only *sídhe* still able to use magic — limited though it was — in this reality, who could be relied upon to do as they were told.

Well, most of the time anyway.

Not that Plunkett O'Bannon was very reliable. His idea of entertainment was appearing to drunks and drug addicts in alleys late at night and coaxing them into handing over their valuables in return for vague promises of good fortune, wealth and even the odd pot of gold. They'd been living on stolen credit cards since they arrived, procured magically by Trása's larcenous little companion. She didn't think he'd given that up just because — at this very moment in time — their hotel bill wasn't due.

'Patrick be the patron saint of Ireland.'

'What's a saint?'

'Not sure, t'be honest.'

'Then who made him one?'

'The Christians, I think.'

Trása shook her head and picked up the room service menu, the part of her not listening to Plunkett debating whether to have breakfast sent up or to brave the restaurant. 'I will never understand how a ragtag bunch of Hebrew outcasts managed to end up in control of half this realm,' she remarked. The various religions of this reality were even more confusing than the rules of celebrity. Surely the deities of her reality had existed here at some point? Had they not resisted the notion that one of their number was more powerful, more worthy of worship, than all the others? Or had the gods faded here — like the magic — leaving only their human worshippers with their human delusions of grandeur to carry on in their names?

'Ye should watch the History Channel more often,' the *Leipreachán* advised. 'Ye'll find Christians ruling the world is no more strange a thing than a score of other odd occurrences that have happened in this realm.'

'I suppose.'

'If ye can't find *The Simpsons*, *Road Runner* will do.'

Although they both regularly viewed the History Channel with something approaching awe as they watched documentary after documentary detailing the bizarre past of this realm, Plunkett was almost as fond of cartoons as Trása was of soap operas and the E! Channel. Fortunately, she controlled the remote. For some reason — possibly the magic that infused every cell of the *Leipreachán* — when

Plunkett tried to use anything battery operated, it shorted out. As a consequence, Plunkett watched what she wanted, and if Plunkett wanted to watch cartoons, he had to earn it.

One did what they must, to control a creature as fickle as a *Leipreachán*.

'What do you want for breakfast?' she asked, tossing the remote on the bed as she reached for the phone. With a *Leipreachán* for company, a public dining room was a bad idea.

'Bacon,' Plunkett announced. 'Mounds of it.'

Trása wondered why she'd even bothered to ask. In some things, Plunkett was as predictable as a rainy summer in *Tír Chonaill*. She muted the TV with its breathless descriptions of the designer dresses worn by the celebrities attending last night's star-studded movie premiere and dialled room service.

'Room service. How can I help you?'

'This is room five-fourteen,' she said, pleased she was now able to do this as if it was the most natural thing in the world. It had taken her months to gain the confidence to use a telephone with ease, something Plunkett took a certain degree of malicious glee in reminding her. 'I wish to order breakfast.'

'Of course, madam,' the oddly accented male voice on the other end replied. 'What would you like?'

'Um ... two American breakfasts,' she said, even though she considered it a silly description. If every American ate bacon, eggs, hash browns, tomato and beans for breakfast every day, they'd all be as fat as those little Chinese Buddha statues, and all the Americans she'd seen on TV were quite thin. Some of them seemed to be actually starving. 'One with extra —'

'Holy Jaysus, Mary and Harry!' Plunkett suddenly exclaimed. He'd been experimenting with the curses of this reality ever since they arrived. This was his latest favourite, having heard it a couple of weeks ago on TV. Unfortunately, he could never remember the last name that belonged in the phrase so he usually added whatever he thought of first. Trása thought the right name might have been John or Jerry. She was quite certain it wasn't 'Harry'.

'Do you mind!' she hissed, putting her hand over the receiver. 'I'm on the phone!'

The *Leipreachán* didn't answer her. He was jumping up and down on the bed, red coat-tails flapping, pointing at the TV, his little eyes fairly bulging out of his head. He was nigh on apoplectic with excitement.

'Extra bacon,' she said to the room service man on the other end of the phone.

'Certainly, madam,' he replied. 'That will be —'

Trása hung up the phone. 'Plunkett! You stupid little *sídhe*! How many times have I told you,' she said sternly, turning to look at whatever it was that had the little *Leipreachán* so excited, 'that when I'm talking to real people in this world, you need to keep qui— Oh, by the Goddess *Danú*!'

Trása grabbed the remote, unmuted the sound and sat on the edge of the bed, staring at the screen, almost as apoplectic as the *Leipreachán*. On the TV, wearing an expensive, beautifully tailored tuxedo, his dark hair falling across his achingly familiar sapphire eyes, and on the arm of a stunning older woman, was the young man she'd come here looking for.

Darragh of the Undivided.

Or, rather, Darragh's twin brother, Rónán. Darragh was back home where he belonged. In her own realm.

Her heart pounding, Trása turned up the volume. '... *and here comes the star of* Rain over Tuscany *herself*,' the female presenter was gushing. '*The fabulous Kiva Kavanaugh, escorted this evening by her son, Ren.*'

'His name be Rónán, not Ren,' Plunkett told the reporter on the screen, a little miffed they got it wrong.

'Shhh ... I'm trying to listen.' Trása wasn't really surprised — or concerned — to learn Rónán had a different name in this realm. It would have surprised her more if he'd had the same name. And it was easy to guess where the diminutive came from. After all, the twins' Druid mother, Sybille, was from Gaul. Although Trása had never known her, Sybille probably called Rónán by the French version of his name — Renan. Perhaps that's all Rónán remembered about who he really was.

'*My, hasn't he grown into the handsomest young man*,' the presenter's male counterpart sighed.

'*That's right, Clive. But it's rare to see Ren in public.*' Sally smiled and winked at her unseen audience. '*Well, I'm sure he's thrilled to be here, sharing this moment with his mother.*'

Trása thought that highly unlikely. The young man in question seemed anything but happy. In fact, he looked as if he'd rather be *anywhere* but standing next to the star of the night, blinded by a hailstorm of flashbulbs, fending off his mother's screaming fans.

'The triskalion! The triskalion! Can ye see the triskalion?'

'Not unless he waves at the camera, idiot,' Trása pointed out, her gaze glued to the TV.

Reporter Clive nodded enthusiastically to his co-host. '*You're right, Sally. If you remember, this is the boy Kiva rescued from drowning in that terrible boating accident while she was filming* Fire on the Water *up in Northern Ireland.*'

'It's him!' Plunkett shouted, jumping up and down on the bed even harder. 'It's him! It's him! It's him!'

'Shut up! I told you … I'm trying to listen!'

'*… Seems hard to credit that was … what?*' Clive was saying. '*Fifteen, maybe sixteen years ago, now?*' He gave his co-presenter no time to answer. '*And here she is! The star of tonight's premiere, the fabulous and beautiful Miss Kiva Kavanaugh! How are you this evening, Kiva?*'

The actress was dressed in flowing red with a train that billowed behind her like a cloud of warm blood. A matching cascade of rubies — that in Trása's reality would have marked her as a sorceress of unthinkable power — graced her earlobes, and a diamond and ruby bracelet, worth more than Trása could calculate, sparkled at her slender wrist. Kiva Kavanaugh turned to the camera, her eyes bright, and smiled with practised ease. '*I'm thrilled to be here, Clive.*'

'*Fabulous dress, Kiva. Who's the designer?*'

'*Dior by Hedi Slimane, of course.*'

'*You look fantastic! And how are you feeling about the movie? There's already talk of an Oscar …*'

Kiva Kavanaugh lifted her shoulders in an elegant, self-deprecating shrug. '*I never listen to gossip, Clive. But I do think Xavier Hannigan is the best director of his generation.*'

'*Do you expect he'll get an Oscar nod for* Rain Over Tuscany?' Sally asked, thrusting her mike at the actress. She seemed a little peeved Clive was hogging all the questions.

'*He certainly should,*' Kiva agreed. '*He's so talented.*'

Not to be outdone, Clive thrust his mike in front of Rónán. '*And what about you, Ren? Are you looking forward to seeing your mother's performance tonight?*'

'*Not particularly,*' the boy replied in a flat, emotionless tone. Trása shivered. His voice, even in those two words, was so like Darragh's it was frightening.

'See! I told ye!' Plunkett shouted again. 'It's him! It's him! It's him!'

'I heard you the first three hundred times, you fool. Now shut up and let me listen!'

'*Really?*' Clive was saying, somewhat taken aback by Rónán's answer. '*Why not?*'

Rónán leaned into the mike. '*She's playing a drug-addicted hooker, dude. Would you want to watch your mother shooting up and fucking complete strangers on a forty-foot screen?*'

Clive laughed uncomfortably. '*Oh, well … if you put it like that …*'

Rónán wasn't afforded a chance to make any further embarrassing remarks. His mother's expression hadn't wavered, but she abruptly took his arm, smiled stiffly, waved to the camera, and dragged Rónán away from the reporters toward the theatre.

Chilled and thrilled all at once, Trása muted the TV again, and sat staring at the screen without seeing it.

'I be right!' Plunkett said in a singsong voice. 'We found him, we found him.'

'Plunkett, shut up.'

He dropped himself down beside her on the bed and nudged her with his elbow, grinning broadly. 'I thought ye'd be happy. We found him. We be heroes!'

Trása shook her head. 'We won't be heroes, Plunkett,' she reminded him grimly, 'until Rónán of the Undivided is no longer in a position to destroy us.'

CHAPTER 6

'*Better the blood of two innocents, than the blood of twenty thousand ...*'

Ren woke to a sharp, horribly familiar pain, feeling sick as he realised he'd had The Dream again. He hadn't dreamed The Dream for weeks. He'd even dared to hope, for a fleeting moment, that it might be gone for good.

That had proved a futile wish.

The Dream was back, more vivid and real and disturbing than it had ever been.

The Dream had plagued Ren Kavanaugh for as long as he could remember. It was so pervasive that he capitalised it, even in his thoughts, to differentiate it from other, more ordinary dreams. Sometimes he dreamed it so often he was afraid to go to sleep. He'd woken in a cold sweat from it more times than he cared to count. It had earned him scores of sleepless nights, his very own shrink and a whole lot of medications he lied about taking more often than not.

The pills never worked anyway, so he didn't see the point in them.

Lately, though, The Dream had faded somewhat.

Or he didn't remember dreaming it, which amounted to the same thing.

He remembered this one, though. And he would have given a great deal not to.

Ren grunted and doubled over, feeling something soaking his T-shirt, as he struggled to sit up. It was blood. That was new. Although he was accustomed to discovering injuries he couldn't explain, they had never come with The Dream before. Ren tossed back the covers and forced himself to sit up. It was important he not bleed all over the sheets. A T-shirt he could toss away. Bloody sheets meant questions, lectures and another visit to the shrink, where he would have to talk about The Dream again. Above all else, Ren didn't want to talk about The Dream.

Even if he confessed to his nightmares returning, after last night and his unforgivable quip to the reporter on the red carpet, there was no chance his mother would believe this latest episode was anything other than Ren trying to wriggle out of the inevitable shit-storm he'd unleashed, by responding off-script to that idiot reporter from the E! Channel.

Ren staggered into the bathroom, biting his bottom lip to ward off the scream he could feel building in his diaphragm. He grabbed the edge of the basin, took a couple of deep breaths and gingerly raised his T-shirt to examine the wound. Sure enough, a long, shallow cut had opened up across his ribs on the left side of his body. The wound was bleeding profusely.

On the upside, it didn't seem life threatening.

Life*style* threatening, perhaps, if he was caught with another injury like this.

Ren knew nothing he said — no protestations of innocence, no swearing of a sacred oath on Kiva's wretched Oscars that he wasn't responsible — would convince his mother he hadn't done this to himself.

Ren squinted in the sudden brightness as he flicked the lights on, leaving a smear of blood on the switch. Noting he'd need to clean that off before the housekeeper spotted it, he grabbed a fluffy white towel from the pile by the marble vanity, ran it under the tap and then pressed the damp cloth to the wound, wondering if it would need stitches. He didn't think it would, but these mystery injuries, that appeared with alarming regularity of late, had a nasty habit of turning septic.

'*Christ!*' he muttered through clenched teeth as he applied pressure to the wound, which stung as if someone had poured vinegar into it. His eyes watering with the pain, Ren glanced out of the bathroom window. It was just after dawn, the low-hanging clouds still pink with the promise of the oncoming day.

Dawn meant Kiva wouldn't be up yet, particularly after last night's premiere and their late-night flight home from London. But dawn meant it was only an hour or so before Kerry Boyle arrived for work. Ren might get away with convincing his mother all was well, but nothing got past his mother's cousin and housekeeper.

There was really only one place to go for help. Only one place he was guaranteed assistance that wouldn't be reported to his mother ... or the tabloids. Wincing, with the damp towel pressed to his side, Ren headed back to his bedroom. He threw open the wardrobe, pulled out his Nikes and tracksuit, a clean pair of socks and a clean T-shirt, and shoved them in his gym bag. Still pressing the towel to his side, Ren tiptoed out of his room, down the hall to the staircase, past the priceless antiques of his mother's Georgian mansion, and out through the kitchen to the garden.

The grass was damp, the dew icy on his bare feet. Ren didn't care. It was more important he get across the lawn to the high hedge bordering the property on the eastern side of the estate.

As with many of the estates in this part of town, there were gates in the fences of adjacent properties that allowed the residents to call on their closest neighbours without the inconvenience of having to trek up and down the pavement or the long gravelled driveways that protected the residents from the riff-raff who used the public streets. Ren reached the small, arched gateway in the high brick wall separating their property from the estate next door, grunting with the effort to force the wooden door open as it pulled on his wound and set it bleeding afresh. He left the gate open, certain nobody would notice. Patrick Boyle, Kerry's husband and the family's chauffeur-cum-gardener, had mowed the lawns only two days ago. There was no reason for him to be out this early. Besides, Kiva's manager was arriving today from the US. Patrick would be leaving for the airport first thing to pick him up. He'd be more interested in making certain the Bentley was spotless than weeding the perimeter of the property.

The house next door was barely visible through the trees, the grounds not nearly as well kept, or manicured, as the Kavanaugh estate. Running toward the main house, Ren noticed a light coming from the glasshouse at the back of the garden. Knowing Jack had no live-in household help, it meant only one thing. The old man was up and about already, pottering about with ... what?

Ren wasn't sure. The old bloke was pretty cagey, as a rule, about what he was up to. Ren didn't know if it was because he really *was* up to something, or he just liked to foster an air of mystery to help his book sales.

'Jayzus!' Jack exclaimed with his back to Ren, as he opened the glasshouse door. 'Shut the effing door! You're letting all the heat out, boy.'

Ren hurriedly closed the glasshouse door, letting out an involuntary grunt of pain.

Jack looked up, examined Ren oddly for a moment and then shook his head. 'So, there's likely going to be a grand tale behind the reason you're paying me a visit at the crack of dawn, bleeding like a stuck pig.'

'It happened again,' Ren said, limping a little as he made his way between the rows of hothouse flowers toward the back of the glasshouse where Jack seemed to be re-potting a rather forlorn looking *coleus*. In addition to the pain from his side, Ren's feet were freezing and the sudden, aromatic warmth of the glasshouse set off pins and needles in his toes.

'How bad?' the old man asked, wiping his hands on a dirty towel he kept on the bench beside the potting mix that probably made his hands dirtier than they were before he wiped them. He was shorter than Ren, compact and wiry, with white hair and the weight of seventy years of pain and secrets etched onto his weathered face.

'It's not fatal,' Ren assured him. 'But it hurts like hell.'

Jack sighed and beckoned the boy closer. 'Better give us a look then.'

Ren dropped the gym bag, lifted his T-shirt and moved the towel. The bleeding had slowed to a welling of beaded crimson along the cut. Jack leant in to examine the wound, his lips pursed.

'Looks like you've been stabbed,' the old man remarked, as he straightened with an obvious effort. He spoke with an odd, clinical detachment. 'Or grazed in a knife fight. What were you doing?'

'Sleeping.'

'If you're going to have dreams that turn real, me boy,' Jack advised, rubbing his chin thoughtfully, 'you should try to concentrate on getting laid.'

Ren tried to smile, but given the pain he was in, he suspected it looked more like a grimace. 'Yeah … I'll do that next time.'

Jack looked at him oddly. 'Is there something you're leaving out here, lad?'

'No. Why?'

'I can spot a liar blindfolded at fifty paces, Ren.'

Ren shrugged, not sure how much it mattered. 'I was dreaming when it happened.'

'About what?'

He shrugged. 'You know … the usual stuff.'

'I know what *my* usual stuff is. What's yours?'

'Nothing exciting. Does it need stitches?'

Jack shook his head. 'I don't think so. It's a clean cut, and fairly shallow. But it'll need to be dressed. And kept clean. Does your mam know about this one?'

He shook his head. 'She's not awake yet, Kerry doesn't start work for another hour, and it's still the holidays, so no school for another couple of weeks, either.'

'So, we have time to patch you up and get you home again before they decide you're a complete loon, then.'

Although he'd never doubted Jack would help him, Ren couldn't help but feel relieved. 'Thanks, dude.'

'You don't have to thank me, lad,' Jack said, tossing his dirty towel back onto the bench. 'And you certainly don't have to keep calling me *dude*.'

The kitchen was a mess, the marble floors sticky, the sink piled with dishes, even though there was a perfectly functioning dishwasher under the counter. Jack flicked on the lights and began looking through the kitchen cupboards until he located a large metal toolbox, which Ren knew from experience contained Jack's alarmingly well-provisioned first-aid kit.

Ren shoved a pile of empty pizza boxes aside and made room on the counter near the sink. As he sat himself up on the counter, Jack opened the box, took out the antiseptic, swabs, sterile strips and wound dressings, laying them out on the counter beside Ren.

'Would it be easier if we do this at the table?' Ren asked, grateful Jack hadn't questioned him further. The old man was washing his hands in the sink, and taking his time to be thorough, too, Ren noted with relief.

Jack shook his head. 'No room.'

Ren glanced through the door to the dining room. Sure enough, the elegant antique table he could just make out in the gloom, seemed piled high with boxes. 'You moving?'

'Nah ... gotta autograph a whole bunch of books for the publisher. Going on tour in the US come September. Take off your shirt.'

Ren lifted the T-shirt gingerly over his head, tossed it on the counter, exposing several faint scars across his chest and arms from similar inexplicable injuries. He raised his left arm to let Jack get to work. 'Do you like America?'

'Hate the place,' Jack said without looking up. 'But they love me. So I do fifteen cities in ten days. Book signings, lectures to political science and criminology students trying to pretend they're cool, and the occasional police department. And I get to smile and pose with snooty-nosed, Irish–American society ladies who've never known a moment's want in their entire fecking lives, who want to be able to tell their friends they've met a real terrorist.'

'But you served your time, didn't you?' Ren said, glad Jack was in such a garrulous mood. It helped keep his mind off the pain. And the residual uneasiness from his dreams. 'You're not with the IRA these days. So technically, you're not a terrorist anymore.'

'Jayzus, lad, don't say that too loud,' Jack said. 'You'll give me publicist a coronary!'

Ren smiled and then hissed at the sting of the antiseptic as Jack dabbed it on the cut. 'You know what I mean.'

'Aye. And the truth is, I much prefer kissing society ladies to being a guest of Her Majesty, but ... well, you know ...'

Actually, Ren had no idea, but he nodded sympathetically. Old Jack might be a bit odd, but he was one of only two people in the world who believed Ren when he claimed he wasn't carving himself up for fun and attention.

And — thanks to Jack's shady past — the old man had enough medical knowledge to render aid when Ren didn't want to draw attention to his injuries. Even so, it was hard to credit that Jack O'Righin had once been counted among the most dangerous men in Europe. Even harder to believe he'd spent thirty years in prison, quite a few of them in the infamous H Blocks.

When Jack was released in 1998 — along with a whole lot of other prisoners as part of the Good Friday Accord (or so it claimed on the dustcover of his book) — he moved south to Dublin. There he sat down and wrote about his experiences as a poor, disenfranchised child, as a prisoner in The Maze, and as an active member of the Provisional IRA. A year or so later, the only slightly repentant terrorist found himself with a *New York Times* bestseller on his hands and a whole new career on the speaking circuit where he commanded a six-figure fee. He had more money now than he ever imagined he would see in one lifetime, let alone every six months in a cheque from his agent in London.

He'd bought the house next door to the Kavanaughs' place last year, upsetting the neighbours who considered the old ex-convict and self-promoting terrorist a blight on their once perfect neighbourhood.

Ren liked him almost as much as the rest of the residents of Blackrock despised him. The old man was interesting. And he could whip up a damn fine field dressing, something Ren seemed to be more and more in need of lately.

Reaching for the sterile strips to bind the skin closed, Jack glanced up at Ren's pain-etched face. 'Saw you on TV last night.'

'I thought you don't have cable?'

'This wasn't on cable, laddie. This was the evening news on the RTÉ. They must have shown you mouthing off to that reporter a half-dozen times before I went to bed. Did your old lady give you much stick for dropping the F-word on national television?'

Ren grimaced, only this time it wasn't from the pain. He'd known as he uttered the words that he would pay for them, but it had been worth it. The tantrum Kiva threw in the car on the way to the airport was monumental. It ended with her declaring he would never, *ever*, set foot on another red carpet as long as she lived, which was just fine by Ren. 'The words *military school* and *Utah brat camp* were bandied about during the discussion.'

Jack looked surprised. 'Seriously? Don't those brat camps make you live on mung beans and dog shite until you've seen the error of your ways?'

Ren nodded. 'If I had to choose, I'd opt for military school, myself, but I'm guessing that won't happen. My mother doesn't like the idea of me being armed. Even under controlled conditions.'

'You know they're gonna hound you, now, don't you?' Jack warned. 'The press, I mean. Waiting for you to open that potty mouth of yours and change feet.'

Ren nodded, as the old man began to tape a long, narrow piece of gauze over Ren's stab wound. 'They'll get sick of me, soon enough,' he said. 'I'm not all that interesting.'

'Well, you weren't until last night, lad,' Jack said, tearing off another piece of tape with his teeth. 'Still, if you stay out of the way for a few days, they'll find someone else to bother, I suppose.'

'That's what I'm hoping.'

Jack finished off the dressing and stood back to admire his handiwork. It was completely light outside now, a slight mist rising off the damp grass.

'You'll need to come over tomorrow so I can change the dressing and check there's no infection,' he said. 'Unless of course you're planning to tell your mam about this and she's taken you to a real hospital by then.'

'Not likely.' Ren picked up his discarded T-shirt and tossed it to the old man. 'Can you ditch that for me? I brought my tracksuit and joggers with me. If Kerry catches me sneaking back in, I'll tell her I've been out running.'

It wasn't such an outrageous plan. Jogging was an acceptable way for him to escape the house. Staying fit was an admirable goal, after all. As Kiva Kavanaugh lived on a permanent diet — only the endorsement deal varied — Ren's announcement that he was following her example had proved a very popular move, even though he'd declined his mother's offer of his own personal trainer.

'You gonna be okay?'

Ren nodded. 'Yeah. Thanks. When's your housekeeper due?'

'Not until next Friday. I gave her the school holidays off. Something to do with her grandkids.' Jack tossed the T-shirt onto the pile of empty pizza boxes. 'You know ... there's got to be a reason this keeps happening, laddie.'

'Bring it on,' Ren said with heartfelt sincerity. 'And then let's make it stop.'

As soon as he was in sight of his own house, Ren jogged from the garden into the kitchen, glad the codeine tablets Jack had given him were taking the edge off his pain. The sun was fully up now, the mist vanishing from the damp lawn almost as quickly as it had formed. He was still sweating with the pain, but that worked in his favour. It made it look like he really had been out jogging.

Kerry Boyle looked up and glanced over her shoulder as the door opened. She was cooking toast. The smell of it made Ren's stomach rumble. As he walked into the kitchen, he discovered why she was cooking toast. It certainly wasn't for Kiva. His mother had been carb-free for weeks now, in preparation for the various movie premieres she had to attend and the insanely expensive designer dresses which she intended to squeeze into.

Kerry's two children were with her: Neil, her red-haired, freckle-faced twelve-year-old son, and Hayley, her seventeen-year-old stepdaughter. Hayley looked more like her father than her brother, dark-haired and green-eyed. She also happened to be the only other person besides Jack O'Righin who believed Ren when he claimed he wasn't slicing himself up for attention.

'Ah, here he is,' the housekeeper said with a smile, as she placed a plate piled with buttered toast in front of Neil who was sitting at the granite-topped kitchen island next to his sister. 'The red carpet terror with the filthy mouth. I'm surprised you're up early. Didn't your flight not arrive until the wee small hours?'

No need to ask, then, whether Kerry had seen the news.

'We got in about two,' Ren confirmed. 'Kiva said not to wake her until Jon gets here.'

Neil grinned at him, shaking his head. 'Man, I cannot *believe* you said that in front of your mother.'

'And on national television,' Hayley added through a mouthful of toast.

'She'll never let you attend another premiere,' Kerry warned, placing a plate of freshly buttered toast in front of an empty stool for Ren.

He pulled out the seat and sat down with relief. 'Then my work here is done,' he said, reaching for the marmalade.

Neil was appalled. 'You said that on *purpose*?' He shook his red curls, pretending to be horrified, probably to mask the burning hero worship he'd developed for his older cousin in the last few months, which Ren studiously ignored to save embarrassing them both. 'You are so *bad*, Ren.'

Kerry put her hand on Ren's shoulder, a gesture that was both comforting and sympathetic. 'Foolish, rather than bad, I think, Neil. But it wasn't a wise thing to do, Ren. In fact, after this, I'll be surprised if your poor mother doesn't finally act on her threat to send you to that camp in Utah she's always going on about.'

Ren shrugged. 'I told her I didn't want to be paraded down the red carpet like her newest handbag.'

'And you don't think you could have found a more subtle way of making your point?' Kerry asked, turning to lift the kettle off the range as it began to sing. His mother's cousin was the complete opposite of Kiva — plump and dark-haired, calm and comforting where Kiva was blonde, angular and nervy. If Ren had grown up in any way normal, it wasn't thanks to Kiva's well-meaning but erratic parenting, it was because of the stability and down-to-earth practicality of Kerry Boyle.

But it was time to get off the topic of last night's premiere. He glanced at Neil and Hayley. 'How come you two are here?'

It wasn't unusual for Kerry to bring her kids to work but, as a rule, she didn't let them hang around all day during school vacations — particularly not on a day like today when Kiva had just returned from her latest travels and likely to be a little fractious.

'Neil needs new shoes before school goes back,' Hayley explained, as her brother devoured his toast as if he'd not been fed for a month. 'Mum figured we could go across to the Blackrock Shopping Centre while she's working today, or find something over the road at the Frascati mall.'

'Cool,' Ren said, spying a perfect opportunity to be gone for the day. 'Can I come?'

'*You* want to help Hayley shop for shoes?' Kerry asked, making no attempt to hide the scepticism in her tone.

'Actually, I want to be far, far away from here when my mother wakes up,' Ren told her honestly. 'Neil's endlessly expanding feet seem as good an excuse as any for being elsewhere.'

'Hey!' Neil exclaimed, looking wounded.

Hayley grinned at him. Kerry studied Ren for a moment, her eyes filled with a mixture of sympathy and concern. 'All right, then,' she said.

'But if she asks me, I'll tell Kiva where you are, Ren. I won't lie to her.'

'You don't need to lie for me, Kerry,' he said, relieved beyond words he had managed to delay the inevitable confrontation over his behaviour. 'I just need to give her time to calm down.'

'I'm not sure there is such a time,' Kerry said. 'But at least with you there, Neil won't be able to bully his sister into buying him anything with *Lord of the Rings* characters on them.' She turned to open the cupboard where the coffee mugs were stored. 'Now who wants a cup of tea with their toast, and who wants hot chocolate?'

CHAPTER 7

'There are things you need to know, Brydie,' the queen said, straightening the folds of her white cloak as the wagon trundled through the ring of earthworks surrounding *Ráith Righ*, 'before we get to *Sí an Bhrú*.'

Brydie nodded, expecting some sort of explanation before they arrived at the Druid stronghold. She hadn't expected the size of the escort, however. It was only seventeen miles or so to *Sí an Bhrú* through friendly territory. If you stood on top of the *Ráith's* tower, on a clear day like today, you could actually see the white quartz stones of its entrance glistening in the sunlight. It hardly seemed necessary for the queen to have an escort of enough men-at-arms to defend them against a small army.

Álmhath's son, Torcán, wasn't riding with his mother in the wagon. The tall, dour prince rode at the head of the column, his future bride, Anwen, at his side, leading their progress.

Anwen will be loving that, Brydie thought, *unless she's peeved that I'm in here with the queen.* Brydie couldn't imagine why she'd rather be in the wagon. Álmhath was a daunting figure at the best of times. Much better to be riding at the head of the column in a place of honour with your future husband, than sitting here suffering the unrelenting scrutiny of your future mother-in-law.

'Do you know why we're headed to *Sí an Bhrú*?'

Brydie shook her head. She had a few suspicions, but really didn't know anything. As she was dressing for this journey, in her best kirtle and the fine linen shift her stepmother had given her before she left home, Brydie had racked her brains for some hint of the reason for this summons, but could think of none. She had no special gifts, no unique talents; she had nothing she could imagine the goddess couldn't find in a score of other girls at Álmhath's court. 'I assume it has something to do with the recent visit of Lord Tarth of the *Daoine sídhe*.'

'It has everything to do with it,' Álmhath agreed, scowling. 'The *Tuatha* have found something they weren't meant to find. We are now in somewhat of a bind, because of it.'

'What did they find?' Brydie asked, as the wagon clattered over the wooden road that connected Temair to *Sí an Bhrú*, winding through the low hills as it followed the natural contours of the landscape. It was a glorious day, warm and clear, but sunset was approaching and the chilly wind was back. Had it not been for the breeze carrying the faintest hint of winter on its breath, it would be hard to credit it was only a few weeks until *Lughnasadh*.

'That is something you don't need to know, just now,' the queen told her. 'In fact, it's rather important you don't know. But it is directly related to the honour *Danú* has chosen for you.'

For a sacrilegious moment, Brydie wondered if it really was the goddess who'd marked her, or if this honour simply suited the queen. In Brydie's experience, when the goddess spoke, she usually did so on a grand scale, sending things like floods, famines and plagues to make her will known — a will that required Druids with years of mystical training to interpret. *Danú* wasn't in the habit, as far as Brydie was aware, of handing out specific instructions to individuals.

She knew better than to point this out to her queen, however.

'What must I do, *an Bhantiarna*?' she asked. And then she added, almost as an apology to the goddess for her blasphemous thoughts, 'Whatever honour the goddess has chosen for me, if it is in my power to do it, I will do it willingly.'

The queen nodded her approval and then glanced around, as if making certain they could not be overheard, either by their escort or — Brydie was certain — by any agent of the *Tuatha* lurking in the shadows in animal or bird form. Then she turned to Brydie and met her gaze evenly. 'She wants you to bear a child of Darragh of the Undivided.'

For a long moment, Brydie didn't answer, mostly because she couldn't think of anything to say.

Her silence apparently frustrated the queen. 'Is that all you're going to do, girl? Sit there and gawp at me?'

'I ... I don't *know* what to say, my lady,' Brydie told her honestly. She truly didn't. She'd known ever since coming to court that she was destined to bear the sons of the next generation of rulers, but she'd expected a husband, and a little more fanfare. The blunt announcement caught her by surprise.

'Gods ... you're not still a virgin are you?'

'Of course not.' Brydie had happily surrendered her innocence at last year's *Lughnasadh*, almost a year ago.

'Well, that's a start, I suppose,' the queen remarked, a little sourly. 'Are you going to ask me why?'

'If it's the will of the goddess ...'

'Oh, don't give me that,' the queen scoffed. 'I saw the look you gave me this morning in the grove, when I suggested Ethna and Morann were blessed by *Danú*. You didn't believe it for a moment.'

'Do you believe, *an Bhantiarna*?' Brydie felt compelled to ask, a little bothered to learn the queen could read her so easily.

'I believe *Danú* gave our people a gift, Brydie,' the queen told her, lowering her voice as she leant forward. 'It's a gift wrapped in a package we might not have chosen for ourselves, but it is a gift nonetheless. A precious gift, but one that can all too easily be taken from us, if we loosen our grip on it. We believe it is *Danú*'s will that we use the wit she gave us, to hold onto it.'

Brydie wished she understood what the queen was telling her, but Álmhath really wasn't making much sense.

'I'm not sure I understand of which gift you speak, *an Bhantiarna*.'

'I speak of the gift of *Tuatha* magic,' the queen said, leaning back in her seat.

Brydie frowned. 'But that is a gift bestowed on

the Druids through the Undivided, my lady. Not mere mortals like you and I.'

Álmhath's brow furrowed with irritation. 'The Druids *are* us, you foolish girl,' she said. 'As I say, the gift comes in a package I would not have chosen, but the Undivided are human, just like you and me, as are the Druids who channel the magic because of their link to the twins. If we lose their bloodline, we lose the magic. You may not think that would make much difference to you, but consider for a moment what our world would be like if we lost the ability to travel instantly through the stone circles, from one place to another. If rift runners couldn't visit other realms to warn of dangers facing this one. Think of the famines we would have suffered, if we hadn't been warned in advance and known to stockpile food? The lives that might have been lost in a flood, had we not seen it coming in another realm so we could evacuate people and livestock to higher ground. Imagine if our healers were forced to heal people with nothing but herbs and dubious surgical tools rather than with magic.' She shook her head, sighing. 'If you've ever seen the aftermath of a battle where there was no magically gifted *Liaig* to heal men's wounds, Brydie Ni'Seanan, you'd not so lightly dismiss *Danú*'s gift to us.'

Brydie had truly never thought of the Undivided in that way before. Or the Druids. But one thing puzzled her about the queen's impassioned speech. 'You said the bloodline needed to be preserved, my lady. I didn't think the Undivided were related to their predecessors. I thought psychic twins were something random that happened at *Danú*'s whim?'

'*Danú*'s whim and the will of the *Matrarchaí*,' the queen said, frowning.

'The *Matrarchaí*?' Brydie asked, puzzled by the queen's comment.

'The *Matrarchaí* are the reason the line has never been broken, Brydie. The reason why, after sixty-six generations, humans still occupy *Sí an Bhrú*.'

Brydie stared at the queen as she realised what Álmhath was telling her. 'The *Matrarchaí* know the secret of producing the psychic twins needed to preserve the Treaty of *Tír Na nÓg*.'

The queen nodded, smiling grimly. 'Your father said you were a bright girl.'

'That's what you meant about my mother's line.'

'There is more than one bloodline,' Álmhath told her. 'There has to be, or those who have a vested interest in there not being a new set of twins to take over channelling the power would have wiped out the line a thousand years ago. Yours happens to be one of the stronger ones. Fortunate indeed that your last bleed was near a fortnight past,' the queen added. 'We may not have much time, so it's important you conceive as soon as possible.'

'Why is time suddenly a problem?' Brydie asked. She couldn't see what the rush was. Darragh of the Undivided had been living a mere seventeen miles away all his life. Surely, if it was so critical to preserve his line, Álmhath could have slipped a fertile woman into his bed anytime in the last four years, or so.

'The *Tuatha* have forced our hand,' the queen told her, frowning. 'If we don't act soon, there may not be a line to preserve.'

Brydie's eyes widened with surprise. 'Is Darragh in some sort of danger?'

'He's always in some sort of danger. He is one of the Undivided,' Álmhath said, glancing around as the canopied wagon slowed. She turned to look over her shoulder. 'Why are we stopping?'

Brydie rose to her feet to find out if she could see past the forest of pikes carried by their mounted escort. 'I think there is something blocking the road.'

It was hard to tell, and she didn't think it was a dire threat, because the mounted guards still had their pikes pointed at the sky, rather than lowering them, as they would if they thought the queen was under attack.

By the time she sat down, the wagon had come to a complete stop.

'Did you want me to find out what's going on?' she asked.

Álmhath didn't answer. Instead, she leant over the side of the wagon. 'Seamus! What's going on! Why have we stopped!'

'The fault is mine, I fear, *an Bhantiarna*.'

Brydie yelped in fright. On the other side of the wagon, the *sídhe* lord, Marcroy Tarth, had suddenly appeared. He was dressed in a fine embroidered linen shirt and a dark emerald cloak held together at his throat by a deep purple amethyst and gold filigree brooch.

'I was on my way to *Sí an Bhrú* when I saw your party approaching and thought I might prevail upon your hospitality for a ride.'

'How convenient for you,' Álmhath remarked with a scowl. There was no way, Brydie realised, the queen would be able to refuse Marcroy's request for a lift to *Sí an Bhrú*, which effectively put an end to the discussion they were having. Brydie was destined to remain in the dark about her queen's sudden need for a child from the Undivided for some time yet, it seemed.

'Do you travel alone, my lord?' the queen inquired, looking about for any other of the *Tuatha* that might accompany the Faerie lord.

'I thought it better under the circumstances,' Marcroy said, smiling. 'I didn't want to alarm anybody at *Sí an Bhrú*.' He turned his attention to Brydie. 'Well met, Lady Brydie. You are honoured indeed to ride with the queen this fine day. You will not object to me joining you, I hope?'

It was phrased as a question, but there really wasn't any polite way for Brydie to answer, except in the affirmative. She glanced at Álmhath for help. The queen let out an exasperated sigh and offered Marcroy a seat with a wave of her hand.

With a smile and a nimble leap, the *sídhe* jumped into the wagon, barely making it rock as he took his place beside Brydie. The guards relaxed and Seamus headed back to the head of the column to ride with Torcán and Anwen.

'So, what are we discussing?' Marcroy asked the silent and decidedly peeved women with a pleasant smile. 'The weather? The latest fashions at court? How long it will be before Atilis is run through by one of his neighbours?'

'We speak of nothing that would interest you, Marcroy,' Álmhath told him, settling back in her seat. Brydie judged that to be a monumental lie, but she took her cue from the queen and made no attempt to resume their earlier discussion.

'Oh, but you judge me too harshly, *an Bhantiarna*,' he said, his hand on his heart. 'I am always fascinated by what humans find interesting.' He turned to Brydie. 'What is it that *you* find interesting, my lady?'

Brydie wasn't sure how to answer him, or even if she should. In the end, she shrugged. 'I don't know … lots of things.'

'What sort of things?' Marcroy insisted. He was enjoying her discomfort. She could tell.

'Just … things …'

Marcroy's smile widened. Although she'd seen many a *sídhe* since coming to Álmhath's court, she still couldn't look at their cat-like eyes without feeling a little awkward. She glanced away, fixing her gaze on the Faerie lord's brooch, which seemed the safest place to look. The wagon bumped over the wooden road at a steady pace, but it was going to be a long journey in this company.

'My brooch seems to fascinate you,' Marcroy remarked, as if he knew what she was thinking.

'It's lovely,' she agreed, wishing she could just curl up and not look at the Faerie at all.

Marcroy reached up and unclasped the brooch. 'Then you shall have it, my dear.'

He held the brooch out to her on the palm of his hand.

Brydie didn't know what to do. She looked at the queen for help. Álmhath seemed a little suspicious, but after a moment, she shrugged. 'You should thank Lord Tarth for such a valuable gift.'

Taking the brooch gingerly from his hand, Brydie smiled uncomfortably. 'Thank you, *tiarna*.'

'It is my pleasure, Lady Brydie,' Marcroy said, looking inordinately pleased with himself. 'I hope my gift will bring you many hours of happiness.'

'I'm sure it will, my lord,' she said, closing her hand over the jewel, wondering why, in this crisp breeze, the stone felt so remarkably warm.

CHAPTER 8

By the time breakfast was almost done, the plans for Ren and Hayley's shopping trip were well under way, with one unfortunate complication. When Hayley's father came into the kitchen, shrugging on the grey, double-breasted jacket he always wore when he was playing chauffeur, he kissed her mother's cheek, waved to her and Neil and then turned to Ren. 'Hope you're not planning any excursions today, Rennie, me boy.'

'Why not?' he asked.

'The vultures are already starting to gather at the gate,' he warned, stealing a piece of Neil's toast as he sat down beside her.

Seeing them side by side, it always struck Hayley as amusing that the older they got, the more her father and her stepmother seemed alike: stocky, dark-haired and solid. Her father, a former stunt man, had worked for Kiva since marrying Kerry some fourteen years ago, not long after he fished a drowning child out of a lake on the set of Kiva's first film. That movie was Kiva's big break, after a Hollywood director, visiting Ireland to scout locations, discovered her on local television and cast her as his leading lady.

'They're out there already?' she asked, glancing sympathetically at Ren, even if he had brought this on himself with his foolish outburst last night. Still, Hayley wasn't surprised to learn the paparazzi were waiting at the gate. For the next few days, they would not leave anything remotely connected to Ren Kavanaugh alone. Even her father would be quizzed for his opinion as he left for the airport later this morning. There was probably another clutch of them waiting at the airport, too. 'Don't those people ever sleep?'

'They're like vampires, love,' her stepmother sighed. 'They only come out at night to suck the life out of you.'

'If they're vampires, how come they're down there this morning and the sunlight isn't setting them on fire?' Neil asked as he chewed his toast.

'Dunno,' Ren said, winking at Neil. 'Let's go down to the gate with a can of kerosene and some matches and find out if they're flammable.'

'Ren Kavanaugh,' Kerry scolded, shaking her head. 'It's idiotic comments like that one that gets the vultures gathering at the gate in the first place. Didn't you learn anything from last night?'

'That's a lesson Kiva's going to deliver as soon as she wakes up,' Hayley predicted. She didn't envy Ren the lesson either.

Her father laughed and ruffled her hair. 'You've got the fey gift of the Faerie, Hayley,' he said. 'It's a well-known trait in our family.'

'Fey, my arse,' Kerry scoffed, putting a fresh mug of tea on the counter in front of Patrick. 'Blind Freddy could have worked that one out.'

'Still,' he said, picking up the tea and taking an

appreciative sip, 'the Boyles are known for their gift with the Sight.'

'You and your brothers getting pissed at Christmas and bragging about being fey doesn't make it a fact, Patrick Boyle,' Kerry said. She winked at Hayley, who was well used to her father's insistence — usually when he'd had a few pints — that they were descended from Celtic seers from back in some distant time when that might have actually meant something.

But her stepmother had delivered her pronouncement on the matter, and clearly wasn't planning to discuss it further. She turned to Ren. 'Is your mam still asleep?'

Ren nodded. 'I suppose. She took something when we got home from the airport last night. You could probably detonate a nuke in the next room, and she'd sleep through it.'

'If you detonated a nuke in the next room,' Hayley pointed out, reasonably enough, 'she wouldn't wake up at all, Ren.'

Ren pulled a face at her. 'Nobody likes a smart-arse, smart-arse.'

Hayley grinned at him and then turned to her father. 'Ren and I are taking Neil shopping, today. To buy shoes.'

'Dear God, woman!' Patrick exclaimed to his wife in horror. 'Have you no respect for the manhood of these boys? *Shoe* shopping?'

'I'm sure the experience will turn both of them gayer than Kiva's stylist,' Kerry replied calmly, as she started to clear away the breakfast dishes. 'Maybe when they get back you can take these poor emasculated lads out to the garage, smear them in grease and have them dance naked around the Bentley. Just to even things up.'

Hayley burst out laughing at the mental image *that* conjured up, spitting out a mouthful of hot chocolate which splattered all over the counter. Kerry hurried over with a cloth to wipe up the mess. Neil and her father were laughing, too. Then she noticed Ren's grimace.

Ren looked as if he would have laughed only it might hurt too much, which made Hayley instantly suspicious. Or maybe he was just feeling a little left out. Hayley thought there must be a special sort of loneliness that came from living on the fringes of someone else's family, especially one as warm and close as hers. Although the Boyles treated him like one of their own, she knew Ren felt as if he didn't belong in their tight-knit unit, just as she knew he felt he didn't belong with Kiva, either.

Ren belonged to some unnamed and never identified couple who considered it cool to tattoo the palm of a toddler's hand, and who had presumably perished in a boating accident when he was three years old.

Maybe.

Nobody knew Ren's age for certain, either. It was the doctors who examined him after Patrick dragged him hypothermic and half drowned from the lake, who had assigned him his age. And his date of birth.

December tenth, 1983. That was the day they found him, backdated by three years. It was 2001 now, so that meant in a couple of months, he'd turn eighteen. Legally, at any rate. Ren might be older, or even younger, but nobody would ever really know for certain.

'Ah, well ...' her dad was saying, as Hayley dragged her attention back from Ren's misty age and origins to the conversation. 'If you insist on ruining these boys, I suppose the least I can do is help them run the gauntlet.' Patrick pushed up his sleeve to check his watch. 'I have to leave for the airport in a few minutes to pick up Jon. If you kids are ready to go, I'll drop you off at Frascati Road on the way.'

'What about the paps?' Ren asked.

'You can hide in the Bentley's trunk. It's big enough to hold a party in there. We'll just sail on past 'em, waving to the ravening whores on the way out. They'll never even know you're in the car.'

'Don't you mean the ravening hordes?' Kerry asked.

'Clearly, my love,' Patrick replied with a perfectly straight face, drinking down the last of his tea, 'you've not seen what's waiting outside the gate this morning.'

Neil's shoes, as it turned out, were not a problem. They found a pair at Clarks, the first store they visited, which fitted the bill of being functional, school-appropriate, and not having any *Lord of the Rings* characters emblazoned on them. After Hayley paid for them with the credit card her mother had entrusted her with, the three of them window-shopped for a couple of hours around the Blackrock Shopping Centre to kill time until lunch. At least Hayley window-shopped. Ren and Neil dutifully tagged along, munching on hot cinnamon donuts, making rude comments about girls and shopping, which Hayley loftily ignored.

They ran into a clutch of girls from school at around eleven o'clock, who zeroed in on Ren like heat-seeking missiles. He wasn't the only celebrity offspring at their school, but after last night, was probably the most notorious. Even more annoying for Hayley was that Ren should have run like hell at the very sight of them, but he didn't. He stopped and chatted to them, smiling self-deprecatingly, brushing off his now apparently world-wide TV appearance with a shrug, and — in Hayley's opinion — taking entirely too much pleasure in being swarmed by a clutch of bimbos. She stood there, tapping her foot, glaring at the ringleader — future beauty therapist Shangrila McGill — until the girl got the hint, gathered up her faithful followers and headed off down the mall in search of something new to obsess over.

'You could have signed autographs,' Hayley said, watching them leave. 'I have a pen.'

Ren turned to stare at her. 'What's up with you?'

'Nothing.'

'Yeah ... right.'

'Okay ... I just think that for someone who complains how much it sucks being harassed by your mother's fans, you're pretty quick to flirt with your own.'

'I don't have fans. I go to school with those girls.'

'I go to school with them, too, Ren. They didn't even acknowledge I was here.'

'That's 'cause you scare them,' Neil chimed in.

Ren grinned. 'You know, I think he's right.'

Hayley grinned suddenly, her anger evaporating at the idea she intimidated Shangrila McGill and her posse. That actually felt pretty good.

They decided to head across the road after that — in part to avoid running into the bimbo brigade again.

'I'm hungry,' Neil announced. He was walking between Ren and Hayley, heading for the travelator down to the car park, so they could cross the road at the pedestrian lights to the Frascati Shopping Centre.

'You're always hungry,' Hayley observed. 'And you just finished a donut. How come you're skinny as a bean pole?'

'Because he burns off all his excess calories talking so much,' Ren suggested with a grimace that might have been meant as a smile. He'd been smiling less and less and growing progressively quieter as the morning wore on, which was probably why the bimbos annoyed her so much. For them he'd managed a smile.

'I do not!' Neil exclaimed, elbowing Ren in the side as hard as he could.

Ren grunted and doubled over with pain.

Neil laughed. 'You are such a big baby, Ren.'

The pain of Neil's elbowing apparently buckled Ren's knees. Ren dropped hard onto the tiled floor, trying to catch his breath. He nodded wordlessly, his eyes watering.

'He can act better than his mother, too,' Neil added, obviously assuming Ren was faking.

When Ren still didn't answer but remained doubled over on his knees, as the crowds of shoppers flowed around them, Hayley squatted down beside him, filled with concern. 'Hey … you okay?'

'I … will … be …'

'Oh, my God!' she hissed, as she noticed blood seeping into Ren's T-shirt. She looked up, glancing around to see if anyone had noticed them. 'We have to get you out of here.'

'What's the matter?' Neil asked, worried, now, that neither Ren nor his sister seemed to be fooling around any longer. 'Is Ren okay?'

'Where are the restrooms?' Hayley asked her little brother, putting her arm around Ren's shoulder to help him up.

'Back the way we came,' he said, sounding worried and a little puzzled. 'What's wrong with Ren?'

'Nothing,' she said, as Ren climbed unsteadily to his feet. 'He just needs a bathroom.'

Neil seemed to understand he'd get nothing more from his sister, so he turned back the way they'd come, cutting a path ahead of them. When they finally reached the passage leading to the public toilets, Hayley turned to her brother. 'Stay here. We'll be back in a bit.'

'What's the matter with Ren?'

'I'll explain later,' Ren gasped. He managed to smile at Neil, which helped. Sometimes a twelve-year-old's hero worship was a useful thing, Hayley decided.

When they reached the men's room, which proved blessedly empty, Ren collapsed against the basin as Hayley turned to find some paper towels.

'Shit!'

'What?' Ren asked.

'They've only got hand dryers here.'

'It'll be okay, Hayley,' Ren assured her. He gingerly pushed back his tracksuit jacket and raised his T-shirt. 'Christ Almighty, your little brother has elbows like a ninja.'

'A ninja elbow didn't do that,' she said as she bent down to take a closer look at Ren's field dressing. She'd seen them before and knew the reason without asking. 'Did it happen again?'

Ren nodded, gently lifting the edge of the dressing to see how bad the damage was. Hayley winced at the sight of it. The cut was long and shallow and looked like Ren had been knifed in the ribs.

'This morning,' he explained. 'Not a fun way to greet the day, let me tell you.'

'Who dressed it for you?'

'I went next door to Jack.'

Hayley didn't share Ren's enthusiasm for his neighbour, but she knew Jack was good at keeping secrets. Still, this looked serious and she wasn't sure it was a good idea to hide it. 'Your mother's going to go ballistic when she sees that.'

'The plan was to not let her see it.' Ren frowned. Two of the sterile strips holding the wound closed had lifted. The wound was bleeding, but not profusely. He pressed them back down, and then lowered the T-shirt.

Hayley hoped the small amount of pressure he was applying would be enough to stem the blood flow. But that wasn't their immediate problem. If Ren wanted to keep this a secret, they were going to have to come up with a plausible cover story.

'What are we going to tell Neil?'

'That he has ninja elbows,' Ren suggested with a faint smile.

She didn't return his smile, wishing he'd take this a little more seriously. 'What are you going to tell Kiva?'

'Nothing. I figure she's so pissed off by what I said at the premiere, she won't even think to worry if I've been slicing myself up again.'

And that was the rub. No matter what he said, everyone would think Ren had done this to himself.

'You didn't, did you?' she asked. 'I mean ... slice yourself up?'

Ren turned to wash his hands.

'I'm sorry ... but ... well ... you know ... I had to ask ...'

'No, Hayley. You didn't.'

Hayley wasn't sure how to answer that. She worried about Ren's mysterious injuries, and believed that *he believed* he wasn't cutting himself, but sometimes she really did wonder ...

The look on his face prevented her from probing the matter further. She knew he was about to shut her out completely, and Hayley didn't want that. 'I'd better go check on Neil. You gonna be okay?'

'Yeah. Just give me a minute.'

'Take a few deep breaths,' she advised.

The door opened before Ren could answer and a young man came in, wearing a Superquinn shirt from the centre's supermarket that brought in most of the mall's customers. He stared at Hayley in surprise, glanced at Ren, and then stepped up to the urinal at the far end of the restroom and waited, looking at them impatiently.

Hayley glared back at him. 'Don't let me stop you.'

'This is the men's room,' the lad pointed out.

'So what are you doing here?'

'Hayley ... please ...' Ren said, taking another painful deep breath. He straightened slowly, wincing. Then he closed his jacket, zipping it up far enough to cover the bloodstain on his T-shirt. 'We're leaving.'

Hayley looked at Ren with concern. 'Do you need a hand?'

He shook his head. 'I'll be okay. Do you think Neil will believe he just bruised my ribs when he elbowed me?'

Hayley shrugged, holding the door open for him. 'It's probably better than telling him the truth,' she said.

CHAPTER 9

Normally, Trása loved to fly. Or rather, she loved to fly when she was the one doing the flying.

Climbing into a human-built metal tube that relied on some obscure scientific principle to do with lift and power ratios, driven by a machine constructed by flawed and easily distracted humans that could, she reasoned, fail at any time, was quite another story.

Trása hated airplanes with a passion and every moment she spent trapped inside one was a special sort of claustrophobic hell.

She had no choice, however.

In this realm she was more human than Faerie.

In this realm, she could only fly to Dublin from London with the assistance of an international airline.

The flight attendants sensed her unease. After she refused breakfast, determined to sit still, white knuckles gripping the armrest, one of them approached her, smiling sympathetically.

'Don't like to fly?' the perfectly groomed, redheaded woman asked, sounding genuinely concerned, which surprised Trása a little. Her nametag said 'Anthea'. She looked more like a Kathleen or a Mary.

'Not like this,' Trása said. 'How much longer?'

'We should begin our descent into Dublin in the next ten minutes or so.'

Trása nodded, not the least reassured. Most plane crashes, they claimed on *Air Crash Investigation*, happened when a plane was either taking off or landing.

'Can I get you anything?'

Trása shook her head mutely. *Just go away and leave me alone.*

'You'll have to stow the *Leipreachán*,' Anthea added with an even wider smile.

'What?'

The flight attendant pointed to the seat beside Trása where Plunkett was slumped. He'd cast a glamour over himself to give his skin the texture of woven cloth. By remaining inert and letting Trása carry him around like a stuffed toy, he was able to travel with her openly, a very useful thing for someone who didn't have a proper passport.

'Your doll,' Anthea said. 'You'll have to stow him under the seat. Or I could put him in the overhead locker for you, if you like.'

Oh, that's a grand idea. Lock the little devil in a small dark place and expect him to lie there quietly ...

'No ... it's okay,' Trása said, snatching him up. 'I'll stow him under the seat.'

'He's quite fabulous, isn't he?' the woman said. 'Can I have a closer look?'

Trása wasn't sure if she could reasonably refuse such a politely worded request. She nodded and, with some trepidation, handed over the *Leipreachán*.

'The workmanship is amazing,' Anthea said, as she admired the little man, turning him back and forth and upside down, even peeking under his waistcoat. 'He looks so real.'

'How could he be real?' Trása asked with a nervous laugh. 'He's a *Leipreachán*.'

'That's true,' Anthea laughed. 'Still, he's beautifully made. Where did you get him?'

'From my uncle,' Trása replied, quite truthfully. It was Marcroy Tarth, after all, who'd assigned Plunkett to aid her.

'You're a very lucky young lady,' Anthea said, handing him back to Trása. 'Is your uncle meeting you in Dublin?'

Trása shook her head. 'No. He lives … quite a way from Dublin. I'm going to visit … the brother of a friend.'

'Well, I'm sure you'll have a grand time,' Anthea said. 'You've still got a few weeks before school goes back, haven't you?'

'Can't wait,' Trása agreed, wishing the woman would go away.

'Do you go to school in —' Anthea stopped abruptly at the sound of a call button further down the aisle. 'Sorry … duty calls. Don't forget to stow your little friend when the seatbelt light comes on.'

The flight attendant moved off to see to her other passengers. Trása sat Plunkett's limp form on her lap and stared at him. There was no sign of life coming from the *Leipreachán* although she knew he could see and hear everything that was going on about him.

'Did you make the call button go off?' she whispered.

The inanimate Plunkett, of course, did nothing

but sit there, staring at her blankly through his shiny, apparently glass eyes.

'Good job,' she added with a conspiratorial smile.

Just then, Trása became aware that someone was watching her. She glanced sideways to find a small boy in the seat on the other side of the aisle staring intently at her and Plunkett. Hastily, she shoved the *Leipreachán* under the seat in front of her, ignoring his grunt as she kicked him firmly into place.

Then she checked her seatbelt, leaned back, gripped the armrests again and closed her eyes. She hoped the pilot knew what he was doing, and that she was not about to plummet to a fiery death when he tried to land this unwieldy beast and discovered it was more than he could handle.

The man at the passport counter must have been having a bad day. Given the number of people jostling for a place in the lines at the passport control booths, Trása didn't blame him. Dublin Airport was one of the busiest in the world.

It took nearly half an hour of shuffling along the roped-off lines before it was Trása's turn. Finally, she stepped forward and smiled brightly at the grumpy official. She handed over the passport Plunkett had stolen for her when she first arrived in this realm. Then she set her *Leipreachán* doll on the counter, so he was facing the Customs man.

'Mr Luigi Mario Berekia?'

'Yes.'

The man studied her for a long moment and then shook his head as if he couldn't understand what he was seeing. He hesitated … and then shook his head again. Anybody watching closely might have noticed her toy *Leipreachán* was sitting a little straighter than a rag doll ought to. Had there been any of the *Daoine sídhe* nearby, they would have felt the magic he was working.

'Are you here for business or pleasure?'

'Business.'

'How long will you be staying in the Republic of Ireland?'

'Only until I've found the person I'm looking for.'

The man closed the passport and handed it back to her. '*Fáilte*. Welcome to Dublin, Mr Berekia. Nice *Leipreachán*.'

'Thank you,' Trása replied brightly. 'He likes you too.'

With a cheerful smile, Trása picked Plunkett off the counter, slipped her stolen passport back into her bag and headed out toward the carousels to collect her luggage.

When she finally cleared Customs, using the same trick — or rather, Plunkett's trick — of glamouring the officials, it was almost midday. Trása waited in line outside the terminal, shivering in the afternoon breeze that threatened to bring summer to an early close. After ten minutes or so, she was at the head of the queue. She climbed into the next cab and ordered the driver to take her to a nice hotel. She had quickly learnt that 'nice' hotels had cable TV. On the downside, nice hotels usually wanted credit cards and identification details. Still, she had a stash of those in her backpack, and she supposed Plunkett would have no more trouble acquiring credit cards here in Dublin than he had in London.

As they drove toward the city along the M1, past car parks on one side of the road and green fields bordered by hedgerows on the other, Trása pondered the dilemma of finding Rónán, now she was here in his home city.

Although the film premiere on TV last night had taken place in London, the same programs that delighted in repeating Rónán's obscenity every hour or so were also quick to report he'd flown home to Dublin with his mother after the event where, they said, it was unlikely he would see the light of day again until he was thirty. Parents in this reality, Trása had gleaned, had a unique punishment for disrespectful children, known as 'grounding'. Trása had no idea what it entailed, imagining it meant confining their children in some sort of dark, dank underground cavern until they learned the error of their ways.

If he's buried underground, Trása lamented, *that will make him rather more difficult to locate.*

A check of the Dublin phone directory at the airport had proved fruitless. There were hundreds, possibly thousands, of Kavanaughs listed, but there was no way of telling which one was the actress who had adopted Rónán. Trása would have to do this another way. She needed to find someone who knew where the famous actress Kiva Kavanaugh lived.

'Have you lived in Dublin long?' she asked the taxi driver, wondering if he might know.

'All me life,' the cabbie said, glancing at her in the rear-view mirror.

'Do you know everybody, then?' It was a reasonable question, Trása thought. She knew everyone in *Sí an Bhrú*.

'Jayzus!' the cabbie chuckled. 'There's near two million people in the greater Dublin area. I'd be stretched claiming to know more'n a score of them.'

'What about someone famous, then?' she asked, a little annoyed he seemed to be laughing at her. 'Like people you see on TV. Do you know any of them?'

The cabbie wrenched the wheel, dodging across into the adjacent lane though a break in the traffic only someone with a great imagination could have spotted. It was a constant source of amazement to Trása that the roads of this reality weren't lined with wrecked cars and corpses. It didn't seem possible that so many dangerous vehicles in the hands of so many dangerous people were allowed to occupy the same roads at the same time, and it not result in multiple deaths and bloody chaos.

'Had Bono in me cab once,' the cabbie told her, scanning the traffic for another imaginary gap.

Trása was unimpressed, mostly because she had no idea who or what a bone-oh was.

'What about Kiva Kavanaugh?' she asked, growing impatient with her driver and more than a little fearful that she may not survive this trip. 'Do you know her?'

'I gotta tell you … I wouldn't mind if I did,' the cabbie said with a wink in the rear-view mirror. 'Know what I mean?'

'I need to find out where she lives.'

'You're not some crazy stalker, are you?' This time he looked over his shoulder.

Keep your eyes on the road, you maniac!

'I'm … a friend of her son's.'

'Well, you might as well turn around and go home then, girlie,' the cabbie said. 'If what I heard on the news is right, that foul-mouthed little bugger won't be entertaining company until hell freezes over. Least, he wouldn't if he was my pup.'

Trása was tiring of the cabbie's banter. So was Plunkett, she suspected. She didn't want the *Leipreachán* getting any ideas about glamouring their driver into a stupor while he was wending his way through the streets of Dublin in this sort of traffic. 'Do you know where Kiva Kavanaugh lives, or not?'

The driver reached forward, grabbing a brochure from the dash, which he handed back to her.

'What's this?'

'Dublin Guided Limousine Tours,' the cabbie explained. 'Tell 'em Dennis sent you. They'll take you around, show you all the sights ... you know, Kilmainham Gaol, Dublin Castle and the Guinness Storehouse ... although I suppose you're a bit young for that to be of much interest to you.'

'Will these Dublin Guided Limousine Tours people know where Kiva Kavanaugh lives?'

The cabbie shrugged. 'Maybe. I suppose.'

'Good,' she said leaning back in the seat, pulling her jacket a little tighter against the air-conditioned chill of the cab. She glanced at Plunkett, who was staring into space with a blank expression, and added, 'Then it won't be long, now, before we can escape this crazy place and go home.'

CHAPTER 10

To avoid the paparazzi waiting outside the main gate, Ren, Neil and Hayley took a cab home from Frascati Road and had it drop them outside Jack's place. His porch was out of sight of the Kavanaugh front gates, so they were able to slip into the grounds of Ren's house through the adjoining wall without the vultures out on the street catching sight of them.

The disadvantage of Ren's clever plan was that he failed to notice the grey BMW parked outside the front of his house, which meant he was unprepared for the surprise awaiting him when he stepped into the kitchen. Fortunately, Ren's pain had abated somewhat by then, and the wound had stopped bleeding, but he still needed to get upstairs and change his shirt before anybody spotted the bloodstain. That Hayley knew about his injury was bad enough, but at least he trusted her not to say anything.

His plans were foiled, however, by the visitor at the kitchen bench sipping a mug of fragrant coffee, waiting for them.

'Dr Symes!'

The man fixed his gaze on Ren and smiled as they filed into the kitchen. He smiled a lot at his patients, in that patronising, know-it-all way he had, that made parents feel they were getting their money's worth, and Ren feel like slamming his fist into that smug, pompous face. No amount of argument on Ren's part had ever convinced Kiva that — if she was going to hire a shrink to deal with his 'behavioural issues' — she ought to start by hiring a doctor Ren didn't frequently fantasise about murdering after ten minutes in one of his sessions.

Murray Symes was a tall, elegant man, with a slightly receding hairline going grey in all the right places. He looked the part of the understanding and compassionate child psychiatrist, which is why Kiva trusted him, Ren supposed. He was sure it wasn't because he was a brilliant shrink, despite his hourly rate.

'Ah, Ren,' Murray said, taking a sip of his coffee. 'I thought you might try to sneak past me through the back door.'

'I wasn't sneaking anywhere,' Ren said, scowling.

He knew why Murray Symes was here. Dropping the F-word on national television definitely came under the heading of 'Oppositional Defiant Disorder', which is what Symes had diagnosed Ren as suffering from.

… *With low self-esteem manifested by frequent episodes of self-harm*, Murray's notes said, *which the patient vehemently denies, claiming he has no knowledge of the origin of his injuries, which range from minor cuts to near lethal doses of homeopathic poisons.*

Ren had sneaked a peek at his file once, when Murray left him alone in his office to deal with some ranting parent in the waiting room. Murray Symes was Europe's leading expert on Oppositional Defiance Disorder. *All* his patients suffered from it.

As far as Ren was concerned, the whole ODD diagnosis was a load of complete horseshit. Since when had a seventeen-year-old arguing with his mother become a disease?

'Hello, Neil, Hayley,' Murray said, smiling at them too. Not that it did him any good. The Boyle children were even less impressed by Dr Symes's efforts to befriend them than Ren was.

'Do you know where Mum is?' Neil asked, backing up slightly to stay closer to Ren and his sister, almost as if he felt the need for their protection.

'I believe Kerry is doing the laundry, Neil,' Symes said, placing his coffee on the granite countertop. 'Why don't you and your sister run along and show her what you bought, while Ren and I talk?'

There was no need to ask Neil twice. He fled the kitchen in the direction of the utility room without any further encouragement. Hayley hesitated, spared Ren a sympathetic glance, and then followed her brother out of the kitchen.

'Have a seat, Ren.'

There wasn't much point in refusing. Ren's main job now was to ensure Symes didn't realise he had an eight-inch-long cut on his left side, another injury certain to be attributed to his low self-esteem. He walked over to the island bench, pulled out a stool, and sat down opposite the psychiatrist.

'I think we need to have a little chat, Ren,' Murray said, watching Ren closely. 'Don't you?'

'Not particularly. Is Kiva up yet?'

'She's been up for hours.'

'Ah,' Ren concluded. 'That's why you're here.'

Murray smiled. Ren unconsciously clenched his fists under the counter.

'I'm here, Ren, because you did something very disruptive at your mother's film premiere last night.'

Disruptive was code for naughty. Murray Symes would never dream of telling a child he was naughty. That might have a negative effect on his self-esteem.

'I didn't mean to embarrass Kiva by saying fuck on TV,' Ren lied. 'It just slipped out.'

'Why do you call her Kiva?' Murray asked, using his favourite tactic of abruptly changing the subject to keep his patient unbalanced. 'You hardly ever refer to her as "mum" or "mother".'

'Well, technically, Kiva's not my mother,' Ren said.

Murray smiled even wider, as if provoking Ren was the aim of the discussion, rather than finding out what might have caused this latest embarrassing manifestation of Ren's ODD. 'Do you resent the fact that Kiva is not your birth mother?'

'Only when she tries to drag me down the red carpet to increase her award chances, by reminding everyone what a fucking great humanitarian she is because she adopted the poor kid who washed up on her film set.'

The doctor nodded, not reacting to Ren's obscenity. 'I see. So you set out to undermine her chances at professional success because ...?' Murray let the sentence hang.

Ren was too wily to fall into the trap of completing it.

'Kiva can have all the professional success she wants,' he said with a shrug. 'Just don't try to make me a part of it. Are we done? I want a shower before dinner.' Actually, he wanted to get up to his room and clean the bloodstain from the light switch before Kerry spotted it and reported it to Kiva. With Patrick's offer to smuggle them out the front gate in the Bentley this morning, he never got a chance to get rid of it before they left.

'Not quite. Take off your jacket.'

'What?'

'This house is air-conditioned and climate-controlled, Ren. Winter or summer, it's shirt-sleeve temperature in here and yet there you sit, sweating in a tracksuit jacket.'

'I like my jacket.'

'And a very nice jacket it is, too. Now take it off.'

It occurred to Ren that Kerry may have already found the blood on the light switch, and Murray knew he was hiding something. That, and not last night's *faux pas* on national television, may even be the reason Kiva had called him. If Kerry decided to do the laundry today, she would have checked every hamper in the house. Ren had ditched the bloodstained T-shirt at Jack's place, but his clothes hamper was in his bathroom and Kerry was meticulous, with a nose like a bloodhound for the minutest speck of dirt. A blood-smeared light switch had no hope of escaping her attention.

Still, there was a remote chance Ren could bluff his way out of this.

'Christ,' he said, standing up and taking a step back from the counter. 'You're a fucking pervert.'

Murray was not impressed. 'Don't try that on with me, Ren.'

'Is that how you get your kicks, you sick bastard?' he asked, feigning disgust. 'By molesting the poor defenceless kids in your care?'

'Ren,' Murray warned. 'Stop it.'

'Stop what? Exposing you for what you really are, you dirty old man?'

Murray maintained an admirable air of serenity in the face of Ren's ludicrous accusation. 'This is just your way of acting out. Calm down.'

'Calm down!' Ren yelled, getting right into the moment. After all, his mother was an award-winning actress. A lifetime spent on film sets surrounded by the greatest directors of this generation had taught Ren a thing or two about being dramatic. He raised his voice even louder. 'I will not calm down! You're disgusting. And I'm not taking my clothes off for you! I don't care what you threaten me with!'

As he'd hoped it would, his yelling brought Kiva running into the kitchen. She wasn't looking nearly so immaculate this afternoon. She was barefoot, wearing a roughly tied blue silk bathrobe over her nightdress. Her shoulder-length blonde hair was mussed and stiff and pointing in several odd directions.

'Ren? What's the matter?' she asked, looking back and forth between him and the psychiatrist. 'What are you yelling about?'

'You gotta save me, Mum!' he cried. He hurried around the bench to put Kiva between him and Murray, as if he feared for his safety, even though he stood a head taller than Kiva and had done since he was fourteen. 'This depraved bastard is trying to make me take my clothes off.'

'Murray?' Kiva asked, looking more perplexed than worried.

'Pay no attention to Ren's histrionics, Kiva,' Murray said calmly. 'He's simply trying to divert attention from the fact that he's cut himself again.'

Bollocks, Ren thought. *He knows.*

'All I did was ask Ren to remove his jacket,' the shrink added, 'so I could check his arms for injury.'

Kiva turned to Ren, looking mortified. 'Is that true, Ren? Did you cut yourself again?'

'No,' Ren replied adamantly — and quite honestly. Whatever wounds he was carrying, he hadn't inflicted them on himself. He pushed his sleeves up and held out his bare forearms for examination. 'There! You see! Not a mark.'

'Kerry found blood on the light switch in your bathroom.'

'I cut myself shaving,' he said. 'It happens. Even to people without low self-esteem.'

Murray studied him closely for a moment from across the counter and then shook his head. 'You don't appear to have shaved this morning.'

'How the fuck would you know?'

'Ren! Stop this!' Kiva exclaimed, her eyes welling up with tears. 'Dear God, I don't know where I went wrong with you!'

'How about the day you pulled me out of that lake,' Ren said, a little regretful that the comment would cut Kiva to the core. Deep down, he did love Kiva, and he knew that she, in her somewhat quirky way, loved him too. She didn't deserve such cruel words, but he needed a legitimate reason to flee the kitchen before Murray decided he really must take off his jacket, and Ren's greater lie was exposed.

'He doesn't mean that, Kiva,' Murray said, calm as a frozen lake. 'He's just trying to hurt you to mask his own pain, isn't that right, Ren?'

'If it meant I didn't have to deal with this sort of bullshit,' Ren said, mostly to Murray Symes, who was the true focus of his immediate problem. 'I reckon I might have been better off if Patrick had left me there to drown!'

With that, Ren turned and stormed out of the room before Murray or Kiva could order him to stay, confident the discussion would no longer be about him. Murray Symes was going to have to spend the next hour or so consoling Kiva, and perhaps reassuring her that twenty thousand US dollars would be a small price to pay for a Utah Brat Camp if it meant Ren could be saved from himself.

Ren took the stairs two at a time, locked the door to his room and headed for his bathroom where the light switch was now free of blood smears. He poured a glass of water from the tap then took out of his pocket the two codeine tables Jack had given him earlier. He swallowed them with a grimace and went back into his room, kicked off his shoes and lay on his bed, wondering how long it would be before the pain in his side abated enough for him to keep up the pretence that nothing was wrong.

CHAPTER 11

Somewhat to Trása's amazement, Dublin Guided Limousine Tours had a whole list of celebrity addresses on their tour itinerary, most of which, however, belonged to dead people.

The latest stop had brought the tour to Baggot Street. They were standing on the pavement outside yet another old house. This one was neat and narrow, four storeys tall with a bright blue door trimmed with brass fittings.

'Do you only know where dead people *used* to live?' Trása asked her guide, a plump blonde woman wearing a green uniform with a rather ridiculous four-leaf clover-shaped hat. The woman had introduced herself as Kathleen, which seemed odd to Trása because she looked more like an Anthea. 'Or do you know where some *live* ones can be found?'

Trása had booked the tour with reception at the hotel when she checked in. She'd left Plunkett in her room to amuse himself while she went scouting their quarry. She had been in Dublin for less than three hours. She should have been minutes away from finally laying eyes on Rónán of the Undivided and this foolish woman with her ridiculous hat was wasting time showing her the residence of some pork vendor.

'Francis Bacon is one of Dublin's most famous sons. His paintings have been exhibited in every major gallery in the world, including the Guggenheim Museum and the Metropolitan Museum of Art in New York.'

'But he's dead,' Trása pointed out impatiently. 'So was the last chap, Yeats.'

'You asked for the celebrity tour, miss.'

'I wanted the *live* celebrity tour,' Trása said.

'I'm sorry,' Kathleen replied in a tone that was anything but conciliatory. 'People who take this tour have usually some idea of the depth of Ireland's cultural heritage.'

Trása smiled, which didn't help matters much. *Stupid cow, you don't know the half of it.* 'I want to know where Kiva Kavanaugh lives.'

'Blackrock,' the woman said with a sigh. She clearly thought Trása a complete philistine. 'It's about fifteen minutes from here. Ten, if the traffic's with us.'

'Let's go then,' Trása ordered, jerking open the car door. She climbed into the back of the limo, wishing she'd brought Plunkett along. He might have been able to glamour some manners into her rather put-upon tour guide.

Still ... they were only fifteen minutes from the Kavanaugh house.

Only fifteen minutes from locating Darragh's long-lost twin ...

She cut the thought off before it could form into something more dangerous. Instead, she concentrated on the good things.

Her time in this reality was almost done. Soon she could go back to her own world where her magic worked. A world where she wasn't constrained by the whim of a fickle *Leipreachán*. A world where everything made sense to her.

Well, almost everything …

Trása sank back into the deep leather seat of the limo.

It wouldn't be long now, and she could go home.

'You should have seen it, Plunkett,' Trása told the *Leipreachán* when she arrived back at the hotel a couple of hours later. 'It's like a fortress. It has a high fence and locked gates and there's a whole mob of noisy people camped outside with cameras, waiting to get in.'

Plunkett shrugged indifferently when he heard Trása's tale of woe. He was sitting cross-legged in the middle of the king-sized bed, rifling through the contents of the bar fridge, which he'd emptied while waiting for Trása to return. In addition to mounds of bacon, he was particularly fond of chocolate and potato chips. Outside, the night sky was bright with the lights of the city. That was another thing Trása found disconcerting. In the cities of this realm, it never really got dark and the sky, instead of being a reassuring backdrop sprinkled with familiar constellations, was a washed-out shadow of what it might have been, outdone by gaudy neon lights.

'What did ye expect? A welcome mat?' Plunkett said.

Trása slumped into the armchair by the window, staring despondently over the city. 'I thought I'd at least be able to get a look at the house. And maybe Rónán. To make sure we've got the right one.'

'Aye,' the *Leipreachán* said, nodding sagely. 'Best be sure we got the *right* Rónán, rescued from drowning at the right age, who's the spitting image of the lad who might be his brother in our realm.' He tore the wrapping off a triangular chocolate bar, snapped a piece off, and added, 'Wouldn't want to make that sort of mistake, would ye?'

'All right,' she conceded. 'We have the right Rónán … hopefully.'

'What do ye mean, *hopefully*?' he asked through a mouthful of chocolate.

She turned from the window to look at him. 'Well, if Marcroy and my father tossed Rónán through a rift to be rid of him, what's to say other versions of my uncle and my father, from other realms —'

'Their *eileféin*,' Plunkett interrupted, calling the alternative versions of the same people by their proper name.

'All right, their *eileféin* … what's to say they didn't do the same thing? I mean, how can we be sure he's *our* Rónán, and not a Rónán from somewhere else?'

Plunkett frowned. 'Ye're worried this Rónán is our Rónán's *eileféin*?'

'It's possible.'

'Then maybe we should lead the Druids to him ourselves,' the *Leipreachán* chuckled. 'Can ye imagine the trouble if they brought the wrong Rónán back?'

Trása hadn't considered that. Knowingly bringing someone's *eileféin* back through the rift was a serious crime among the *Tuatha*. It invariably ended in someone's death, usually the *eileféin*'s and often that of the rift runner who had brought them through.

She shook her head. It was a nice idea, but it wouldn't really work. 'The Druids would only be in trouble if someone brings the right one back. And even if they did, how would anybody tell the right one from the wrong one? The real Rónán from our realm is missing.' Trása sighed unhappily. Her enthusiasm for this mission was waning rapidly, a feeling that surprised her, given she was so close to succeeding. She expected, at this point, to have become more excited, not increasingly bothered by the likelihood of success.

Perhaps it was because Rónán looked so much like Darragh. That was a hurt Trása knew would probably never heal. And she knew it was dangerous to think of Rónán as anything other than what he was — a threat that needed to be contained before the others found him.

Or perhaps it was because, although she loved her uncle dearly, she didn't trust Marcroy Tarth much more than she trusted Plunkett.

'Do you think we should send a message back home?' she asked. 'Let them know we've found him?'

'And risk the news getting out?' Plunkett asked. 'I wouldn't, if I was ye. But then, I'm only a hundred-and-eleven years old. Who am I to argue with a halfling *Beansídhe*?'

Plunkett must be feeling the pressure too, Trása decided, surprised to hear the *Leipreachán* sounding so snappy. Or he'd eaten too much sugar.

'How do we get to him, then?' she asked. Plunkett might be right about keeping the news of their discovery to themselves, but she still needed to make contact with Rónán. How else was she going to lure him away from the rift? 'You can't glamour us past *all* those people at the gate.'

'*I* could pay him a visit,' Plunkett suggested, as he continued to devour the triangular chocolate bar.

Trása shook her head. 'He's been raised in a world with no magic. The *Tuatha* are nothing more than a children's story in this reality. If a *Leipreachán* suddenly appears to him, telling him he comes from another reality where he's a Druid with a long-lost twin, he'll think he's hallucinating. It sounds crazy even to me, and I *know* it's true.' She sighed. 'I'm afraid no one raised in this reality is going to go anywhere with you voluntarily, Plunkett.' Still, it wasn't an entirely ridiculous idea. Her forehead creased thoughtfully. 'Do you suppose you could glamour him into compliance?'

Plunkett shrugged. 'Don't know. Can't glamour any kind of Druid in our world.'

'But we're not in our world,' she said, leaning forward a little. 'Maybe here, you *can* glamour a Druid, even one of the Undivided.'

The *Leipreachán* frowned, looking very uncertain. 'Be taking a big risk if it doesn't work.'

'What risk? He doesn't even know what a glamour is, so he won't understand what you're trying to do.' She smiled. 'I've seen the face you make when you glamour humans, Plunkett. He'll probably just think you're constipated.'

'And what's *your* solution, lassie?' the *Leipreachán* asked, scrunching the foil wrapper of the chocolate bar and tossing it at her with a scowl. 'Ye have no power as a *Beansídhe* here.

What're ye thinking? To lure him with feminine *human* wiles?'

The *Leipreachán* had a point. Trása's magic was non-existent in this reality. She couldn't fly, she couldn't shape-shift. She couldn't even tell if someone was dying, although that might have been a good thing. With so many people crammed as closely together as they were in the incomprehensibly large cities she'd visited since she'd been here, she'd have spent *all* her time wailing and crying, if she could sense the end for *everyone* about to die. Trása was stuck in her human form, and that meant that here she was just a seventeen-year-old girl with impressively long blonde hair, rather oddly shaped ears and a charming stuffed toy *Leipreachán* she was fond of carting every place she went.

Rónán wouldn't know what she was. Or who she was.

And how was she supposed to explain herself?

What *would* she say to Darragh's twin if she came face to face with him? *Hello, Rónán, I'm a Faerie — well, half a Faerie, truth be told — from another reality, and I've come to make sure you never get home or meet the twin brother you don't know you have.*

'I think we need to try the glamour option first,' she decided. She bit down on her bottom lip for a moment and then added, 'But I'm not letting you do it alone.'

No need to add it was because she didn't trust him. That was a given.

'Which brings ye back to the problem of getting through the front gate.' Plunkett ripped the top off the small tube of sour-cream-and-onion-flavoured Pringles and began stuffing them into his mouth.

'You're right,' she said, something she'd never admitted to a *Leipreachán* before.

'I am?' the *Leipreachán* said, shocked by her admission.

'The *front* gate is out of the question, but I checked out the neighbourhood, and according to the postman I spoke to, there's an old man living alone in the house next door. Maybe there's a way onto the Kavanaugh estate from his place.'

The *Leipreachán* thought about that for a moment and then nodded. 'He might even know the lad,' Plunkett suggested, chip crumbs spilling out of the side of his mouth and catching in his goatee. 'Maybe ye can lure him out that way.'

'It will solve most of our problems right there, if we can,' Trása said, making her decision. She stood up, thinking it was about time she ordered room service. Plunkett's bar-fridge binge reminded her she hadn't eaten all day. 'It's settled, then. First thing tomorrow, we're going back to the Kavanaugh house in Blackrock and we'll try to make contact with Rónán using the old man next door.' She leaned across and playfully jerked the little *Leipreachán*'s perky red cap over his eyes. 'Time for you to pay your debt to the *Daoine sídhe*, Plunkett O'Bannon.'

The little man shook his head sorrowfully. 'Marcroy sending me here with ye was punishment enough, Trása Ni'Amergin,' he said, pushing the cap up in annoyance. 'Trust me, lassie, I'm paying me debt to the *Daoine sídhe*. Oh, how I'm paying.'

CHAPTER 12

Every morning, just before dawn, Jack O'Righin climbed out of bed, treated himself to a long, luxurious hot bath to ease the aches and pains that came with old age, and then walked downstairs to the kitchen. There, every day without fail, he ate two pieces of thick white toast with butter and honey, brewed himself a cup of good strong tea, shovelled four heaped teaspoons of sugar into it, and made his way out to his glasshouse.

Jack loved his glasshouse. It was the reason he'd bought this particular house. Not because of the neighbours, the posh location or the fact that — thanks to his runaway bestseller — he could have bought his own island in the Caribbean had he been so inclined. As long as Jack could remember, through a childhood filled with hunger and pain, a youth filled with violence and death, and much of his adult life spent behind bars, he had dreamed of being able to do exactly this. Get up, make a cup of tea, and potter around the garden with nothing more important to worry about than whether or not the *bromeliad* needed re-potting. It was his idea of heaven, and no matter where he went after he died — and Jack was certain, given some of the things he'd done, he was heading downwards to a very warm place — he would always be grateful that, for a short time at least, he'd known what it meant to be in heaven.

Well, almost heaven, he thought, as he shovelled sugar into his chipped enamel cup, ignoring the mess in his kitchen. He knew he should at least put the dishwasher on, but Carmel, his cleaning lady, would be back next week. She ought to be grateful he'd left her so much to do. After all, he paid her by the hour.

Jack glanced out the kitchen window, looking for the sun, but the day was overcast and it seemed about to rain. *Perhaps a bit of precipitation will drive away those fools hanging around the gate next door*, he thought.

Living next door to a famous actress had unexpected consequences for a man who liked his solitude and privacy. There were always those wretched photographers lurking in the street, hoping to catch a glimpse of her.

And then there was that poor kid of hers.

Jack liked young Ren, but knew he had problems. He didn't believe for a moment Ren was slicing himself up for attention, or that he had anything else wrong with him other than being a perfectly normal seventeen-year-old boy. That made him a pain in the arse, at times, to be sure, but hardly warranted the attention of that fancy shrink Kiva insisted on sending him to. Jack had spent enough time in The Maze with lads who really *had* lost their marbles to know Ren wasn't one of them. Someone else was inflicting those strange wounds on the young man.

At first, Jack thought it might be Kiva, but he dismissed that notion the time Ren stumbled through the gate, bleeding from a deep cut on his arm while his mother was on location in Italy.

It wasn't a schoolteacher inflicting the injuries. The kids were on vacation until September.

That left the housekeeper and her husband. But that didn't make any sense, either. The Boyles were the only solid things in Ren's life, and their own kids seemed normal and perfectly well adjusted.

That left Jack with nothing to believe but the inexplicable truth.

Something unseen and unknown had the ability to wound Ren — sometimes seriously enough to threaten his life — and the lad genuinely had no idea what or who it was.

The doorbell interrupted Jack's musings. He glanced at his watch, surprised to see it was not yet seven.

Curious as to who could be calling on him at this hour, Jack left his tea on the counter and shuffled through his echoing mansion to the front door. When he opened it, he was confronted with an unexpected sight.

Standing on his doorstep was a creature out of legend. That was his instinctive reaction, but he knew the girl couldn't possibly be that. Even so, the girl standing at his door was just too ethereally perfect to be real. As tall as he was, she appeared to be only sixteen or seventeen years old, with luscious, wavy blonde hair that flowed down past her waist. She was slender and pale with cat-like almond eyes, wearing jeans and a rainbow-coloured T-shirt, and clutching a toy *Leipreachán* in her arms.

'Yes?'

'What's your name, old man?' the girl asked, smiling brightly.

'Jack O'Righin,' he said, never for an instant thinking he should refuse the information.

'Do you live alone?'

'Yes ... well ... the housekeeper comes once a fortnight, but ...'

'Excellent,' she said, holding up her toy *Leipreachán*. 'Say hello to Plunkett.'

She held the doll up in front of him. The toy was so well made he almost seemed alive.

'This is yer granddaughter, Trása,' the *Leipreachán* told him — which was an impossibility, Jack knew. It was just a toy. 'She's come to visit ye from the north. Ye've asked her to stay as long as she likes and ye're not going to ask any questions about why she's here.'

Jack nodded. 'Very well.'

'Oh, and we like bacon for breakfast. Lots of it. Now, say hello to Trása.'

'Hello, Trása.'

'Good work, Plunkett,' Jack's granddaughter said.

Jack stepped back to let her in. He didn't remember having a granddaughter, or even a son or daughter to provide him with one.

But the *Leipreachán* had told him the girl was his, so it must be true.

Jack's granddaughter followed him around for the rest of the day — then all evening, eventually staying the night — asking him questions about himself, his life and how he came to be living in this particular house, especially as it seemed far too large for one person. Jack found himself telling her everything she wanted to know, even things he normally didn't share with other people.

He was enchanted by Trása, but any time he started to wonder about her, the thought seemed to hit a wall in his mind, vaporising like a mist and vanishing into a forgotten memory.

She seemed disgusted by the state the house was in, so she ordered her toy *Leipreachán* to clean up, which Jack considered a bit of wishful thinking, until he came downstairs the next morning to discover a sparkling kitchen with no dirty dishes, old pizza boxes or frozen TV dinner containers lying about.

A part of Jack knew there was something odd about his granddaughter. In fact, deep inside he knew he didn't *have* a granddaughter, but that hardly seemed to matter. He couldn't articulate the words, and when he did try to say something about it, suddenly that damned *Leipreachán* was there, staring at him, and he couldn't remember for the life of him what he had been about to say.

But Jack didn't mind. He found himself enjoying the company, in no small part because Trása was hugely impressed by his beloved glasshouse.

Carrying a cup of tea — complete with four sugars like his — she followed him the next morning through the misty summer rain, anxious to see his collection of exotic flora. He showed her around the benches, telling her the Latin names of each specimen, its origin and where he'd acquired it. She admired the plants he'd so carefully nurtured, ooh-ing and ah-ing with genuine awe over each new species, particularly the *bromeliads*. Jack was thrilled because the *bromeliads* were his favourites.

'They're native to the southern states of the US, like Florida,' he explained, delighted to have an attentive audience. Ren visited him in the glasshouse often, but had no interest in anything Jack was growing. 'You'll find them all through central America and South America, all the way down to Chile. There's even a very primitive species in Africa, but I don't have one of them to show you. It's survived there since before the two continents separated.'

Trása sipped her tea, looking at him oddly. 'When did *that* happen?'

Jack shrugged. 'Millions of years ago, I suppose. Don't they teach you that sort of thing in school?'

She shook her head, and took another sip of the overly sweet tea. 'Not the schools I've been to. We learnt a lot about plants, though.' She pointed to a spiny, pale green plant with a large, rusty yellow seedpod. 'What's this one?'

It was Jack's turn to look at Trása oddly. He put down his tea and picked up the pot with a grunt. It was very heavy. 'Are you serious? You don't know what that is?'

'Should I?'

'It's *ananus comosus*. My God, girl ... it's the most well-known *bromeliad* of all.'

'Oh,' she said. 'Of course.'

Jack laughed, and replaced the *bromeliad* on the bench. 'It's a pineapple, silly! Surely you've seen a pineapple before?'

'No. Should I?'

He shook his head, still laughing, 'Jayzus, it's like you're from another planet.'

'Isn't it?' she agreed, without missing a beat. 'Who lives over there?'

He looked up and followed the direction of her gaze. From the glasshouse, Jack could just make out the lights coming on in the upper storey of the Kavanaugh house through the trees.

Jack sighed. He was about to lose his audience. No teenage girl was going to stay interested in *bromeliads* when there was a celebrity living next door. 'Kiva Kavanaugh,' he said, with a certain air of resignation. 'You know ... the actress. I suppose you want to meet her. Get her autograph ...'

'No,' Trása said. 'But I'd like to meet her son. Do you know him?'

Jack smiled. The request made perfect sense to him. Why had he thought a girl Trása's age might want to meet the revered Kiva Kavanaugh? Of course, she'd rather meet Ren. He was much closer to her age, a good-looking lad, and after the other night, a minor celebrity in his own right. 'I know him.'

'Does he have a triskalion?' she asked, holding out her right hand. 'Here. On the palm of his hand?'

'Can't say I've ever paid that much attention to what sort of tattoo he has on his hand.'

'How could you miss it?,' she asked, impatient with his poor observation skills. 'It's a three-pointed symbol in a red circle bordered with orange. It's green with a yellow centre and a spiral at the end of each of the three legs.'

Jack shrugged. 'I really don't recall it, lass.'

'Well,' she said, with a heavy sigh. 'I suppose I could check for myself.'

That was one request Jack *could* grant his newly acquired granddaughter. 'He comes here to visit me,' he told her. 'I'm sure you'll run into him, sooner or later.'

'Excellent,' she said. 'In that case, why don't we have breakfast?'

'We've already had toast,' he reminded her.

'I know,' she said, 'but Plunkett wants his bacon and if you know what's good for you, old man, you'll know it's not wise to get between a *Leipreachán* and his breakfast.'

CHAPTER 13

It took Trása more than a day to find the tools she needed to construct a scrying bowl. This close to finally meeting Rónán, and with an assurance that — sooner or later — Rónán would come to visit his neighbour, Trása felt confident it was time to report home for further instructions.

She was under orders to find Rónán, after all. Exactly what she was supposed to do once she found him wasn't all that clear.

The first job was to find a bowl suitable for the task. She couldn't use plastic — scrying with a plastic bowl was about as effective as standing on a street corner and yelling loudly in the hope of being heard in her own reality — so she had to find something else. Something with a trace of lead in it.

After rifling through Jack's cupboards the day before, she had found a crystal bowl that felt right, and carried it outside to collect rain. Trial and error had taught her the need for rainwater, too. The amazingly clean water that flowed from the pipes in this realm came at a price. Treated, chlorinated and often fluoridated as well, it was about as useful as scrying with soup. She'd learnt *that* inconvenient fact when her first few attempts to call home had failed miserably.

Like everything else in this realm, the magic in the water had been processed away by progress.

Fortunately, it had rained heavily overnight, clearing with the dawn to produce a spectacularly sunny day. After lunch, while Jack was snoozing in his armchair in front of the TV, Trása carried her crystal bowl full of rainwater over to the marble garden seat on the deck outside Jack's dining room.

She removed all her clothes and dropped them on the deck. Trása had learnt about that the hard way, too. Wearing anything made of artificial fibres interfered with scrying in much the same way that powerlines interfered with TV reception.

And then carefully, so as not to disturb the water, she straddled the bench to make it easier to look into the bowl.

'What are ye going to tell him?' Plunkett asked, materialising on the other side of the bowl, bumping the rim and making the rainwater tremble and ripple. Trása would have to wait until it calmed completely before she could begin.

'That you're very annoying,' she said. 'What are you doing out here?'

'Same as ye. Getting me orders.'

'Your orders are to do as I say, Plunkett O'Bannon. That's all you need to know. Now go check on Jack. I don't want to be disturbed.'

'I already checked on him. He's asleep.'

'Then make sure he stays asleep.'

The *Leipreachán* glared at her for a moment, muttered something under his breath and vanished into thin air.

'Stupid *sídhe*,' she grumbled, turning her attention back to the bowl. The water was almost still again. Trása reached behind her head, pushed her long blonde hair aside and undid the clasp on the only thing she was still wearing — a silver chain and pendant, formed in the shape of a complicated three-pointed Celtic knot. Once she was satisfied the water was completely calm, she dropped the *airgead sídhe* knot into the water and closed her eyes.

Trása cleared her mind and concentrated on the *Tuatha* she wanted to contact. Communicating by scrying was usually a one-way affair across realities, unless both worlds were steeped in magic. That was why she had the talisman. It was infused with enough magic to make the link possible from this barren world. Her uncle, on the other hand — with the benefit of being located in a world saturated in magic — had none of her problems. He'd be able to sense her call and could simply turn to the nearest puddle to answer.

It didn't take him long. It was summer, after all, and her home was a damp and rainy place.

'Trása!'

She opened her eyes. Marcroy Tarth's unnaturally young and beautiful face stared back at her from the bowl, pale and translucent.

Trása sighed with relief, a little surprised by how glad she was to see a familiar face. 'Well met, *Uncail*.'

'You're calling me for good reason, I hope?' He glanced around, frowning. 'It had *better* be important. I'm really not in a position to talk right now.'

It was hard to say where her uncle was because the world behind him was dark. That could mean it was night, but, in theory, it should be the same time in both realities. Historical events and the level of magic differed across worlds, but the relentless progress of time remained constant. Perhaps he was indoors. Or underground. Maybe even at *Sí an Bhrú*, which would explain why he couldn't talk freely.

Dare I ask? Dare I inquire about Darragh?

She decided not to, certain Marcroy would not look favourably on her wasting time asking questions she knew he would refuse to answer. 'I've found him.'

Marcroy's translucent image regarded her warmly. 'Then you are to be congratulated, *a thaisce*.'

My treasure, he'd called her. That was a rare endearment from her fickle uncle, whose trust and affection was hard to gain and even harder to hold. 'I live to serve the *Tuatha Dé Danann, Uncail*.'

'Do you understand what you must do next?'

Trása hesitated. 'I think so.'

'You must be certain, Trása,' he said, his smile fading. 'Since your father betrayed us, we have been battling against time. Chances are high the Druids already have people in that reality, searching for Rónán. It is your job to make certain that even if they find him, they can never get close enough to him to bring him home.'

That was the same instruction Marcroy had given her before she left her own reality to step through the rift into this one. He hadn't missed an opportunity to remind her of Amergin's betrayal then, either.

There was just one thing she needed clarified. '*Uncail*, you don't want me to … kill him, do you?'

Marcroy shook his head impatiently. 'Killing Rónán would kill Darragh. Do that and you will have broken the Treaty of *Tír Na nÓg*. If that happens, *a thaisce*, trust me, I'll see to it you never find your way home.'

'Then what am I supposed to do?' she asked.

Marcroy shrugged. 'Use your imagination. Just don't fail me. Or the *Daoine sídhe*.'

'I won't,' she promised, with no idea how she was supposed to contain Rónán in this reality so that, even if the Druids somehow managed to find him, they wouldn't be able to touch him.

At least, after the fiasco on the red carpet, she thought, *he'll not be making any more appearances in public, so the chances of a Druid spotting him on TV the way I did is much less likely.*

'*Tá mo chroí istigh ionat*, Trása,' Marcroy said, as his image faded from the water. *My heart is within you, Trása.*

'Hey! Jack! You home?'

Trása froze.

He was here. Just as the old man said he would be, sooner or later. The voice calling out to Jack was so achingly familiar she wanted to weep. And she was sitting on the deck, naked as a newborn.

He hadn't seen her yet. The door leading from the kitchen into the garden was around the corner.

Trása pulled her jeans on as she debated calling for Plunkett, but decided not to. This might be the only time she got to see Rónán as he really was. Before Plunkett glamoured him into submission — assuming he could. And before she'd worked out a way to keep him out of reach of the Druids.

Before someone told Rónán the truth.

Forcing a happy smile, Trása pulled on her T-shirt and hurried barefoot through the dining room, past the table laden with books and boxes, to the kitchen.

Rónán was standing there, looking around for Jack. He looked exactly like Darragh, except that his hair was shorter. Rónán was as tall as his brother, but not as broad across the shoulders. That was likely a sign of the easy life Rónán led compared to that of his twin, who had been trained to wield a sword since he was old enough to lift a wooden practice blade. It was Rónán's eyes, however, that almost brought Trása undone. They were sapphire blue and piercing, so like Darragh's eyes that, for a moment, she could barely breathe ...

And then she managed to get a hold of herself.

'Hi, you must be Rónán from next door.'

He stared at her, momentarily stuck for words. 'My name is Ren ... Who are you?'

'I meant Ren,' she said, mentally kicking herself for the slip. Then she added by way of explanation with the friendliest smile she could manage, 'My name's Trása. Jack's my grandfather.'

'Oh,' Rónán said, staring at her oddly. 'I didn't think he had any family.'

His gaze gave her goose bumps. It was curiosity mixed with desire and mistrust. That, in itself, didn't really surprise Trása. She was half-*Beansídhe*, after all. Even though the last of her kind had died out in this world half a millennia ago, there was still some residual influence here, albeit not the magical powers she enjoyed in her own realm. And her race was not forgotten. She'd found a book, not long after she arrived, that described the *Beansídhe* as '*extremely beautiful Faeries, with long, flowing hair, red eyes (due to continuous weeping) and light complexions*'. It also claimed, '*their wailing is a warning of a death in the vicinity, although the* Beansídhe *never actually causes the death*'. That was nonsense, of course, along with the red eyes from weeping all the time, and having nothing better to do all day than foreshadow death. Still, the description wasn't entirely inaccurate. No human male in this reality or any other could resist her if she set her mind to enticing him. Or, at least, not if she had been full-grown and a pure *Beansídhe* planning a life among the *Daoine sídhe*. Even so … Rónán's gaze was like nothing she was used to. He may not have had any magical powers in this realm, either, but she could sense the latent power in him and it frightened her a little. That surprised her. She'd never considered herself afraid of Darragh.

'Did Jack tell you he had no kin?' she asked, hoping to appear nonchalant.

'Actually, it's on the dustcover of his book.'

Trása stared at him blankly. 'What book?'

'*Excuse* me?' Rónán's expression was starting to change from curious to suspicious, and unless she did something about that soon, there was going to be trouble.

A little panicked, Trása suddenly remembered the boxes of books piled on the table in the dining room. She laughed. 'I'm joking, Ren.'

'Why has he never mentioned you?'

'Because until yesterday, he didn't know I existed,' she said, deciding on a modified version of the truth. 'I sort of arrived unannounced.'

'How long are you staying?'

'We haven't really decided yet.'

Rónán was still suspicious. He looked past her. 'Where is Jack? Is he okay?'

She stepped in front of Rónán to distract him. 'Of course he's okay. I have a toy *Leipreachán*. Would you like to see him?'

'I'd like to see Jack,' Rónán insisted, trying to step past her.

Trása forced a laugh, wondering how she was going to ease his suspicions, when she spotted Plunkett materialising on the counter behind Rónán. Now was as good a time as any, she supposed, to find out if the *Leipreachán* could glamour a Druid in this reality. She pointed to the counter. 'Look, Ren, say hello to Plunkett.'

Rónán glanced at the stuffed toy that now sat on the counter, leaning against the toaster. A moment later, Trása felt the *Leipreachán* projecting the glamour. She watched Rónán carefully, looking for some sign it was working. The young man stared at Plunkett for a moment and then turned back to Trása.

'Cute,' he said, apparently unaffected by the *Leipreachán*'s spell. 'He looks real. Where's Jack?'

Trása sighed, and stood back to let Rónán pass. 'I think he fell asleep watching *Oprah*. Did you want a cup of tea?'

The request seemed to puzzle him. '*Tea?*'

'Well, you're obviously going to go in there and wake up poor old Grandad to ascertain I'm not some crazy squatter who's taken over his house. I figure he'll want a cup of tea when he wakes. I might as well make two.'

Rónán stared at her for an uncomfortably long time before asking, 'What did you say your name was?'

'Trása.'

'Milk,' he said, still staring at her intently. 'And two sugars.'

'Jack takes four,' she said, in a further attempt to establish her credentials as a member of the family.

'I know.' He glanced around the kitchen. 'Has Carmel been?'

'Who?'

'Jack's housekeeper?'

'No. We cleaned up.'

'We?'

'*I* cleaned up,' she corrected. 'Jack tried to help, but you know how he is ...'

Rónán said nothing.

On the edge of panic, Trása tried to think of something to say that would allay his suspicions, but could think of nothing that wouldn't make things worse.

The awkward tension lasted a few moments longer, until Rónán broke eye contact and she stepped aside to let him pass. He headed toward the living room where the unsuspecting Jack O'Righin was snoozing peacefully, unaware his home had become the epicentre of the battle between humans and the *Tuatha* from a different reality, and that the first salvo in that war was about to be fired ...

If only Trása had some idea what she was supposed to use for a weapon.

CHAPTER 14

Ren hurried through the dining room, down the long polished hall, past a row of oil paintings of people Jack couldn't even name — they'd come with the house — and into the main reception room where the old man liked to watch TV.

He was certain Jack's granddaughter — if that's who she really was — had been able to read every conflicted emotion on his face. Truth was, he couldn't get away from her fast enough. Not because he didn't want to be in her company, but because he didn't know how much longer he could remain focussed on those amazing, cat-like, almond eyes, and not let his gaze wander to the rest of that spectacular body — the body that only a few moments before had been sitting outside on the deck, stark naked, straddled across a marble garden bench, apparently having a conversation with a salad bowl.

Ren had escaped his own house only a few minutes earlier while Kiva was meeting, yet again, with Murray Symes. He'd tiptoed down the stairs, cut through the kitchen and across the lawn to the back gate before anybody noticed — except for Neil, but he'd shushed him with a finger to his lips as he sneaked out, confident his young cousin would not betray him.

He slipped unobserved through the gate in the garden wall. Not finding Jack in his glasshouse, Ren figured the reluctant celebrity was probably stuck in the dining room, signing books.

Ren's plans didn't extend much beyond escaping his own house. He had a vague plan in the back of his mind to call a cab from Jack's house, although he didn't have a destination in mind. Still pondering the problem, he'd rounded the corner of the house and stopped dead when he spied the strange naked girl on the terrace.

Ren had no idea what to do. He had no inkling who this odd vision of loveliness with her Lady Godiva-esque hair might be, or why she was engaged in such a strange pastime. After a moment of stunned surprise, he backed away quietly, took a few deep breaths and headed for the kitchen door, announcing his presence as loudly as he could manage.

When she'd emerged to greet him a few moments later, Trása — who seemed disturbingly familiar, although he couldn't pinpoint why — was decently dressed, to Ren's intense relief. That didn't lessen the effect she had on him, but it did make it a little easier to concentrate on forming whole words and remotely coherent sentences.

Jack, somewhat to Ren's surprise, was doing exactly what Trása had said he was doing — snoring in his armchair, the credits rolling on the Oprah show. Ren bent over him and shook him awake gently. Jack was an old man, after all. He didn't want to startle him into a heart attack.

'Hey, Jack … you okay?'

The old man blinked and glanced around vaguely for a moment. 'I must have fallen asleep,' he yawned.

'You did,' Ren said, squatting beside the big leather recliner. 'Your granddaughter let me in.'

'Who?' Jack asked blankly.

'Your granddaughter,' Ren said. 'Trása.'

'Oh, Trása,' Jack said, shaking his head as if to clear it. 'Of course. Trása is my granddaughter.'

Something made Ren glance over his shoulder; a feeling of being watched. On the credenza under the window was Trása's toy *Leipreachán*. The one she'd tried to show him in the kitchen. It looked freakishly alive. And he couldn't imagine how it had arrived here before him. Trása hadn't moved it. She was still in the kitchen making tea.

'You never said you had a granddaughter.'

'Trása is my granddaughter,' Jack repeated. 'She's from the north.'

'You mean from Belfast?'

'She's from the north,' Jack said again. It seemed an odd response and although Jack sounded a little vague, he was quite adamant.

Unable to shake the feeling of being watched, Ren glanced at the toy *Leipreachán* again. 'Don't you find that thing creepy? I mean, it's like its eyes are following you.'

'That's Plunkett,' Jack said, still sounding a little distant. Maybe it was because he'd just woken up. 'Trása's *Leipreachán*.'

'Ren!'

He looked up to find Trása standing at the door, looking a little alarmed. 'What?'

'There's a very angry-looking woman coming across the back lawn from the direction of your house.'

Shit, Ren thought. *Kiva's found me*. Maybe Neil had given him away after all.

'Sorry, Jack. Gotta bolt.'

'Why don't you and Trása take off?' Jack suggested. 'I'll cover for you.'

Ren looked at him doubtfully and then glanced over at Trása.

'You've got about thirty seconds,' she warned.

'Are you sure, Jack?'

The old man nodded, smiling as if he was looking forward to the confrontation. 'Aye, son. Off you go with Trása. I've tangled with the British SAS. I can take care of the Kiva Kavanaughs of this world.'

Ren stood up, just as the pounding on the back door started. It was all the encouragement he needed. With a final glance at Jack, he ran for the front door with Trása, closing it behind them as they heard his mother's decidedly angry footsteps on the polished boards of Jack's hallway, as she stormed through the house angrily calling Ren's name.

They didn't stop running until they were several houses down the road, in the opposite direction to the photographers camped outside Ren's front gate. Trása was laughing as they ran, as if this was a grand adventure. Ren eventually had to grab her arm to pull her up. The wound on his side was objecting to the exercise and he was afraid of opening it up again.

He collapsed against the tall, ivy-covered wall surrounding the O'Day residence, just out of sight of the paparazzi, breathing hard. Trása turned to look at him, as if she was surprised he'd stopped.

'What's the matter?'

'I ... need a minute,' he gasped in pain, holding his side.

'You don't have the stamina of your —' she began, and then stopped herself.

'Of my what?' Ren asked, wincing.

'Nothing.' She moved a little closer, examining him with a worried expression. 'Is something wrong, Ren? You're looking very pale.'

Ren lifted his shirt and showed her the bloodstained dressing underneath. 'Not pale. In pain.'

Trása pulled a face. 'Ouch! What happened?'

'I wish I knew,' Ren said, lowering his shirt. 'I get these weird injuries sometimes. Cuts, bruises ... and a couple of times they've had to pump my stomach. I woke up this morning with this beauty.'

Trása stared at him for a long moment. She didn't scoff at his words or seem to doubt him. 'Do you feel anything else?' she asked. 'Or just the wounds?'

'I get the wound, I feel the pain. What else is there?'

'You don't sense anyone else's thoughts, do you? Or anyone else's feelings?'

'What are you?' he said, looking at her oddly. 'My shrink now?'

'I'm sorry,' Trása said quickly, as if she was afraid she had offended him. 'It's just ... I don't know ... I figured that maybe if you're manifesting someone else's wounds, it would make sense you might be getting their thoughts, too, or maybe their dreams ...'

He stopped and stared at her. There was not a hint of condescension or disbelief in her tone.

He was stunned. For only the second time in his entire life, someone didn't immediately jump to the conclusion he was disturbed, suicidal or just plain crazy.

This girl he'd known for all of ten minutes believed him.

Even Hayley didn't always do that. The relief Ren felt was indescribable.

'Why do you think they're someone else's wounds?'

Ren had never contemplated the possibility. Could that be the reason for his mysterious injuries? Perhaps even his nightmares? For as long as Ren could remember, he had considered his nightmares simply an expression of his own twisted psyche. It had never occurred to him his recurring dreams, which often woke him in a cold sweat in the middle of the night, wondering what sort of sick monster lurked inside him, might belong to someone else. He wasn't sure he believed it now.

'I ... don't know *why* I think they might be somebody else's wounds,' Trása said, so uncertainly that Ren was positive she was lying. 'It just seems ... likely. I mean, if they're not your injuries, they have to be coming from somewhere, don't they?' Then she added with concern, 'Do you need help?'

He shook his head. 'I'll be okay once I catch my breath. Provided we don't do any more running.'

'We can walk,' she said, offering him her hand. 'Which brings up an interesting question. Where are we walking to?'

The pain was more manageable now, and he felt able to continue. 'Nowhere in particular. I just wanted to get out of the house for a while.' He took a cautious breath before he pushed himself off the wall, his mind still swirling with the possibilities Trása had opened up for him. Was it possible he was simply dreaming someone else's dreams; that there wasn't a monster who dreamed of murdering babies lurking inside of him? Was he suffering somebody else's wounds?

'I can understand you wanting to get out,' Trása said as they resumed walking. 'You people spend far too much time cooped up indoors.'

'You people?'

'You celebrity types,' she said.

He looked at her askance. 'Excuse me? Have you *seen* what's camped outside my house? Anyway, I'm not a celebrity. My mother's the celebrity.' It suddenly occurred to him this strange girl didn't believe his story about his mysterious injuries, she was just playing along because she believed he was famous. Or worse, because his mother was famous.

They headed away from Jack's house, Trása holding his hand as they walked. Ren tried to be cool, but he liked the idea of walking down the street with a pretty girl who didn't think he was crazy.

'I saw you on TV the other night,' Trása said, looking at him sideways.

Of course you did. 'Yeah ... you and the rest of the world.'

'I thought you were funny.'

'You should tell my mother that,' he said. 'She thinks my "funny" warrants sending me into the wilds of Utah until I learn the error of my ways.'

'What's Utah?'

Ren stared at her for a moment, wondering if she was trying to be funny or if she was simply a dumb blonde. 'It's a state in the US where everything even remotely fun is illegal. My mother has been threatening to send me to a camp there for wayward teenagers. Sort of like a cross between Alcatraz and the next season of *Survivor*.'

'Is she evil?'

'Who? My mother?' Ren shook his head. 'No. Of course not. A bit loopy at times, maybe. Her heart's in the right place. She's just not coping well with being a parent, I think. There's no script she can follow.'

'So she's sending you away,' Trása said, frowning. 'I know how that feels. What will happen to you in the wilds of Utah?'

'I'll be eating nothing but mung beans and dog shite, according to your grandfather,' Ren said as they walked. 'Completely cut off from the outside world or any semblance of civilisation, you know ... like phones, the internet, internal plumbing ... that sort of thing.'

Trása seemed utterly intrigued. '*Completely* cut off from the outside world?'

'There's no need to sound so thrilled about it.'

'I'm not ...' she said hastily. 'It's just ... I mean ... you poor thing. That's terrible.'

'It's like a prison sentence,' he agreed.

'Are people in prisons completely cut off, too?'

'I suppose,' he said. 'Why not ask your grandfather? He's the expert on doing hard time.'

'You know,' Trása said, sounding unduly pleased for no reason Ren could fathom, 'I think I will.'

CHAPTER 15

They ended up simply walking around the block, but it was quite a long way and took the better part of an hour and it was almost dusk by the time they got back. Trása was surprised how quickly the time went. She had so many questions for Rónán, and thought he'd be suspicious of them, but he seemed happy to talk and willing to answer pretty much everything she asked him, although he did get a little testy when she asked him about his dreams. In that respect, he was just like his brother. Darragh was just as guarded about his dreams, partly by nature and partly a result of the world he'd grown up in.

It was moot, in any case. Darragh would never have been permitted to spend an afternoon alone with a *Beansídhe* — even a half-human one — casually going for a walk. It was unthinkable. Even her own father would not have allowed it when he was alive and still Vate of All Eire. The Druids might turn a blind eye when other men bedded one of the *Daoine sídhe*. They'd not held it against her father, and he'd gone so far as to marry one. The Undivided, however, must never be compromised. The risk of a Druid heir being born with the powers of a *Tuatha* was too horrifying to contemplate.

That was much of the reason Trása had been sent away from *Sí an Bhrú* as soon as she turned fifteen. It was why she wasn't allowed to be there when her father died. By then, she'd reached an age where her innocent childhood friendship with Darragh was no longer indulgently smiled upon as a step toward breaching the gulf between the *Tuatha* and humanity. By that time it was regarded as dangerous.

She caught a movement in the leaves of one of the oak trees lining the street and realised Plunkett was sitting in the branches, watching them. The Druids would find out soon enough, Trása thought, as she pretended to ignore the *Leipreachán*, that sending her to Marcroy might prove far more dangerous than leaving her in close proximity to Darragh.

'Will you be in trouble when you get home, Ren?' she asked, as they neared his house and the photographers' cars parked outside the Kavanaugh residence.

'Probably,' Rónán replied with a shrug. 'But what more can Kiva do? She's probably already booked my ticket to hell.'

'Where I come from, you would be considered a man, and nobody would be able to send you anywhere you didn't want to go.' Trása figured if she dropped a few hints now, it might make it easier later on, if she had to tell Rónán the truth about who she was.

Rónán slowed and turned to look at her curiously. 'And where exactly is it that you come from?'

'North.'

138

'I come from the north, too,' he said, as if he expected her to volunteer something further.

She smiled at him, refusing to take the bait. There was dropping hints, after all, and then there was giving the game away completely. She wasn't ready to do that yet.

'That's where they found me,' he added, when she didn't answer. 'In a lake up in County Donegal.'

That wasn't what she'd heard. 'They said on TV that you'd been found in Northern Ireland.'

'Well, it's north,' he said. 'They got that much right.'

'Did your mother really save you from drowning like they said on TV?' She had no doubt Rónán was Darragh's twin brother, but by clearing this up now, Marcroy could never accuse her of not checking her facts once she returned home.

She even had a vague plan forming in the back of her mind about how she would carry out her orders so she *could* go home. But it worried her that Plunkett was following them. Things were going well. The last thing she needed was the *Leipreachán* taking matters into his own hands.

Rónán shook his head at her question. 'Actually, it was one of the stunt men.'

By Danú, *these people have some strange occupations.* 'What's a stunt man?'

'Seriously?' he asked. 'It's someone who's paid to dress the same as the actors in a movie and do the dangerous stuff. The insurance companies insist on them.'

Only about half of the sentence made sense to Trása, but she got the gist of it. 'And it was her stunt man who found you?'

He nodded. 'They were filming a scene where Kiva was supposed to be drowning. Needless to say, she wasn't. She was tucked up nice and warm in her cabin on the production barge, having her Tarot cards read, probably.'

'What happened to him?'

'Who? The stunt man? He married Kiva's cousin.'

'That's ... nice.' And convenient. Trása had no idea why her father had tossed Rónán through the rift at the exact point that he had, only that Marcroy had made him promise to ensure Rónán survived on the other side. From what she'd seen of Kiva Kavanaugh on TV, she doubted Amergin had intended her to become Rónán's guardian, but it was possible there was something about the stunt man that made him special, a suspicion made even more likely given he was still in Rónán's life. Not for the first time, Trása wished she'd been there when her father died. She would have given much to have questioned Amergin, before he passed on, about what he'd intended for the child he so callously tossed through a rift into an unknown realm.

Rónán shrugged as he walked along slowly, happier to talk about others than himself, it seemed. 'Kerry was on set with Mum when Patrick dragged me out of the water. Kiva was certain I'd been sent by God — or whatever deity she was into at the time — so she decided to adopt me. Patrick kinda felt responsible for me, I think, so he started hanging around her trailer. That's how he got to know Kerry. He had a kid the same age as me, that his first wife had just dumped on him, and one thing led to another ... you know how it is.'

'I see … and is he still a stunt-double man?'

Rónán shook his head. 'No. He quit just after he and Kerry got married. Kerry used to worry about him getting hurt, I think, which is why Patrick gave it up. Mum hired him on as her chauffeur.'

'That was nice of her.'

'Yeah,' Rónán said, with a faint smile. 'I'm not sure if it was because of all that useful stunt-driver training he had, or because she figured with Patrick on the payroll, Kerry wasn't going to up and leave her alone to fend for herself.'

'So you know Patrick well?'

'Closest thing I have to a father,' he said. Rónán stopped walking and studied the swarm of cars parked further up the street. He frowned and took her hand again. This time he walked on the other side of her, and the hand holding hers was the hand with the triskalion. Trása could feel the faintest hint of the magic it could channel still lingering in the design, even here in this reality, where there was no magic to speak of. 'Let's walk on the other side of the road. With luck we might even get back to Jack's place before anybody notices us.'

'Is Patrick the one who named you Ren?' she asked, as they stepped up to the kerb. Behind her, she heard leaves rustling in the branches of the leafy oak. Plunkett was still following them, she guessed. *Don't you dare let him see you*, she warned the *Leipreachán* silently, knowing he couldn't hear her, but wishing he could. She'd have a lot of explaining to do if Plunkett suddenly dropped out of a tree and landed at their feet.

She dragged her attention back to Rónán, who was shaking his head. 'Ren was the only coherent thing I could say after Patrick dragged me out of the water.' He glanced both ways and then, hand in hand, they jogged across the street to the path on the other side. Almost without thinking, Rónán moved to Trása's right, placing her between him and the photographers further up the road, adding, 'Kiva renamed me when I was officially adopted. My full legal name is Chelan Aquarius Kavanaugh.'

Trása wasn't sure how to respond to that.

Rónán sighed at her silence. 'I think Chelan is a Native American name meaning deep water, and Aquarius —'

'Is Latin,' Trása said. She knew that one. 'The water bearer.'

'It could have been worse,' he said. 'She could have named me Evian Perrier Kavanaugh.'

Trása waited, thinking there was more to his comment, but the joke went completely over her head. 'So how is it everyone calls you Ren, if your name is really Chelan?'

'I refused to answer to anything else. They gave up trying to call me Chelan in the end.'

'Do you think Ren's your real name?' she asked, as she caught a flash of red tartan in the branches of the tree just ahead of them. 'The one you're supposed to have?'

He shrugged. 'I don't know. But at the very least, it's way easier to spell than Chelan Aquarius.'

'You don't mind talking about this, do you?' Trása was anxious to keep his attention on her. Plunkett was being very careless.

Rónán seemed unconcerned. He wasn't paying attention to the movement in the trees ahead of them, but to the gauntlet of photographers they would soon have to run. 'Not really. It's no big secret, and to be honest, I don't remember anything about it. I only know what I've been told.'

'Don't you ever wonder how you came to be in the water?' Trása hoped she sounded curious rather than desperate to know the answer to that very important question. 'Did they never find any clue as to how you came to be there?'

Rónán shook his head. 'Not a thing. They assume I was on a boat with the rest of my family and it sank without a trace — even though they dredged the lake — because nobody even lodged a missing person complaint afterward, for me or anybody else.'

'That's so sad,' Trása said, thinking the complete opposite, and a little sorry they were almost home. It had been a very enlightening conversation. She risked a glance at the tree. They were almost under it. She couldn't see Plunkett. With luck he'd tired of them and had returned to the house to keep an eye on the old man.

'My theory is they were crazy hippies who'd dropped out of society — hence the reason nobody reported them missing.'

'Why would you think they were hippies?'

Rónán let her hand go and opened his left palm to reveal the triskalion tattoo she'd been able to feel, but not examine closely. There was not the remotest chance this wasn't the Rónán she was looking for.

'Who else would tattoo a baby like this?'

Fortunately, Trása didn't have to pretend she couldn't answer his question. Their walk had brought them past the tree where Plunkett had been lurking and almost opposite the high locked gates of Rónán's house. So far, the photographers weren't paying any attention to them. To the waiting paparazzi — who'd barely glanced at the couple on the other side of road — they probably seemed nothing more than local kids out for a walk on a bright summer afternoon. Their quarry — as far as the paparazzi knew — was still safely holed up inside the house and their long lenses were pointed in that direction, while they talked and joked among themselves, waiting for something to happen.

'Keep your face turned away,' Rónán advised, as they drew level with the crowd of photographers gathered around the gates on the other side of the road. They were mostly men, but there were one or two women, as well as a couple of American tourists hoping for an autograph, if their loud shirts and sandals worn over socks were anything to go by. Rónán thrust his hands deep into the pockets of his jeans, hunched his shoulders and lowered his head, making himself as inconspicuous as possible.

Across the road, Trása could hear someone's phone ringing. A few moments later, she heard the photographers ribbing the recipient of the call. It was his wife calling, she gathered, demanding he pick up some milk on the way home.

Then two things happened almost simultaneously. The gates of the Kavanaugh house began to swing inwards.

And somebody called Ren's name.

It was like throwing a crust of bread into a flock of seagulls. The photographers began simultaneously pushing and shoving, to see who was coming out of the Kavanaugh estate, and looking around for Rónán.

But it wasn't a paparazzo who'd called Ren's name, Trása realised, it was Plunkett.

What was he thinking?

Trása looked around for the *Leipreachán* but couldn't see him. Across the street, however, was a girl of about sixteen or seventeen with dark hair pulled up into a ponytail and features so familiar that for a moment, Trása was rendered speechless. The girl was standing near Jack's driveway, waving to them, and shouting something Trása couldn't make out. Then a sleek silver BMW appeared behind the opening gates of the Kavanaugh house.

'Oh, crap,' Rónán said, with a panicked look. 'That's Murray's car. I thought he'd left hours ago.'

'Who's that girl?'

'Hayley,' he explained. 'Shit ... Neil must have said something about me leaving. Come on,' he added, grabbing Trása's hand. 'We're gonna have to run for it.'

'There he is!' one of the photographers cried.

At the cry, the paparazzi went into a frenzy. Half of them were determined to get a shot of whoever was in the car, while the rest set off after Rónán. They were tripping over each other, calling out Ren's name, yelling questions about who Trása might be, and where his mother was. They shouted and shoved, flashbulbs exploding with painful light. The driver of the BMW leant on the horn, and gunned the engine threateningly as he forced his way through the pack.

I am going to kill you, Plunkett, Trása promised herself silently. *As slowly and as painfully and as many times as I can manage.* She couldn't see the *Leipreachán,* but she could feel him nearby.

Trása didn't have time to wonder why Plunkett had alerted the photographers to Rónán's presence. All she could do was hang on to Rónán as they ran, only a few steps ahead of the mob. Unfortunately, they were trapped on the wrong side of the street, making it impossible to return to either Rónán's, or Jack's, house.

Hayley saw their dilemma. Still waving and calling out to Rónán — as if there was anything she could do to rescue him — she ran across the road toward them.

Trása felt it before it happened. Whether or not there was magical power in this realm, she was still half-*Beansídhe*. She knew when someone was about to die.

The dread washed over her and instinctively she stopped, forcing Rónán, who was still holding her hand, back onto the kerb just as the BMW suddenly accelerated forward, slamming into Hayley, throwing her in the air like a rag doll.

CHAPTER 16

The day dragged for Darragh, made worse by the wound in his side that suddenly seemed to get worse as midday approached, making him double over with the pain. By the time the queen of the Celts and her party arrived at dusk with Marcroy Tarth — who was inexplicably unaccompanied by any other *sídhe* — it had subsided, somewhat, and then, miraculously, just as the evening's festivities were getting underway, the pain faded away completely.

Darragh smiled, and not just because of the relief. He knew what the pain meant. The pain he felt wasn't his, he realised. And that filled him with a sense of giddy anticipation.

Unfortunately, his smile coincided with his introduction to one of Álmhath's countless court maidens. Everybody in the hall immediately took his delighted smile to mean he found her pleasing, and without causing the young woman enormous shame and embarrassment by saying otherwise, Darragh had no choice but to play along.

Not that the maiden wasn't lovely to look at. She was his age — perhaps a year or two older — with a mass of thick dark curls that tumbled down to her waist, wide blue eyes framed by long dark lashes, a sprinkling of pale freckles across her creamy skin and a smile that hinted at a sense of mischief. She curtseyed low as the queen introduced them, meeting his eye in a manner suggesting that, far from being awed or frightened of him, she was enchanted.

'I don't believe you've met my court maiden, Brydie Ni'Seamus, *Leath tiarna*,' Álmhath said, watching Darragh closely. 'She's Mogue Ni'Farrell's daughter.'

Darragh tried to wipe the smile off his face, but it was too late. The damage was done. 'I've not had the pleasure, *an Bhantiarna*.' He'd heard of Mogue Ni'Farrell, a legendary beauty to whom Amergin, in his day, had composed more than one popular ode celebrating her magnificence.

'She's pretty enough to be one of the *Daoine sídhe*,' Marcroy remarked from his seat further down the table — a high compliment indeed from the *Tuatha* lord. 'Are you sure your Mogue was faithful to her husband, Álmhath?'

Darragh expected Álmhath to explode at the suggestion but, rather than take offence, the queen of the Celts laughed aloud. 'If you knew my prudish little friend Mogue well, *tiarna*, you'd wonder not that she might have lain with a *sídhe*, but how she came to lie with any man at all.'

That was an odd thing for Álmhath to say ...

Regrettably, Darragh was still smiling — it was hard not to — so he leant forward and offered Brydie his hand. 'Do not listen to them, my lady. Your beauty is all your own.'

That's done it, good and proper, Darragh thought, as Brydie rose to her feet, smiling at him

148

with an open invitation. Quoting a line from one of Amergin's epic love poems about her mother — however innocently — would have this girl in his bed by moonrise.

Any other time, that might not be a bad thing, but he had plans for the coming days, and they didn't involve bedding the court maiden of the Celtic queen, no matter how enticing.

'Why don't you ask Brydie to join us, Darragh?' Torcán suggested.

Darragh glanced at Torcán in surprise. The prince was sitting between his mother the queen, and his betrothed, Anwen. On the other side, Marcroy Tarth was leaning back in his seat nursing a cup, looking a little concerned. Torcán sipped his mead, feigning innocence, though not very effectively.

Darragh turned back to Brydie. Even without the Sight, he would have smelt the trap. Brydie was here to entice him and, in all likelihood, Torcán knew about it. He may have even been the one who suggested it.

Among the *Tuatha*, one never discussed business until the festivities were done, so there'd been no hint, until now, why Marcroy had asked for this meeting nor why Álmhath had agreed to be party to it. There was no good-mannered way for Darragh to inquire about the nature of their business, either, before the partying was finished. Darragh suspected it would be something frivolous. Some trivial matter that could have been handled by far lesser ranks than the lord of the Mounds, the queen of the Celts and the Undivided.

But perhaps this wasn't about treaties. Perhaps this was about getting a pretty girl, who owed her loyalty to someone other than the Druids, into the bed of a young man too blinded by desire to care that she might be a spy.

What have I ever done to make these people think I'm so stupid?

'I think that's a wonderful idea,' Darragh said. *Two can play this game.* He turned to Colmán. 'Have another place set for the Lady Brydie, my lord Vate.'

'No need to go to any trouble,' Marcroy told the Vate with an oily smile. 'There's already an empty place right next to Darragh. Lady Brydie can sit there, can't she?'

Silence descended on the hall as every eye expectantly turned to Darragh. The empty place Marcroy was referring to was Rónán's place; the place that had remained vacant for the past fifteen years, waiting for Darragh's brother to return.

Darragh understood, now, what introducing him to Brydie was about. Forcing Darragh into making this very public gesture was one way of having him admit, in front of his own people, the Celts and the *Tuatha Dé Danann*, that the power of the Undivided was broken.

If he allowed Brydie to take Rónán's seat, he would be telling the whole world his brother was lost forever. But what would such an acknowledgement achieve? While Rónán lived, even though he wasn't in this realm, the power still flowed to the Druids through the twins, and if they killed Darragh, Rónán — wherever he was — would die too. That would render the Druids powerless ...

Of course. This wasn't about the Undivided. This was about Álmhath's resentment of the

Druids. She was queen of the Celts but it was the Druids who made the laws, recorded history and, in many ways, ruled her kingdom. She was an absolute monarch, but the Druid sorcerers and bards who roamed her kingdom had the power to overrule her, and quite often did.

Not being a Druid, she had no real concept of how the destruction of their magical power would decimate them and their world. Or perhaps she did.

Marcroy Tarth, on the other hand … what would he get out of this? The sacred nature of *Tuatha* law meant he could never knowingly break the Treaty of *Tír Na nÓg*, which guaranteed the sharing of *Daoine sídhe* magic with humans. *But if the treaty became irrelevant because there were no more Undivided to bear the power-sharing burden?* Yes, Darragh could see Marcroy embracing such a plan with great enthusiasm.

What must it be like, Darragh wondered wearily, *to live in a world with no magic and the politics that went with preserving it?*

Rónán might know. Some said he'd been thrown into a reality where his power meant nothing. What would it be like, to be free of the burden?

When we find him, will he want *the burden of his magical powers thrust upon him?*

Darragh didn't allow the dread fear of not finding his brother take root in his mind. They would find Rónán.

They *had* to find Rónán.

He glanced at Colmán — who looked paler than a worm found under a freshly turned rock — trying to imagine him doing what Amergin had done.

And then Darragh became aware of the heavy air of silent anticipation focussed on him. He forced himself to smile even wider, looking around the hall at the sea of expectant faces. The whole court was holding its breath, waiting for him to stumble.

He was still holding Brydie's hand. With a bow, he indicated Rónán's vacant seat. 'The lord of the Mounds is right, my lady. We'll not be needing my brother's seat tonight. Why don't you sit here?'

One immediate benefit of Darragh's decision to put Brydie in his brother's vacant seat was that Colmán was rendered speechless, and the evening progressed very nicely without the constant interruption of the Vate's appallingly bad verse, chronicling the details of their meal. Colmán was, in fact, quite apoplectic, but it was hours before he would be able to get Darragh alone and inform him of his displeasure. In the meantime, Darragh enjoyed a pleasant meal with the delightful Brydie by his side, while the guests muttered ominously about him, and Álmhath, Torcán and Marcroy barely contained their glee.

Neither could Darragh, but for entirely different reasons.

The Vate finally cornered Darragh in the hall outside his room as he was heading for bed. Darragh let him rant for a few minutes, knowing the old man would feel better for it, and that while he was ranting, he wasn't likely to throw in another verse. After the third time Colmán called him a mindless fool with his brains in his genitals — so angry he didn't even attempt to make the insult a rhyme — Darragh decided he'd heard enough.

'Stop!' he commanded, putting his hand over Colmán's mouth — an unpleasant sensation, given how much grease the old man used to fork his beard. 'I get it. You're angry with me.'

He took his hand away. Colmán looked ready to burst something. '*Leath tiarna*, have you any idea what you've *done*?'

'I know exactly what I've done, Vate, and one day you'll be singing about it. In the meantime, can you get me some *Brionglóid Gorm*?'

Colmán was instantly suspicious. 'What do you need that for?'

Darragh grinned. 'In case she snores.'

'*Leath tiarna*!' the Vate gasped in horror. 'You can't mean you're …?' He stopped and glanced around to be certain they were alone. 'Are you insane? You're planning to render the Celtic queen's court maiden unconscious in order to have your way with her?'

'Quite the opposite, Colmán,' Darragh said, lowering his voice. Although he was certain there was nobody listening, there were *Daoine sídhe* in *Sí an Bhrú* tonight. One couldn't be too careful. 'I want to render the Celtic queen's court maiden unconscious to *stop* her having her way with me.'

The old man took a deep breath. 'Darragh,' he said, one of the rare times Colmán had ever addressed him by name. 'I don't know what game you think you have going here, but I must warn you, it will not work.' He threw his hands up in despair. 'By *Danú*, where is Ciarán when I need him?'

'Ciarán would tell you not to worry,' Darragh assured the Vate, hoping the old man's concern wouldn't prompt him to go looking for the missing warrior.

Fortunately, Colmán was too distressed to even wonder where Ciarán was. 'You have weakened your position tonight,' Colmán warned, 'all for the sake of a smile from a pretty girl. To compound the error by even allowing that sly little vixen into your bed, let alone thinking you can keep the upper hand by drugging her ...' He threw his hands up again helplessly, his voice trailing off as if he didn't have the words to explain how he felt, a cruel situation for a man who lived by his ability to find words for every occasion.

Darragh sighed to cover his frustration. Amergin would not need to have this explained to him. 'Lord Vate, what did Amergin tell you about me?'

The old man looked away, unable to meet Darragh's eye. 'I don't know what you mean ...'

'You were Amergin's apprentice for a decade before he died, Colmán. You discussed my progress with him often. Amergin told me that himself.'

The Vate shrugged, unable to deny it.

'And didn't he tell you I'm smarter than I look?' Darragh knew that to be case, because Amergin had joked about it afterward.

'Even so, *Leath tiarna* ...'

'All I'm asking is that you give me the benefit of the doubt, Colmán,' Darragh begged, wishing this man would take him seriously, as Ciarán did. '*Trust* me. Trust that I knew exactly what I was doing when I surrendered my brother's seat to Lady Brydie tonight.'

Colmán frowned, his eyes filled with doubt.

'And if that isn't enough for you, trust that Ciarán would not have left me here to deal with

Álmhath and Marcroy alone, if he didn't believe I knew what I was doing.'

It was hard for Colmán to argue with that. He shook his head, still not convinced, but not able, in his confusion, to think of an argument to counter Darragh's logic. '*Leath tiarna*, it is arrogant in the extreme to think you alone — a mere boy — can outwit the *Daoine sídhe*, the Celtic queen and even those among our own order who believe that without the other half of the Undivided, you have no right to sit the Twin Throne. Regardless of what Ciarán may have to say on the matter, you gave Álmhath a gift tonight, and all you seem capable of thinking about is your own carnal pleasure.'

Darragh smiled, hoping to reassure the old man, but suspecting his smile would only reinforce the Vate's suspicion that he was a young, politically naïve — and dangerously lustful — fool. 'I can tell you this much, Vate,' he said. 'If you trust me, all will be well. And of one other thing I can assure you — I won't be alone.'

CHAPTER 17

When Ren gave his statement to the Gardaí several hours later he was hard-pressed to remember the details of the accident. By then it was night. The ambulance had taken Hayley away in a wail of urgent sirens, the Gardaí cars with their flashing blue lights had dwindled to a lone patrol car parked in the circular driveway outside the house, and the paparazzi had thronged to the hospital. A gentle rain pattered softly onto the street, washing away the last traces of Hayley's blood.

All Ren could remember was the sound of Murray's car hitting Hayley. And her scream — cut short by the crack her head made when it smacked onto the roadway, several metres from where the BMW had skidded to a stop.

'And you're sure that's all you can remember, Ren?' the officer asked, as she closed her notepad.

Ren nodded mutely, not sure what else to say. He was numb — lacking the energy for even the simplest exchange. Across the hospital waiting room a muted wall-mounted TV was previewing the upcoming football season while beneath it, a frazzled mother tried to keep several tired kids, all in their pyjamas, under control.

'It all happened so fast,' he finally said, because the officer was looking at him so expectantly.

They were sitting in a tucked-away corner of the Emergency Department. They had been brought here to make their statements against a background of whimpering children, belligerent drunks and weary mothers, probably wishing their children's illness were a little more serious so they'd get bumped up the triage list and not have to wait so long in this depressing place.

Ren glanced at Trása sitting beside him. She nodded and squeezed his hand comfortingly.

'What about you, Trása?' she asked. 'Can you remember anything else?'

Trása's eyes were red from weeping. Hayley's accident seemed to have wounded her more than it affected Hayley's own cousin, Ren.

Trása shook her head. 'It's like Ro … Ren said. It happened so fast. It was very crazy out there. All those excited people. All those bright flashing lights.'

The Gardaí officer nodded in agreement. 'I can imagine,' she said. 'Must be awful, living in a fishbowl.' She smiled sympathetically. 'I'll get your statements typed up and bring them over to the house for you to sign tomorrow. Normally, I'd ask you to come into the station to sign them, but in light of your … special circumstances, it's probably better if I bring them to you.' She glanced over her shoulder toward the door. Hospital security were keeping the wolves at bay, so for the time being at least, there were no paparazzi waiting outside.

'What special circumstances?' Trása asked, looking puzzled.

'She means not everyone has a rabid mob of hyenas camped outside their front gate waiting to get a saleable shot of the freak show,' Ren told her bitterly, and then he turned to the officer. 'Thanks, sergeant, we'd appreciate that.'

'What will happen to the man driving the car?' Trása asked.

'Not up to me.' The officer climbed to her feet and straightened her jacket. 'I'm guessing not much, though,' she added, pocketing the notebook beside the pen. 'Dr Symes wasn't drunk, he has a clean driving history and the paparazzi had a lot to do with it.' She looked down at Ren sympathetically. 'Accidents happen, Ren. Don't go blaming yourself over this. It's not your fault.'

'I'm not,' he assured her. 'Symes floored it.' He'd been adamant about that in his statement. Of the few things he did remember, the sound of Murray Symes revving the engine of his BMW to scare the paparazzi away was one of the things that stuck in his mind. 'I wouldn't be surprised if he'd been planning to hit one of the photographers.'

'Well, unfortunately, he hit your cousin instead,' the officer said. 'And I'm quite sure he wasn't planning to do that. So be careful making accusations, Ren, unless you are certain you can back them up.'

'He still ought to pay,' Trása insisted, letting Ren's hand go to wipe her eyes with a scrunched up tissue that was long past its useful life. 'An innocent soul should not be snuffed out so carelessly without some recompense to the goddess.'

'She's not dead, Trása,' the officer repeated, a little impatiently. Trása seemed to be writing off Hayley too easily. 'Are you kids going to be okay?' she asked, picking up her car keys from the vinyl waiting-room seat. 'It's been a fairly harrowing day for you. Did you want me to call someone?'

Ren shook his head. 'We'll go back upstairs to the ICU in a bit. My mother's up there with Hayley's parents.'

'Okay then,' she said. 'I'll see you tomorrow.'

'I'll walk you out,' Ren offered. 'I could do with some fresh air.'

The woman thanked him for the offer, said goodbye to Trása, and then walked with Ren toward the Emergency Department entrance. She checked once again if he'd be okay, and then said goodbye. Ren waited as she ran across the driveway in the drizzling rain, and then climbed into her patrol car which was parked in one of the reserved emergency places at the front of the hospital. As she drove away, Ren pulled up the hood of his sweatshirt and headed in the opposite direction, toward the car park. There were a few photographers gathered on the other side of the road, but it was wet and they were sitting in their cars, not paying attention to the lone figure heading away from them. They were waiting for Kiva.

'Is the Gardaí officer gone?'

Ren turned. Trása had followed him. The wretched *Leipreachán* was tucked under her arm. 'Yeah,' he said.

'What will happen now?'

'We wait,' Ren said, glancing up at the multi-storey building where Hayley was fighting for her life. The hospital car park was almost deserted. He glanced at his watch. It was past midnight. 'You don't have to stay with me. I'll be okay, Trása.'

'I'm so sorry about Hayley, Ren.'

He adjusted his hood, so he wouldn't have to face her. 'She'll be okay, Trása. This is the best hospital in the country, she's under the best doctors, getting the best care.' He thrust his hands into his pockets. 'Kiva won't skimp on making sure Hayley gets whatever she needs. The Boyles are family.'

Trása seemed truly bewildered. 'But surely Hayley's injuries are so bad nothing can be done for her now, except make her comfortable until she dies?'

Ren stopped and turned to look at her. 'You give up on people pretty easily, don't you?'

'I'm not giving up, Ren,' Trása said, as if she was afraid she'd made him angry. 'I'm just being realistic. There was so much blood. And Hayley's head was badly injured. The men driving the ambulance said so. You have no magical healing in this world to fix her.'

'Yeah, well a few million bucks' worth of hi-tech medical equipment and a hospital full of specialists ought to have the same effect as magic. In *this* world.' Ren turned and continued to walk through the misty rain, wondering why Trása would comment on "this world". As if there was another one out there somewhere.

Trása put her hand on his shoulder. 'The officer was right, Ren. It's not your fault.'

'Of course it's not my fault,' he said, shaking her hand off. 'Hayley steps in front of speeding fucking cars trying to get across the road to me all the time. Even when I'm *not* there.' Ren stopped and closed his eyes for a moment.

'Ren, don't blame yourself.'

'Then who *should* I blame?'

'The man driving the car?' Trása suggested. 'You said it yourself ... he was trying to hit someone. He wielded the weapon. He was aiming for those men who were blocking his path. He is the one who hit her. He is the one who should pay. He is the one we will *make* pay.'

The strident tone of her declaration made Ren open his eyes and stare at her in alarm. 'Settle down there, Rambo.'

She wasn't smiling. 'I don't know what that means, Ren. I just know that where I come from, such an act would not go unpunished.'

'And *where* is that exactly?'

She smiled. 'North.'

Red couldn't help but smile, too. He didn't feel like it, but there was something about Trása, even with her swollen, tear stained eyes, that was hard to resist.

'North, huh?'

'It's a very nice place,' she said. 'You should visit it sometime.'

Her vagueness irritated him a little, but then he frowned, as another thought occurred to him.

'Hey ... shouldn't you be getting home? It's past midnight. Jack'll be worried about you.'

'He knows where I am,' she said. Then she leant across, quite unexpectedly, and kissed him on the lips.

Ren said nothing. His brain seized up like a badly maintained engine, gluing his tongue to the roof of his suddenly dry mouth. She tasted of raindrops and promises.

His silence seemed to confuse Trása. 'What's the matter? Did I do something wrong?'

'Um … no … of course not,' Ren managed finally. 'I was just wondering … you know … why you did that?'

'I like you,' she said, as if it was the most reasonable thing in the world. 'Where I come from, we comfort the people we like when they're in pain.'

He smiled wistfully. 'Makes me kinda wish I'd broken my leg.'

Trása cocked her head sideways. 'What?'

'Nothing,' he sighed. 'I'm just not used to … well, girls I've known for less than a day kissing me out of the blue.'

She seemed a little miffed at his reaction. 'Look, if it upsets you so much that I kissed you, I'm sorry. I'll know better than to try to comfort you next time. I'll see you later.'

'Please, Trása … I'm sorry.'

Trása turned to stare at him, frowning. 'For what?'

'For snapping at you. I'm not …' He let the sentence hang, uncertain how to explain himself. He had never felt so lost. Or so alone. Everyone was upstairs in the ICU, worried sick about Hayley. As they should be. *It's where I should be.* Ren reached out and grabbed Trása's arm.

She debated his apology for a moment in silence, her dark almond eyes giving away nothing, making him wait a few moments longer, before asking, 'Can I hang out here with you?'

He shrugged. 'If you want.'

Trása reached up to gently touch his face. 'I know someone just like you,' she said softly. 'When he gets upset, he does the same thing.'

'What thing?' he asked, with no clue who she might be referring to. A boyfriend, perhaps? Her hand was unnaturally warm against his skin.

'He disappears outside, saying he wants to be alone.'

'Do you follow him and randomly kiss him too?' Ren asked. He wished he hadn't said it, almost as soon as the words were out, but her hand was burning his cheek where it touched and he really wasn't thinking straight.

But Trása didn't seem offended. She stepped a little closer to him, rose up on her toes and kissed him again, squashing her creepy *Leipreachán* doll between them. Ren slipped his arms around her, pulling her closer. As he tightened the embrace, part of him thought the damned toy had grunted in pain.

CHAPTER 18

Brydie came to Darragh's room later that night. She let herself in, padded barefoot to the end of the bed where she stood and waited for him to notice her. He turned over at the sound of the door closing and waved his hand to magically light the oil lamp beside the bed. He silently studied his guest for a time.

Ciarán had taught him that trick. When you weren't sure of the right thing to say, it looked wiser to say nothing at all.

His silence worked. After a few awkward moments, Brydie tried to fill the silence.

'What happened to your legendary protector?'

'Excuse me?'

'The great warrior, Ciarán. Legend has it he sleeps on the floor outside your door.'

'Ciarán makes up those rumours to scare off people who want to sneak into my room in the dead of night,' Darragh said, pushing himself up on his elbows. Brydie was standing at the foot of the bed in a nightgown made of gossamer, her rich auburn hair down. She unclasped the amethyst-and-gold filigree brooch at her throat, dropping her cloak to the floor to reveal her comely body clearly outlined through the thin fabric. Anybody who had seen Brydie traversing the halls of *Sí an Bhrú* dressed like that would have no doubt she had a lover's assignation in mind.

'Apparently, the legend's not working as well as it should,' Darragh said.

'Are you going to send me away?' she asked with a slight tremble in her voice. She seemed much less certain of herself now than she had been in the hall earlier.

Darragh clasped his hands behind his head because it made him look more in control of the situation than he felt, and was the best way to ensure she couldn't see them trembling. 'That depends.'

'On what?'

'On whether you're here because you *want* to be here, or because Álmhath's threatened you with something you dislike even more than the idea of sleeping with me.'

Instead of answering him, Brydie tugged at the laces on her nightgown, letting it fall to her feet. Her body was flawless, pale and enticing. Her breasts were round and full, the dark bush between her thighs a sure sign that the rich dark tone of her hair was natural and not the result of being dyed, the way the Greeks and Romans dyed their hair.

'I volunteered,' she said with a small smile.

Darragh swallowed hard, trying to give the appearance of nonchalance. 'Call the Vate.'

'Pardon?'

'Go to the door,' he said. 'Call for Colmán. He'll be hovering around out there somewhere. He's very annoying like that.'

'You're sending me away?'

Darragh shook his head. 'Not at all. I want you to give the old fool a message.'

'What message?'

'Tell him we're going to be busy.'

'Until morning?' she suggested, with a smile that promised so much Darragh could feel himself growing hard at the mere thought of what this girl might want to do to him.

'For the next few days,' he corrected with a grin. 'Tell him to bring food, later, too. And that only he is to deliver it.'

'That's a harsh thing to ask a man in Colmán's position.'

'What do you care?'

'Well, now you mention it …'

Brydie went to the door, called for Colmán, took great delight in telling the mortified Vate of All Eire she and Darragh would be busy for the next few days and that he was now charged with serving them. Then she shut the door in the old man's face, and turned to lean on it with a laugh.

'I enjoyed that.' She sauntered back to his side of the bed and stood there looking down at him, hands on her hips, her breasts pushed forward provocatively. After a moment, she ran her tongue over her full, pink lips with the faintest hint of a smile. 'You're not what I was expecting.'

Danú *give me strength* … 'What … were you expecting?'

'I'm not sure, really,' Brydie said, studying him curiously. 'You're more … human than I was expecting, I suppose.'

Darragh laughed at that. 'Human? What made you think I wouldn't be?'

Brydie shrugged. 'I don't know. It's probably

because you're one of the Undivided. You have to admit, you're not really like the rest of us.'

'You don't know that. You don't know me at all.'

'I'd like to,' she said, holding out her hand.

Danú, *but she's gorgeous.*

Darragh leant forward and took the offered hand, pulling her down on top of him. He let her kiss him, open mouthed, relishing the taste of her, delighting in the feel of her firm body as he ran his hands over her creamy skin, wishing it was going to end the way she seemed to intend. For a time he gave in to her caresses, telling himself he had to act as if he really intended to make love to her, otherwise she'd be suspicious. After a few moments of increasingly frantic kissing and urgent groping, they rolled over in a tangle of furs so that he was on top of her. Her legs were open, wide and inviting, silently begging him to enter.

He sat astride her, breathing hard, with no need to fake the desire he felt. A part of him marvelled at his own self-control for stopping now; another part of him — the part of him ruled by his little brain, not the big one, as Ciarán was fond of saying — was whispering, *what's a few more minutes ... why not? ... after all, she volunteered ...*

'Close your eyes,' he ordered.

It was time to get this done. He didn't have *that* much self-control.

Brydie smiled up at him languorously. 'Why?'

'Humour me.'

'Nobody warned me you were the type who likes to play games,' she said. Brydie closed her eyes, however, still smiling. 'Do you have a surprise for me?'

'Oh, yes,' Darragh told her, as he reached for the small pouch of blue powder sitting on the side table beside the lamp. 'I most certainly do.'

'Will I like it? Is it fun?'

'I don't know,' Darragh said. He poured the powder into his hand and blew the *Brionglóid Gorm* into her face, and watched as she fell into a deep sleep. He sat back on his heels and smiled at her. 'But I'm pretty sure *I'm* going to be smiling about this for some time to come.'

The *Brionglóid Gorm* did its job. Brydie was out cold. Darragh had a few hours before she stirred. He stayed still, astride her for a moment. What a waste ... still, he had things to do, and only a few hours to do them. With a regretful sigh he climbed off her, walked around the bed and kicked aside her cloak with its amethyst brooch into the corner by his trunk.

Time. He had only a short window of opportunity to contact Ciarán with the scrying bowl.

A few hours to find out if there was any news.

A few hours to find out if Ciarán had received word from the rift runners searching for Rónán, that they had found him and were bringing his brother home.

CHAPTER 19

'What the hell is going on here?'

The flash of headlights and a shout tore Trása back to reality. For a moment there, she'd been lost in a delightful fantasy … a fantasy in which Darragh was kissing her, the way she'd tried to get him to kiss her before … before they'd banished her from *Sí an Bhrú*. She pulled away from Rónán and blinked in the bright light of the headlights of a car which had stopped in front of them. The driver's door was open, the driver standing beside the car, wearing a suit with a loosened tie, yelling at them.

'Jesus Christ!' the man exclaimed. 'You are un-fucking-believable, Ren! Your cousin is lying in intensive care — thanks in no small part to your stupidity — and you decide the best way to deal with it is to party with some random skank you probably found roaming the streets!'

Trása didn't know what a skank was, but she gathered it wasn't meant as a compliment. Rónán pushed Trása aside and walked around the car to confront the man, standing almost nose to nose with the driver. Rónán was the taller of the two. Trása didn't know who the angry man was, but he clearly felt he had the right to chastise Rónán. Was it Patrick? The stunt man who rescued Rónán as a baby?

'Fuck off, Murray,' he said.

Not Patrick then. Murray Symes, Trása realised. *The man who ran Hayley down.* Trása hurriedly tossed Plunkett — who'd been mashed between her and Rónán during their embrace — into the darkness beyond the circle of light from the car's headlights.

'I'm warning you …' the man began. His face was red with fury.

'You're warning me?' Rónán taunted. 'Of what? What are you going to do? Run me down, too? Beat some sense into me, maybe? How's that going to look? Go on, tough guy. I dare you.'

They glared at each other for a long, tense moment; long enough for Trása to look around for Plunkett, thinking she shouldn't have rid herself of him quite so hastily. He may yet need to intervene. The *Leipreachán* had no luck glamouring Rónán, but this Murray Symes shouldn't prove any trouble. After all, Plunkett had already seen him once. And the confontration between Ren and Murray Symes might get ugly. She'd seen Darragh toe-to-toe with an enemy like this, and it invariably ended in bloodshed. Rónán's similarity to Darragh in that moment was frightening.

But just as she was expecting them to come to blows, Symes backed down.

'I wouldn't give you the satisfaction, you arrogant little bastard,' he said in a tone that indicated he knew Rónán was baiting him. 'I'll not sink to your level. Go on, be an arsehole. Party with your girlfriend. You'll get what's coming to you, soon enough.'

'She's not my girlfriend,' Rónán said. 'This is Trása, Jack O'Righin's granddaughter.' He glanced at Trása apologetically. 'Trása, this is Murray Symes. The guy who runs down girls who step in front of his car.'

Murray turned to Trása, seeing her properly for the first time. He studied her for a moment with suspicion and disdain. 'The ungodly spawn of your friendly neighbourhood terrorist, eh?' He shook his head and turned back to Rónán. 'Didn't take you long, did it?'

With that, Murray turned on his heel and headed back to his car.

'How's Hayley?' Rónán asked Symes's retreating back.

The doctor stopped and turned to look at him. 'Oh, so *now* you're worried about Hayley?'

'How is she?' Rónán repeated. It seemed he could contain himself too, when the occasion called for it.

'She's still critical,' Murray said. 'Your mother's in the ICU with Kerry and Patrick. I imagine they'll be there for a good while, yet.'

'Is she going to be okay?'

'I don't know, Ren. I'm not her doctor.'

'Didn't they tell you *anything*?'

'I'm not her physician,' Symes repeated with a shrug. 'I've no right to be told her prognosis.'

'But you know,' Rónán said with utter certainty.

Murray sighed, as if suddenly weary of the conversation. 'And if I thought for a moment that you cared about anybody else but yourself, Ren, I'd probably tell you. Clearly, however,' he added, fixing his contemptuous gaze on Trása, 'you have other priorities. How old are you, young lady?'

Trása was a little taken aback by the question, unsure what her age had to do with anything. 'Old enough.'

Murray looked at Rónán. 'Have sex with that girl and I'll personally see to it that you are charged with, and convicted of, unlawful carnal knowledge of a minor. To hell with what your mother thinks it'll do to her career.'

Rónán rolled his eyes, clearly not believing the threat. 'Jesus, Murray, we were just kissing. Get your mind out of the gutter.'

The man didn't appreciate Rónán's easy dismissal of his threat. 'Laugh all you want, wise guy. Because after I've had you charged, I'll pull every string I have to make certain your case isn't heard until you've turned eighteen so I can be *absolutely* positive they'll send you to an adult prison. A couple of years as some axe-murderer's bitch may even cure your ODD.' Then Murray glanced at Trása and added, 'What you do in your grandfather's house is his concern. Don't bring his violent politics or your questionable morals into other people's homes.'

'You can't tell her what to do,' Rónán said, sounding just like Darragh.

'Pity,' Murray said. He turned away, not interested in any further conversation. As he climbed back into his car, he added, 'At least show your mother some respect by finding somewhere less public to make out with your girlfriend. There are still photographers around. You've caused Kiva enough problems for one day.'

Rónán watched him leave, his fists clenched at his sides.

Trása felt sorry for Rónán, but it was time, she decided, for her to make a strategic withdrawal. 'He's right, you know, Rónán. Perhaps I should go home.' Plunkett could glamour away human memories, after all, but he couldn't erase photographs.

She saw Rónán force himself to relax. He unclenched his fists and managed a thin smile. 'I'm sorry he called you a skank. Why do you keep calling me "Rónán"?'

'I don't know. Maybe you remind me of someone.' She hoped she sounded as if the slip meant nothing and covered it by walking over to Plunkett. 'You don't need to walk me back to the hospital. I can catch a cab home.'

Ren frowned at the *Leipreachán* sitting on the kerb as if it were watching them. 'You really are attached to that horrid thing, aren't you?'

Trása didn't answer. Instead, she rose up on her toes and kissed him, lingeringly this time, leaving Rónán speechless. Before he could recover his wits or do anything that would spoil the moment, she fled, tucking Plunkett under her arm, not waiting to find out if Rónán was following.

'What were you thinking, you stupid, *stupid* little *sídhe*?' Trása finally demanded of the *Leipreachán*, once they were settled into the back of the cab and heading back to Jack's place. 'You could have killed someone!'

Plunkett crossed his arms defiantly and glared up at Trása.

The cab driver gave them an indifferent glance and kept his eyes on the road. Trása didn't really care. Plunkett could glamour away his memory of their ride — and the fare they owed — once they got home.

'At least I be doing something,' Plunkett muttered, 'other than moonin' over some lad I can't ever have.'

Trása looked away angrily. 'You could have killed her! For that matter, if I hadn't stopped Rónán from stepping onto the road, you might have killed him!'

'Well, that would have solved our problem right there, wouldn't it?'

Trása was so frustrated she wanted to strangle him. 'Marcroy said we're not to kill him. He was very clear about that. If we kill him, we'll have broken the treaty. We're just supposed to contain him. Find a way to stop the Druids bringing him home, that's all. You almost ruined everything by interfering!'

'I didn't do nothin' wrong,' the *Leipreachán* insisted.

'Really? What about making that car speed up? No way could you have done that without Murray seeing you.'

Plunkett shrugged. 'What if he did?'

'You wouldn't have had time to glamour away his memory of you.'

'So what?' the *Leipreachán* said with a shrug. 'He ain't going to say anything 'bout it.'

'You don't know that.'

Plunkett rolled his eyes impatiently. 'The man just ran down an innocent lass, and now he has to convince everyone the whole fiasco be an accident. He won't go announcing to all and sundry that a *Leipreachán* made him do it, now, will he?'

The little man probably had a point, but that didn't make Trása feel any more kindly disposed toward him. 'You've ruined all my plans.'

'Plans? What plans?' Plunkett scoffed. 'Ye've not a clue how to contain the lad, and I doubt ye're even looking for one. Ye're just trying to find a way to become his sweetheart, 'cause ye're not allowed to have his brother in yer own realm.'

'That's ridiculous!'

'Then why did ye kiss him just now?'

Trása hesitated, and then shrugged, not sure how to answer in a way that wouldn't confirm the *Leipreachán*'s suspicions. 'I'm *Beansídhe*. I'm *supposed* to lure men to their doom.'

'It's ye luring me to mine I worry about. What's yer plan, then?'

'I'm not going to sit here in a cab discussing it,' Trása said, turning to look forward. The rain was gentle but it had been relentless and she was soaked through and chilled to the bone, from standing in the car park kissing Rónán. 'You shouldn't be here, anyway. You need to go find that Gardaí lady and the doctor and glamour away their memory of me. And the memory of the statement I gave the Gardaí. And destroy her notes.'

'Ye've nothing to discuss, is what ye really mean,' the *Leipreachán* accused. 'Ye can distract me with other things, but I'll be telling ye *uncail* as much next time he contacts me to check on ye.'

Trása turned to look at him. She knew the *Leipreachán* was more than capable of carrying out his threat. The consequences would be dire if Marcroy thought she had failed him, particularly after bragging she was on the brink of success. 'I was planning to find a way to lock him up in gaol.'

'How are ye going to manage that?'

That, of course, was the bit she hadn't figured out yet. But there was no need to confess that to Plunkett. 'I was working on it, actually, right up until *you* came along and screwed everything up by causing that wretched accident.' Trása crossed her arms against the chill and stared down at the little man, somewhat relieved she'd found a way to make her lack of progress his fault.

Plunkett didn't react to her accusation. Instead, he looked up at her, stroking his pointy little beard thoughtfully. 'Ye know ... that notion has real potential.'

'*Had* potential,' she pointed out.

'It may still be workable,' Plunkett said, furrowing his brow. 'Do ye know for certain what ye have to do in this realm to be incarcerated, or are ye just guessing 'cause ye've watched a lot of television?'

Trása shrugged. Her plan hadn't advanced much further than a fleeting idea while she had been talking to Rónán earlier in the day, when he compared the camp in Utah with prison. Then she remembered something else Rónán had said. 'I was planning to ask Jack,' she told Plunkett. 'According to Rónán, he's the expert on doing hard time. He should know what we have to do.'

Plunkett nodded slowly. 'Go ask him, then, so we can get this done.'

'Don't be ridiculous. It's the middle of the night. I'll ask him tomorrow. It won't seem suspicious that way.'

The *Leipreachán* nodded reluctantly, in agreement. 'All-righty then, but ye see ye do, Trása Ni'Amergin, or I warn ye, I'll be informin' ye *uncail* of ye preference for kissin' the Undivided, rather than doing what ye were sent here to do with him.'

CHAPTER 20

'What does one have to do to get thrown in gaol here?' Trása asked Jack the next morning, as they did their regular round of the glasshouse.

Jack sipped his sweetened tea as he poked about in the shrubbery with his pruning shears. A gentle rain pattered on the glass roof and ran down the misty walls in rivulets. The old man thought about her question for a moment and then shrugged. 'Lots of things, I guess. Depends who you are, where you are ...' He grinned suddenly. 'And on how many Loyalists you've blown up.'

'What did *you* do to get thrown in goal?'

'I blew some Loyalists up,' the old man replied matter-of-factly.

'So killing someone will get you imprisoned?'

'If you get caught.'

Trása pondered that for a moment, sipping her own overly sweet tea — which she was growing to like — as they moved on to the next plant requiring Jack's attention. 'What does "unlawful carnal knowledge of a minor" mean?'

Jack stopped pruning and turned to stare at her.

'I want to know what it means,' Trása repeated.

The old man turned back to his *bromeliad*. He looked very uncomfortable and was silent for a long time. Trása was wondering if Plunkett would have to glamour Jack again to make him answer her question, when he mumbled, 'It means they can send you to gaol if you're caught ... y'know ... fooling around ... with someone under the age of consent.'

'What's the age of consent?'

'Seventeen, these days, I think.'

'Oh.' It seemed a bit arbitrary. What gave the law the right to decide such a thing? Among the *Daoine sídhe*, it was the female who decided when she was ready, and it had much to do with the individual nature of the *sídhe*. It was her body, and she was the only one with the right to determine how it was to be treated. Trása's mother was *leanan sídhe* and she was almost twenty-five before she found an artist who took her fancy enough for her to give up her maidenhead to become his muse.

'Where did you hear about unlawful carnal knowledge of a minor, anyway?' Jack asked, unsettled by her line of questions.

'Murray Symes.'

The old man shook his head unhappily. 'Jayzus ... I'm not sure I'm game to ask why. Was he talking about you? And young Ren?'

'I suppose.'

Jack shrugged. He turned back to the plants to avoid meeting her eye. 'I dunno. A couple of kids fooling around ... it's not exactly the end of the world. Even if they bothered to take it to court and found the lad guilty, if it's two teenagers having a good time, they're both willing and about the same age ... say, your age or thereabouts ... I doubt he'd get more than a few months. Maybe not even that. Just a slap on the wrist and some community service. At worst, the lad'd get a couple of years, maybe, if the judge was a real bastard.'

Two years, Trása thought. *That's not nearly long enough.*

'How long were you in gaol, Jack?'

'Too fecking long.'

'You said you killed someone?'

He nodded, and kept pruning. 'Several someones.'

Ah, that's more like it. 'And the penalty for killing several someones? What was that?'

'For murder? It's life, usually. For each count.'

That was much more to Trása's liking. Locked away for life, confined and out of reach. That should satisfy Marcroy.

'A whole life?' she asked, making certain she had this right.

'I'm tempted to ask why you're so interested in this, girlie. You're not planning to murder someone, are you?'

'I might be,' she admitted, confident Plunkett could glamour away Jack's memory of this conversation later. 'If I can find someone who deserves it.' Trása pondered the possibilities for a moment. There was one flaw she could see that needed clarifying. 'You were sent to gaol for life, Jack, so how is it you're here now, pottering among the *bromeliads*?'

'Politics,' Jack said with a shrug. 'Trumps justice every time.'

'So …' she mused, sipping her tea thoughtfully. 'Without political interference, someone sent to gaol for life would have to stay there, right?'

'That's the way it's supposed to work.'

Trása nodded. That's what she wanted to hear. She caught a movement among the *coleus* behind Jack and realised Plunkett was there, watching and listening.

'Do you still have many criminal friends in gaol?' It had been Plunkett's idea that she ask Jack that. Plunkett figured — rightly so, Trása was forced to concede — that it would be much quicker to stage a crime Rónán could be blamed for if they had professional help.

Jack smiled, this time not too embarrassed to meet her eye. 'More than I'd like to admit.'

'Excellent,' Trása said, drinking down the last of her tea. 'Then let's finish up here and make some calls, old man. We have plans to make.'

'There's an awful lot that could go wrong,' Trása said later that day, as she continued to brush her hair, something that took so long she wondered if she ought to do what many women in this reality did — cut it short.

'Ye're too much of a pessimist, Trása. It'll be fine and, by tomorrow, we'll be home.'

'How am I supposed to convince Rónán to do this?'

'You could use those legendary *Beansídhe* wiles ye were so proud of last night,' the *Leipreachán* said.

Trása stopped brushing to look at Plunkett in the mirror. 'But what if he's not the sort that cares about vengeance?'

'Then he surely not be the twin of Darragh the Undivided,' Plunkett said as he sat down beside her on the bed, his little legs dangling over the edge. 'This be his chance for redemption. Ye heard him. He thinks the accident be his fault. Even the man driving the car accused him of as much. Ye can tell, just by looking at him, the lad's riddled with guilt and remorse over the girl being hurt. Ye know Darragh, Trása, and trust me, his twin be made of the same stuff. If it be Darragh in the same position, he'd do anything he could to redress the balance.'

She thought about that for a moment, then added with a puzzled frown, 'I can't understand why she's not dead, though. I felt her death approaching when the car sped up.'

'That would be those legendary *Beansídhe* powers, again, would it?'

Trása had to resist slapping the *Leipreachán* with her hairbrush. 'You are getting very close to overstepping yourself, Plunkett. Marcroy put me in charge.'

'They have their own healing magic in this world,' the *Leipreachán* said, conceding that she might have felt the approach of death. Trása smiled — this was the closest Plunkett would ever come to apologising for getting above himself. 'Perhaps in our world her injuries would have been fatal, but here, with their machines and their unnatural drugs ... who knows?'

That made sense. Still, it was unsettling. She was *Beansídhe*, after all. Trása was not used to being wrong about things like that.

'Things would be a lot easier if you hadn't interfered in the first place, Plunkett.'

'Ye're making excuses.'

'I'm being thorough. What if you tried to glamour Rónán again?'

'It won't work,' the *Leipreachán* insisted. 'And it will cause problems if we try. He already be suspicious of me.'

Trása resumed brushing her hair. 'Rónán's never said a word about you. Except that you're creepy. Which isn't actually that far off the mark.'

Plunkett pulled a face at her in the mirror. 'That be because I have to keep up the pretence of being a toy when the Half-Lord be nearby. I canna move a muscle when he's looking at me. The glamour doesn't work on him, Trása, as well ye know. He sees me as I be, so it be yer job to make certain he does what we need him to do.'

'He trusts Jack, I suppose,' Trása said with a defeated sigh. She wasn't sure why she was uneasy about their plan. It was, after all, her plan. And her mission for being in this realm in the first place. 'What if you glamour the old man and he convinces Rónán? I'm pretty sure Rónán will believe him.'

'And if he *doesn't* believe Jack?'

'He has to.' Trása lowered the hairbrush to look at Plunkett and remind him of the dire nature of their predicament. 'You're right about one thing, Plunkett. It's time we went home. I'm not sure how much of a lead we have on the others who are searching for Rónán. Darragh was with my father when he died. He heard Amergin's deathbed confession. He knows where Rónán is now and he wants his brother back even more than Marcroy wants him kept away. You can bet your wretched pot of gold there are Druids here looking for Rónán, right now. If we can find him, so can they.'

'Then let's get this done,' the *Leipreachán* said. He hopped off the bed and added with a frown, 'Just so long as ye don't blame me if ye plan doesn't work, girlie. I be in enough trouble with Marcroy Tarth as it is.'

CHAPTER 21

Brydie woke with a dreadful headache. The room was dark, but she could hear voices. She moaned softly with pain, trying to remember what had happened. The last thing she could recall was lying on the bed, Darragh sitting astride her filled with passion and desire, and then everything went blank. She didn't think she'd drunk enough to pass out. In fact, she was sure she hadn't.

Peering through the darkness, Brydie saw a pale light at the foot of the bed. She wondered what it meant. Only magical light shone with that distinctive blue radiance.

'… would have expected you to hear *something* by now,' said Darragh's voice. As Brydie's eyes grew accustomed to the darkness, she realised Darragh was sitting on the edge of the bed, his back to her, hunched over the source of the pale light.

He was scrying, she realised. Talking to someone through water.

Brydie had no magical ability, but she'd seen Malvina using a scrying bowl to contact other Druids. Ossian, the old Druid stationed in her father's *Ráith*, would often chat to his distant colleagues in the same manner.

Why, though, was Darragh talking to someone now? In the middle of the night? In a whisper?

Brydie remained still, lying on her side, able to see only a little of the room lit by the pale blue radiance of the scrying bowl. She strained to hear what Darragh was saying. She was certain the queen would be interested in this secret late-night conversation.

'Surely they've located him by now,' Darragh whispered to the bowl. 'I know he's close, Ciarán. I can feel him.'

So Darragh was talking to Ciarán, his mentor, teacher and bodyguard. The man who should have been here in *Sí an Bhrú*, watching over his precious charge. Álmhath would be fascinated to find out what Ciarán was up to.

'Aye, Darragh,' Brydie heard the older man say. It was hard to pinpoint the source of the voice. It was as if it came from nowhere and everywhere, all at once, muffled and distorted by the water of the scrying bowl. 'But you mustn't get your hopes up. Even if they've found him, it's going to be difficult making him leave everything he knows in the other realm.'

Who were they talking about? Someone trapped in another realm? A lost rift runner, perhaps? Or a rift runner turned rogue?

Brydie had heard of that happening. Rift runners visiting other realms had been known to become so enchanted with the alternative version of their world they didn't want to come home. Some did it for love. Others for avarice. Some simply for the adventure.

But what would it matter to Darragh? He was one of the Undivided. His existence allowed the

Druids to send rift runners to other worlds, but he wasn't responsible for them. He probably didn't even know most of them.

Still, a rogue rift runner was a dangerous problem, particularly if they were lost in a world of forbidden technology. It explained why Ciarán was away from *Sí an Bhrú*.

'They'll find a way,' Darragh said, although it sounded as if he was trying to convince himself as much as Ciarán. 'They must. Soon.' He glanced over his shoulder at Brydie, who shut her eyes, feigning sleep.

'Are you not alone?' she heard Ciarán inquire.

'Álmhath sent one of her maidens to my bed. I'm not sure what she hopes to gain by it, though.'

'Álmhath is at *Sí an Bhrú*?' Even through the distortion of the scrying bowl, the older man sounded concerned. 'Why?'

'I don't know,' Darragh said. 'We haven't got past the festivities yet. But she brought Marcroy Tarth with her, so it's not going to be good news, I'll wager.'

There was silence for a moment, before Ciarán spoke again. 'You need to get rid of the girl. She's Álmhath's spy.'

'Why, thank you, Ciarán,' Darragh replied. 'I'd never have worked that out for myself.'

Brydie cautiously opened her eyes again, as Ciarán chuckled. 'Sorry, lad. I'm sure you're being careful. Is she pretty?'

'Of course she's pretty,' he said, a little impatiently. 'What did you expect Álmhath to tempt me with? A dog? She's gorgeous. The legendary Mogue Ni'Farrell's daughter, no less.'

'The one Amergin wrote so many odes about?' There was a note of wistful longing in his tone. 'I remember when I was a lad and she was a court maiden. She was a rare beauty, right enough. I take it the lass can't hear us, then?'

Darragh shook his head. 'I knocked her out with *Brionglóid Gorm*. She shouldn't wake up for a while yet.'

You bastard, Brydie thought. Still, it explained her headache. And why she couldn't remember her night of unbridled passion with Darragh. There simply hadn't been one.

It never occurred to Brydie until then what a good liar Darragh might be. Although she didn't really have any basis for the impression, she'd always imagined the Undivided to be above the petty politics of ordinary men. Was he pretending *everything* he'd said since she met him? Even at dinner, when he'd smiled at her like he desired nothing more in the world than her company? When he'd given up his brother's place at the table to have her by his side? And later? When she came to his room? When he'd kissed her like he might die for the wanting of her?

Brydie felt a surge of anger at his deception, even as it occurred to her that she had been no more honest with Darragh than he had been with her. She was in his bed, after all, to steal his seed. To preserve a precious bloodline the *Matrarchaí* could ill afford to lose.

Which brought up another interesting problem. What was she going to tell Álmhath? *I'm sorry, my lady, I remain barren and the bloodline is lost because Darragh is up to something so secretive and dangerous, he drugged me and left me to sleep it off, while he made his plans in the dead of night.*

It was easy to imagine what Álmhath's reaction would be to that.

And even if Brydie told the queen about this odd conversation, even if there was nothing sinister in it at all, Álmhath would want to know what Darragh was up to. She'd want to know about this rogue rift runner — if that was what Ciarán was searching for — and why he was so important to the Druids.

More importantly, the *Matrarchaí* wanted a child. If Brydie gave them what they wanted, she was assured of a shining future in Álmhath's court. If she failed … what then? The spectre of Ethna's future stuck in some Gaulish backwater as the bride of a pig like Atilis was still fresh in her mind.

Could she do both? Brydie wondered. Her first instinct was to leap out of the bed, slap Darragh for his deceit, snatch up her clothes and storm out of his chamber full of righteous indignation.

But what if she stayed?

What if she lay here and pretended to sleep? What if she woke in the morning and pretended to be completely innocent, and enticing, and managed to do what she'd been sent here to do? Brydie certainly wasn't averse to the notion. Unlike Atilis, Darragh wasn't some uncouth barbarian looking for a bride and a treaty to help hold off his equally barbaric neighbours. Darragh was young, and healthy and strong and agreeable to the eye — something she'd been weak-kneed with relief to discover when she first spied him across the hall the previous evening. Far worse fates might befall a woman of her station than being asked to bear the child of one so important. And so pleasing.

I wonder if I could entice him to ask me to stay in Sí an Bhrú after the queen leaves?

Brydie was a little shocked to discover she might consider the notion. She hadn't come here to be made Darragh's mistress. She wasn't a Druid. Her loyalty lay with the queen of the Celts. If anything, she shared her father's opinion that the Druids — and the Undivided who were the source of their power — were an annoying necessity. The reasons Álmhath had given about why humans needed them were true enough. But she'd often heard her father remark that life would go on — a little less comfortably, perhaps — if they lost the Undivided, but surely it wouldn't mean the end of civilisation.

'You might have some trouble if Álmhath discovers you thwarting her plans for you, lad,' she heard Ciarán say. 'And right now, it'll not pay to do anything to make her, or that damned *sídhe*, Marcroy Tarth, suspicious.'

'You're not suggesting I let her think she can manipulate me so easily, are you?' Darragh asked his mentor softly, sounding a little wounded by the suggestion. 'It was almost insulting the way they threw the girl at me, thinking I'd be so easily diverted by the sight of a pretty face.'

At least he thinks I'm pretty. Brydie moved her head fractionally, afraid the furs tickling her nose would make her sneeze.

'Be grateful they did,' Ciarán told him. 'It shows they know nothing about what's afoot, or indeed, anything about you, either. Play along with them, lad. Use the tools that come to hand. Haven't I always taught you that?'

Darragh sighed. 'I suppose. When are you scheduled to open the rift again?'

'Tomorrow night,' Ciarán told him. 'Whatever scheme Álmhath and Tarth have cooked up between them, it would be useful if you could delay them until after that.'

'They'll be there waiting this time, Ciarán,' Darragh said with complete confidence. 'I know they will.'

'Is that your Sight speaking, lad, or are you just hoping for the best?' Ciarán asked gently.

Brydie strained to hear the answer. She was very interested to know that too. Was Darragh simply hoping for something to happen or had he Seen it?

For that matter, if he had the gift of Sight, why hadn't he Seen her in his dreams, or had some inkling as to why she'd been thrust in his path?

Prescience, Brydie decided, wasn't all it was cracked up to be.

She moved her head slightly, to hear a little better, but this time Darragh caught the movement out of the corner of his eye. He spun around faster than Brydie would have thought possible. The bowl tumbled to the ground, plunging the room into darkness, the scrying magic evaporating as the link with Ciarán was severed.

Darragh leapt astride Brydie, his hands at her throat, before she could utter a sound.

'Tell me everything you heard,' he demanded, his sapphire eyes sinister and dangerous in the darkness. 'And trust me, I'll know if you're lying.'

She stared up at him in fear, her heart pounding, her breath strangled. Should she betray her queen or save her own life?

It should have been a difficult decision to make, but she decided she wouldn't be in a position to report anything to her queen if she was dead.

Brydie did not doubt that Darragh was capable of carrying out his threat.

'I heard you talking to Ciarán. I gather he's hunting some rogue rift runner for you, and he's planning to bring him home soon. Or at least you're hoping he will.'

He squeezed her throat a little tighter. Brydie could barely breathe. 'Is that all?' he said.

'What else was there to hear?' Brydie gasped, struggling to drag air into her lungs.

'Why did Álmhath send you here tonight?'

'She ... she wants me to have your child.'

Darragh stared at her for a moment and then released his grip on her throat and stood up. He waved his hand, setting the candle by the bed magically alight. The meagre flame did little to dispel the sinister cast to his angry expression.

'What are you talking about?' he demanded.

'Álmhath wants a child from you,' Brydie repeated. 'She says your line is too precious to lose.'

'Why?'

'You are one of the Undivided,' Brydie reminded him. 'I would have thought the *why* was self-evident.'

'Why now, then?' he asked, echoing the thought Brydie had had when the queen first marked her for this task.

'I don't know,' she said. 'I only know what Álmhath told me. "The *Tuatha* have found something they weren't meant to find." Those were her exact words.'

Darragh frowned as he considered her information. Brydie wondered if the rift runner Ciarán was searching for had anything to do with

the thing the *Tuatha* had discovered, the very thing
that had precipitated her presence in Darragh's bed.

'So you're not really a volunteer, then?'

'No ...'

'Get out.' He said it in a flat, emotionless tone.

She was shocked. She'd told him the truth.
'But ... *why*?'

He sat on the edge of the bed and began to pull
on his shirt. 'Álmhath might want my seed bad
enough she's willing to take it by force, but I'm
not having any woman against her will. Go.'

Brydie couldn't believe he was kicking her out
because he was so principled he didn't want to
take a woman against her will. Laudable as that
was, Brydie couldn't go back to Álmhath empty-
handed. Or with an empty womb, for that matter.

'But Ciarán just told you to play along with
Álmhath,' she said, afraid she sounded like she
was begging to stay. 'You should be keeping me
here to allay her suspicions, not sending me away.'

He looked at her over his shoulder. 'You heard
that much, then?'

*Hmmm ... I probably shouldn't have admitted
that.* 'Yes.'

'I thought you weren't a volunteer.'

'So now I *am* volunteering,' she said, sitting
up to look him in the eye, conscious the furs had
fallen to her waist and her breasts were exposed.

Darragh studiously avoided looking at anything
but her face. 'You're spying for Álmhath.'

'So, don't tell me anything of strategic
importance.' Brydie smiled, figuring if she couldn't
entice him with her fabulous breasts, a smile was
about the only weapon left in her arsenal. 'At
the very least, don't give Colmán ammunition

193

to compose some dreadful epic poem tomorrow about your inability to keep a woman satisfied.'

Even Darragh cracked a small smile at that suggestion. 'I can see why Álmhath picked you.'

Brydie smiled a little wider. 'I have a better idea. You want to stall Álmhath and Marcroy Tarth until Ciarán opens his rift tomorrow night? Then stay here with me as you planned. Don't come out of your room at all.'

'Why?'

She climbed onto her knees, warming to the idea. She could still get Álmhath the child she wanted, and also remain in the good graces of the young man who, a few moments ago, had his hands around her throat and might still be considering killing her to ensure her silence. 'You've already had me tell Colmán you're planning to be here for days. So let's do it. They can't hold a meeting with the Undivided if you're not there, can they?'

He stared at her in silence.

'I'm up for it, if you are ... and if you aren't ... well, I know a few tricks that could help with that, too.'

Darragh continued to study her with a puzzled expression. 'Just whose side are you on, Brydie Ni'Seanan?'

'The truth?' she asked him honestly, thinking of Ethna and her grim future as Atilis's bride. 'Mine.'

CHAPTER 22

Hayley wasn't sure when she became aware of her surroundings again. For a long time she floated in a world of emptiness ... a warm cocoon where nothing seemed to matter. Reality resolved around her slowly. It took a while for her to register she was lying in a hospital bed and that there seemed to be some dissent as to her prognosis. She had heard people talking in the distance in hushed, frightened tones. Then the soft beeping of countless electronic monitors lulled her back into unconsciousness, while voices she didn't recognise whispered about her as if she wasn't there.

When she tried to move, she discovered a strange heavy feeling in her limbs, holding her down, but the cottonwool cocoon kept her warm and safe so she didn't feel the need to panic. She did want to know why her stepmother was crying, though, and why her normally jovial and talkative father was so ominously silent.

Hayley deduced that people were upset, and they seemed to be upset with her. She wasn't sure why. She wanted to tell everyone she was fine. She wanted to sit up and demand to know why she was surrounded by electronic beeps and whispering voices, because she had no idea how she got there.

Hayley's last memory was seeing Ren with that girl. He was holding her hand.

In the distance, the faint beeping seemed to grow more strident …

Hayley drifted in and out of consciousness, unable to tell anyone she was awake. Her head pounded constantly when she emerged from the darkness. Unconsciousness was a relief. Such a relief she was disinclined to do anything that might prolong her fleeting bouts of awareness.

Not that Hayley had any control over that, either. She couldn't move a muscle.

Her dreams were jumbled and chaotic, never focussing on any one thing for long. Her world was defined by haunting images interrupted occasionally by a reality so painful she prayed for the dreams to return. Her dream world was bewildering, but painless.

In her dream world, Ren wasn't holding that pretty blonde girl's hand. He was holding Hayley's. Ren featured a lot in Hayley's dreams which was why she preferred them to the real world. In them, he seemed much happier than the Ren she knew in her waking life. In her dreams, Ren wasn't haunted by dark nightmares so terrible he couldn't even tell his best friend what he dreamed about …

In her dreams, Ren noticed she was alive.

Even in her befuddled state, Hayley knew that wasn't fair. Ren didn't ignore her. Of course he knew she was alive. He was her best friend, after all, and she was his.

But that's all he was, she knew; that was how it was meant to be. Hayley had resigned herself to that long ago, and some days it even seemed a good idea. Ren had few real friends, thanks to his suspicion, not entirely unfounded, that people only wanted to know him because of his mother. He protected those few friendships jealously.

But he wasn't nearly so careful of casual relationships with girls, as their encounter in the mall with Shangrila had proved. In that respect, he was like every other boy who had ever drawn breath. Kerry had once hugged her and told her to stop worrying about it. *Besides*, Kerry said, *it's not like you have to care, darling. He's your cousin.*

Adopted cousin by marriage, Hayley wanted to remind her, but she stayed silent. It hurt less if people thought she was just being a critical friend, questioning her cousin's taste, rather than a jealous fool with a crush on a boy she could never have.

Hayley once woke to a world she didn't recognise. Ren was there, as he was in all her dreams, except this time he wasn't the Ren she knew. He was a different Ren, with longer hair, and a more muscular build, as if he'd spent all summer working out, instead of playing that PlayStation of his. The Ren in her dream was dressed strangely, too. He was different, stronger, more serious. But every time she called to him, every time he turned to look at her, the dream vanished and she was back with the pain, the electronic beeps and the hushed, worried voices of reality.

'Hayley ... can you hear me?'

Ren's voice pierced the fog and she realised she wasn't dreaming this time. She was stuck in the limbo between unconsciousness and waking where the pain hadn't quite returned, but she could hear the beeping that had become the soundtrack of her dreams.

Ren ...

Hayley said his name in her mind but nothing came out. Her tongue was dry, stuck to the side of her mouth, forced there by a tube that took up most of the space between her teeth. She was aware of the tube, mildly surprised she wasn't gagging on it.

But she could do nothing about it.

And she certainly couldn't speak.

'They say you can hear me.'

Yes, Ren, I can hear you. God ... my head is pounding ... it hurts so much to think ...

'I'm so sorry, Hayley. This is all my fault.'

Hayley might have agreed with him, had she been clear-headed enough to figure out exactly to what Ren was referring. She guessed it had something to do with the headache and the tube and the beeping and the fact that she couldn't feel her fingers or toes ...

'They told me to just tell you good news ... you know, like you'll get better, and keep on fighting, and all that crap ... but ...' His voice faltered.

But what? Hayley wanted to scream at him. *Don't stop there! Tell me what's happening!*

'Jesus, you'd better not die on me, Hayley.'

Die? I'm dying? Thanks for the heads up, Ren ...

She sensed him leaning in a little closer. 'We're gonna get him for you,' he whispered.

Get who? Make some sense here, Ren.

'Trása's called in a few favours from Jack's old prison cronies.'

Trása? Who is Trása? Is that the skanky ho I saw you walking down the street with? Hand in hand?

'Turns out Murray is a first-rate sleazebag,' he said.

Like somebody else, I could mention. If I could talk.

'One of Jack's buddies has some info on a deal he's got going this afternoon,' Ren continued, still talking in a whisper, as if he was afraid he'd wake her.

God, Ren, stop going on about Murray Symes. Tell me what's wrong with me ...

'The cops said they're not going to do anything about what he did to you, but we can get the bastard disbarred, or dismembered, or whatever it is they do to doctors caught dealing shit under the counter.'

Is that what's wrong with me? Murray Symes gave me something? The thought didn't make much sense to Hayley. The last thing she remembered was seeing Ren trying to cross the road amid a sea of photographers.

Was Murray Symes even there?

Hayley knew the answer was there somewhere, but in her pain-fogged mind, she couldn't quite make the connection. She wondered if Ren was holding her hand. If he was, she couldn't feel it.

He was still talking, but Hayley found it increasingly difficult to concentrate on what he was saying. She wished she could open her eyes but there seemed to be something over them, blocking out the light, and she couldn't move her hands to check. By the time she finished that thought, she felt something on her forehead ... Ren's lips, she decided, not sure if he was kissing her goodbye or she was back in another dream ...

'Why isn't she awake yet?' Hayley thought she heard Ren ask, except he wasn't talking to her. His tone was no longer soft and conspiratorial. Now he sounded angry. Or maybe worried.

'There's nothing to worry about,' she thought she heard Kiva tell him. *Was Kiva here too? Why?*

Hayley might have panicked at that point — if she'd been able to. *God, I must be dying if Kiva's the one handing out sage advice.*

'She's in an induced coma, sweetheart,' Kiva explained to Ren in a low voice. 'The doctors will bring her out when they're satisfied she's stable.'

'But it's been more than a day ...'

'And it may be a few more,' his mother told him comfortingly. 'There's nothing to worry about.'

'Yeah ... 'cause they induce comas for the *craic*, don't they?'

'Ren ... please ... not in here ...' That wasn't Kiva. It sounded like her father. Was Patrick there too? Was everyone in the room, clustered around the bed, talking about her as if she was on her deathbed?

'I'm sorry, Mum,' she heard Ren say after a moment. 'About everything.'

'It's okay, Ren,' Kiva whispered.

'No ... really. I'm sorry. About the red carpet. Accusing Murray of being a pervert. For getting Hayley into this mess.'

'It's not your fault, Ren,' Hayley heard her father say.

What? What isn't Ren's fault? Somebody tell me what's happening and why I can't make you hear me!

'Patrick's right, darling. Hayley's injuries are not your fault. As for Murray ... he only wants the best for you. We all do. You just make it so hard, sometimes.'

'I know,' Ren said. He sounded worn down and defeated. *Do you sound like that because of me?* Hayley wondered.

'I do love you, Mum,' Ren added in a low voice. 'You know that, don't you?'

'You have an odd way of showing it sometimes, darling.'

'Look ...' Hayley heard Patrick say in a loud whisper. 'Much as it's nice to see you two hugging and making up, can we move it outside? She can hear everything, you know.'

'Then perhaps it's a good thing she hears us talking,' Kiva said. 'Hayley should know she's loved and that those who love her love each other.'

'And she will,' Patrick assured Kiva. 'But really, if we crowd her, the doctors won't let any of us in here.'

'I could have my naturopath call in ...' Hayley heard Kiva begin. But she didn't hear the rest because the voices faded and Hayley could no longer make out what they were saying. Or perhaps she'd fallen asleep again, and had dreamed the whole thing.

Any time now, Hayley decided, *I'm going to wake up at home in my bed and everyone is going to laugh themselves senseless when I tell them about this crazy dream I'm having.*

Except if it's a dream, why does my head hurt so much?

CHAPTER 23

'Anything coming?'

Ren glanced out of the warehouse window at the rain-slick cobbled alley. He shook his head.

'Nothing.'

'Like you were even looking,' Trása said, tossing Plunkett the Creepy Leprechaun Doll ahead of her before climbing up the stack of abandoned freight pallets to where Ren was sitting. She wore a very tight T-shirt that didn't quite cover her midriff, which Ren found distracting. 'Some lookout you are.'

Trása shoved the doll aside and clambered forward on the stack of old pallets to look out the window. It was still raining, but there was no sign of any cars yet. Ren wondered why she wasn't wearing a jacket. It was chilly in the warehouse, but the temperature didn't seem to bother her.

'Are you sure Jack is right about this?' he asked, still wondering why he'd allowed himself to be talked into this foolishness. Trása was far too good at persuading him to do things against his better judgement and he couldn't understand why. He'd only known her a couple of days.

In fact, the rational Ren inside him suggested —

the one he wasn't listening to — *if you had any brains at all, moron, you'd leave now. Before anybody else arrives.*

And before his mother's manager, Jon van Heusen, discovered Ren borrowed his rented Ferrari while he was back at the house discussing Kiva's next movie offer with her.

But Jack had been adamant this was the real thing. And as Ren was helpless to do anything else for Hayley, getting Murray Symes off the road seemed as noble a quest as any.

'This is a matter of honour,' Trása reminded him. She was very determined about this — so determined, Ren found it impossible to disagree with her.

'I wonder if that's reasonable grounds for breaking and entering,' Ren mused, glancing around the rubbish-strewn building. There were a few cardboard shelters beside a couple of old shopping trolleys over in the far corner of the cavernous warehouse. He guessed a number of homeless people camped here at night. He wasn't sure how the homeless men found their way inside the warehouse. Ren and Trása had broken a lock to gain entry. 'That door didn't pop open on its own, you know.'

Trása shrugged. 'You worry too much.'

'Are you sure this is the right place?'

'It's the address Jack gave us.'

'I still don't understand how Jack even knows about Symes selling drugs.' Ren still wasn't clear on that point. Since Trása had thrown a stone at his window in the early hours of the morning, motioning him to come down to meet her, things had moved very fast. As soon as he'd sneaked out of the house, she'd taken him by the hand, pulled him through the gate in the wall to Jack's place, and then demanded her grandfather tell Ren what he'd apparently just told her.

Murray Symes is peddling drugs, Jack had informed him.

And Jack went on to say there was a fair chance the holier-than-thou Dr Symes had been high on something when he hit Hayley.

Ren was appalled. The man who'd made his life a misery, the man who'd run Ren's best friend down in his haste to escape a few photographers, was dealing amphetamines on the side, and one of Jack's shady friends knew all about it.

Not only that, Jack informed Ren. He knew where the deal was going down. That very day.

'Jack already explained how he knows,' Trása said, a little impatiently. 'One of his old associates from prison is in on the deal. He saw Murray on the news and realised the accident happened next to Jack's place, so he called him to tell him that he knew the chap, and how he knew him.'

'Yeah ... I know that's what he told us, it just seems a little ... convenient, don't you think?'

She glared at him in annoyance. 'Why are you asking me, Ren? I'm just the messenger.'

But Trása was more than just the messenger. She was driving this careening bus and the rational part of Ren had a feeling it would end badly.

That hadn't stopped him borrowing the Ferrari without permission — easier than taking the keys for the Bentley which Patrick never let out of his sight — and driving down to this abandoned warehouse to find out if Jack was right. Maybe, if he and Trása were lucky and they got away quickly enough — not a hard thing to do in a Ferrari — the only person this would end badly for was Murray Symes.

It was high time *something* went badly for Symes. The cops weren't going to do a damn thing about him. The policewoman had told them as much.

Ren sat a little straighter. 'There's a car coming.'

Trása leant forward to look, leaning on Ren's thigh to balance herself. She craned forward until Ren's face was almost smothered in her luscious, long, blonde hair, her hand on his thigh dangerously close to his groin. He breathed in the scent of her hair until he was giddy. She smelled like a warm summer day.

Ren turned to look out of the window again; a far safer option than drowning in the heady scent of Trása. A silver Mercedes had pulled up in the alley. It sat there, its wipers on, but nobody had emerged from it. Although there was nothing happening, the presence of the car made Ren feel a little better. Clearly, something illegal was about to happen. People who drove cars like that did their legitimate business in offices, conference rooms and hotel bars, not out the back of abandoned warehouses.

'One down, one to go,' Trása said in a low voice, leaning back to make sure she wasn't seen from the alley below. 'Are you sure this is going to work, Ren?'

'*Now* you're having second thoughts?'

She pulled a face at him.

Ren shrugged, watching the car from the shadows. 'If Jack's right, the game is on. All we have to do is ring the cops once Murray arrives.'

Trása nodded. 'Ring the cops.'

Ren shook his head. 'No point. Right now, there's a car sitting in an alley. We need someone else to turn up before we have anything happening. *That's* when we'll call the cops.'

'Suppose the Gardaí don't come?'

'I'll tell them there's a man with a gun. Cops always respond faster when you mention guns.' He'd learned that on the set of *Angel of Justice* in LA when he was eight, from the ex-cop acting as the movie's technical advisor.

Trása looked a little sceptical, but didn't argue the point. Ren wondered what she was thinking. Was she worried about being caught in a place where neither of them belonged? Or was she — like Ren — thinking only of Hayley, lost in a coma because she got in the way of Murray Symes's speedy getaway?

Suddenly there was a crash. They both turned to look for the source of the noise. On the other side of the warehouse, a man stood watching them. He wore a long, grubby coat, and was pushing an overloaded shopping trolley, stuffed with plastic bags. Ren guessed it was one of the homeless men who squatted here. The man stared at them suspiciously for a moment and then shoved his trolley behind a couple of sheets of corrugated iron that were leaning against the wall. He must have come in through another door at the back of the warehouse. Fortunately, he no longer seemed interested in what Ren and Trása were doing.

'The other car is coming,' Trása hissed.

Ren turned his attention back to the window as a vehicle pulled into the alley behind the Mercedes.

'Call the cops.'

Ren hesitated, wondering if he should wait. All they had down there, really, were two cars minding their own business in a lane between a couple of abandoned warehouses, and neither of them was Murray's BMW. There was no sign of anything illegal going on. If he called the Gardaí and they arrived too soon, they wouldn't find anything amiss. Murray Symes would get away.

Down in the alley, the car doors opened.

'Call them,' Trása insisted.

Ren reached into his pocket for his mobile.

He dialled 999. The phone rang a couple of times.

'Emergency. Please state the service you require.'

'Gardaí.'

Four men stepped out of the cars, despite the rain. They were too far away to tell if any of them was Murray.

The phone rang again, followed by a female voice.

'Please state the nature of the emergency.'

'There's a man with a gun,' Ren said, trying to inject a little panic — and something more of an Irish accent — into his voice. He gave them the address, and then added urgently, 'Please be quick. I think there's some sort of drug deal going down. They're gonna shoot someone!'

Ren cut the call as the operator was asking for his name. Trása grinned from ear to ear. The glee of vengeance about to be served. In bucket loads.

'Time to go,' Ren said, shoving the phone into his backpack. Already they could hear sirens. Only they weren't in the distance, they were loud and near and close enough for them to see the pulsing blue lights, reflecting off the warehouse walls.

Trása looked surprised. 'That was quick.'

'Too quick,' Ren said with a frown. He'd made the call only seconds ago. For the Gardaí to be already here … he tossed the backpack to the floor. 'Shit! We've gotta get outta here, Trása. Now!'

'What's the hurry?' she asked, as Ren jumped from the pallet stack to the floor. 'Don't you want to see what we started?'

'I don't think it was us that started it,' Ren said, scooping up his backpack. There were voices outside. Shouting. The sirens were loud enough to drown out the tattoo of rain on the warehouse's metal roof. 'If the cops are already here, they didn't need us to tell them about this.' Trása didn't seem to get how urgent this was. 'Come on!'

Finally, she jumped to the floor, grunting in pain as she landed, leaving Plunkett on top of the pallets.

'You okay?'

She nodded. 'Twisted my ankle a bit, that's all, you go ahead. I'll catch up.'

Ren didn't want to leave her, but she pushed him away. 'Go, Ren. I'll be fine.'

He did as she bid, glancing backward after a moment. Trása was limping, rapidly falling behind. Ren hurried back to her, took her arm, placed it over his shoulder, and pulled her toward the door they'd broken through to get into the warehouse.

The Ferrari was parked just outside. They had to get to it before the police did, because even if Ren and Trása remained undetected, the police would know who'd rented the car the moment they checked the licence plate.

About thirty seconds after they called the rental company, they would call Kiva's manager and they'd know Ren Kavanaugh was somewhere in the vicinity.

The paparazzi had radio scanners. It would take them another thirty seconds to be on the scene and then ... well, who knew what might happen next.

Then Ren remembered Trása's damned toy. She'd left the creepy thing on top of the pallets. If there was any way it could be traced back to her, it would lead them right back to Ren ...

When he glanced back at the pallet, however, the doll was gone. 'What happened to Plunkett?'

Trása looked at him oddly. 'What?'

'That creepy toy of yours,' he said. 'Where is he?'

'Don't worry about him, Ren,' Trása said as she hobbled along beside him. 'He'll be fine.'

Ren couldn't have cared less about the *Leipreachán*'s welfare, and it certainly wasn't why he was asking, but before he could clarify the reason for his question, the door ahead of them burst open. Police spilled into the warehouse like a river of dark ink, wearing helmets and bulletproof vests emblazoned with ERU across their backs.

Emergency Response Unit. Great.

Their presence removed any doubt Ren might have had about whether or not his call had been responsible for this ambush. He was certain he'd had nothing to do with it.

The Gardaí didn't send out the ERU on the strength of one anonymous phone call.

The ERU men carried semi-automatic weapons with laser sights that sprayed red dots around the warehouse walls like lethal confetti, which very quickly focussed on the two teenagers trying to flee the scene.

'Halt or we'll shoot!'

Ren glanced down at the score of red lights dancing across his chest. He let go of Trása and raised his hands in the air, wincing as the action pulled on his wounded ribs.

'Drop the bag!'

Ren did as ordered. He dropped his backpack. It spilled open on the damp floor. The phone was screwed, he guessed, as it rolled into a puddle.

'On the floor! Face down! Now!'

Ren knew better than to argue with a bunch of trigger-happy ERU officers. He lowered himself to the ground, pressing his face against the cracked concrete floor. It was cold and damp and smelled of kerosene and feral cats.

On the edge of his awareness, oddly enough, he thought he smelled smoke.

He turned his face toward Trása as the police swarmed over them, roughly pulling their arms behind them, slapping cold metal cuffs on them with a great deal more enthusiasm than Ren thought the situation warranted. Then they grabbed his backpack and pulled them both to their feet. Trása didn't look so much scared as fatalistic about the whole thing. But Trása's mugshot wasn't going to be appearing on the front page of all the major daily newspapers the next morning.

Trása looked at Ren apologetically. She seemed genuinely remorseful. 'I'm so sorry for doing this to you, Ren.'

'Not your fault, Trása.'

'Shut up!' the officer holding Ren ordered.

'There's a bright side to this, you know,' Trása said, as if she was determined not to let the police intimidate her.

'I told you to shut up, kid!'

'A *bright* side?' Ren asked. Neither of them was paying any attention. It was a small act of defiance but an important one.

'You'll be safe now,' Trása said.

'Safe?' *That was one name for it*, Ren thought as he was manhandled outside and into the back seat of a Gardaí car for his trip downtown. They put Trása in a different car, and he soon lost sight of her as the cars pulled away in a flurry of flashing lights, misty rain, the squeal of sirens, and for some reason Ren couldn't fathom, fire engines heading at high speed back the way they had come from.

CHAPTER 24

'I'll kill you if I have to, to stop this.'

Ren smiled down at the baby twin girls, dismissing the empty threat. 'Even if you could get across this room before the deed was done, you can't kill me without killing yourself, which would achieve precisely what I am here to prevent.'

He moved the blade a little, repositioning his grip. The candlelight danced across its engraved surface, mesmerising the baby. Ren was happy to entertain her with the pretty lights for a few moments. His mission was to kill her and her sister, afterall, not to make them suffer.

There was a drawn-out silence as he played the light across the blade. Behind him, the presence that was both his conscience and his other half remained motionless. There was no point in him trying to attack. They were two sides of the same coin. Neither man could so much as form the intent to attack without the other knowing about it.

The girls would be dead before anybody could reach the cradle to stop —

'Chelan Aquarius Kavanaugh.'

Ren was jerked rudely from the dream. He sat up, blinking furiously, his eyes watering, trying to focus in the sudden bright light. He'd been leaning his head on the cold metal table as he dozed. He was still cuffed and his shoulders ached from the unnatural position in which he'd been resting. 'What?' he mumbled.

The detective took the seat opposite Ren, dropping a file on the table. Ren had no idea what time it was, only that he'd been there long enough to doze off. There was no clock. The room was bare, but for the table, two cold metal chairs and a two-way mirror on the cream-coloured wall behind the detective. And the fluorescent light overhead.

'Got quite a history, haven't you, Chelan Aquarius?'

'Yes, sir.'

The officer they'd sent to interview him was fairly young, late twenties maybe. They probably figured Ren would bond better with a younger officer than with an older one.

'Want those cuffs off?'

Ren gritted his teeth. He hated the police who pretended to be his friend.

'No, thanks. I quite enjoy having my shoulders forced back at an unnatural angle.' He looked around for the video cameras and the recording equipment. 'Aren't you supposed to be filming this interview? Reading me my rights? Asking me if I want a lawyer?'

'We haven't charged you with anything yet.'

'Then I can go home?'

The detective shrugged. 'That depends on what you were doing in that warehouse.'

'We weren't doing anything wrong.'

'Which would be why the ERU brought you in. They were just cruising the streets looking for innocent bystanders to take into custody, I suppose.'

'Someone should do something about that, officer. That's a waste of taxpayers' money, isn't it?'

The officer wasn't amused. He opened the file and glanced down at the charge sheet. The inside cover of the file had Ren's unflattering mug shot stapled to it. It was the same one the tabloids delighted in blowing up and pasting on the front page of national newspapers whenever they got wind of him being in trouble. 'Says here you're a real smart-arse.'

Ren leaned forward with interest. 'Does it really? I didn't think you'd be allowed to use words like "arse" in official documents.'

'You think you're real funny, don't you, Kavanaugh?'

Ren shrugged, which proved a rather stupid and painful thing to do, given his hands were still cuffed behind his back. 'I'm not trying to be funny, officer. I'm trying to co-operate.'

'This is your idea of co-operating?' The officer looked back down at the file. 'You celebrity kids are all the same. You think you're above the law because you're famous.'

Here we go again ...

'I'm not famous,' Ren said patiently. 'My mother is. That's not actually my fault, you know.'

The cop studied his file as if Ren hadn't spoken. 'How long have you been involved with Dominic O'Hara?'

The question was completely unexpected. 'Who the hell is Dominic O'Hara?'

'The scumbag drug dealer you were acting as a lookout for today.'

Ren stared at him, dumbfounded. '*What?*'

'Is he your boss?' the officer asked. 'Your platinum Amex not enough for you, rich boy, so you thought you'd earn a little extra cash on the side dealing coke?'

'What the fuck are you talking about?' Ren asked, alarmed at the line of questioning. *Damn you, Jack O'Righin. So much for your inside information.*

How could Jack have got it so wrong? What happened to Murray Symes and his sideline in amphetamines?

'If you weren't involved in O'Hara's little enterprise, what was a kid from a posh suburb like yours doing in that part of town?'

Ren frowned as it occurred to him that, for the first time, he was in trouble so serious that not even his mother's smooth-talking lawyer could negotiate his way out of it. 'I want my lawyer.'

The detective was growing impatient. 'You wanna hope your lawyer can help you, Kavanaugh, 'cause you sure aren't helping yourself, right now.'

Ren hoped he was projecting an air of quiet innocence, which was no mean feat, because on the inside he was bordering on blind panic. If he couldn't talk his way out of this mess, he'd probably die an old man in Utah.

His mother might forgive the time he was caught spraying graffiti on the windows of Harrods in London a couple of years ago. It helped that he'd been protesting seal clubbing with several of Kiva's co-stars at the time, who were much more high profile than Ren and who got most of the resulting publicity. Criminal acts for noble causes were easier to forgive than the time he'd filled all the umbrellas on the set of *Rain Over Tuscany* with talcum powder, which shut down shooting for a whole day while they cleaned up the mess, and got Ren sent back to school in disgrace. She'd even forgiven the time he'd stolen a realistic and bloody dummy corpse with its throat punctured by bite marks from the prop van and left it in the elevator of the hotel where they were staying. But Kiva was going to take a very dim view of a front-page headline announcing her son was caught acting as a lookout for a notorious drug lord.

He took a deep breath. Maybe it would be better if he co-operated. Or at least gave the appearance of doing so. Although he'd been warned — more times than he could count — to say nothing if he was arrested again, he decided to ignore the advice.

'We just wanted somewhere quiet to hang out. We found the warehouse —' he started.

'You *broke* into the warehouse,' the officer corrected.

'Not us,' Ren said, trying to look innocent. 'Someone else must have busted that door, officer. We found it like that.'

'Yeah … right,' the officer said, shaking his head. 'Why do you keep saying "we"?'

'I meant me and Trása.'

The cop stared at him blankly. 'Who?'

'My friend. The girl they arrested with me.'

He looked at Ren oddly. 'Are you on drugs, kid?'

'No.' Ren started to worry. 'What happened to Trása?'

The officer shook his head. 'There is no Trása,' he said. 'They picked you up alone, Kavanaugh.

There was nobody else in that warehouse. Everything that happened today you did all on your lonesome.'

'That's not true. Trása was there ...'

The officer shook his head, as if he'd heard it all before. 'It's a bit late to start working on your insanity plea,' he said, 'by inventing an imaginary friend.'

'This is bullshit!' Ren cried, wishing now he'd asked for the cuffs to be taken off, so he could shake some reason into this man. The police were playing games with him, he was certain. Trying to rattle his cage to get a confession out of him for something he knew nothing about.

'There was no girl,' the officer insisted.

'She was there! Right beside me! She's about five six. She's pretty ... really pretty. With incredibly long blonde hair. She was wearing jeans and a blue tank top. They put her in the other car. What have you done with her? You'd better not have hurt her!'

'I see.' The officer was studying him with a strange expression. 'Who do you claim she is?'

'Her name's Trása,' Ren told him, realising he didn't even know her last name. 'She's Jack O'Righin's granddaughter.'

'Really?' The officer leant back in his chair, smiling like he'd just won the lottery. 'Jack O'Righin's granddaughter? That crazy old terrorist-turned-media-whore who lives next door to you? Are you serious?'

'No ... I'm making it up because I think it's cute,' Ren snapped. 'Of course I'm fucking serious!'

'Watch your mouth, Kavanaugh.'

'Then stop trying to fuck me about. What have you done with her?'

'Jack O'Righin doesn't have a granddaughter,' the officer said flatly. 'His wife and three daughters were murdered in the Troubles up north long before you and I were even born. Do your homework, smart-arse, before you go making up bullshit that won't hold up to even the most cursory examination.'

'I'm not making this up! Christ, the cop who took my statement after Hayley's accident took one from her, too. She was going to bring it to the house.'

The detective consulted his file for a moment and then shook his head. 'No mention of her here.'

Ren slumped back in his chair. He didn't understand what was going on. He thought they were just messing with his head, but the officer genuinely seemed to believe Ren was arrested alone.

But Ren had seen Trása in cuffs. He'd watched them loading her into a patrol car.

'Is there any chance they took her somewhere else? To another station, maybe, or —'

'For chrissakes, give it up, will you?' the officer snapped. 'There is no girl, there *was* no girl, and if you have any brains at all, Kavanaugh, you'll do a deal with us to give up O'Hara's cocaine operation tonight, so we can all get out of here before morning.'

Ren shook his head helplessly. 'I have no idea who you're talking about.'

The officer laughed sceptically. 'So … you were just driving around in a stolen car with your imaginary friend, seeing how the other half live, I suppose, and Dominic O'Hara just happened to pull up with a carload of cocaine?'

'That's exactly what happened, officer. I even called it in. Check my phone. Better yet, check your records with the nine-nine-nine call centre. I was the one who made the call.' Then he added as an afterthought, 'And I didn't steal the car. I borrowed it from my mother's manager.' Picking up the keys off the counter in the kitchen while Jon was in the study with his mother didn't make it stealing, Ren reasoned. After all, he was planning to return the car.

'Yeah,' the officer said, glancing down at the file. 'Funny ... borrowed is not the word he used when he reported it missing.'

Bastard.

The door to the interview room opened and an older female cop walked in before he could be asked any more questions. She was accompanied by a very sleekly groomed, mid-thirtyish woman in a business suit, who Ren knew all too well. Eunice Ravenel, his mother's lawyer — she was usually dispatched to deal with the Ren problem.

'My client has nothing more to say,' Eunice announced in her clipped and perfectly correct Swedish accent. She glared at Ren as she slammed her briefcase onto the metal table. Ren wasn't sure why, but she always slammed her briefcase down. Maybe she liked the noise it made. More likely she enjoyed the idea of seeing cops — every one of whom she was certain was either corrupt or incompetent — jump.

The officer who'd been interviewing Ren looked at his boss. The inspector shrugged. 'Sorry, Pete.'

'Yeah, Pete,' Ren said. 'I'm sorry, too. We were just starting to bond, I thought.'

Eunice turned to Pete, her eyes blazing with indignation. 'Why is this boy still in cuffs?'

Pete looked to his boss for help. 'He said he liked them.'

'Is this your idea of revenge? Because my client is the son of a celebrity?' Eunice turned on the inspector, who wore a pained look that spoke of long experience with Eunice Ravenel and her righteous indignation. 'You can be sure I'll be lodging a formal complaint about this, Inspector Duggan. Ren is a minor. And you've kept him here, interrogating him like a prisoner of war, alone, without representation and chained like a common criminal. This is police brutality!'

Ren rolled his eyes, glad Eunice had her back to him and couldn't see him doing it. *Police brutality.* For once, he sympathised with the police. Although he supposed he shouldn't. Eunice was here to bail him out, after all.

The inspector sighed and nodded. 'Why don't you do that, Ms Ravenel? In fact, I can give you a form. You can fill it out while we book your client for dealing in commercial quantities of prohibited substances, breaking and entering, trespassing, arson, and maybe even murder, if the homeless man they pulled out of the warehouse your client burned down doesn't make it through the night.' She turned to the detective who'd been interviewing Ren. 'Unlock the cuffs, Pete.'

What fire? What are they talking about? Homeless man? Did they mean the guy with the shopping trolley?

With a grunt of disapproval, Pete produced the keys to the cuffs and freed Ren's wrists from the restraints. Ren eased his shoulders forward, glad to be free, but fairly certain it wasn't because they were about to let him go.

Eunice stared at him, dumbstruck. 'God, Ren, you tried to kill someone?'

So much for innocent until proven guilty.

'No. I don't know what they're on about.'

Eunice shook her head with a heavy sigh, not believing him any more than Inspector Duggan or Detective Pete did.

'How long before I can arrange bail?' Eunice asked.

'Bail?' the inspector scoffed. 'There won't be any bail for your boy this time, Ms Ravenel. He's facing serious charges.'

'My client is not a flight risk. His mother —'

'Hasn't been able to stop him doing anything he wanted since he was ten years old. This kid is the very definition of a flight risk. He's not in the slightest bit sorry, he's facing serious time, has a valid passport, easy access to credit cards and a private jet, last I heard.'

'We don't have a private jet,' Ren said. 'It belongs to the studio.'

'Be quiet, Ren,' Eunice ordered. 'You're not helping.' She turned back to the inspector. 'If Ms Kavanaugh could guarantee Ren's good behaviour —'

'Then the little smart-arse wouldn't be sitting here, would he?' Pete said, glaring at Ren.

'I'm sorry, Ms Ravenel,' the inspector said in a tone that suggested she was anything but sorry. 'Your client will be our guest for the evening and if you want to argue what an upstanding member of society he is, you can do it tomorrow. In court. To a magistrate.'

Eunice looked like she might keep objecting, but the inspector never gave her the opportunity. She turned for the door. 'C'mon, Pete. I'm sure Ms Ravenel wants a word with her client.'

Pete gathered up his file, gave Ren a serves-you-right-you-little-smart-arse look, and followed the inspector out of the room, slamming the door behind them.

CHAPTER 25

'I'm very disappointed in you, Ren,' Eunice said, taking the seat recently occupied by Detective Pete.

'I didn't do anything, Eunice.' Ren stared down at his hands, locking his fingers together until they turned white.

'A magistrate will go much more leniently on you if you take responsibility for your actions.'

'I didn't *do* anything, Eunice,' Ren repeated in a monotone. He felt like adding *you have to believe me*, but that just seemed like begging, and he shouldn't have to beg his own lawyer to have a little faith in him.

She sighed heavily. Eunice Ravenel often sighed heavily when she dealt with Ren. 'I've spoken to your mother. She's tempted to let you rot in here, Ren. So unless I can give her a compelling reason to believe you're innocent — no mean feat, given you stole a guest's car from her house — then I'm afraid there's no stopping the natural course of justice.'

'How about you just accept it when I tell you I haven't done anything wrong, and you defend me like you're supposed to. You know ... because you believe me.'

Eunice wasn't so easily persuaded. 'Then tell me what you were doing in that warehouse.'

Ren didn't answer.

'Are you involved with this O'Hara character?'

'I never heard of him until ten minutes ago.'

'Then how is it you happened to be at his warehouse at the precise moment his drug deal was going down?'

Ren was wondering that, too. For a moment, he even thought about telling Eunice everything. About Murray Symes. About where he got the information from about the drug deal ...

But he didn't want to betray Jack until he was certain Jack had betrayed him. The old man had helped Ren too many times, and kept quiet about it, for Ren to hand him over to the police, just to get his own backside out of the fire. Besides, he was more worried about what might have happened to Trása. 'It doesn't matter why we were there, Eunice. Can you find out what happened to my friend?'

'What friend?'

'Jack O'Righin's granddaughter. They arrested us at the same time, but now the cops are saying she wasn't there.'

Eunice let out one of her trademark sighs. 'Jack O'Righin has no granddaughter. If you'd read more than the dustcover of that shameless attempt to rewrite history that he's peddling and were less impressed by notoriety, Ren, you'd know Jack O'Righin's family was killed years ago. Vengeance for their deaths was one of his feeble justifications for the violence he perpetrated on all those innocent people.'

'If you don't believe me, ask Murray Symes about her,' Ren said, sick of everyone trying to convince him that Trása was a figment of his imagination. 'He's met her. He even threatened to have me arrested if I tried to have sex with her.'

Eunice stared at him, saying nothing.

'It's the truth,' Ren insisted. 'If I was lying I'd have thought up something way better than that, Eunice, believe me.'

The lawyer shook her head sadly. 'You've had so many opportunities, Ren. But this time, you've crossed the line. Your mother has spent her life campaigning against drugs. You know how she feels about drug dealers.'

'God! Aren't you listening to me? I wasn't dealing drugs!'

He might as well have remained mute, for all the attention she was paying to him.

She let out another sigh. 'And now you're in danger of taking a man's life. What were you thinking, Ren? Setting fire to that place? Are you so starved for attention you thought you'd give arson a go? Was cutting yourself not getting the results you wanted, so you decided to hurt someone other than yourself?'

Ren closed his eyes, overwhelmed with a feeling of helplessness. How was it possible that everybody got him so wrong? This woman was supposed to be defending him, and even she thought he was a lost cause.

'I swear to God, Eunice, I know nothing about the fire at the warehouse.'

'The Gardaí tell me that when they searched you, they found another cut on your ribs. Is that true?'

Ren hesitated before he answered, knowing the truth was sure to condemn him. 'Yes.'

'I see.' Eunice rose to her feet, with another sigh. 'I'll call your mother and tell her what's happened. I'm sure she'll try to be in court tomorrow, but …'

'I know. She may not be able to get away.' Ren knew that excuse by heart.

'She's still at the hospital with the rest of the family, Ren,' Eunice told him. 'I think poor Hayley's vigil is likely to take precedence over another one of your court appearances, don't you?'

Eunice had that much right. Hayley's fate was far more important than his.

The lawyer picked up her briefcase and knocked on the door. She glanced at Ren as she waited for someone to unlock it, but said nothing further. Pete opened it, looking far too smug for Ren's liking. He let Eunice out, entered the room and closed the door firmly.

'What now?' Ren asked.

'We're going to book you into the five-star accommodation of Chez Watch-house,' Pete informed him, as he pulled Ren to his feet. 'And it seems there's nothing your mother's celebrity lawyer can do to stop it, either.'

'Can I order room service?'

'Keep it up, smart-arse.' Pete shoved Ren toward the door, apparently pleased with the notion that Chelan Aquarius Kavanaugh would spend the night behind bars and that — unless he was kidnapped by aliens — that was where he was probably going to stay for the rest of his life.

The watch-house cells were noisy and brightly lit. There was no window in Ren's cell, so he couldn't tell what time it was. The walls were white, made of some sort of laminated material impervious to graffiti or vandalism. A narrow bed was built into the back wall and had a thin, vinyl-covered foam mattress. There was a stainless-steel toilet in the opposite corner. Ren wore overalls made of paper, presumably to stop him strangling himself with his own clothes. Because he was only seventeen and still legally a juvenile offender, Ren was treated to a solitary cell, rather than a communal one full of drunks and addicts. He thought that was something to be grateful for, until he realised he'd been confined to one of the observation cells they used for suicide watch, which meant they cranked up the heating instead of giving him a blanket — again, he assumed, to prevent him making a noose out of it. He wasn't officially on suicide watch, but he figured he might soon be, if they didn't stop checking on him every thirty minutes to ask if he was okay.

Despite the regular interruptions, Ren had lost track of the time when they made the next round of checks. He even managed to doze off. It was several hours since dinner — which had turned out to be takeaway from the local fish and chip shop down the road — when he was woken by someone saying his name.

'Ren Kavanaugh?'

'Wasn't that my name the last time you checked?' he asked, rubbing his eyes. Then he realised that it wasn't what they'd asked him the last time. The last time they'd called him Chelan Aquarius. He squinted at the newcomers in the sudden brightness. They'd turned on the main light, which he assumed the cops had picked up at a sale of leftover stadium illumination equipment.

'Are you Ren Kavanaugh?'

'Yes,' he said, with a sigh that would have done Eunice proud. 'I am Ren Kavanaugh.' He focussed on his visitors and frowned. They were a man and a woman of indeterminate age, both dressed in dark suits. They looked like door-to-door salesmen.

'Come with us please.'

'Where?'

'Please, do not question us.'

Had he been less exhausted, Ren decided later, he might have started to worry when they wouldn't tell him where they were going. Given Trása had already vanished — seemingly without a trace — he had reason to be concerned. Not until he followed the suits out into the corridor and past the door at the end of it that normally needed a card and a PIN to get through, did it occur to him that something was amiss. The watch-house desk was abandoned, too, and an elderly sergeant was slumped over the keyboard of his computer, where he'd apparently been playing Solitaire before falling asleep.

Ren looked around the deserted reception area. 'What's going on?'

'You are being evacuated,' the woman said. She seemed to be in charge.

'To where? For what?'

'Please. Be patient.'

'Can I have my clothes, then?' Ren asked, pointing at the white paper overalls that crackled as he walked.

'Clothes will be arranged for you when we reach our destination,' the woman assured him.

'Destination? What destination? Where are we going?'

'Your questions will be answered soon enough, Ren.'

'Has someone called my lawyer? She'll be royally pissed if she finds I've been moved and nobody's notified her.'

'Everything has been taken care of. You have nothing to fear.'

'Who are you guys?' Ren asked, as they hurried him into the elevator.

Suit One looked at Suit Two for a moment and then the woman smiled. 'We are with Interpol.'

Interpol! Ren thought in alarm. *What the fuck have I done now?* 'Show me some ID.'

'Very well.'

The woman reached into the pocket of her jacket and took from it not a wallet with a badge as Ren was expecting, but a handful of blue powder.

Before Ren had time to turn away, the woman blew the powder into his face and he slumped unconscious into the arms of the man behind him.

PART TWO

CHAPTER 26

Groggy and unsettled by his nightmares, Ren woke to the worst headache he had ever experienced. It was beyond pain. It was as if someone had drilled into his skull through his eyeballs and was digging out the grey matter with a jackhammer. He couldn't think. He couldn't speak. He could barely breathe. In the end, he passed out again, with only the vaguest notion of what had happened to him.

He woke again some undetermined time later, feeling much better. The jackhammer had faded to a dull thudding.

Ren jerked awake at the sound of a relentless whooping alarm. He sat up sharply, banging his head on the bunk above. Looking around, he figured he might be on a boat. He was in a cabin — possibly below the waterline, given there was no porthole — the sloped walls of which were painted khaki in places and bare metal in others.

Warily, Ren swung his legs around and put his feet on the floor. There was a slight trembling movement underfoot that indicated they were under way. The alarm was still going, but his headache was easing.

I'm dreaming, he decided, rubbing his gritty eyes. His hands came away with a fine blue powder on them. He stared at the blue powder for a moment, wondering why it seemed familiar ...

And then he remembered the Interpol agents.

Fighting back a sudden rush of panic, Ren took a deep breath, trying to remember what he'd been told about situations like this.

When Ren was eleven, Kiva had acquired a stalker, who was utterly convinced she was speaking to him directly from the screen. He believed she was begging him to save her from the terrible life in which she was trapped, where she was held captive by an evil demon named Norman. The guy was a complete nutter — a paranoid schizophrenic who'd gone off his meds. For over a year — until the security guards had tasered him as he was climbing the wall of their rented house in Prague where she'd been filming a movie about the French Resistance in World War Two — Kiva and Ren had been virtual prisoners.

And not without cause. The stalker — when they'd caught him — was armed, manic, and carried two cyanide pills, which he later told police he was planning to use on the Spawn of Satan — Kiva's son — whom he believed was an agent of the demon, Norman. Ren was there, the stalker claimed, to guard his beloved Kiva like a Doberman Pinscher, expressly to stop the man she truly loved from coming to her rescue.

For much of that year, they had lived surrounded by high walls, bodyguards and extraordinary security measures. Ren hadn't been allowed out of the house without an escort, not even to play in the garden with Neil and Hayley.

Kiva had taken him out of school and brought in a tutor. In fact, after a couple of months of living on a knife edge, jumping at every unexpected sound, Kerry had hired a local housekeeper to look after Kiva and taken her own children back to Dublin. Ren had been desperate to go with them, but Kiva wanted him close by.

How to behave if he were ever kidnapped had been drilled into Ren during that time. He racked his brains now, trying to remember the rules.

Avoid being restrained. That was the first rule. *Once you're tied up, it's much harder to escape.*

Second rule: fight. Do it immediately. The moment they grab you. Windmill your arms. Kick. Scream. Punch. Scratch. Go for the eyes ... the genitals ... Do whatever it takes. You may not get a second chance.

Well, I blew that one ...

Rule three. Pay attention. Ren remembered Kiva's bodyguards drumming that into him. *Remember as much as you can about your kidnappers — what they're wearing, eye colour, hair colour, tattoos, scars ... If they have guns, don't look down the barrel. Look at their faces. Look them in the eye.* People generally fix on the weapon when it's pointed at them, they told him, and later find they can't describe their abductors at all.

Listen. If they're speaking a language you don't understand, try to make out individual words, they'd urged. *Listen for names. Better yet, never travel to a country where you don't know at least a few key phrases you might need if you find yourself in trouble.* Ren remembered that rule well, because he could pick up whole languages in a couple of weeks, if he heard enough of them.

Learning of that gift was the only time Ren could ever remember impressing those big, surly, humourless men charged with protecting his life.

Run if you get the chance, they said, *even if they have guns. Kidnappers motivated by money don't want to kill you*, the bodyguards assured Ren. *Neither do sexual predators. They have even more reason to keep you alive.*

Never run in a straight line.

Make a ruckus.

Get somewhere public as fast as you can.

Ren was surprised how well he recalled the rules. For all the good they were now. Nobody had mentioned phoney Interpol agents, blue dust that knocked you unconscious or what to do if you found yourself held captive on a ship.

This wasn't a stalker on the loose, Ren was certain. This was organised. Premeditated. Well thought-out.

Organised crime, maybe? Or perhaps this was about that drug dealer … what was his name? O'Hara? Maybe Ren had been abducted by some drug lord's enemies.

Bad call if they think I know anything useful, Ren thought sourly.

He sighed. Would anybody even notice he was gone? With Hayley's life in the balance, his fate wasn't that important. Although his abduction was a distraction the Boyles didn't need right now. Murray Symes would probably accuse him of arranging to get himself kidnapped as some sort of attention-seeking behaviour.

Ren pushed himself off the bunk. Time to get this over with. *Kill me or let me go.* Forcing himself to ignore his headache, he crossed the cabin in two steps.

He banged on the door with his fists. 'Hey! Who are you guys! Where am I! Let me outta here!'

The door opened almost immediately and the alarm miraculously stopped screaming at the same time. There was a man standing outside in the passage wearing jeans and a plain black T-shirt. Last time Ren saw him, he had been posing as an Interpol agent. He looked much younger without the suit. Not much older than Ren.

'There's no need to shout, Rónán. If you'd tried it first, you'd have discovered the hatch wasn't locked.' The man spoke in an accent not unlike Trása's indefinable brogue.

Ren stared at him, stunned into silence by the unexpectedly friendly greeting. What was going on? Were they hoping to win him over? Was this the first stage of their plan to seduce him to their cause? If they were being extra nice, hoping for the Stockholm Syndrome — which had been explained to him in excruciating detail by Kiva's bodyguards — to kick in by giving a bit of a push, they were very optimistic.

'My name's not Rónán.'

'You'd rather we called you Ren? As you wish.'

'Where am I? What was that alarm?'

'You're on a barge,' the young man said pleasantly. 'The alarm was … well, I'm not sure. Mechanical things aren't really my area of expertise.' Then he smiled and shrugged apologetically. 'I realise you're probably used to better treatment than this. Sorry we couldn't come up with anything more salubrious, but it won't be for long. Did you want to bathe? Have something to eat?' He was staring at Ren intently, almost as if he couldn't believe what he was seeing. But whatever it was about Ren that seemed odd, it was making this kidnapper very happy, because he didn't seem to be able to wipe the smile off his face.

Ren studied him warily. He was talking as if they were old friends. 'I want to call my mother,' he said.

The young man nodded, still grinning stupidly. 'Why don't we get you cleaned up and have something to eat, first? Follow me.'

'Where are we going?'

'To the showers.'

Ren didn't budge from the door of his cabin. 'That's what the Nazis said to the Jews getting off the trains at Auschwitz,' he said.

'Nazis?' His kidnapper squinted at him blankly for a moment. Then he nodded and smiled even wider. 'Ah, yes! A regime that achieved some notoriety in your twentieth century.'

Your twentieth century, the man had said. Not 'the twentieth century' or 'our twentieth century', but *your* twentieth century.

Brilliant. I've been kidnapped by a bunch of ... what? Looney conspiracy theorists? Aliens?

'The Nazis killed millions of people,' Ren felt compelled to point out. Whatever crackpot theories these people held about time, there were certain facts here that couldn't be disputed. 'A lot of them in showers, incidentally.'

The kidnapper seemed amused. 'I can assure you, Ró— Ren, our showers are quite safe, if a little temperamental. Much like the rest of the ship.' He turned and headed down the corridor. He didn't bother to check if Ren was following.

Ren debated staying put. He didn't debate it for long, however. There didn't seem much point. Whoever these people were, they didn't seem hostile. It was probably just about money.

Whatever ... Ren thought. He wasn't in handcuffs and they were offering him a shower and food and hopefully a change of clothes. He might as well play along.

I wonder what they think I'm worth?

'Do you people have names?' Ren asked, as he followed his kidnapper down the rusty companionway.

The ship creaked and groaned alarmingly. If these people had abducted him in the hopes of making money out of him and had hidden him on a rusty barge, they clearly thought the negotiations were going to take time, despite his captor's assurance he wouldn't be here long. Were they planning to move him? Or were they chugging across the Irish Sea, about to meet up with another ship sailing under a foreign flag and he'd never be heard of again?

They didn't seem bothered about him being able to identify them. That could mean they were confident of not being caught. Or that their politics were such that getting away wasn't an option ...

Ren hoped the latter wasn't the case. People with political agendas weren't squeamish about death, or about taking their hostages with them when they died.

'*Brógán is ainm dom.*'

Ren stared at the young man in surprise. His abductor was speaking Gaelige. Or a strangely accented version of it. That meant they were locals. Irish.

Oh God, no ... I've been kidnapped by the IRA. Aliens might have been better.

'Brógán is my name,' the kidnapper added in English. He glanced over his shoulder, and pointed to a metal staircase leading upward. 'My ... colleague's name is Niamh.'

'Ah ... the lady with the deadly blue powder.'

Ren grabbed hold of the cold handrails, which left flakes of paint on his palms, and began to climb the gangway after Brógán. 'What was that shit, anyway?'

Brógán glanced over his shoulder and grinned at him. 'A deadly blue powder.'

'Great,' Ren muttered. 'Not just a *cheerful* IRA grunt ... this one thinks he's a comedian, too.'

'It's called *Brionglóid Gorm*,' Brógán added.

'Blue dreams, huh?' Ren translated, to make certain he'd heard right.

'Brógán!' a tinny, female voice called over a loudspeaker. 'You'd better come up here.'

The woman, too, had spoken Gaelige. It was a somewhat different dialect to the one Ren was used to hearing, the one they taught at school, but alike enough for him to make sense of it. Maybe they were from one of the Gaeltacht regions outside Dublin, Ren thought, where the locals spoke Irish first and English as an afterthought. That would account for the difference between the formal language Ren was used to, and the much more colloquial version these people spoke.

'I guess this means we're going to the bridge first,' Brógán said with a sigh. They reached the next deck and headed up another set of rusty metal stairs. There was no sign of any other crew. Were these two and he alone on this rusty old barge?

The idea gave him hope. How hard could it be to get away from only two of them? Particularly as they didn't seem to be armed.

Ren followed Brógán silently, wondering what the temperature of the Irish Sea was at this time of year. If he jumped overboard, would he get away? Or would he drown before anybody could rescue him? Die of hypothermia?

When they finally stepped onto the rain-swept deck a few moments later, Ren guessed the answer was '*you'll die of hypothermia*'. The sea was dull and relatively flat, but a steady, icy rain was falling, making the deck slippery and treacherous. Ren shivered as he grabbed the slick rail and followed Brógán forward, doubting he'd last even ten minutes if he tried escaping over the side. A quick scan of the horizon confirmed his suspicion they were out of sight of land.

Jesus ... where are they taking me?

Wherever it was, Ren consoled himself with the idea that people would already be looking for him. Kiva would be calling in every favour she was owed. And there was the minor matter of appearing to have escaped police custody.

Shit ... what if they don't realise I was kidnapped? What if they think that O'Hara simply busted me out of gaol ...

Ren was still worrying about that when they reached the bridge. It was warmer inside. Brógán slammed the sliding door shut, before fighting with the lock for a few moments to ensure it stayed that way. Niamh didn't look up. Her gloved hands were clamped to the wheel, her eyes fixed on some point on the misty horizon through the rhythmic thump and squeak of windscreen wipers in need of new rubber. She didn't realise, Ren thought, that Brógán wasn't alone.

'This rain is going to make it almost impossible to —' she began. She stopped abruptly when she saw Ren and actually paled a little. '*Leath tiarna!*'

Half-Lord she'd exclaimed. 'Excuse me?'

Niamh recovered herself quickly. 'I am sorry, Rónán,' she said in English. 'I wasn't expecting you.'

'Who were you expecting?' he asked. *Pay attention. Look at what they're wearing, how they speak, eye colour, hair colour ...*

Niamh would be easy to remember, he thought. She had long, wavy dark hair flecked with the occasional strand of grey, sharp blue eyes and an air about her that suggested she was used to being in charge. She was much older than Brógán, too, he realised, now he had time to notice. She was closer to his mother's age.

Niamh didn't answer Ren's question. 'Has Brógán fed you, yet? Offered you a chance to clean up? Is there anything you want?'

'You could drop me off at the nearest port,' Ren suggested. 'And let me go home.'

Niamh smiled. 'Never fear, Rónán,' she said. 'If I can promise you nothing else, I can promise you this, *Leath tiarna*: we are taking you home.'

CHAPTER 27

'*Better the blood of two innocents, than the blood of twenty thousand.*'

Ren extracted his finger from the soft, determined grip of the baby girl, her skin so soft and warm, her gaze so trusting and serene; it was heartbreaking.

But not heartbreaking enough to stay his hand. He raised the blade, transfixed by the guileless blue eyes staring up at him. And then he brought it down sharply, slicing through the swaddling and her fragile ribs into her tiny heart without remorse or regret.

He was quick and, he hoped, merciful, but the link between the sisters was quicker.

Before he could extract the blade from one tiny heart and plunge it into another, her twin sister jerked with pain and began to scream.

The next time Ren woke he was no longer on the rusty old barge tossing around on the Irish Sea. As the wisps of his unsettling dream faded, he looked about and discovered he was lying on a rank, straw-filled mattress in what seemed — and smelled — like some sort of rude shepherd's cottage. There were no windows. The only light came from cracks in the split-log walls.

For a few moments, he struggled to recall how he got here. The last thing he remembered was sitting with Brógán in the galley of the barge, eating a perfectly ordinary ham sandwich. It was about ten in the morning, and Ren was freshly showered and dressed in borrowed jeans and a sweatshirt, none the wiser about what his captors wanted. Niamh's voice had come over the PA again, announcing they were almost there. Brógán's grin broadened. He was excited. Full of anticipation.

'Where exactly is "there"?' Ren asked.

Brógán was hard-pressed to contain himself. 'You'll see. Finish your lunch.'

'Why?'

'You'll have to come up on deck. Then you'll see.'

Ren swallowed the last of his sandwich, drained the lukewarm can of Pepsi Brógán had given him, and then followed the young man onto the deck to join Niamh. But almost as soon as he appeared, she hit him with that deadly blue powder again.

That was the last thing Ren remembered.

He pushed himself up on his elbows to look around. There was no sign of Brógán or Niamh and — through the pounding headache that was a *Brionglóid Gorm* hangover — he discovered that under the smelly woollen blanket, he wasn't wearing any clothes.

He didn't want to think about why.

The door opened and Brógán walked in. Still smiling like a fool, the young man was no longer dressed in jeans and T-shirt. Now he was wearing a tan hooded robe made of a rough woven fibre.

'Where're my clothes?' Ren demanded, horrified at how panicked he sounded. 'Who took them?'

'I'm sorry,' Brógán said, surprised. 'Oh ... Of course ... you wouldn't know. We couldn't bring them through the rift.'

'What rift?'

'Ah ...' Brógán paused, as if choosing his words more carefully. 'We are ... in a ... *different* place ... to the one you are used to, Rónán,' he said slowly, considering every word. 'We have rules here that make the apparel you were wearing ... dangerous.'

Ren's panic evaporated in the face of such a ludicrous suggestion. '*Dangerous?* Dude, I was wearing jeans!'

'With a zip fastener,' Brógán said. 'And your T-shirt was a blend of synthetic fibres. Neither of those technologies is permitted here.'

'A zipper? *Technology?* Are you kidding me?'

Brógán looked appalled. 'Of course not, *Leath tiarna*!'

'And that's another thing ... why do you keep calling me Rónán? And Half-Lord? Where is Niamh by the way? And what happened to the boat? Wait ... let me guess! The damn thing sank, didn't it?'

Brógán shrugged. 'Possibly. I don't know what happened to it after we left.'

Brógán wasn't making any sense and Ren's head hurt too much to puzzle it out. He just wanted some aspirin, some clothes and a ride home. He was long over being a kidnap victim.

'Look ... can I just —' Ren let out an involuntary yelp as the pain in his head suddenly spiked. 'God ... that blue crap you people keep blowing in my face is some serious shit. My head is killing me.'

Concerned, Brógán hurried to Ren's side. 'Here, let me fix that for you.'

Before Ren could stop him, Brógán placed his hand on Ren's forehead and closed his eyes.

Miraculously and without warning, the headache vanished.

Ren stared at Brógán in surprise. Brógán was instantly concerned. 'Is something wrong?'

'No … I mean … Christ, what did you do, Obi Wan? Use the Force?'

'I don't know what that means,' Brógán said, looking puzzled. 'I healed your pain, Rónán, that's all. It's what I do.'

'I thought what you did was kidnap people?' Ren said sourly.

The young man smiled. 'Not people. Just you.'

'What makes me so special?'

Brógán's grin threatened to split his face in half. 'You'll see. Did you want to get dressed?'

'Didn't you ditch my gear because of the evil zipper?'

'We did,' Brógán said, without a hint of irony. 'I have clothes that will fit you.' He hurried to the other side of the small hut where a folded pile of clothes sat on a roughly carved three-legged stool by the unlit fireplace. He picked them up and brought them to Ren. 'Here.'

Ren eyed the pile warily before taking it from Brógán. It consisted of a sleeveless sheepskin vest and a pair of brightly coloured, speckled blue trousers made of soft wool. There was a shirt too, laced with a leather thong, made of a fabric that felt like linen, embroidered along the cuffs and collar with beautifully worked blue climbing roses and soft, equally embellished, ankle-high boots.

There was no underwear. Ren shook his head in despair. 'Dude, that has to be the gayest outfit I've ever laid eyes on.'

'I'm glad the clothes please you, Rónán.'

Ren sighed. He had always thought he spoke Gaelige pretty well, but something was clearly getting lost in the translation. He studied Brógán's expectant expression and shook his head. 'You seriously expect me to wear this stuff, don't you?'

'Of course.'

'How do you know it'll fit?'

Brógán's face split into that insufferable I-know-something-you-don't-know grin again. 'They'll fit.'

There didn't seem to be much choice. Silly or not, any clothes were better than no clothes. Ren pushed back the rough blanket, shivering a little in the chill air, and pulled the shirt over his head. Brógán watched, still grinning stupidly. As his head poked through the neck, Ren glared at him. 'Having fun there, pal?'

Brógán looked at him oddly for a moment and then shrugged. 'I'm sorry ... you're used to privacy, aren't you?'

'If you don't mind ...'

Brógán backed out of the small hut, closing the door — which was hung on thick leather hinges — behind him. Ren dressed as quickly as he could, surprised by how accurately they'd guessed his size. The trousers took some working out, though. They were much tighter-fitting than he was accustomed to and were held down at the ankles by a slender strap passing underfoot. The shirt looked like a frock coat, but it had no collar. It reached a little below the hips, with a leather girdle at the waist. The clothes weren't as comfortable as he was used to, but the boots felt as if they'd been custom-made for him, and the rest of the gear fitted almost as well.

When he was finally done, Ren glanced down at himself, shaking his head. 'Oh my God ... Hayley ... if you could see me now ...'

Ren wondered what would happen next. Brógán seemed excited rather than worried — but that could mean anything. And there was no sign of Niamh. It occurred to Ren that if Brógán was alone out there, perhaps now was his chance to overpower him. Ren wasn't defenceless. He'd been taught to fight by Kiva's bodyguards — who were masters of dirty tricks rather than the Marquis of Queensbury rules — and he'd spent some time on the school boxing team. At least until he realised competition boxing meant answering awkward questions about those wretched cuts that kept appearing on his arms, legs and torso.

Ren flexed his hands, wondering how hard he'd have to hit Brógán to incapacitate him. There wasn't much he could use as a weapon in the hut. He'd done enough boxing to know a single blow to the head resulting in unconsciousness would be — in his case — more good luck than anything else.

He lost his chance to do something about Brógán while he was still wondering about it. The door opened and Niamh came in. She was also dressed in a long tan robe. She eyed him warily for a moment and then stood back to let another man in.

Ren stared at the newcomer, whose powerful presence filled the hut. The man was a little taller than Ren, his face scarred and weather-beaten, making it hard to guess his age. He was dressed in a similar fashion to Ren, with the addition of a chainmail vest that reached to mid-thigh, golden bracers at his wrists, and rings on almost every finger. And he was wearing a sword. A very large sword.

He stared at Ren for a moment and then shook his head. 'By *Danú* ... except for the hair ... it's uncanny.'

'What's uncanny?' Ren asked.

'Nothing ...' Niamh said, with a warning look at the big man. She fixed her gaze on Ren. 'This is Ciarán. He's here to watch over you. Let's go outside. There is someone coming to meet you soon and we need to explain a few things before then.'

Here we go, Ren thought. *This is where they tell me 'it's nothing personal, son, but if your mother doesn't arrange for the release of every political prisoner in the entire freaking world by tomorrow morning we're going to start sending you home, one finger at a time'.*

CHAPTER 28

Filled with trepidation, Ren followed Niamh and the big scary guy outside, mindful that escape would be easier out in the open. It turned out his guess about being in a shepherd's hut was right. The tiny shelter was located on the side of a small hill. The countryside fell away in a postcard-pretty sweep of emerald green fields, dotted with a few trees and a dozen or so scrappy-looking sheep grazing contently. Nearby was a lathered mare cropping at the grass close to the hut, although there was no sign of a saddle or bridle to indicate she'd been ridden recently. Ren could just make out a thin blue ribbon of water on the horizon. The day was cool and cloudy and seemed to be mid-afternoon. They weren't that far inland, he calculated, given he could smell the salt air on the breeze, but there was no sign of civilisation. No powerlines, no roads, no smoke haze in the distance. They were far from everywhere.

'Who's coming to see me?' he asked, blinking as he emerged into the sunlight.

'That will be obvious when you meet him,' Niamh said. She pointed to a fire pit where Brógán was turning a lamb on a spit over a bed of glowing coals. 'Are you hungry?'

Ren shook his head. The creature still looked quite raw.

'Sit down,' she said.

He looked around. 'On what?'

Niamh looked at him oddly. 'The ground. What else?'

Ren sighed. *Ask a stupid question …* He did as Niamh suggested, and sat down cross-legged — no mean feat in those trousers — on the grass near the fire, close enough, almost, to reach it. Maybe, when Brógán turned his back to stoke the fire, Ren could grab a burning stick for a weapon …

But a glance at the newcomer in the chainmail who was here to 'watch over him' made Ren think better of that plan. Ciarán looked like he could break tree-trunks in half with his bare hands.

Niamh sat opposite him, much more gracefully. The man with the sword folded his alarmingly well-formed arms across his chest and remained standing behind her.

'The first thing we must explain to you, Rónán,' Niamh said, arranging the folds of her robe, 'is that there is no point in trying to run from here. This is not the world you know. You are in danger from threats you cannot imagine, which is why Ciarán is here. I want your word that, at least until you meet your …' she hesitated, as if searching for the right word, 'your visitor … you will not try to run away.' She spoke Gaelige, as she had almost continuously since he had first met her, although it was oddly accented and Ren wasn't sure he was getting all the words.

He nodded in response to her request, easily making a promise he had no intention of keeping. Not that he had much choice in the matter with Ciarán standing there ... *looming*. 'Okay,' he said.

'The next thing I need to explain is that we are not from the realm you know.'

That seemed something of an understatement. 'I see ...'

Niamh frowned. 'I am serious, Rónán. This is a different Earth to the one you are familiar with.'

'This is not your reality, is what she means,' Ciarán said. He added, speaking to Niamh, 'He won't understand realms, Niamh. You should call them realities.'

'You're talking about *alternate* realities?' Ren asked. He was expecting a political manifesto. Even some rant about how Kiva didn't deserve her Oscar, and that he was stuck there until she gave it back, would have made more sense. He wasn't expecting a physics lesson.

'You know of alternate realities?' Niamh said in surprise. 'I wasn't aware they knew about such things in your realm.'

'We have theories about them,' Ren said cautiously, deciding he'd be better served not antagonising the guy who looked like he ate small children for breakfast. 'Sci-fi shows on TV like to use them when they run out of other ideas,' he added in English. 'Get to the bit where you busted me out of gaol. And why.'

'There are certain things you need to understand about this place,' Niamh replied in Gaelige. 'Differences between our realm and the one you came from. These differences are critical, Rónán ... differences on which your life will depend.'

Something about Niamh's tone warned Ren she was serious, and that was frightening. She truly believed what she was telling him, even if it was insane. Ren decided to at least give the impression he was listening attentively, figuring it wasn't a good idea to anger the insane people who just kidnapped you.

Pay attention, he reminded himself silently. *Remember as much as you can. Listen. Listen for names. Listen for key words that tell you useful things about your kidnappers.*

Such as they're completely off their collective rockers and think they're from an alternate reality …

'Okay,' he said in a conciliatory tone. 'Lay it on me.'

Niamh glared at him crossly, before she continued. 'This reality differs from the one you've known in many respects, but the true point of diversion seems to be a Roman occupation of Britain.'

Ren waited. She was looking at him as if her statement should mean something to him. It didn't.

Ciarán seemed frustrated that Ren wasn't getting the significance of Niamh's revelation. 'Two thousand years ago, the Romans failed to take Britain, Rónán,' he said. 'They failed to eradicate the Druids.'

Ren eyed them warily. 'Okaaay … So you're Druids, huh?' That, at least, explained the outfits.

'I know what you must be thinking,' Brógán said cheerily, taking a seat beside him on the ground. The roast on the spit didn't need his complete attention, although it was starting to smell delicious.

'I'm thinking you guys have been skipping your meds.'

Even Brógán didn't crack a smile. Perhaps they were from the Totally Lacking a Sense of Humour reality. Ren remembered Murray Symes once telling him that at least two percent of the world's population were psychopaths. Looking at these three, he started to wonder if the percentage wasn't a lot higher.

'Please, Rónán, you must take this seriously!' Niamh sounded more than a little frustrated.

Ciarán nodded in agreement. 'There are things you must learn yet, Rónán, skills you need to master, to survive here.'

'You have been gone a very long time,' Brógán added, 'and there are those, like the *Tuatha* for one, who have benefited enormously from your absence.'

'*I've* been gone?' Ren asked, glancing back and forth at the three of them suspiciously. He didn't bother to ask who or what the *Tuatha* was, because for some reason he knew who they meant. And that worried him. Even feigning interest in their politics was the short ride to insanity, but now he had actually understood one of their words. 'You think *I'm* one of *you*?'

'There is no doubt,' Brógán said, looking ready to burst with glee.

Ren was tempted to ask why they were so certain, but he was afraid they might tell him and he really didn't want to buy any further into their delusion.

An unexpected scene from his recurring nightmare flashed unbidden through his mind. Ren suddenly felt ill. The clothes he was wearing —

the clothes they'd just given him — were almost identical to those he wore in his dream …

Niamh must have mistaken his expression for scepticism. With a frustrated snort, she rose to her feet. 'This is a waste of time,' she said to Ciarán, brushing loose grass from her robe. 'There is only one way he's going to be convinced. I'm not interested in wasting my time trying to tell him something he'll only believe when he sees it with his own eyes.'

Ren climbed to his feet. 'Show me then. Prove it.'

He needed proof, either that this was really happening, or that he was going mad.

Dear God, please let me be going mad. The idea that his nightmare had become a reality was more than he could bear. Just knowing he had the capacity to imagine killing those unnamed babies had haunted him most of his life, making him fear the darkness secretly dwelling in his soul. He wasn't sure he'd be able to deal with the idea that his nightmare wasn't actually a nightmare, but something he really might do some day …

Niamh looked at the older man, who nodded slightly. She nodded back, glancing up at the sun that rested on the edge of the horizon in the west. 'I suppose it's almost time.'

'Time for what?' Ren asked.

She didn't bother to answer him. She turned to her younger companion. 'Give me your robe, Brógán.'

The young man looked at her questioningly.

'She can't parade him openly through the village, can she?' Ciarán explained impatiently.

'Oh!' Brógán said. He jumped to his feet, untied his woven belt and slipped off his robe, handing it to Ren. Beneath it, he was wearing tight red trousers and a linen frock coat similar to the outfit Ren was wearing.

'Put it on,' Niamh ordered. 'And pull the hood up so nobody sees your face.'

Small wonder they didn't want him recognised. They must know the police would have circulated his photo and that by now his face would be on every news broadcast, every newspaper front page and probably every milk carton in Europe. Ren hoped that was the reason for the disguise. He desperately needed to believe that was the reason and that she was lying about the alternate realities.

Ren did as he was ordered. 'So ... there's a village nearby?' he said in what he hoped was a casual tone.

'About three miles from here,' she said.

He glanced around. Except for the one horse, there was no sign of a vehicle, although it would take a four-wheel-drive with some serious torque to climb this hill. He glanced at the horse. 'How are we getting there?'

'Walk, of course.'

Niamh set off without any further ado, not even bothering to check if Ren was following. He supposed that meant she took him at his word when he said he wouldn't try to escape. *Fat chance. First public place we come to in the village, I'm outta here ...*

Even if the village was too small to have its own Gardaí station, there was sure to be a pub or a store. Some place with people and a phone.

Ciarán wasn't quite so trusting. He waited for Ren to move off, before coming up the rear, leaving Brógán to tend the roast on the spit.

Ren hurried to catch up with Niamh and put some distance between himself and Ciarán. It would take them half an hour maybe to walk to the village.

In half an hour, Ren figured, he would be free.

Ren was soon forced to rethink his escape plan. The village of Breaga didn't even have a sealed main road, just a muddy, rutted street separating a cluster of thatched roundhouses no more salubrious than the shepherd's hut they'd left behind. A pall of wood smoke hung in the air, and the few people he did see were dressed like brightly coloured extras from a Conan the Barbarian movie. But the residents of Breaga seemed to want to avoid Ciarán's eye and scurried indoors as soon as they appeared.

So much for asking someone to help. Ren couldn't see anything in the village that looked like a pub or a shop. Not even a public phone. And if there was electricity in this village, then the lines were underground.

Not that they ventured far enough into the town for Ren to be sure about that. Their destination proved to be a small ring of stones on the outskirts of the village. As they approached, Ren studied the circle curiously. Some of the stones were taller than he was, the lowest of them only waist-height and flat on top. Although moss-covered and weathered, he could see they were covered in intricate Gaelic knot-work. Maybe this was the local tourist attraction, Ren thought, rubbing his tattooed palm against his thigh. For no apparent reason it prickled with pins and needles. If the village was hoping to encourage tourists, a cafe and a souvenir shop, along with a useable road, would go a long way to improving their chances.

The grass around the site was trimmed, or grazed down by sheep. The ground inside the circle of stones seemed to have been used for a bonfire. There was a small stone platform in the centre, and around it, the earth was scorched and dead and dry, in contrast to the damp ground outside.

Ren turned to Niamh. 'What's with the poor-man's Stonehenge?'

She looked at him in surprise. 'You've been to Stonehenge?'

Ren nodded. 'Kiva did a photo shoot there once. Some perfume endorsement she had going at the time. I don't remember much about it. Except playing around the set and getting underfoot.' He said it in English, not sure if there were even words in Gaelige for 'photo shoot' or 'endorsement'.

'Did you feel anything?' Ciarán asked him curiously.

'Feel anything?' It seemed an odd question, but then, pretty much everything about his current circumstances was odd. 'Not that I recall.'

Niamh shook her head with a sigh. 'It is a very strange world you've grown up in, Rónán. I hope it has prepared you for this one.'

'Here's hoping,' he agreed in English, playing along with her as he glanced over his shoulder toward the village. He wondered if he could make it to the first house — dressed as he was — before Ciarán caught him. Assuming, of course, he wasn't armed and didn't shoot him in the back to stop him. 'Last time I —' Ren stopped abruptly, as every hair on his body suddenly stood on end and the tattoo on the palm of his hand started to burn.

The area inside the small standing stones began to crackle with red lightning.

Alarmed, Ren took a step backward, which brought him up against the solid bulk of Ciarán, who placed a firm hand on his shoulder.

Niamh didn't seem in the least concerned by the lightning. In fact, she was smiling expectantly as she moved closer to the circle. Ren glanced over his shoulder again, eyeing the houses on the edge of the village warily. The burning in his hand intensified. Was now the time to run? While the standing stones danced with that arcing red light and Niamh's attention was elsewhere?

Will I get more than three steps without Ciarán lopping my head off with that sword?

Before Ren could decide, the lightning stopped as inexplicably as it had started — no wonder the ground was singed. He looked at the standing stones. A hooded figure now stood on the stone platform in the centre of the circle.

Neat trick.

The figure pocketed something he held in his right hand and then walked toward them until he was only a few feet from Ren. He hesitated, then he pushed back the hood of his robe.

Ren stared. He knew this person's face as well as he knew his own reflection.

Shocked, he briefly glanced at Niamh, then fixed his attention on the young man who'd emerged from the lightning.

When he finally found his voice, 'What the *fuck* …?' was all he could manage.

CHAPTER 29

Darragh took the better part of a day to reach the village of Breaga. He took a circuitous route through a number of villages north and west of the coast, to confuse anybody who thought they saw him briefly appearing in the standing stones, as he moved from one place to another.

Anybody who did report seeing him — either to his own people or to agents of the *Tuatha* — would be laughed at. It was common knowledge by now, after all, that Darragh the Divided was currently locked in his room at *Sí an Bhrú*, keeping company with Queen Álmhath's court maiden, the lovely Brydie Ni'Seanan, and that — both being young and virile — they probably wouldn't emerge for days.

Even so, he'd almost been discovered more than once, the closest call being on his way through Naase. Like all the stone circles used for opening rifts, it was located outside the village, its entrance facing northeast, directly opposite the lowest stone, the only one in the circle with a flat top. It was raining when he arrived, and moments after he stepped through the rift, from the standing stones at *Sí an Bhrú*, the red lightning began to arc a second time, indicating another rift was about to open. Darragh dived for cover on the outside of the stones, squatting to flatten himself against the wet rocks. He held his breath as two of the *Tuatha* emerged from the rift, unaware they were observed. The two — a male and a female — were deep in conversation, picking up their discussion mid-sentence as they emerged, as if the rift was nothing more than a minor interruption. The male *sídhe* pocketed his jewel as soon as the lightning stopped, and the two moved off, heads bowed against the rain. They pulled up their hoods to cover their pointed ears and long hair, and hurried down the muddy track toward the town, and whatever business they had there.

Darragh didn't waste any time wondering what the *Tuatha* were doing in Naase, although Ciarán might have been interested to hear of it. As soon as they were out of sight, he stepped back into the centre of the standing stones and opened his palm to reveal the small red jewel he carried, etched with the intricate knot-work spells that allowed him to open the rift. He quickly scanned the standing stones until he found the symbol for Breaga, sparing a thought for the young woman currently ensconced in his chambers back in *Sí an Bhrú*, with promises of keeping up the illusion she was there with him.

He'd spent much of the night lying awake, talking to Brydie after he'd discovered her eavesdropping on his conversation with Ciarán. She was by turns frustrating and oddly willing to help. There had been no further talk of trying to steal his seed, although it was clear that, had he shown the slightest inclination, Brydie would have been more than happy to oblige. She'd been chosen that morning, she claimed, by Álmhath, looking for someone to thrust into his bed, selected merely because she was in the right part of her menstrual cycle. Darragh thought there might be a little more to it than that. The girl was stunning. Even if the sacred grove had been full of fertile maidens, Darragh suspected Álmhath would still have chosen Brydie.

One baited a trap, after all, with the most delicious bait at one's disposal.

Even after talking with her for hours, Darragh still wasn't sure whether he'd met the girl of his dreams, or the most conniving little vixen ever to darken the halls of *Sí an Bhrú*. Brydie was either the best ally he could have found to hide his absence, or she was, at this very moment, betraying him. His only consolation, if that proved to be the case, was knowing she still thought Ciarán was searching for some rogue rift runner, not his long-lost brother. But Darragh knew that for the time being at least, Brydie wouldn't betray him. She had been given a mission by the queen of the Celts and until she managed to consummate her union with one of the Undivided, she wasn't, Darragh suspected, planning to go anywhere or betray anyone.

Who knows, maybe, if luck is with us, she'll have two of us to choose between by tonight.

It was a fleeting thought, however, and Brydie was far from his mind when he arrived in Breaga, filled with both anticipation and trepidation.

After months of fearing they would never find his brother, Darragh was suddenly afraid of what Niamh and Brógán might have brought back.

What if Rónán turned out to be uninterested in his true origins?

Even worse, what if he was a fool? Or a fop? Or so corrupted by the technology of the reality where Amergin and Marcroy had abandoned him, he wasn't capable of dealing with the reality where he belonged?

What if he hated the idea of having a brother?

What if he didn't want to know his twin?

What if they couldn't stand each other?

Darragh forced himself to stop thinking like that. It was pointless. Rónán would be what he was and there was nothing Darragh could do about it now. When he stepped onto the stone platform for the last leg of his trip to Breaga, he forced himself to be calm and contained, and had almost convinced himself there was nothing to be concerned about.

His serenity lasted long enough to draw on the power of the stones, focus it through the jewel to open the rift, and to connect with the stones in Breaga. But as soon as he stepped through the rift and saw a hooded figure standing in front of Ciarán, with the big man's hand on his shoulder, Darragh's knees threatened to give way.

He took a deep breath, tucked the jewel safely into the pocket of his robe, and walked forward, pushing back the hood, barely able to contain his excitement.

Rónán stared at him for a painfully long moment. Then he exclaimed, 'What the *fuck* …?'

Darragh stared back. He didn't understand what his brother was saying. Rónán spoke a language he didn't know, but the shock in his expression told him what the words probably meant.

'Well met, brother,' he said warmly, hoping Rónán remembered enough of his native tongue to appreciate the sentiment.

Rónán said nothing. He just stood there, speechless.

'It is up to me, I suppose, to make the formal introductions,' Niamh said. 'Rónán, this is your twin brother, Darragh. Darragh, your long-lost brother, Rónán.'

Darragh wanted to grab Rónán in a bear hug. He wanted to check he was real. To hold him so he could be certain he was actually a real, live, warm, breathing person and not a figment of his tormented imagination. Rónán was clearly flabbergasted to learn he had a brother. Darragh, on the other hand, had spent a lifetime knowing that his other half was lost to him. To have him back, to have him standing there, whole and solid, was almost as overwhelming for Darragh as it was for his twin.

'What the *fuck* …?'

'Why does he keep saying that?' Darragh asked Ciarán in a low voice, frowning.

'He's shocked, that's all,' Niamh explained. 'He didn't believe me when I tried to explain about this being a different realm to the one he knows. So we gave up explaining and brought him here to meet you.' She shrugged. 'Sometimes it is better to show, rather than tell, don't you think?'

'I have … a *twin*?' Rónán managed to stutter, asking the question in Gaelige, much to Darragh's relief, although his accent was strange. Darragh hadn't considered the possibility his brother no longer spoke his native tongue, but clearly some vestige of it remained. It wouldn't take long, Darragh knew, for him to recover the knowledge.

The Druid gift for languages was one of the reasons their order was so respected among the nations of the world.

Or at least they *had* been respected — until Amergin and Marcroy Tarth had tried to circumvent the Treaty of *Tír Na nÓg* by separating the Undivided.

Darragh studied Rónán closely, drinking in the sight of him. Except for his hair, which, although exactly the same shade of dark brown, was cut short the way the Romans preferred it, looking at Rónán was like looking in a mirror.

'No f-freakin' way ...'

More stammered words Darragh didn't understand. He smiled. 'You were not expecting this, I think.'

'This isn't real,' Rónán said in Gaelige, shaking his head, pale and wide-eyed with astonishment.

Darragh, in answer, pushed his robe aside, and unsheathed the table dagger he carried on his belt. Rónán stared at him warily as Darragh opened his palm to reveal the triskalion tattoo. Then he held his arm out, and carved a shallow cut across his left forearm.

'*Jesus Christ!*' Rónán cried in pain, clutching his own arm.

Rónán pushed back the sleeve on his robe to reveal an identical cut — and tattoo — the blood beading across his skin. He stared at the blood.

'No *fucking* way ... this is insane.'

'As is standing here in the open, chatting like a couple of gossipy fishwives,' Ciarán warned, looking toward the village. 'We should head back to the hut. You and your brother can catch up while we walk, *Leath tiarna*.'

'It was you!' Rónán accused Darragh, in a mixture of both languages, with a look of dawning comprehension. He pulled his shirt out and lifted it to show Darragh the long slice across his ribs.

Darragh opened his robe and lifted his shirt to reveal a perfectly matched slice across his own ribs. 'We are more than brothers, Rónán — we are the Undivided.'

That clearly meant nothing to Rónán. He was still getting over the realisation that his many and varied injuries over the years were also Darragh's. Rónán said something else in the tongue Darragh didn't understand, and then repeated it in Gaelige when he saw Darragh's blank look. 'It's you! *You're* the reason for all the cuts. Getting my stomach pumped …'

'I have my share of injuries caused by you, brother.' Darragh smiled, understanding how startling this must be for his twin, but anxious that Rónán accept the truth as quickly as possible. There was so much to catch up on. So much for Rónán to learn.

So much they could achieve as the Undivided.

'I fell off my bike a couple of times. But you tried to kill yourself! Thanks to you they sent me to a fucking shrink.'

Niamh impatiently translated Rónán's rapid, excited accusation. He seemed able to speak his version of Gaelige only when he was calm. Darragh smiled when he realised what Rónán was so upset about, glad he could clear that up. 'I never tried to kill myself, Rónán. That was others trying to kill me … us actually, given that if one of us dies, we both do …'

'We must leave here now, *Leath tiarna*,' Ciarán

said, even more firmly, before Darragh could add anything more. 'The locals are starting to wonder about us.'

Darragh looked toward the village. The residents of Breaga were starting to emerge from their houses, warily watching the Druids who were using their stones.

'You speak wisely, old friend. Let's go.'

Rónán was too dumbstruck to object. Still clutching his stinging arm, he turned without protest in the direction of the hut. The curious villagers would go back inside as the Druids walked through the village. Darragh wasn't too worried as the people here would know it was unwise to interfere in Druidic business. Álmhath was unlikely to have spies this far from *Sí an Bhrú*. Breaga's relative isolation — and its proximity to the sea — was much of the reason he'd chosen this place to rendezvous with his brother.

Even so, Darragh found himself hard-pressed to care if someone did report to Álmhath. Rónán was back and, right now, that was all Darragh cared about.

'Do you remember anything about your life before you were taken?' Darragh asked, falling in beside Rónán. Niamh walked on the other side and Ciarán behind. It was a silly question. He knew that. Rónán was only three years old when they threw him through the rift.

It didn't seem fair, though, that Rónán had lost all memory of Darragh, when not a day in the last fifteen years had gone by when Darragh hadn't thought of Rónán.

'Taken?' Rónán asked in the foreign tongue. 'You mean from the Gardaí station?'

Confused, Darragh looked at Niamh again for a translation. 'Rónán was imprisoned when we found him,' she explained. 'I think he's confusing his original abduction with his most recent one.'

'Does he not remember our mother tongue?' Darragh asked.

Niamh shrugged, glancing over her shoulder at Ciarán. 'They teach a version of it in the schools of the other realm, but what they call Gaelige is only a first or second cousin to the language we speak.' She smiled reassuringly. 'Give it time, *Leath tiarna*. He is your twin. He has your gift for languages. It won't take him long to remember.'

'I'm right here, you know,' Rónán said in his oddly accented Gaelige, a little annoyed, apparently, by a conversation that excluded him. 'And I understand enough to know what you're saying. Why does she call you *Leath tiarna*?'

'For the same reason she calls you *Leath tiarna*,' Ciarán replied grumpily.

Darragh smiled at Rónán's blank look. 'Individually, brother, we are the Half-Lords of All Eire. Together we are the Undivided.'

Rónán considered that for a moment, before thrusting his hands deep into the pockets of his Druid robe. 'There's no chance, I suppose,' he said after a time, his command of his native tongue improving noticeably with every sentence, 'that I was the one Murray Symes ran down, and it's me — not poor Hayley — lying in hospital in a drug-induced coma?'

'No, Rónán,' Darragh said. 'You're not in a coma. You are home.'

Rónán sighed. Darragh recognised the gesture. He'd done it himself a million times. 'I know ...

it's just … well, the coma thing would have been easier to swallow,' Rónán said.

'I've no doubt,' Darragh agreed. 'You must have many questions for us.'

Rónán nodded warily. 'Do we have parents?'

'Of course,' Darragh said, glancing at Rónán with an odd expression. 'Do they not have parents in the reality where they found you?'

'Yeah … but …' Rónán sighed. 'Dude, I've spent the last fifteen odd years wondering where I came from. It'd be nice to have some answers.'

'Our mother was a Gaulish Druidess. Her name was Sybille.'

Rónán's eyes suddenly glistened with tears. He brushed them away impatiently, as if showing emotion over the mother he didn't remember was a sign of weakness. 'You say "was". Past tense. That means what? She's … not around now?'

Darragh shook his head. 'She died not long after you disappeared.' He hoped that was explanation enough for his brother. There would be time later — perhaps after the *Comhroinn* — when Rónán had come to grips with his new circumstances, to explain the manner of her death.

'Do we have a father?'

'Naturally.'

'Does he have a name?'

'Undoubtedly.'

Rónán stopped walking and stared at Darragh in annoyance. 'And …?'

'I'm sorry. I'd tell you his name if I knew it, but, as is often the case with the Undivided, we were conceived during the Summer Solstice festival. Our mother lay with many men during the festivities and all were masked.'

'So you're saying you don't know?'

Darragh wasn't sure why the mystery of their paternity bothered his brother so much. 'What does it matter? We are children of the people, and they are of us. It is as it should be.'

Rónán resumed walking, his expression forlorn. But after a moment, he seemed either to come to terms with the idea he could never know the identity of his father, or to put the matter aside for more practical concerns. Darragh suspected the latter. It's what he would have done.

'Do we share anything else?'

'Like what?'

Rónán was silent for a moment. 'Dreams ... nightmares ... maybe?'

Darragh hesitated before he answered, wondering if Rónán was asking a general question or if he had a specific dream in mind. 'I'm not sure,' he said, figuring that was the safest way to answer the question. Once they'd shared the *Comhroinn*, he would know if his visions involving his brother were true visions of the future or just a vivid nightmare he shared with his twin.

'Do you eat the same food in this reality?' Rónán asked after a while. If he had any other questions about sharing dreams, he seemed content to wait for the answer.

'Actually, it's better,' Niamh said. 'We sing to our crops, to encourage them to grow. Happy food always tastes better.'

'Good,' Rónán said, in a tone so reminiscent of Darragh's own, it gave Darragh the chills. 'Because I'm starving and, brother, you have a shitload of explaining to do.'

CHAPTER 30

Trása was intensely relieved to be heading home. She stepped through the rift, ready to announce the successful conclusion of her mission to prevent the Druids ever finding the lost Undivided twin.

Her return was not unexpected. Someone had to open the rift from the other end, after all. There wasn't enough magic left in the other realm to do much more than keep a *Leipreachán* amused, and the effort of sustaining an open rift for an indefinite time from this side was impractical, even for the *Daoine sídhe*. Her *marra-warra* cousin, Abbán, had been given the task of opening the rift when she was ready. He was waiting for her as she and Plunkett splashed into the icy water beside the rift-raft. She was convinced he'd moved the vessel at the last moment to be certain she got a dunking.

Abbán helped Trása onto the floating wooden platform with its carved stone circle, ignoring the *Leipreachán* who followed Trása through the rift and landed with a loud yelp and a splash a few feet away. *Leipreachán* hated water but Plunkett didn't hang around and object to his inelegant re-entry. As soon as he surfaced, he vanished into thin air.

Abbán wasn't quite as tall as Trása. His upper body was muscular and well-tanned, and only the gills running in line with his ribs marked him as different from other *sídhe*. His legs, however, were spindly and pale, a sure sign he spent as little time as possible on land. Once he slid back into the water, his fishtail would return and he would once again be the magnificent specimen he fancied himself to be.

'I'm sorry, cousin,' Abbán said insincerely, as Trása wrung the icy water from her long hair. She was naked, but unconcerned by the merman's gaze. For a *sídhe* to step through the rift wearing anything produced by the technology of another realm was a crime punishable by death. Besides, among the Faerie, clothes were an affectation most of them only bothered with when they had business in the Land of Men.

'I must have misjudged the location of the rift,' he added with a helpless little shrug, his gills exhaling apologetically. 'What with the waves, and the motion of the raft ... well, you know how it is.'

Trása knew exactly how it was, which is why she didn't believe him for a moment. Abbán was a merman. He could sense the movement of the water the way Trása could sense the wind. The rift would have opened directly over the centre of the floating stone circle the *marra-warra* had constructed to travel around this realm. For her not to land on the raft, meant the raft had been shifted sharply and quickly out of the way.

Trása had no intention of giving Abbán the satisfaction of thinking he'd bested her, however. Shivering a little in the crisp, offshore breeze, Trása smiled. 'And here was I, cousin, thinking you'd thoughtfully moved the raft clear of the rift to ensure I'd have a soft landing.'

Abbán smiled, as if he knew her sentiments were as suspect as his apology. He stepped away from the edge of the small platform, making it rock alarmingly, threatening to send Trása straight back into the water. Trása grabbed at the nearest standing stone, its etched granite warm under her fingers from the recent infusion of the magic Abbán had channelled to open the rift.

She stared at her cousin, wondering why, of all the *Daoine sídhe*, her uncle had sent Abbán to open the rift for her. It wasn't as if they were friends, even though they shared the same bloodline. Like Trása, Abbán was the offspring of one of Marcroy's many *leanan sídhe* sisters. He'd inherited his *marra-warra* father's pale colouring, his mother's dark eyes and blonde hair and, like Trása, his ears were not so pointed they raised comment when he walked among humans, if no one examined them too closely. He was a striking creature, and he knew it, which made him insufferably conceited.

'Of *course* you misjudged it,' she said, glancing at the small jewel sitting in the exact centre of the circle. It was still glowing with magic, its etched triskalion pulsating with rapidly fading light. She drew on a little of the dissipating magic to dry her hair — thrilled to feel magic coursing through her again — and took a step nearer to the raft's centre where it was a little more stable. She bent down and picked up the dark red jewel for a closer look, frowning. 'This is Marcroy's own talisman.'

'He opened the rift you went through,' Abbán said with a shrug. 'It was safer to bring you back the same way.'

That made sense. But it was an act of extraordinary trust, for Marcroy to let the talisman out of his sight.

Trása refused to let the thought stir her to jealousy. She didn't need to be jealous of anybody. For once, she had the better of her cousin. 'Our uncle will be pleased with your efforts, Abbán, given the news I bring.'

Abbán leaned forward and plucked the jewel from her fingers. 'Yes, Marcroy says you are the bearer of great tidings.' There was a note of scepticism rather than congratulation in his tone.

'I found the Undivided twin and sent him to a place where he will not bother us again,' Trása announced. She had rehearsed the announcement in her head a thousand times since watching Rónán being driven away from the burning warehouse in a Gardaí car.

It felt marvellous to say it aloud.

Abbán set the raft moving toward the shore, the tingle of his magic making Trása's skin prickle. It was wonderful to breathe in magic with every breath, instead of the fumes of the other realm.

She would miss television, though.

'What was he like?' Abbán asked.

'He's like Darragh,' she said. And then she shrugged. 'Only different.' Trása realised she'd be hard-pressed to pinpoint exactly what it was about Rónán that made him different from his brother, other than the obvious, superficial changes wrought by his upbringing. But there was something else, too, something she couldn't put her finger on.

'That's to be expected, I suppose,' Abbán said. 'Are you sure you confined him well?'

Trása nodded. Of that, she was certain. The penalty for murder in Rónán's reality was life imprisonment. She and Plunkett had watched enough police shows like *The Bill* and *Law and Order* in her six months away to be sure of that, and Jack had confirmed it. They took murder very seriously, had many inexplicable scientific tricks for discovering the truth, and invariably sentenced the culprit to life in prison.

Although she'd thought Plunkett had ruined everything when he caused Hayley's accident, it turned out perfectly in the end. Thanks to Hayley's injuries and Rónán's guilt, thinking he was in some way responsible, Trása and Plunkett found a reason to coerce him into thinking he could avenge his cousin. Plunkett couldn't glamour him, so it had taken every bit of skill Trása owned to convince him he should take the rented Ferrari and drive to the address Jack had given him, believing he would catch Murray Symes in a criminal act. Trása knew they'd been lucky. Rónán was in a vulnerable state of mind and probably not paying enough attention to the flaws in her story. And there were plenty of flaws. He just hadn't seen them, because he was so distraught at the thought his cousin might die, or be permanently injured, that he was ready to believe anything that even smelled of redemption.

The doctors had told Hayley's family she was suffering from a bilateral trauma to her primary visual cortex, Rónán had said. Trása wasn't entirely sure what that meant, only that when Rónán had heard about it, he became even more upset than he had been the night of the accident. His distress was fertile ground for Trása's scheme to take root.

Lure him somewhere he shouldn't be, make it look like he's killed someone and then lead the authorities to him, Plunkett had suggested after Trása decided Rónán would be best hidden if he were imprisoned.

Plunkett had burned down the warehouse, setting the fire just before the ERU arrived. He'd glamoured the old homeless man into staying put as the flames engulfed his cardboard lean-to, and Rónán — caught red-handed at the scene of a drug bust just as the building began to burn — was considered responsible.

Poor Rónán, she thought, feeling a twinge of guilt. He hadn't known anything about the homeless man. Or the drug deal going on between one of Jack's old criminal associates from his prison days and the drug lord, Dominic O'Hara. It hadn't taken Plunkett long to glamour the police. He glamoured away the memory of her presence and reinforced the idea that Rónán was the criminal responsible for the whole sorry mess. Whatever he said, no one would believe Rónán.

But prison didn't sound like much fun. Rónán didn't really deserve such a fate, but saving his life by sending him away would save Darragh, too, and Trása was prepared to go to extraordinary lengths to preserve Darragh's life. She reminded herself again that Rónán would be under guard, confined, and out of reach of the Druids if they discovered the reality of where Marcroy and Amergin had sent him.

'So ...' Abbán prompted, as he magically guided the raft toward the shore.

The wind was cool, but flavoured by the sweetest hint of impending autumn, something she'd missed in the other realm, where the air smelled like burnt dead things, and the magic was so thin even Plunkett was hard-pressed to find it.

'What did you do with him?'

Trása crossed her arms against her body and turned to look toward the misty dark-green line of the land in the distance. She was reluctant to reveal her secret to Abbán. She wanted to wait until everyone was assembled before she announced her solution to the Undivided problem that plagued the *Tuatha Dé Danann*.

'I sent him away.'

'Sent him where?'

Trása hesitated, wondering what Abbán's reaction would be to her news.

'I had him sent to prison,' she said. 'For murder,' she added. 'He'll be there for life.'

Her cousin didn't react immediately, no doubt trying to find some flaw in her plan. 'Are you sure life means life?' he asked, after a time.

'I have it on the best authority,' she said. Trása was satisfied he would stay where she sent him, until the fates conspired to end his life, or his brother's.

Abbán said nothing, turning his attention to getting the raft safely back to land. Trása closed her eyes to let the cool, sweet-smelling breeze caress her face, and realised that for once, she'd got the upper hand on her cousin.

Of course, the downside of beating Abbán at anything was that he would spend the rest of the journey back to *Tír Na nÓg* trying to find fault with her plan.

The trick then, was to not give him time, she thought. She was back in her own reality now.

Every breath she took was infused with magic. For the first time in months, Trása felt whole.

Spreading her arms wide, she let the thrill of simply *being* overwhelm her.

Then, before Abbán could stop her, Trása shifted form into a white owl and took off from the raft. She soared upwards, filled with ecstasy and glee, circled the raft once to laugh at Abbán in a raucous squawk and then turned and headed north toward the Giant's Causeway and home.

CHAPTER 31

Ciarán came at Rónán with a vicious flurry of sword strikes, driving him backward, but never quite breaking through his guard. Rónán was too busy to be frightened, too focussed on staying alive to wonder how he managed to parry even half the blows the Druid warrior was trying to land on him. One semester of fencing at school with Olympic foils, endless lectures about safety and head-to-toe protective gear, had in no way prepared him for the real thing.

Ren stumbled backward, the sloped, uneven ground doing nothing to help him, until finally Ciarán landed a blow that sliced deep into the muscle of his forearm. With a cry of pain, he dropped his sword and fell backward, grabbing his arm, trying to put pressure on the cut to stem the bleeding.

Ciarán stepped back, lowered his sword and shook his head. 'This is never going to work, *Leath tiarna*.'

Ren was doubled over with pain, sweating despite the chill. These people, he decided, were crazy. Instead of telling him anything about this reality, the first thing they did was stick a sword in his hand and try to kill him.

Darragh came forward, squatted beside Ren and grabbed his arm. He examined the wound critically for a moment, apparently unaffected by it.

'How come you're not bleeding all over the scenery, too?' Ren asked.

Darragh seemed a little surprised to discover his brother needed an explanation. 'Because Ciarán's blade is simple iron.'

'You left out the bit about bloody sharp, too.'

Darragh seemed amused. 'The link between us is magical, Rónán. It takes a magical metal to affect us.'

Ren still wasn't used to being called Rónán. He was about to remind Darragh that his name was Ren, when his brother took his wounded arm and healed the deep slice as he watched, the pain vanishing along with the cut. Darragh then did the same to the cut on his ribs. Ren's skin and the tattoo on his palm prickled with the sensation, as it had when Brógán cured his headache on the boat. The feeling was much sharper here, much more intense, almost thrilling.

Flexing his hand in wonder, Ren examined the bloody mark on his arm where the cut had been. 'Wow ... Thanks.'

'It is my honour, *brother*,' Darragh said with a grin.

'Can I do that?' he asked, wiping his other, still bloody, hand on his trousers, still not convinced he had any sort of magical powers.

Darragh shrugged. He offered Ren his hand and pulled him to his feet. 'The Undivided have many talents. Your arm feels better now, does it not?'

Darragh was being polite. He didn't need to ask how Ren felt, any more than Ren needed to ask how Darragh felt. Although conscious knowledge of their link was still very new to him, he realised — now he knew what it was — he had always been able to sense his twin in a way that was impossible to describe. It wasn't telepathy. It was more an *awareness*. He'd only just begun to understand the reason for a feeling he'd experienced all his life, never considering it odd, because he couldn't imagine what life would be without it.

'So how come the blade you used in your little demo earlier cut us both?'

Darragh withdrew the small knife from his belt and handed it to him. Ren turned it over in his hands, examining both sides. It was a thin dagger, with a leather-wrapped hilt, the silver blade etched with unfamiliar symbols.

'That blade was forged from *airgead sídhe*.'

'*Faerie* silver?' Ren looked at the three of them, trying to detect some indication they were pulling his leg. He didn't know where Niamh had gone. She'd headed back to the village not long after Ciarán and Darragh decided to see how well Ren could defend himself. The sun was almost set, and the roast that had been turning on the spit for most of the day appeared to be ready, which was a good thing because Ren was starving. But try as he might, he could detect not a hint of amusement in any of them.

'This is never going to work,' Ciarán said, planting the tip of his sword in the earth. 'We can't take him back to *Sí an Bhrú* like this. He knows nothing.'

'He'll learn,' Darragh said with absolute confidence, his gaze fixed on his brother. 'Once we've shared the *Comhroinn* —'

'The co-rin?' Ren asked, but neither his twin nor the Druid seemed to notice his question.

'It won't matter,' the big man warned Darragh. 'He'll be killed — and you along with him — long before he can learn anything useful. The *Comhroinn* will give him knowledge, not the experience to use the knowledge wisely.'

Ciarán was — so Ren gathered — something of a cross between a teacher and a bodyguard, assigned to protect and tutor Darragh, which gave his assessment of Ren's chances of survival a lot of weight.

'Killed by whom?' Rónán asked. '*Faeries?*'

'Amongst others,' Darragh replied, as if Ren had meant it as a serious question.

'Dude ... I was joking ...'

'You see,' Ciarán said, looking displeased. 'He doesn't even understand the most basic threats, let alone have any notion how to deal with them. By *Danú*, he doesn't even know what a threat looks like!'

'It will be your job to teach him.'

Ciarán shook his head. 'I can't protect you and train him at the same time. We need help. Someone we can trust. Someone who'll keep him alive while he learns.'

Darragh turned to the warrior curiously. 'Who did you have in mind?'

'Sorcha.'

His brother didn't answer immediately. He glanced at Ren, squinting a little in the setting sun behind him, and then turned his attention back to the warrior. 'Would she come?'

'For this she might. She has no love for the *Tuatha Dé Danann*.'

'I wasn't aware she had any great love for her own kind, either,' Darragh said, frowning.

'Who's Sorcha?' Ren asked.

'The oldest Druid warrior alive,' Ciarán said. 'In this realm or any other.'

'Sounds like a plan,' Ren said, wondering exactly how much help one little old lady Druid would be against apparently evil Faeries bent on killing him.

'It does sound like a good plan, doesn't it?' Darragh agreed, not getting Ren's ironic tone or else deliberately ignoring it. 'Having my brother finally take his place at the head table a month from now, with Sorcha by his side, will give even Marcroy Tarth pause.'

'A month from now?' Ren asked, a little alarmed at the speed with which his life was being taken over. 'What's happening a month from now?'

'*Lughnasadh*,' Brógán explained, as he returned to his spit-roasting lamb. 'The autumn equinox.' He turned to Darragh. 'Are you wishing, *Leath tiarna*, or have you had a vision of Sorcha helping us?'

'Wishing, I fear,' Darragh said with a shrug. 'But that doesn't mean it won't happen.'

'You have visions?' Rónán asked.

'Your brother's gifts include the Sight,' Ciarán explained.

Rónán looked at Darragh warily. 'You see the future?'

'Sometimes,' said Darragh. 'The future is not so fixed it can be predicted with any great accuracy. I dream dreams of possible futures.'

'You can't seriously mean to do this.'

'It has to be done. You know that.'

283

'They are innocent.'

'They are our death.'

Ren shook his head to drive away the lingering memory of the dream that had haunted him for much of his life. Was it a dream? Or had he, like his brother, been dreaming of a possible future?

'Rónán?'

'Yeah?'

'Are you unwell? You've gone quite pale.'

Ren nodded. He wondered if he really had paled, or if Darragh was simply sensing his unease. A part of him wanted to get Darragh alone for an hour or two and demand some real answers. Another part of him didn't want to know. *Would I rather discover my nightmare was just the result of watching too many horror movies, or discover I can see the future and know that one day my own brother is going to have to threaten to kill me, to prevent me murdering a couple of babies?*

Ren couldn't decide.

'I'm fine,' he lied. Darragh knew he was lying, too. Ren could feel his scepticism.

He didn't make an issue of it, though. Instead, Darragh turned to Ciarán. 'Do you know where to find Sorcha?'

'I think so.'

'I'd ask her myself, but we have visitors in *Sí an Bhrú* tonight,' Darragh added. 'And if I'm to maintain the fiction I'm currently entertaining Lady Brydie in my chamber, I need to get back before she decides to change sides. Again.'

Ren stared at Darragh for a moment, almost afraid to ask for an explanation of that particular statement.

'Rónán can stay here with me until Ciarán

gets back with Sorcha,' Brógán offered. 'And then we can move him somewhere a little more comfortable until it's time to present him at *Sí an Bhrú*. Nobody knows he's back. He'll be safe enough.'

'It's going to be a full moon,' Ciarán pointed out.

Ren wasn't sure why that was important, but it seemed to bother the warrior. He was a little concerned, thinking anything that bothered Ciarán was probably something to be bothered about.

Brógán shrugged. 'I can handle a few weremen. Assuming they're about.'

Darragh turned to Ren. 'Is that all right with you, Rónán?'

Ren shrugged. 'I guess. What's a wereman?'

Darragh glanced at Ciarán briefly. 'Nothing you need to worry about, brother. Brógán is right. He can probably handle any danger you might encounter.'

'So they're dangerous?'

Darragh didn't answer, stooping to collect his robe from the damp grass. The temperature was dropping and the air was already thick with moisture.

As Darragh tied his robe, Ren turned to Brógán, wondering if he could get a bit more information from the young Druid once the others had departed. 'Does that mean we can eat?'

'Of course.'

Unconsciously, Ren rubbed at the triskalion tattoo on his palm. The one that matched Darragh's tattoo. When he looked up, he saw Darragh mirroring Ren's gesture without even noticing.

Creepy, Ren thought, wondering what else he shared with his twin besides the same genes, a tattoo, and an impressive array of scars.

And dreams of a possible future where he was a killer.

It was dark by the time his brother left. Darragh hugged Ren briefly, before he headed off with Ciarán, promising to return as soon as possible. The warrior offered no signs of affection, just a curt nod, a warning to Brógán to remain vigilant, and then he and Darragh turned and headed back through the darkness toward the village and the standing stones — Darragh to see to the Lady Brydie and Ciarán to bring back Ren's bodyguard, Sorcha.

And what of the life I've come from, Ren wondered as he watched them walk away? What of his own realm ... his own reality ... or whatever the hell they were calling these different worlds? *Is this a one-way trip? Am I stuck here forever, while my life at home chugs along merrily without me? Am I still wanted for attempted murder back in my own reality?*

What a choice. A lengthy trial and a good chance of spending the prime years of his life behind bars for a crime he knew nothing about, or stay where he was, and confront the possibility that his frightening dream wasn't a dream but an event yet to happen.

The thought made Ren ill.

And then he thought of Kiva. What of his mother? The Boyles?

What of Hayley?

Ren's heart constricted as he thought of his cousin Hayley. Would she wake to learn he'd disappeared? Would she spend the rest of her life wondering what happened to him? Would she even *wake* from her coma, and if she did, was her brain damage permanent?

Ren needed time alone. Time to work out what went wrong with Trása's grand plan to take vengeance on Murray Symes. Time to work out what had happened to Jack's apparently imaginary granddaughter. Time to figure out why the cops insisted he had been alone at the warehouse. Time to wonder if Kiva was worried sick that he'd disappeared, or just chalking up his absence to more attention-seeking behaviour.

He needed time to consider something else, too.

Is the dream going to happen if I stay here?

Or if I go?

CHAPTER 32

'How did you find me?'

Brógán looked at Ren sitting by the fire trying to soak up some warmth. It was getting chilly, for all that it was still summer. For the last little while, Ren had watched the Druid pace out a circle around the hut and their campfire, marking it with a white powder he apparently kept in his pocket for occasions such as this.

'We searched your realm for the better part of a year,' Brógán told him, as he continued to scatter the powder. 'Niamh found you about three months ago.'

'You've been stalking me for three months? That's creepy.'

'It was ... educational.' Brógán brushed the powder from his hands. He examined his handiwork and nodded with satisfaction. 'That should do it.'

'What should do it?'

Brógán pointed to the faint white circle. 'I've marked out a perimeter. If there are any weremen about, it should keep them at bay.'

'What is it? Salt?'

'Good lord, no!' Brógán laughed. 'The last thing

those creatures need is a salt lick. We'd never get rid of them if we laid out salt.'

'How silly of me,' Ren said, still unsure what the threat was, although he was wondering how bad the threat could be if some white powder was enough to scare them off. He glanced up at the sky, but the night was cloudy and there was no sign, yet, of the moon.

Brógán smiled. 'It's aconite powder.'

'Of course,' Ren said. 'What else would it be?'

'Wolfsbane,' the Druid added, by way of explanation. 'The weremen hate it.'

'Good to know. What *is* a wereman, exactly? Are you talking werewolves?'

'Sort of.' Brógán turned to check the roast before he answered. 'They're Faerie.'

'Faerie werewolves, huh?'

The Druid looked up at Ren, frowning. 'The *Daoine sídhe* in this realm are nothing like the Faerie you think you know, Rónán.' As if to emphasise his words, Brógán produced a savage looking dagger from under his robe. He waved it at Ren. 'You'd do well to listen and learn, *Leath tiarna*.'

'Absolutely,' Ren agreed hurriedly, the blade glinting dangerously as it caught the firelight. 'Listening and learning from now on. Count on it.'

Brógán turned his attention to their meal and to Ren's relief began to carve slices of roast meat from the spit, dropping them on a wooden platter from the hut. After a few moments, Brógán offered Ren the platter and then took a piece of meat with his fingers. Ren followed suit, guessing knives and forks weren't a priority in this world.

Ren sat on the ground. 'So how come you didn't just come up to me on the street and ask me to go with you three months ago?' he asked, figuring it was a safer subject than Faeries. 'Would've been a lot less trouble than a gaol break.'

'Would you have come without protest if two strangers had accosted you on the street and asked you to get in their car?' the Druid asked. 'Would you be sitting here, sharing a meal, discussing the situation with me so calmly, if we'd taken you by force?'

Ren shrugged. 'Probably not.'

'Anyway,' Brógán added with a thin smile, 'neither Niamh or I can drive a car.'

Ren smiled too, because seeing Brógán dressed like a Jedi, he couldn't imagine him behind the wheel of a car stuck in Dublin's peak-hour traffic. 'I guess that explains a few things, although not why you busted me out of goal.'

'Niamh decided we couldn't wait any longer to retrieve you,' Brógán said, through a mouthful of meat. 'Once you did something that caused your face to be broadcast across the world, the chances of the *Tuatha* finding you before we could bring you home became a real danger.'

'You broke me outta gaol to save me from the Faeries, huh?' Ren said, eyeing Brógán warily. 'That doesn't sound in the least bit crazy.'

Brógán was no longer smiling. 'You may poke fun at us, *Leath tiarna*, but the danger is real, and you mock it at your peril. Had the *Daoine sídhe* decided to take you, you would have been powerless to resist them. Just be thankful that in the realm we rescued you from there is so little magic left, no true *Tuatha* can survive there.'

'If they can't survive in my reality, what were you worried about?'

'There are mongrels aplenty who can cross between the worlds.' Brógán's tone was cold; filled with bitterness and contempt.

'So ... these mongrel *Daoine sídhe* ...' he asked warily, not sure what reaction his question would provoke. 'They can teleport across realities too?'

Brógán nodded. 'The half-breeds can. Some of them. But crossing the rift between realms is not a teleport in the sense you mean.'

A blood-chilling howl suddenly split the air. Ren jumped.

Brógán carried on as if he hadn't heard a thing. 'Teleports such as those we saw on television in your reality are purely mechanical. Such a machine would be massive and would require the power of a small sun to make it operational.'

'Then how do yours work?' Ren asked, glancing over his shoulder. He wasn't sure which direction the howling had come from. The first call had been answered by a second, just as chilling, which seemed to come from the opposite direction.

'Magic.'

Another howl rent the night.

'Should we be worried about that?' Ren asked. The howls seemed to be getting closer.

'The aconite will keep them at bay. Did you want some more meat?'

'No ... I'm good ...'

'There's nothing to worry about, Rónán,' Brógán assured him, reaching forward calmly to carve himself another slice off the spit. 'Did you want me to explain about the rift?'

He's trying to change the subject. Distract me. While the hounds of hell are descending upon us.

Okay ... I'll play along ... 'Can you jump through time, too?'

'Of course not. Everyone knows that.'

'Here, maybe everyone knows it,' Ren agreed, scrambling to his feet at the sound of something moving in the dark. 'In the reality I come from ...' he added, peering into the darkness, 'we're still pretty much content with the whole idea of not being able to travel between dimensions at all.' Despite a lighter patch of sky behind the clouds indicating the hidden full moon, it was too dark beyond the circle of firelight to see much of anything.

'It's not possible to travel through time ...' Brógán explained patiently. He seemed oblivious to the shadows Ren could sense creeping closer and closer to the faint perimeter. 'Otherwise you run the risk of running into yourself, and that's a paradox *Danú* just won't allow.'

Ren jumped at another howl that seemed to come from just over his shoulder.

'But you can run into yourself in another reality, can't you?' he said, trying to sound as if he wasn't freaked by the nearness of the unseen weremen. 'Are those things going to kill us?'

Brógán looked around for a moment and then shrugged. 'While they're howling like that, they're nothing to worry about.' He glanced up at the overcast sky and shrugged. 'We'll be perfectly safe, provided the rain holds off. We call them *eileféin*, by the way.'

'Cellophane?' Ren asked, wondering if he'd misheard the Druid.

'*Ella-phane*,' Brógán corrected.

'Okay ... what are these *eileféin*?'

'The alternate-reality version of oneself,' Brógán explained. 'We have very strict laws in this realm about bringing *eiléféin* through the rift.'

'Good to know. If they're not actually werewolves, exactly *what* are they?' Ren asked, turning a slow circle to see if he could spot one. He could sense them, but still couldn't make out much more than darting shades in the darkness, and Brógán had a valid concern about the rain. The Wolfsbane circle protecting them wouldn't last a minute in even a light shower.

'Shapeshifters, originally,' Brógán said, with a complete lack of concern. 'Legend has it they broke away from the *Tuatha Dé Danann* after falling out with Orlagh over some matter or other.'

'Who's Orlagh?'

'The queen of the *Tuatha*.'

'So ... they changed their shape and then got stuck in it?'

The howling had picked up in pitch to the point where Ren's hair was standing on end.

'No, of course not,' Brógán said, wiping the grease from his knife on the grass. 'They usually only take on wolven form during a full moon. The rest of the time, they're just ordinary, everyday Faerie.'

Ren eyed him askance. 'Seriously? Ordinary, everyday *Faeries*?'

'Something you're going to have to get used to,' Brógán reminded him calmly.

Ren shook his head, trying to spot one of the elusive shadows. The howls were so close, Ren couldn't believe the creatures weren't snapping at his ankles.

'Yeah ... about that whole magic thing ...' *How is this happening? I shouldn't be here waiting for* fairy werewolves to rip my throat out. *I should be home ...*

No, I should be at the hospital with Hayley ...

I should be in a reality where nightmares are just dreams and not a glimpse of the future ...

'Magic is a natural force like any other, *Leath tiarna*,' Brógán explained patiently, mistaking Ren's silence for interest. 'It just requires a creature with the ability — such as yourself — and of course, in the case of the Druids, the training as well, to tap into the power of *Danú* to make it happen. The idea in your realm of ever being able to break people down into their component parts and reconstruct them somewhere else with a machine is really quite absurd, when you think about it.'

'Unlike *magically* moving people around,' Ren said distractedly. The howls were growing ever more frantic. 'Which makes perfectly good sense?' Ren's head swivelled, trying to follow the sounds, hoping to see one of the creatures before they came at him, teeth and claws ready to devour him. Right now, even though he was hard-pressed to believe in it, a bit of magical intervention seemed like a splendid idea. 'Tell me, how long does it take to learn this "tapping into the power of *Danú*" thing? I think magically moving us somewhere other than here seems a grand plan right about now.'

'Mastery of magic is the result of years of training, *Leath tiarna*. However, once you and Darragh have shared the *Comhroinn* it should become much easier for you.'

Ren looked up at the feel of raindrops on his face, acutely aware of Brógán's warning about the rain washing away their protective barrier. He backed closer to the fire until his heels were almost touching the glowing coals. 'So, there's nothing you can teach me in the next … you know … three minutes or so, that might be useful if I was looking not to get devoured …'

Brógán sighed heavily, holding a hand out to confirm it really was starting to rain. 'I am *Liaig*. I couldn't teach you that, even if I wanted to,' he said. 'My power is —'

Without warning, the howling abruptly stopped.

The Druid lowered his hand with a frown. For the first time since the howling started, Brógán looked worried. 'Ah … that's not good.'

'Not good?' Ren asked, looking about in a mild panic as the rain began to fall a little harder. A moment ago, he had thought he'd give anything for the howling to stop, but the silence seemed infinitely worse. 'What do you mean, *not good*?'

If Brógán answered him, Ren never heard it, because at that moment, a dark growling blur launched itself at Ren, slamming him hard into the ground in a snarling swirl of hair, teeth, red eyes, slobber and breath that smelled like rotting meat.

CHAPTER 33

Killing things always evoked mixed feelings in Sorcha. If she hesitated, it wasn't because she feared the kill or lacked the ability to deliver a decisive killing stroke. It was the faint suspicion that, no matter how good at it she was, she didn't have the right to take another life, even though the goddess *Danú* had clearly gifted her with an exceptional talent in that area.

Sorcha held her breath, the taut string of her bow tickling her cheek as she waited for the right moment to loose her arrow. The hind in her sights still had no inkling of her presence. The dappled twilight in the clearing and Sorcha's almost supernatural ability to move silently through the forest meant the creature had no notion its death was a mere heartbeat away.

And still Sorcha hesitated, silently thanking the goddess for her bounty, wondering if she should let the creature go …

A loud snapping behind her startled the hind and it dashed off, crashing through the undergrowth and out of sight.

Sorcha lowered her bow and released the string, neither angry nor disappointed.

Danú had spoken. The hind, this time, was meant to live.

'There's no point in you sneaking about out there,' she called, returning her black-fletched arrow to the quiver at her belt. 'You're making enough noise to wake the dead.'

There was more clumsy crashing through the undergrowth. A few moments later a familiar figure emerged from the trees, his beard threaded with golden trinkets, his muscular forearms encircled by gold bracers engraved with the triskalion insignia.

'I should have known it was you,' Sorcha said, shouldering her bow. 'You thunder through the forest like an elephant.'

Ciarán smiled at her, but wisely stayed out of her reach. 'I've never seen an elephant.'

'Well, you'll know it when you meet one,' Sorcha assured him. 'You have the same boot size. What's the matter?'

The big warrior stared at her, all full of wounded innocence. 'Why do you assume something is wrong, my lady?'

'Because you're here, Ciarán,' she replied, putting her hands on her hips, which placed them — conveniently — nearer the knives she carried at her belt. 'You know better than to seek me out for mere social intercourse.'

He smiled tentatively. 'I bring wonderful news, my lady.'

'I was sixteen the last time anybody shared their wonderful news with me, boy,' she reminded him. 'That cost me everything and everybody I knew and loved.'

The pain of that discovery was long behind her now, but Ciarán didn't know that, and it suited Sorcha to let people think she still bore the emotional scars. It made them wary of her and meant, as a rule, they gave her a wide berth, which was exactly how she liked it. She turned to pick up her waterskin, not caring much for whatever wonderful news the Druid warrior brought. There was little, these days, that inspired Sorcha. Even less that she considered 'wonderful'.

'We have found the missing twin,' Ciarán announced with barely contained excitement.

Sorcha hesitated. That was not something she'd expected.

'Good for you,' she said, straightening as she shouldered the waterskin on the opposite side to her bow and began to walk back down the faint game trail along which she'd followed the hind. 'Come see me when you have him.'

'We do have him, Sorcha.'

This time she stopped, turning to look at the warrior. She'd taught him when he was a mere lad, and could tell at a glance if he was lying. Even in the fading light of the forest, she could see him nodding, barely able to control his joy.

'You *have* him?'

'Rónán is alive and well and back where he belongs.'

'He's at *Sí an Bhrú*?' she asked, a little incredulous. Sorcha chose to remain aloof from human society as a rule, but she couldn't imagine news that the missing twin of the Undivided had returned to *Sí an Bhrú* was about and she'd not heard it from someone.

Ciarán shook his head. 'No, of course he's not there. We have him stashed in a hut just outside

Breaga. You are only the fourth person, including Darragh himself, who knows of his return.'

Sorcha didn't answer immediately, not sure how the magical reappearance of the long-lost Undivided twin affected her. She had lost any desire for life at any ruling court, Druid or otherwise. Were it not for the oath she'd once sworn to the Druids, she'd have had nothing to do with them at all.

'Why bring *me* this news?'

'I bring a request on behalf of Darragh, my lady,' he said with a formal and not inelegant bow. 'He wishes to engage your services as his brother's protector.'

'Does his brother need protecting?' she asked, her curiosity piqued. Although she had little interest in the goings-on at *Sí an Bhrú*, she knew how much the *Tuatha*, and Marcroy Tarth in particular, would like to rid themselves of the Undivided. To be there when he learned his most recent efforts had been in vain … well, for that, it was almost worth heading back to *Sí an Bhrú*.

'The traitor, Amergin, threw Rónán through the rift to a realm with no magic,' Ciarán explained. 'He seems as intelligent as his brother and, naturally, has the same physical abilities, but he has been raised in complete ignorance of his heritage. He is untrained and unprepared for the life ahead of him. He needs someone who can protect him while he learns. Someone who can teach him.'

'There are Druids for that. Have Darragh perform the *Comhroinn* on his brother. He has no need of my help.'

'The *Comhroinn* will give Rónán knowledge, not experience, Sorcha. Even with all his brother's knowledge, he'll need training. And protection.'

'I'm no sorcerer,' she reminded him. 'What can I teach a Druid — one of the Undivided, no less — of magic?'

'Darragh is not asking you to teach him magic. He needs you to keep his brother alive while others teach him,' Ciarán said. He glanced up at the sky. Night was closing in on them and he was clearly in a hurry. 'Will you come?'

'I'll think about it,' she said, turning back to the path. Undivided or no, Darragh couldn't just arbitrarily send for her and expect her to drop everything for him.

'It's a full moon tonight, Sorcha.'

'Then you'll have a few weremen to contend with on your way back to the stones,' she said over her shoulder, unsympathetically. 'Do keep your eyes open, lad. They're particularly hungry at this time of year.'

'Rónán is alone in Breaga under the protection of a single *Liaig*. If we don't get back to him before moonrise, there may be no *Leath tiarna* left to protect.'

Sorcha frowned. 'And whose stupid idea was it to leave the unprepared and untrained lost twin of the Undivided alone with a herb-peddler on a night like this?'

'Darragh suggested —'

'Darragh is a fool,' she snapped, annoyed the decision had been taken from her, although she realised Darragh wasn't a fool at all. He just knew her far better than she thought. He must know the danger his brother would be in and that she would feel honour-bound to protect one of the Undivided.

Curse his wretched Druid soul. He must have been supremely confident I would come to his aid.

300

That boy really is too clever for his own good.

'Where is Darragh now?'

'He had to return to *Sí an Bhrú*. Marcroy Tarth and Queen Álmhath are currently visiting. He couldn't tip them off about Rónán's return by going missing for any length of time.'

Sorcha let out an exasperated sigh. 'I will meet with Rónán,' she announced, to save face, if nothing else. She'd make Darragh pay for playing on her sense of duty like this. She wasn't sure how, just yet, but she would see he did not get away with this manipulation unscathed. 'But I'll make no promises about staying. Rónán may have been spoiled beyond redemption by this other realm. I'll not agree to anything until I've had a chance to take his measure myself.'

'That seems fair.'

'And you can tell Darragh I don't appreciate being played like this.'

'You can tell him yourself, *a Mháistreás*.' Ciarán looked mightily relieved.

Sorcha wasn't surprised. Already she could hear the first faint calls of weremen in the distance.

'Then we'd best hurry,' she said. 'Breaga is east of here. The moon will rise there sooner than here. If I am to have a *Leath tiarna* to protect, we don't have much time.'

It was full dark by the time they emerged from the stones in Breaga. Ciarán took his arms from around Sorcha — who could not travel through the stones without the help of a Druid — pocketed his jewel, and took off at a run. There was a fine rain beginning to fall, the moon misty behind the clouds, and the howling they could hear in the distance was the frenzied howling of a were-pack closing in on a kill. It seemed colder in Breaga than in Sorcha's forest. The tiny village was little more than a few round dark shadows pierced here and there by the blur of yellow light from a tallow candle in a window.

Sorcha easily out-distanced Ciarán, running with the ease of a seasoned warrior, her lighter, more supple frame — and the fact that she carried less in the way of armour and weapons — making her much faster.

The howling stopped abruptly as they caught sight of an orange glow in the distance. The cook-fire would keep a wereman at bay only if one was actually standing in the middle of it.

Sorcha withdrew two long knives as she ran, certain, now, that *Danú* had scared away the hind earlier today because she had other lives in mind for her warrior daughter to collect on her behalf.

It was time to kill some weremen.

She leapt into the fray with a terrifying ululating cry. She aimed for the nearest one who appeared to have a human pinned to the ground beneath him. Sorcha didn't know if the human was Rónán, the Druid healer they'd left him with, or some random shepherd who happened to be caught outdoors on a full moon. She didn't even know if she had arrived in time to save him.

Sorcha slashed at the beast, jumping on its back as she sliced her blades sideways. A hot rush of blood gushed over her arms and the beast's terrified victim as she laid open its throat. The beast collapsed onto the human and she left it there as she leapt up, looking for her next kill. Whoever it was pinned beneath the hairy wolven corpse was safer trapped under the bulk of the dead wereman while she took care of the rest of the pack, than stumbling around panicked, frightened and getting underfoot.

Ciarán joined the fight. He killed another beast with a single blow of his Roman sword, while Sorcha turned her knives on a creature that seemed torn between attacking the man brandishing a burning branch on the other side of the fire, and the roast lamb.

She dispatched the creature with a sharp thrust to the spine. Its blood-curdling scream distracted some of the other weremen. They knew what that scream meant. Only *airgead sídhe* weapons could cause that sort of pain in a dying Faerie creature.

Sorcha and Ciarán disposed of another two each before the beasts fled howling into the darkness, looking for less troublesome prey. Prey that wasn't armed with blades forged from *airgead sídhe*.

Breathing heavily, Sorcha turned to survey her handiwork. Now they were dead the weremen had returned to their true form. No longer frightening, drooling beasts, they were pale, slender, long-limbed creatures, dirty and bloody, but unmistakeably Faerie.

Sorcha bowed her head, offered their souls to *Danú*, and then turned to the first corpse she'd killed, under which was trapped — and hopefully still alive — the long-lost twin of the Undivided.

CHAPTER 34

Hayley's fog lifted slowly to be replaced by light-headedness and a bewildering darkness. Her bizarre dreams faded as she clawed her way back to consciousness. She realised she was in hospital, had a pounding headache, and for some reason, couldn't see.

Her father and stepmother were with her. She felt her father's hand gripping hers. Her stepmother was whispering her name, drawing her back from her cottonwool cocoon, coaxing her gently back to consciousness as the drugs relinquished their grip on her mind, and allowed the pain of her headache to come rushing back.

'Hayley, love ... can you hear me?'

'Mum ...' she tried to say, but it came out as an unintelligible grunt.

'She's back,' Kerry said to someone else in the room, her voice filled with relief.

'Take it slowly,' she heard her father say. Hayley smiled. Or, at least she tried to. It wasn't easy smiling around the tube in her mouth.

A moment later, she felt someone fiddling with the hardware filling her mouth and she coughed reflexively as the tube was withdrawn and she started breathing on her own.

'Did you want some water, pet?' Patrick asked.

Hayley nodded, her throat dry and painful now the tube was gone. She raised her head a little and took a sip from the drinking straw her father guided into her mouth, and then lay back down, letting the cool water trickle down her raw throat, while she tried to make some sense out of her surroundings. It was still dark in the room, and she could feel the bandages over her eyes, which didn't make much sense because they seemed to be the only part of her that wasn't aching.

'What happened, Dad?' she asked after a moment. Her memories of the past few hours or days were too jumbled and unreliable to count on them to provide a reason for her being in this state.

'There was an accident,' Kerry said. 'You were hit by a car.'

'Ren was there ...' Hayley said, trying to piece together the last thing she remembered.

'Aye,' Patrick agreed, in a rather odd tone. 'He was there.'

'Is he okay?'

There was a moment of silence as a look she could sense but not see passed between Kerry and Patrick. 'He's fine, sweetie,' Kerry said finally. 'You need to concentrate on getting better, and stop worrying about your cousin.'

'Can I see him?' she asked. 'When they take the bandages off, of course.'

'Let's just wait and see how you're doing, lass,' Patrick said, gripping her hand even more tightly. 'How are you feeling?'

'Like I was run over by a bus.'

'Well, actually, it was a BMW, but I'll not quibble with you over the details,' Patrick chuckled. 'Are you in pain, love? The doctors can give you something.'

She shook her head. Or at least, she tried to. That's when she discovered how stiff it was. And how thick the bandages around her eyes were. 'I'm feeling woozy and I've got a headache, but it's not that bad. Did I crack my skull?'

'You surely did,' her father replied with only the slightest hesitation. 'Tried to dig a hole in the road with it, according to the doctors.' Only the faintest tremor in Patrick's voice betrayed how worried he was.

'Am I going to be okay?'

'Of course you are,' Kerry said. 'Few weeks and you'll be as good as new. They're saying you'll be out of hospital by the end of the week.'

Funny how easy it was to tell when Kerry was lying. Probably because she didn't do it much. She really wasn't very good at it.

Hayley turned her head in the direction of her father's voice. 'But I'm *not* as good as new, am I, Dad?'

There was a thick silence for a time before he answered. 'It's too early to tell, pet.'

'Why is it too early?'

'You hit your head pretty hard, love,' he explained. 'Hard enough to make your brain swell. The doctors put you in a coma until the swelling went down.'

'But …' she prompted when her father paused, quite certain there was more to that statement.

'You have a mild traumatic brain injury,' Neil

announced proudly, as if he'd been rehearsing the phrase to make sure he got it right.

'*What?*'

'Out,' Kerry ordered in a firm voice.

'But Mum …'

'Now,' her father added. A moment later she heard Neil muttering and a door slamming shut.

'Was he serious?' Hayley asked.

'They did an MRI while you were unconscious,' her father said, his voice choked.

'They're worried the blow to your head may have damaged your occipital lobe,' Kerry added, when Patrick seemed unable to go on.

Hayley was grateful for her practical, unemotional tone. 'What's that mean in English?'

'Nothing to worry yourself about, pet,' her father assured her. 'The doctors are saying the effects are probably temporary.'

'What's "probably temporary"?' Hayley asked, directing her question at her stepmother. Patrick Boyle was a loving father, but he'd never been good at delivering bad news. It was always up to the ever-practical Kerry to tell Hayley what she needed to know.

'We'll talk about it when you're feeling a little better,' Patrick said.

'No. I want to know now.' *You can't wake a person up from a coma and drop something like that on them without an explanation.*

There was a strained silence for a moment before Kerry, as always, answered her difficult question. 'The occipital lobe is the part of the brain that takes in what you see and makes sense out of it,' she explained.

Hayley took a moment to digest that information and then frowned when she realised what it meant. 'You mean there's something wrong with my eyes?'

'No, no ...' her father hastened to assure her. 'Your eyes are fine. It's just the part of the brain that helps it all make sense, that's all. Until the swelling goes down, the doctors won't know the full extent of the damage.'

'Is that why my eyes are bandaged?'

'It's only while they make sure there's no other damage, love,' Patrick said. 'They're hoping that as the swelling recedes, the pressure will ease and you'll be fine again. In the meantime, they want to protect your eyes. You could accidentally look into the sun, or do some other damage without realising you're doing it.'

'But in the meantime, I'm blind,' Hayley said with admirable calm. It was probably the drugs, she realised, because the news should have made her distraught. There was definitely something in the drip, feeding into the vein on the back of her left hand, that was taking the edge off her emotions.

'They'll do another MRI in a couple of days,' Kerry told her. 'And a whole lot of other tests too, they're saying. But you're awake and talking, so that's a good sign you're not suffering permanent brain damage.'

Hayley's mind reeled at Kerry's casual mention of brain damage. *Brain damage? Oh my God, I have* brain *damage ...*

'I dunno, the lengths some people will go to in order to get out of going back to school, eh?' said her father with a forced laugh.

Hayley didn't know what to say, so she fell back on a reliable topic. 'Does Ren know?'

'We haven't told him yet,' Kerry answered. She sounded very terse.

'But you told Neil?' Hayley asked.

'Did you want him back in here?' Kerry asked, a smile back in her voice. 'For a wee while? He's been beside himself with worry.'

'Really? He was worried? Not asking if he can have my room if I die?'

Patrick chuckled and squeezed her hand. 'It's good to have you back, sweetheart.'

'It's good to be back,' Hayley said. 'And it's going to be even better when they take these damned bandages off and I can see.' *Assuming, of course*, she added to herself, *I don't have permanent brain damage*.

Kerry let Neil into the room, then she and Patrick went to speak with the doctors. Neil sat on the edge of the bed, and poked her on her arm as he tested whether or not she really was awake.

'Hey, ratbag,' she said with a smile. 'Watcha up to?'

'Nothing,' Neil said. 'Except hanging around here. Are they going to let you come home now you're awake?'

'I hope so,' she said. 'Why? Do you miss me?'

'I miss everything,' he lamented. 'All we've done since Doctor Symes ran you down is hang about here waiting for someone to tell us something, and talking to the cops about Ren. Can you ask Mum if we can stop at McDonald's on the way home? She'll say yes to anything you ask for the next few days.'

'Why are the cops asking about Ren?' Hayley asked. 'This wasn't his fault, you know.'

'Nah … it's nothing to do with you. He's mixed up in some drug deal. Someone died, too. They arrested him, but he got away and now we're supposed to ring the cops if we see him or if he tries to call us.'

Hayley fell silent. The Ren she knew wasn't into drugs. He used to joke that he had problems enough to deal with, without chemically enhancing them. What had happened since her accident to turn the world so radically on its head?

Still, it explained Kerry's terse dismissal of her questions about Ren.

'What about Kiva?' she asked. 'What's she up to?'

'I dunno. She held a couple of press conferences. Then after Ren disappeared she locked herself in the house and won't come out, but that's probably because all the paparazzi in the known universe are camped outside her gate at the moment.'

Hayley felt a moment of pity for her. 'And nobody's seen Ren at all?'

'Not a whisper,' Neil confirmed. 'It's like he's vanished. I heard the cops telling Kiva he hasn't used any of his credit cards, and nobody's spotted him anywhere. I think the cops think the drug bosses got him and have killed him for ratting on them about the —'

'Neil, that will be quite enough!' Kerry cut in, before Hayley's brother could finish the sentence. 'You've seen your sister, now you can go.'

'But Mum …'

'Now, Neil.'

Hayley sensed Neil lean forward and then felt his cool lips as he placed a brief and unexpected kiss on her cheek. 'I'll see you round, Hayley,' he said, adding in a whisper, 'and I'll let you know if I hear anything about Ren.' His weight lifted off the bed and the door closed behind him as he left.

'Mum?'

'Yes, sweetheart?'

'Was Neil right about Ren disappearing?'

Kerry hesitated. 'It's true he's missing, love, but don't start reading things into it. Ren blamed himself for what happened to you and he always manages to find trouble when he's troubled. I'm sure he'll be back when he's ready.'

'You don't think he's dead, do you?'

Kerry sat on the edge of the bed. 'That boy's survived being half-drowned, living in a fishbowl, being dragged all around the world and having my loopy cousin as a mother. Don't you worry about that young man, sweetheart. Ren will be fine.'

Hayley didn't believe it. For one thing, Ren didn't do drugs. And, for another, Ren would never have left her in hospital alone, if he knew she was hurt.

And that meant something had happened to him. But Hayley's head was aching too much for her to even attempt to figure out what it might be.

CHAPTER 35

Most of the blood in which Ren was drenched wasn't his, he discovered, when they finally hauled the dead weight of the slain wereman off him, and he was able to scramble to his feet, soaked from the cold rain and the warm blood of his attacker. He looked around, breathing harder than if he'd run a mile, stunned by both the ferocity of the attack and the unlikely appearance of his saviour.

'You are the lost twin,' the woman said.

Ren nodded, not sure if it was a question or an accusation. The rain was pelting down now, chilling him to the core, washing the blood from his face and making the fire spit and hiss. He rubbed his face and stared at the woman who'd rescued him. No older than twenty or twenty-five, he guessed, she was dressed in a similar fashion to Ciarán: tooled leather armour and trousers with gold trimmings, a bloody Roman sword in her hand, a quizzical expression on her face. She seemed oblivious to the rain.

'I suppose,' he said.

'Ciarán was right,' she said, bending down to wipe her blade on the wet grass. 'You have no skills. You'll not last a day in *Sí an Bhrú*.'

Ren wasn't sure how to answer that. She didn't give him the opportunity in any case. Instead, she turned to Ciarán, who was unceremoniously slashing the throats of the dead weremen. The creatures were slowly morphing back into pale-skinned, naked, man-shaped creatures. She ordered him to run them through the heart as well with his *airgead sídhe* dagger, to be sure they were dead. Ren watched the gruesome task, almost too overwhelmed to grasp what their transformation back into human form meant.

Ren turned to find Brógán standing beside him, nursing a wounded arm that looked as if one of the wolves had taken a piece out of him.

'One of them got you,' he said. 'Are you going to turn into one of them, now?'

The Druid shook his head. 'Of course not. You can't catch shape-shifting.' He smiled. 'You have some of the strangest ideas about the *Daoine sídhe*, *Leath tiarna*.'

'He has no idea at all,' said the woman who'd come to Ren's rescue, sheathing her sword. 'That's the problem.'

Ren studied her, not ungrateful for her assistance, but a little annoyed by her tone. He wondered who she was. He was under the impression Ciarán had gone to fetch an eighty-year-old Druid warrior to be his bodyguard. This woman was tiny — barely reaching his shoulder — dark haired, lithe and cranky. Maybe she was Sorcha's great-great-great-great-granddaughter or something.

'He will learn, *a mháistreás*,' Brógán assured her.

'But will he survive the lesson?' Ciarán asked as he joined them, wiping his dagger on the leg of his trousers. He added to the woman, apologetically, 'I think one of them got away.'

She frowned. 'You'll never track him in this rain. Was he wounded?'

'Bleeding like a stuck pig.'

'Then let's hope he won't make it through the night. In the meantime, we should get our fragile *Leath tiarna* here into the hut and dry him off. It would be a shame to save him from the weremen only to lose him to a common cold.'

Ren didn't appreciate being described as fragile, but he was all for getting out of the rain.

'Pity about the roast,' Ciarán said, eyeing the drenched carcass. 'No point leaving it out for scavengers.'

Ren hurried up the slope to the hut. Ciarán lifted the spit from the fire, slung it over his shoulder, and strode up to the hut, throwing open the leather-hinged door. It was very crowded inside. Ciarán would fill any enclosed space on his own, Ren supposed, but with Brógán and Sorcha crammed in too, there was barely room to move.

'Take your clothes off.'

'Excuse me?' Ren stared at the young woman.

'This is Sorcha,' Ciarán explained. 'You'd do well to heed her, lad. Your life will be in her hands when we get back to *Sí an Bhrú*.'

Ren stared at the young woman in disbelief. '*This* is your eighty-year-old warrior?' He shook his head. 'She's not much older than me.'

'How do you know?'

'I have eyes,' Ren said.

'And they see nothing,' Sorcha replied. She took the flaming branch from Brógán and squatted down at the tiny fireplace to set fire to the tinder-dry wood in the hearth, filling the hut with a warm orange light. Ren thought it odd that she'd lit the fire like that when Brógán and probably Ciarán could have waved an arm and done it with magic. Sorcha fed a few more sticks onto the fire and then stood up and turned to Ciarán. '*This* ignorant ingrate is what you wanted me to protect? I should have stayed home.'

'It's not his fault, Sorcha,' Ciarán said, 'that he knows nothing of our ways.'

'And whose fault is it that he lacks any manners?'

'I do not lack manners,' Ren protested.

'You do,' Sorcha said, turning on him. 'And you also appear to lack the ability to follow a simple instruction. Take off your clothes. I'll not have you dying on me, for such a mundane reason as catching a chill. I am not, however, averse to running you through myself, should your conduct convince me that this world would be better served by the discontinuation of your line.'

Ren stared at her, not sure he believed her threat, and then he looked at Brógán. 'Is she for real?' he asked in English.

'Most definitely, *Leath tiarna*,' Brógán said with a smile. 'She is every bit as capable of killing you as she claims.'

Ren still hesitated, but in the end decided to do as she commanded, in part because he was freezing and in part because Ciarán and Brógán had begun to peel off their own wet clothes. Ren did the same. Sorcha snatched the clothes from the men as they undressed, wrung them out, shook them, and then draped them around the fire on the low stools that served as seating in the hut. The others didn't seem to mind sitting on the dirt floor. The rain beat down relentlessly, dripping through the thatched roof, but the hut was surprisingly warm, helped, no doubt, by the body heat of four people.

Ciarán attended to Brógán's wounded arm. He held the Druid's arm, closed his eyes and, a moment later, Ren watched as the mangled skin began to knit together. The whole process took no more than a few minutes and Brógán's arm was as good as new, only a faint scar and a few bloodstains left behind giving any indication of the nasty bite.

Ciarán smiled. 'Not as good a job as a *Liaig* would do, lad, but it'll do.'

'I'm just grateful you know enough to heal, Ciarán,' Brógán said. 'Thank you.'

'Don't thank me. Just be glad a bit of healing is a useful thing for a warrior to know. And that you weren't suffering from anything more than a flesh wound.' He caught the look on Ren's face. 'What's the matter, *Leath tiarna*? You look like you've seen a ghost.'

'What you just did … it's … unbelievable,' Ren said, shaking his head. 'I saw it before, but it's … unbelievable.'

'Why?' Sorcha asked. She was studying him intently, awaiting his answer as if his life depended on his next few words.

'Because … well, you just can't fix things like that in my reality.'

'This is your realm, Rónán,' Brógán reminded him.

He glanced at the Druid healer and shrugged. 'You know what I mean.'

'I don't see how it's different,' Sorcha said. 'What happens to people who are injured in this other realm you've been living in?'

'We have doctors and nurses and paramedics and hospitals —'

'So, what you're saying is that injuries and diseases are healed by men and women who spend years studying their craft?' she cut in.

'Well ... I suppose.'

'What makes you think it's any different here?' she asked, turning to stoke the fire again as the wind picked up outside, rattling the walls of the tiny hut.

'But ... well, he used *magic* to fix Brógán's arm. It was healed in a few minutes.'

'And I'm sure some of the cures used by healers in your world would seem equally miraculous to us,' she said, sitting back on her heels. She turned to Ciarán. 'Keeping him alive may prove the least of your troubles. Imagine trying to teach him anything.'

Ren decided to ignore that remark. He really wasn't in the mood to argue with her.

He was, however, fascinated by the idea of magical healing.

'Can I do that?' he asked Brógán.

The young Druid nodded. 'It is all a matter of training, *Leath tiarna*. I am a *Liaig*, which is similar to a doctor in your reality, but we use plants and some magical intervention to heal. Here, unlike your realm, surgery is a last resort.'

'Does everybody use magic here?' he asked.

'Not everyone,' Brógán said. 'Of course, there are many of the Druid caste who do, like the *Brithem*. They're similar to a judge or an arbitrator in your realm. They specialise in lexichemy. That's magic using the spoken word.'

'Of course it is.'

Brógán continued in a lecturing tone. He seemed to be enjoying this chance to show off his knowledge of Druid society. 'Niamh is also one of us, although she is *Cainte*. A master of magical chants and incantations. Our Vate comes from the Bardish caste, whose job it is to maintain our history and the history of all the important events and people in our world. There are also the *Deoghbaire*. They specialise in intoxicating and hallucinogenic substances, such as the *Brionglóid Gorm* we used to knock you out.'

'So you have your own version of the paparazzi and drug dealers? Some things are the same all over, I guess.'

Brógán frowned, but ignored the interruption. 'Ciarán is of the Warriors. All those involved in the trades and in agriculture belong to the Producers.'

'What's Darragh? And what am I?'

'The Undivided stand outside the Druid castes, *Leath tiarna*, embodying all of them, yet being no part of any one cast.' Brógán glanced at Ciarán, who gave him an almost imperceptible nod. 'The power of the Druids is vested in the Undivided through the Treaty of *Tír Na nÓg*,' Brógán went on. 'In theory, you can do anything. In practice, even with access to all that power, it's not something one does without training. Traditionally, because of their role as leaders of the Druids, the Undivided are trained in more ... esoteric disciplines, such as philosophy and ethics.'

That sounded deadly dull. 'They're trained as warriors too, aren't they?'

'What makes you ask that?' Ciarán asked.

Ren held out his arm to reveal the fine web of scars he'd collected over the years from his brother's injuries. 'I didn't get these because Darragh doesn't know how to handle a steak knife.'

'The Undivided are taught to defend themselves like any other warrior,' Ciarán conceded.

'Why not just use magic?'

'What do you mean?' Sorcha asked, frowning.

'I mean, if you're chock full of magic and can do anything, then why not just defend yourself with it?'

The three of them stared at him for a long, silent moment.

Eventually, Sorcha turned to the fire and tossed another small log on it from the pile by the hearth saying, 'There are those who thought the Treaty of *Tír Na nÓg* was in danger with one of the Undivided missing.' Then she added cryptically, 'They are going to pine for the good old days when they realise the danger it is in, now that he's back.'

CHAPTER 36

Darragh managed to sneak back into his chamber at *Sí an Bhrú* before Brydie woke, but only just. She was stirring as he tiptoed across the darkened bedchamber to her side, undressed and slid under the covers. He breathed a sigh of relief, grateful she hadn't seen how he'd returned to his room. That was a secret Darragh had not even shared with Ciarán. Had Brydie witnessed him appearing out of nowhere like a *Leipreachán* he would have had no reasonable explanation for her. He shouldn't be able to do it, and he didn't think any other Undivided had ever been able to perform such a feat. He'd have a great deal of explaining to do, if word got about that Darragh of the Undivided had a power known to only occur naturally in the *Daoine sídhe*.

Would Rónán have the same ability? he wondered as he closed his eyes. Brydie stirred against him. He slid his arm around her as if he didn't want to let her go. Then he felt her turn, lift her head slightly …

He realised he'd left the candle burning. He extinguished the flame with a thought, hoping Brydie hadn't opened her eyes, or if she had, that the flame was burning so briefly she barely had time to register it before the room was plunged into darkness.

'Darragh ...'

'Mmmm ...' He pulled her closer.

'When did you get back?'

'A little while ago,' he told her. 'I tried to be quiet so I wouldn't wake you.'

'Did you find what you were looking for?'

He shook his head. 'No. Our lost rift runner remains lost.' It was easier to play along with her assumption that a rift runner was what he was looking for, and it was certainly safer for her to believe Ciarán was still out there looking for him. The last thing he needed right now was Brydie and her divided loyalties discovering the truth about Rónán.

She turned to face him, snuggling down under the blankets. 'Colmán came by just after midday yesterday, to ask when I was leaving.'

'What did you tell him?'

'Not a thing,' she said with a mischievous giggle. 'I just pounded the headboard as loudly as I could, moaned in ecstasy and shouted your name a few times. He probably went away to compose an ode to your legendary prowess as a lover.'

Darragh smiled. 'I really only needed you to keep him believing I was still here for a day.'

'Oh, trust me, *Leath tiarna*, he believed it.'

Darragh wasn't sure what he was going to do with Brydie. She was the only person in *Sí an Bhrú* who knew he'd sneaked out. Would she keep his secret? Or betray him the moment he let her out of his sight?

Or would she hold it over him, in order to force considerations from the Undivided? And if she did that, what would she want? Wealth? Power?

He studied her in the darkness. Brydie seemed very pleased with herself. So he kissed her, thinking that the best way to head off any discussion that might start with 'And now for the favour you owe me …' Brydie kissed him back with parted lips, sliding her hand down his belly toward his groin.

'I'll see that Álmhath knows you were diligent in your duty,' he whispered through the kiss. Brydie had helped him, after all, by keeping Colmán away. It was the least he could do to let Álmhath think Brydie had done her duty by her queen, too. Although if Brydie wasn't with child a month from now, she might have some awkward questions to answer. He tried to sit up, but Brydie moved onto her knees, threw back the covers, and grabbed his stiffening penis with her hand and lowered her mouth over it. His back arched and he gasped, before letting out a startled cry which was interrupted by Colmán rushing into the room with a lantern in one hand.

'*Leath tiarna*!' he cried, and then he stopped dead as he took in the scene before him. 'Oh … I'm sorry … I thought perhaps …'

Brydie raised her head and glared at him. 'You thought *what*, old man?'

Colmán's appearance put an immediate end to Darragh's burgeoning desire. With a sigh of regret, he pushed himself up on his elbows as Brydie sat back on her heels. She didn't seem to care that Colmán was staring at her nakedness.

'I thought perhaps the *Leath tiarna* was finished

with his amusements. I fear I was being overly optimistic.'

'There's nothing to worry about,' Darragh said.

'Perhaps not in here, *Leath tiarna*,' Colmán said, glaring at Brydie with disgust as he changed the lantern to his other hand. 'But you have been far too long, my lord. The Council of Druids has been convened.' He closed his eyes and began to intone the opening lines of his next Bardic composition, 'The Undivided turns from his duty, the *Tuatha* scheme, while he lusts after —'

'Enough!' Darragh cried.

Why had the Council been convened?

He muttered a curse, spared Brydie an apologetic grimace and swung his legs over the side of the bed. 'When did they convene?' he asked, reaching for his trousers.

'Just on dawn,' Colmán told him. 'They'll just about be finished with the formalities. If you hurry, you can get there before Marcroy addresses them. I will compose something along the way to announce you.'

'That will help no end, I'm sure.' Darragh stood up and pulled his trousers on, hopping on one leg, then the other. 'How did Marcroy manage to convince the Council of Druids that he should be heard?'

'The same way he does everything, *Leath tiarna*,' the Vate said. 'By sounding reasonable. You must hurry.'

'What about me?' Brydie asked. 'Are you just going to run off and leave me?'

'Of course not,' Darragh said, pulling his shirt on. He leaned over and kissed her on the cheek. 'You can go to the kitchens and tell them I said you could have whatever you want.' He winked at her and added, 'You'll need a good feed after the exercise we've had.'

Without giving her a chance to object, Darragh scooped up his boots and hurried out of the bedchamber, pulling them on as he went.

'No good will come of your licentiousness, *Leath tiarna*,' Colmán warned as they hurried down the corridor toward the main hall.

'You sound like one of those Christians,' Darragh told him, tugging his boots on as he hopped his way down the hall. 'Do you remember them? The ones who arrived here just before the Spring Equinox last year and demanded we denounce the *Imbolc* festival and embrace the one true god?'

Colmán nodded. 'I remember.' The old man loathed their cult with a passion out of all proportion to their small numbers. 'We should have killed them.'

'They're entitled to worship their own gods, Colmán.'

'That wasn't why I wanted them killed, *Leath tiarna*.'

Darragh didn't have time to discover the real reason. He had a council meeting going on without him. 'What happened after word got out that I was locked in my room with Brydie?'

'What do you think happened?' Colmán asked crossly, and more than a little breathlessly, as he hurried to keep up with Darragh. 'Marcroy started talking to anybody who would listen. They made much of you allowing Brydie to sit in your brother's place the other night. Your rudeness in locking yourself away all the following day to sate your carnal needs while the queen of the Celts and a prince of the *Tuatha* are guests in *Sí an Bhrú* will have consequences, *Leath tiarna*.'

'What consequences?'

'Marcroy claims he has an announcement to make. He's claiming to have solved the problem of the missing Undivided twin.'

That's not possible. How could he know? Rónán's been back barely a day!

'Did he give an indication as to how he has solved this dilemma?'

Colmán's brow furrowed and he began tugging on his forked beard, a sure sign he was nearing the edge of panic. He hadn't even tried to compose an epic since they'd left his bedchamber. 'I don't know. He said he and the Celtic queen have an announcement to make — one that will solve all our problems — but I can't imagine what he means by that, or why Álmhath has allied herself with him.'

Neither could Darragh, and that was a problem. What was it that Brydie had told him? *The* Tuatha *have found something they weren't meant to find.* He cursed under his breath for allowing himself to become too distracted by the search for his brother. One could not risk taking one's eyes off Marcroy Tarth for a second, if one expected to stay even half a step ahead of him. 'I wonder if he's trying to modify the Treaty of *Tír Na nÓg*.'

'Could he do that?'

Darragh nodded. 'He's never been happy about Druids being able to wield *sídhe* magic, and would very much like that power restricted to the *Tuatha* once more — assuming he could find a way to void the treaty without breaking any *Tuatha* laws.'

Colmán frowned. 'Is that even possible?'

'Maybe it is,' Darragh said, cursing softly under his breath. He needed more time. He needed to stall this inevitable confrontation until Rónán was ready to meet his destiny. Right now, his brother barely spoke his mother tongue. If he brought him back too early, Rónán would never be able to navigate the treacherous politics of the Druids and that might be the death of both of them, just as surely as Marcroy Tarth's politicking.

Darragh closed his eyes for a moment, wondering if there was some glimpse of the future to be had that might suggest whether or not he was on the right path, but nothing came to him. With no other course open to him, Darragh squared his shoulders and continued down the long stone hall to confront the untrustworthy Faerie who was responsible for Darragh's predicament in the first place.

CHAPTER 37

The Giant's Causeway at sunset looked exactly like the entrance to a magical kingdom, which was appropriate, Trása thought, as she circled the rock formation, looking for the entrance to *Tír Na nÓg*. The tallest of the staggered steps were as high as the pillars of a Greek temple, while others were barely big enough to stand on, weathered by the relentless waves that threw themselves against the stones, as if they, too, sought entry into *Tír Na nÓg*.

It was low tide when Trása arrived, the flat stones brimming with puddles of luminescent water that reflected the setting sun like a pile of rubies scattered at random by some careless giant striding along the edge of the sea. The rock pillars formed a series of steps that climbed to the cliff top where many humans had lost their lives, searching for something only a Faerie could see.

There were other entrances to *Tír Na nÓg*, of course. Other places closer to the veil, where Trása could have entered the Faerie realm. But there were none so majestic, none so evocative of the power and majesty of her kind.

And none quite so much fun to fly over.

Birds squawked at her as she rode the thermals down to the shoreline. The causeway was a haven for noisy black-and-white cormorants, blunt-beaked razorbills and a score of other sea birds. Tucked amid the weathered rock formations were a host of rare and unusual plants, much sought after by human herbalists, including sea spleenwort, frog orchid and vernal squill. Ignoring the temptation to go fishing for her dinner, Trása landed on the first row of stones poking out of the water, the chill air cooling her naked skin as she resumed human form. She stood looking up at the rocks with the retreating sea at her back, admiring the pathway into the Faerie kingdom in the light of the setting sun.

Trása smiled, anticipating her welcome. Marcroy would be pleased with her, she knew. Not only had she succeeded in finding the lost Undivided twin, but she'd found a way to keep him trapped in an alternate reality, one from which he could never escape.

That was a good thing, Trása knew, although exactly why it was a good thing had never really been explained to her. In any case, it wasn't her job to question her uncle. Marcroy Tarth was a prince of the *Tuatha Dé Danann*. His only interest, Trása was certain, was the safety and security of their people. If the Undivided were a threat to the *Daoine sídhe*, and breaking the Treaty of *Tír Na nÓg* an act of treason no sane Faerie could contemplate, then he was doing what he must, she reasoned, to save them from ... well, whatever it was that would happen if the treaty were broken.

Trása wasn't very clear on that point, but as

no half-*Beansídhe* would dream of questioning a cousin of the Faerie Queen, unless Marcroy volunteered the information, she wasn't likely to be told the consequences. Unlike humans with their republics, and their congresses, and their empires and their constantly shifting forms of government, the ruling line of the *Tuatha* was constant. There had not been any change in the way the Faerie conducted their political business in ten thousand years.

Trása was not going to be the one responsible for changing that.

She skipped up the stones, leaping across the magical pathway, invisible to the human eye. The tops of the thousands of columns formed stepping-stones emerging from under the sea that led to the cliff — a natural formation humans were fond of trying to explain. The most popular story about how they came to be was that the legendary giant, Fionn, had been trying to create a bridge to Scotland after he was challenged by another giant who was eventually outwitted by his wife.

Trása thought it interesting that even in legend, despite the power of a giant capable of building something on the scale of the Giant's Causeway, in the end, it came down to a woman using her brains, to save the day.

Of course, if she believed what she'd seen on television in the reality where Rónán was now trapped, then the causeway wasn't magical at all, just forty thousand or so interlocking basalt columns, the result of a volcanic eruption over sixty million years ago.

Trása thought the legend of Fionn the Giant much more plausible.

She reached the top in twilight, not long after the sun had disappeared below the horizon. Her skin tingled as she passed through the magical veil that separated the *Tuatha* kingdom from the realm of man. It wasn't so dark here, the magic glimmering from everything that lived. Even the trees pulsed with life, showing Trása the way to the centre of *Tír Na nÓg* where the majestic trees that housed the *Daoine sídhe* grew. She didn't know how long it would take to get home — time had no meaning here in any case — but it always seemed different. Some journeys seemed endless, others so short it was as if *Tír Na nÓg* was perched right on the edge of the Giant's Causeway, others so long it felt as if she'd travelled all the way to Avalon.

Today the journey seemed to lie somewhere in between the two extremes. Trása couldn't be certain — only a true *Daoine sídhe* was completely immune to the time dilation effects of *Tír Na nÓg* — but it seemed she reached the sacred trees just on dawn. Intoxicated by the magical air of the forest, she made her way up the curved stairs the *sídhe* had coaxed the sacred trees into growing, hoping her mother was home. After all, it wasn't long since Amergin's death. Hopefully, Elimyer had yet to take another human to feed on. She'd loved Trása's father. At least as much as a *leanan sídhe* could love a human. Why else did she restrain herself so? Elimyer could have drained Amergin's life force in a matter of months, had she cared nothing for him. But she hadn't. She'd kept him for fifteen years. Lived among humans with him. Allowed him to raise his half-breed daughter among his own kind, until she was too old to play innocently with the playmates of her childhood.

Surely, Elimyer would take some time, Trása hoped, to grieve her beloved human husband before consigning the memory of him to history, and moving on?

The sacred trees of *Tír Na nÓg* were full of hollowed-out caves and broad boughs wide enough to act as platforms. When Trása reached the branches belonging to her mother, high among the magical leaves, there was a young man sitting cross-legged on the wide branch, painting feverishly, using a thick brush to dab paint across a large canvas. She watched him for a moment, recognised the intense, almost obsessive look in his eyes and sighed. Elimyer, it seemed, hadn't waited long at all.

'*A Stóirín*!'

She looked up to see her mother emerge from the dark entrance of her quarters in the sacred tree. She was as beautiful as Trása remembered. Like Trása, Elimyer had long, white-blonde hair and eyes that seemed carved from emeralds, but the points on her ears were far more pronounced than her daughter's. Naked like Trása, she held out her arms to embrace her daughter.

Trása moved forward cautiously. She looked at the young man as she approached her mother. Instinctively, her eyes filled with tears. Whoever he was, the man was not destined to live long. His end was so near, Trása could taste it like the metallic tang of blood in her mouth. She wondered if she should say something to him, but she never got the chance. Elimyer was smiling, revealing her tiny pointed teeth. 'Trása, my darling! You're home!'

Trása stopped just short of embracing her mother. Elimyer glanced past her daughter at the young artist working so intently and smiled even wider. 'You've nothing to fear, daughter. As you can see, I'm not starved for affection.'

It wasn't her mother's need for affection Trása was worried about. She loved her mother, but Trása was half-human. Elimyer was *leanan sídhe*. That made her just as capable of consuming her daughter's life force as she was of consuming the young man's.

'Who is he?'

'His name is Éamonn,' her mother told her. 'I found him in the markets of Crúachu. He's very talented.'

Trása smiled. 'With you as his muse, *Máthair*, how could he be anything else?'

Elimyer laughed. 'I trade inspiration for life force, Trása, not talent. And I've known many a *leanan sídhe* who didn't understand the difference. Are you hungry?'

Trása nodded, wishing she'd eaten before she arrived. Faerie food was often as ephemeral as the magic from which it was conjured. After using the energy of a bird to get here, she was famished. 'There's no need to fuss, Mother. I can find something myself.' She glanced over her shoulder at Éamonn, caught in a trance so inspirational that he would stay that way until he fainted from hunger and thirst. 'And you're feeding at the moment.'

'It's all right, darling,' Elimyer said, waving her arm in Éamonn's direction. 'I'm sated for now.' The young man suddenly looked up, as if he'd just woken from a deep sleep. He stared at his half-finished canvas blankly, and then looked over at Elimyer. When he saw her, although drained and pale, his face lit up.

'Rest now, Éamonn,' she told him. 'Eat. And don't forget to bathe. You can finish it later.'

He nodded, put the canvas down and climbed to his feet, stumbling so close to the edge of the branch, Trása feared he might fall. He righted himself and staggered toward them.

'This is my daughter, Trása,' Elimyer told him as he stopped and stared at her suspiciously. He would be jealous, Trása knew, of anybody who might compete with him for Elimyer's affection.

'You never said you had children,' he complained, eyeing Trása warily. 'Will she be staying long?'

'Not long, dear,' Elimyer assured him. 'Now run along. We have family business to attend to.'

Still glaring at Trása, Éamonn pushed his way past them into the tree cave.

'You're draining him too quickly,' Trása accused her mother, recognising the signs of obsession that came with an artist utterly consumed by his muse. That had never happened to Trása's father. Elimyer had restrained herself out of genuine affection for Amergin. As a consequence, he'd lived until he was in his mid-forties, before the strain of sustaining a magical muse destroyed him. This young man was doomed to die. Sooner, rather than later.

At the rate Elimyer was draining Éamonn, he'd be lucky to see his next birthday.

'He's a snack, dear,' Elimyer said. 'Not a life-long commitment. Have you been back long?'

Time meant little to Elimyer, so the question was more out of politeness than real interest. Nor was her mother concerned about anything

333

she might have seen or done in the reality where she'd been living these past few months. A world without magic was inconceivable to a pure *Daoine sídhe*. Trása would have no luck explaining it, and Elimyer wasn't interested, anyway.

'Not long,' Trása said.

'And your mission for your uncle was successful?' Elimyer asked, waving a hand to produce a magical bowl of fruit that was pretty and perfect but hardly enough to sate Trása's appetite. This question was also asked out of politeness. Elimyer had no interest in politics. Even after living for fifteen years in the inner circle of the Druids, she had little or no care for their business — a source of endless frustration for her brother. Her mother's lack of interest in human politics was what had caused Marcroy to turn to Trása, of this she was certain. As helping her uncle gave her a purpose in life, Trása was silently thankful Elimyer was only interested in artists, and what they could do for her.

'Very successful,' Trása said, taking a perfect apple from the bowl. She bit into it, the taste sublime, but the meat of the apple dissolved almost as soon as she began to chew. Elimyer had forgotten, apparently, that her daughter was half-human and, when in human form, needed human food to sustain her. 'In fact, that's why I'm here. To report my success.'

Elimyer nodded. 'He'll be glad to hear of it, dear,' she said, 'but he's not here.'

'Where is he?'

Her mother paused thoughtfully. 'He did tell me, I'm sure ... but you know how I am with things like that.'

'Mother,' Trása said firmly, taking her by the arms. 'Concentrate. Where did Marcroy go?'

The *leanan sídhe* paused for a moment, her face creased into a thoughtful frown. Then she smiled. 'I think he went to *Sí an Bhrú*. Something about a meeting with Álmhath and Darragh. Do you remember Darragh, dear? You and he used to be such good friends when you were smaller.'

Trása nodded. 'I remember, Mama. Did he say when he'd be back?'

'Who? Darragh?'

'No, Marcroy,' Trása said patiently.

'He might have, darling. But I don't remember.' She gasped as if suddenly struck by a grand idea. 'Why don't you go to *Sí an Bhrú* and find him? I'm sure Darragh would like to see you, too.'

'I'm not allowed to visit *Sí an Bhrú*, Mama. Don't you remember?'

'Why not?'

Trása stared at her mother for a moment and then let it go. If Elimyer didn't remember the reason Trása was sent away from *Sí an Bhrú*, she wasn't going to open any old wounds by reminding her.

'Perhaps I will go,' she said, wondering why she ever expected anything more from her mother. She was *leanan sídhe*. There was no fighting her nature. No trying to change it. No point in lamenting it. 'Will you tell Marcroy I'm back if you see him before I do?'

Elimyer looked at her blankly. 'See who, dear?'

CHAPTER 38

Marcroy Tarth was an oddity among the *Tuatha Dé Danann*. He loved politics. He loved scheming and plotting and manipulating affairs in a way that was rare among his kind. The *Daoine sídhe* as a race enjoyed amusing themselves with humans, true enough, but for Marcroy, it was more than a game. It was what he lived for.

Orlagh had once accused him of being part human, such was his fascination for politics and the pursuit of power. Although somewhat insulted by the comment, Marcroy couldn't deny there was a glimmer of truth in the idea. It was that glimmer of truth that gave him the power he now enjoyed. Orlagh had chosen him as the instrument of her treaty. Marcroy alone, she believed, understood humans well enough to deal with them on a daily basis. The queen had no such talent or inclination. She had done what she must to protect the *Daoine sídhe*. She wasn't bothered about what happened afterward.

Marcroy was able to convince Orlagh that the Treaty of *Tír Na nÓg* needed constant vigilance. No member of the *Tuatha* race was capable of breaking the treaty, but the treaty was with humans, and they were known to keep their word solemnly — right until the moment it suited them to break it. She had appointed her cousin the *Tuatha* envoy, and then left him to administer a treaty he despised and would have given anything to destroy. The magic was safe and Orlagh had negotiated a settlement that would keep it that way. She had no further interest in human affairs.

That the treaty was still in place after nearly two thousand years was proof Marcroy didn't have a drop of human blood. If he had, he'd have found a way to circumvent the damn thing centuries ago.

He was always looking for loopholes. It was an amusing pastime that had become urgent, Marcroy thought as he watched Darragh approaching the Council of Druids, with the birth of this young man and his missing twin brother.

The irony was not lost on Marcroy. He was the very *sídhe* who had discovered the unique ability of psychically linked twins to channel the power of the *Daoine sídhe*, as if they had one foot in the world of man and another in the world of Faerie. The Romans under the Emperor Claudius were gathering their forces and would likely succeed in their invasion of Albion and, if that happened, Eire itself (or more importantly, *Tír Na nÓg*) would be directly threatened, unless drastic action was taken.

The *Tuatha* had seen the different outcomes in other realms. They could travel between worlds. The realms where the Romans had prevailed were already starting to lose their magic, a combination of the destruction of the *Tuatha Dé Danann*, and the rampant consumption of natural resources required to fuel their relentless progress. And the

Tuatha's fears had proved more than justified two thousand years later. There were realms where the *Tuatha* could no longer survive, drained of magic as the forests that replenished the source of their power were cut down to make way for machines. Lesser *sídhe* such as that annoying *Leipreachán* Plunkett O'Bannon, and mongrels like his niece Trása, were the only ones who could travel to those realms now and live to tell about it.

For all that Marcroy despised sharing his magic with these wretched humans, the treaty had been — and still was — the lesser of two evils.

Marcroy glanced up. It was almost midday, and the vast wooden arches of the circle where the Council had gathered cast almost no shadow. The sky was clear, the previous night's rain a distant memory. The day was warm, cheery and at complete odds with the solemn nature of the ritual taking place on the crest of the hill overlooking *Sí an Bhrú*.

Soon, he consoled himself, *it will be done. Soon Darragh and his brother will no longer be a problem.*

He just needed the twins separated for a little longer, perhaps only a few days …

Afraid his thoughts would betray him, Marcroy forced himself to concentrate on the ceremony. Each of the Druids in the Council held a thick staff made of elm, which they thumped rhythmically on a small wooden pedestal on the ground in front of them, to alert the gods to their presence in the sacred circle. But the drumming, which normally Marcroy found quite soothing, set his teeth on edge today. Although he had no prescient ability to speak of, something felt awry. Something, somewhere, he feared, was not going according to plan, although he could not imagine what, because right now, everything was going exactly as he wanted.

He glanced across at Álmhath, who was standing next to her son, Torcán. The prince looked bored, having no idea of what was to come. Marcroy had insisted on that. Torcán was a fool, incapable of keeping his mouth shut. The best way to ensure he kept a secret was to be certain he wasn't privy to it. The Celtic queen was looking her age today. Her face was lined, her blue eyes puffy and red rimmed, as if she'd suffered a sleepless night. She obviously couldn't wait for what was coming.

He understood her anticipation. For a *sídhe* limited so severely by the laws of his own people, things could not have worked out better for Marcroy. Darragh was right where they wanted him — in danger of losing his seat through his own foolishness.

Or he would be, if the Druids had been able to find another set of psychically linked twins to take his place. A generation lost, and the power would slip away from man. The Treaty of *Tír Na nÓg* guaranteed the sharing of power only while the twin line remained unbroken. Miraculously, the Druids had always managed to produce another set of psychically linked twins, generation after generation for the past two thousand years.

The search for heirs to the Undivided kept the Druids endlessly occupied. And somehow the *Matrarchaí*, the caste of Druid women charged with finding these rare and precious twins, had always found another set. Until now.

Marcroy was never quite sure how they'd managed. The reason he had not objected to the treaty clause that continued the magical sharing with the Druids after the Roman threat was defeated, was Marcroy's belief that psychically linked twins were so improbable, there was little or no chance the Druids would be able to keep the line going. It didn't seem to be an hereditary skill. Over the years, many of the Undivided had produced twin offspring who shared little more than a name and an uncanny resemblance to each other. Just as many Undivided heirs had appeared out of nowhere, from human family lines with no history of twins, or magical ability. Druid women seemed a little more able to produce psychically linked twins more often than ordinary women. Marcroy recalled that RónánDarragh were the get of the lovely Druid Sybille — but it was by no means a certain thing.

As Marcroy puzzled over the history of the Undivided, the Druids chanted in a monotone. Finally, Darragh entered the circle. By then, the prayers calling on the gods and goddesses had been going on for the better part of an hour.

'*Siuil linn a* Danú,' the Druids chanted as they thumped their staves. '*Siuil linn a* Uathach.'

Walk with us, *Danú*. Walk with us, *Uathach*.

Marcroy mouthed the words of the chant, but his mind was in other places as he reflected on the contribution he'd made to this awkward situation. And he *had* contributed to it. He was prepared to admit that much to himself.

'*Siuil linn a* Rhiannon.' Walk with us, Rhiannon.

It wasn't that there hadn't been enough magic to defeat the Romans back then, simply that there hadn't been enough *Tuatha* to deliver it. It was Marcroy's idea to enlist the Druids as allies. He'd heard of other *sídhe* in other realms, saving the day in a similar fashion — although if he'd known how it would end, he would have thought twice about suggesting they follow the same course. Druids knew a little magic, although only a few of them could truly wield it, they worshipped the same gods as the *Daoine sídhe*, and shared a similar outlook on many fundamental beliefs.

They had seemed perfect allies.

All the *Tuatha* had to do was find a way to allow the Druids access to their magic — using psychically linked twins — as they had in other realms, and their effective numbers would increase tenfold. It was enough to send Claudius scurrying back to Rome, leaving their islands safe and the humans who made up the fractured tribes of Britain, Ireland, Scotland and Wales, free to continue to do what they did best, which was — in Marcroy's opinion — to fight each other.

It made for little progress but it kept the Druids from growing too strong.

Let the Romans attack Persia and recreate Alexander's glory. Let the Djinn fight off the Roman desire for empire. Let Claudius take his legions to China and face the wrath of the *Tianwang*. Let them see how far they got attacking the islands guarded by the *Youkai*. The *Tuatha* just wanted to be left in peace.

'*Siuil linn a* Ogma.' Walk with us, *Ogma*.

If only they'd seen how the balance of power would shift so dramatically in favour of the Druids. Who would have imagined the whole world might one day turn to them, and not the *Tuatha Dé Danann*, for guidance and direction?

Marcroy frowned as Darragh came closer, thinking the boy seemed cockier than the situation warranted. Was he just being a foolish child or was there a reason for the boy's confidence?

'*Siuil linn a* Telta.' Walk with us, *Telta*.

It had been almost two thousand human years since the Treaty of *Tír Na nÓg* was shaped, although for Marcroy and his people, time was a fluid thing. For the *Daoine sídhe* it was not measured nearly so inflexibly as humans measured it, with their clocks and calendars and constant arguments about the movement of the planets around the sun.

Sixty generations of Undivided had come and gone since then.

Sixty generations passed before this young man and his missing brother were born.

Sixty generations to find a pair of twins who didn't need the *Tuatha* to bestow their power on them.

Sixty generations to find a pair of twins powerful enough to use magic without help from anyone.

Marcroy remembered well the ceremony that had marked Rónán and Darragh with the magical triskalion that would allow the magic to flow into them and, through the twins, to every other Druid marked the same way. The three-legged symbol merged the power of three worlds: the Otherworld, the Mortal World and the Celestial World. It was on the Celestial plane that the rifts to other realms could be opened.

'*Siuil linn a Gráinne.*'

Marcroy had never imagined the Druids would find such a use for that magical power. It was something, he realised, they should have foreseen.

It had happened a long time ago, but he still clearly recalled the tall stones of Beltany casting their shadows over the stone platform where the infant heirs lay. As tradition demanded, when the new heirs had passed their first birthday, they were branded with the magical triskalion that allowed the power to flow from the *Daoine sídhe* to the human realm. That way, should anything happen to the reigning Undivided, the flow of magical power to the Druids remained uninterrupted.

It was a ceremony Marcroy had presided over sixty times before. A boring ceremony full of absurd ritual having little to do with the business at hand. He'd been stifling a yawn when Orlagh stepped forward and took each of the year-old twins by the hand — Rónán by the left and Darragh by the right — and branded them magically with the symbol that would act as a conduit between the *Tuatha* and the Druids. The magical symbol that gave the Druids, and all those similarly branded, access to the Three Worlds.

He'd waited, expecting the children to howl with pain. After all, it was much more than a surface tattoo the *sídhe* queen was bestowing on them. She was branding them to the bone, searing the magical symbol so deeply that even losing that limb would not interrupt the flow of power.

But the boys hadn't cried. They cooed and smiled as if feeding at their mother's tit.

'*Siuil linn a* Eostre.'

It was only then that Marcroy started to pay attention. It was only then he realised the danger the *Tuatha* were in. It was only then that the need for a plan to contain the Undivided came to him.

Jamaspa came to him a few days after the branding to warn him of the danger he had glimpsed for himself. These children, the Undivided twins, would be their undoing, the Djinni warned. They had seen it happen in other realms. It would not be permitted to happen here. Either Marcroy did something about it, or the Brethren would.

It had taken Marcroy the better part of two years to find a way to reduce the risk of the Undivided without breaking his oath to uphold the Treaty of *Tír Na nÓg*. It had seemed such an elegant solution, too. Break the boys apart. Never let them discover how powerful they would be if they acted together. Keep them contained until the line died out or they could be replaced.

These boys — these psychic twins born of a human woman — obviated the need for the treaty. There was no need for spells or magical tattoos, Jamaspa told him. These children could take from the *sídhe* that which had, until now, been given only under very specific conditions.

'*Siuil linn a* Bel.' Walk with us, *Bel*.

Darragh finally stopped before the gathered Druids who were, for the most part, wearing animal masks making them look like a horned herd of demonic creatures. The drums fell silent.

The young man seemed undaunted. Marcroy wanted to believe it was because Darragh had grown up with ceremonies such as this that they held no fear for him. He worried Darragh's confidence meant he was up to something.

He's nothing more than an irritating boy, Marcroy reminded himself, hoping his uneasiness was simply a reaction to the awful food in *Sí an Bhrú*, and not something more worrying. *That*

*which makes him dangerous, his twin, is in
another realm, trapped and unable to return.*

Trása had seen to that. His mongrel halfblood
niece, of whom he had despaired for most of her
growing years, worrying her affection for Darragh
would lead them all into even worse trouble should
she share her mother's fascination for humans.
It was a condition of the treaty — for obvious
reasons — that no *sídhe* would ever produce a
child with one or other of the Undivided. Until
Marcroy had arranged to remove her from *Sí an
Bhrú* and bring her back to *Tír Na nÓg*, where she
couldn't make trouble — innocent or otherwise —
he'd never really breathed easy. And now ... to his
great surprise, she'd proved to be useful.

He'd sent her to look for Rónán to get her out
of the way. He'd even sent her with that fool,
Plunkett O'Bannon, the most useless *Leipreachán*
in this realm, certain she'd get herself — and
probably Plunkett — killed in a world she didn't
know or understand.

And yet it was Trása who'd found the missing
twin he'd cast into another realm, and it was Trása
who had promised him the boy would remain
trapped there, out of reach of the Druids, forever.

*You'd not be looking so smug now, young
Darragh*, he thought, *if you knew that.*

Farawyl, Druidess and High Priestess of *Sí an
Bhrú*, now stepped forward. She wore a stag-head
mask, which distorted her voice as she finished the
prayer that would enable congress to commence.

'*Danú* bring peace to the north,' she chanted.
'*Danú* bring peace to the east. *Danú* bring peace
to the south. *Danú* bring peace to the west. *Danú*
bring wisdom and peace to the Undivided.'

Darragh didn't answer her. No response was required. But he flexed his hands at his side, the only indication that he might have been even a little nervous.

Farawyl lifted her mask, so that she could look at Darragh. 'You have been missed, *Leath tiarna*.'

CHAPTER 39

'Have you been to many other realities?' Ren asked, as the four of them emerged from the shepherd's hut into a misty sunrise. 'You know ... where the Dark Ages actually ... finished?'

Brógán shook his head at the incomprehensible question, and then headed over to the dead cook-fire to see if he could stoke some life into it. Ren stretched appreciatively, glad to be out of the close and smelly confines of the hut. Both Ciarán and Sorcha made for the nearby bushes to relieve themselves. Ren supposed he ought to do the same. The rain had stopped sometime during the night and the early morning chill was making his breath steam as he spoke. He took a step forward and tripped over something in front of the hut — he recoiled in horror when he realised it was a dead body.

'Christ! The werewolves are still here!'

Brógán looked up from the fire. 'What did you expect? Phantoms to spirit them away during the night?'

Ren hadn't thought about it. Gingerly, he stepped a little closer to examine the body. The pale creature was naked and filthy, with matted

347

hair so fouled it was impossible to tell what colour it might once have been. The body had leaked fluid overnight. The creature's loins were soiled and the tips of its fingers and toes were purpled with pooling blood. Its mottled ears were pointed, as were the small teeth visible through its partially open mouth. It was the creature's eyes, however, that drove home to Ren how alien it was. They were open, staring at nothingness, but even in death they displayed an unusual golden sheen and a vertical iris reminiscent of a cat's eye. Ren poked at the dead Faerie with his foot. It felt solid and real and stank like a cesspit; not otherworldly at all.

'Is that a ritual in the place you come from?' Sorcha asked, coming up to stand beside him. 'Kicking the corpse of your enemy after he is slain?'

'Bit hard to kick his corpse before he's slain,' Ren remarked, regretting the words almost as soon as he uttered them. It was comments like this that used to get him in trouble in his weekly sessions with Murray Symes.

Sorcha glared at him. 'In this realm, you will be required to show respect for the dead, *Leath tiarna*. Even dead enemies.'

'I'm sorry,' Ren said, genuinely contrite. 'I've got plenty of respect for the dead. It's just ...' He glanced around at the other bodies. 'Well ... this is all pretty new to me. I'm still trying to get my head around the whole alternate reality, long-lost brother thing. I'm not sure I'm ready for live werewolves that turn into dead Faeries.'

Sorcha studied him for a moment, as if judging how sincere he was. Then she nodded. 'You must have many questions, *Leath tiarna*.'

Ren nodded. 'That's something of an understatement.'

Suddenly all business, she slapped his arm with the back of her hand and pointed to the nearest corpse. 'You can ask them while we're cleaning up. Ciarán has gone to hunt us up some fresh meat. After the rain last night Brógán will be a while getting the fire alight, even using magic. It would not do for the *Tuatha* to stumble across these bodies.'

'They attacked us,' Ren pointed out, wondering what 'cleaning up' entailed. He was already feeling queasy.

Sorcha stepped over to the corpse and grasped its ankles. 'Never fear, *Leath tiarna*. A few dead bodies won't spoil your appetite.'

'I'm glad you think so,' Ren muttered, mostly to himself as he bent down and grabbed the corpse under the armpits. He helped Sorcha carry the surprisingly light body away from the hut toward a flat spot a little further down the slope where the corpses could be burned.

It took them the better part of an hour to pile up the bodies and set them alight. Brógán used magic to light the fire. Ren wasn't sure what that involved. One moment he was looking at a pile of dead bodies, the next the tattoo on his hand was tingling and the bodies were engulfed in flames as if they'd been soaked in gasoline.

'So ... which one of us is the evil twin, do you suppose?' Ren asked, as he dropped to the damp ground beside the cook-fire. Breakfast proved to be freshly killed rabbit, which Ciarán skinned with the same ease Kerry Boyle might have displayed preparing a pack of instant noodles.

Brógán, Ciarán and Sorcha turned to stare at Ren. 'Why do you assume one of you is evil?' Sorcha asked.

'I thought that was the way it worked … on TV your evil twin always comes from another reality.'

Brógán smiled. 'In make-believe stories perhaps, Rónán. Here there is no evil. There is light and dark. Safe and dangerous.'

'But not good and bad?'

'Good and bad are intangibles,' Sorcha said. She sucked on a rabbit bone to strip it of its meat. 'They are points of view, not objects one can buy and sell at market.'

Ren was not sure he was ready for such a radical worldview. 'Some things are evil,' he said.

'I'm sure deer think us killing them for food is the height of bad manners,' Ciarán agreed. 'Doesn't make them any less tasty.'

'*Danú* has granted us a world that requires balance,' Brógán added. 'Good requires evil in order that both may exist.'

It was too early in the morning for philosophical discussions, Ren decided. There were other, more practical considerations to be dealt with. Things that had kept him awake most of the night, as Ciarán snored and Sorcha tossed and turned, muttering softly in a language Ren didn't understand. 'When can I go home?'

'Darragh will be able to tell us when he returns from *Sí an Bhrú*,' Ciarán said. 'There are political considerations that make your return an event requiring careful management.'

Ren looked at the big warrior in confusion. 'Political considerations? What political consider- ations? They're just going to think I've lost my marbles when I get back and tell them I've been to another reality. That's not political. It's just something likely to get me prescribed psychotropic medication and a nice long stay in a padded cell.'

Ciarán and Sorcha exchanged an odd look before the big warrior responded. 'You won't be returning to the reality where Brógán and Niamh found you, Rónán,' he said with a frown. 'This is your home. This is where you belong. You *are* home.'

Ren stared at him for a long moment. 'Are you serious?'

'Of course,' Ciarán replied, as if surprised by the question. 'Why would I joke about such a thing?'

'No frigging way!' Ren exclaimed, jumping to his feet. 'I'm stuck here?'

'Stuck would imply you have no desire to be here,' Sorcha said, wiping her hands on her trousers as she rose to her feet. In daylight, the warrior seemed more unlikely than she had last night. Her frame was so slight, she looked like a strong wind might carry her away.

'Why would I want to be here?' Ren asked, shaking his head. He pointed to the pile of burning corpses, and the black smoke being carried away from their campsite on the cool morning breeze. 'So far I've been kidnapped, knocked unconscious, dragged to a world apparently populated by insane Faeries who want to eat me whenever there's a full moon, and little old ladies who behave like Xena, the Warrior Princess. I've been attacked by werewolves and briefly met some kid who may or may not be my evil twin. Exactly which part of that sales pitch is supposed to have me signing up for the full tour of duty?'

Brógán climbed to his feet and stood beside Ren, holding his hand out as if to comfort him. 'Rónán … it will be all right …'

'How will it be all right?' Ren demanded, taking a step backwards. 'Hayley's lying in a coma while we sit here mulling over the philosophical differences between good and evil. Meanwhile, there's a dozen or so dead bodies over there, being cremated as we speak, and you lot are sitting here like it's an everyday occurrence, enjoying breakfast. This isn't funny any more. I want to go home.'

'You are home,' Ciarán repeated. 'Accept it.'

'Get fucked,' Ren said in English, not knowing the Gaelige equivalent. He turned on his heel and stalked away from the fire and hut, heading east, thinking he'd return to the village. If he couldn't find someone there to help him, well, there was always a stone circle. Darragh had used the circle to appear out of nowhere. If he and Darragh truly were magically linked, perhaps from there, Ren could find his way home.

He'd not taken more than three steps before the big bearded warrior blocked his way. Ciarán may not have known exactly what Ren said to him, but he certainly got the sentiment and, apparently, he could move like a ninja.

'You may not like what the future holds for you, *Leath tiarna*,' he said unsympathetically, his hands on his hips, 'but that is your burden, and how light or heavy it becomes is entirely up to you. You are here and you will do what you were born to do, or I will see to it myself that you live to regret your reluctance.'

Ren stared at him in surprise. 'What are you going to do, tough guy? Break my legs?'

'If I have to.'

Ren realised that Ciarán wasn't joking.

The trouble was, neither was he. Ren smiled, hoping reason would work where cussing and bravado had failed. 'Look, big fella, I appreciate you're thrilled you've found Darragh's long-lost twin, but I have a life, dude, and it ain't here.' The impact of his appeal was somewhat lost by the fact that he made it in English, a language only Brógán understood.

'He is asking for consideration of his previous life,' Brógán translated. 'It's not an unreasonable request, I suppose.'

'What does he expect us to do?' Sorcha asked Brógán, glaring at Ren. 'We can't let him go back.'

'I have a family in my reality,' Ren reminded them, speaking their language again. 'My best friend is lying in a coma, and I'm stuck here with …' He stopped and stared at Brógán for a moment, as something occurred to him. 'Jesus! You could fix her!'

'What?' all three of them asked simultaneously.

'You could fix her!' Ren repeated. 'You guys … you could magic her up and she'd be fine.'

Brógán shook his head. 'I'm sorry, Rónán, it's not possible.'

'Why not?'

'There is no magic left in your realm.'

'But you are a healer!'

'No, magic is a natural force,' he explained.

But Ren was excited by the idea that Hayley could be magically healed. The sight of her lying in that hospital bed, her head bandaged, tubes sticking out of her, haunted him. He still felt

responsible. If these Druids could take him back ...
he could heal her ...

'Magic ... the magic we use ... is an elemental
force,' Brógán said. 'It's tied to the *Daoine sídhe*
and the life force of all growing things. In your
world, so many of your forests and rivers have
been destroyed, there is only a small vestige of
the magic left. The lands of the *sídhe* have been
destroyed. There's barely enough magic left in
your realm to sustain a *Leipreachán.*'

'But *you* crossed into my reality with magic,
didn't you?' Ren pointed out. 'How did you get
back?'

'The rifts were opened from this side,' Ciarán
said.

Ren stopped listening for a moment as he
realised he couldn't get home unless someone
opened a rift for him.

'Then why don't you bring her back here?' he
asked. 'You could bring her to this reality, heal
her with magic, and then send her home once she's
fixed.' *And I could go with her. Back to the world
where my nightmare is just that ... a disturbing
nightmare that can be medicated away ... not a
glimpse of the future.*

Brógán glanced at the others before conceding
the point. 'Well ... theoretically, I suppose ...'

'Then you're going to have to do it,' Ren said,
crossing his arms. 'You want me and my twin to
rule your world, or whatever it is the Undivided
do? Fine. You do something for me first.'

Sorcha shook her head. 'The Undivided do not
rule the world, *Leath tiarna*. And even if they did,
your brother will never agree to such a bargain.'

Ciarán, however, didn't seem so certain. 'I fear,

354

my lady, this is Darragh's brother,' he reminded her. 'It's just the sort of harebrained lunacy that would appeal to him.'

That made perfectly good sense to Ren. After all, if Darragh was his identical twin, they probably had a similar outlook on life. Of course, that might also mean that if Ren asked to go back to his own world, Darragh might know he wasn't planning to come back. Or would he? Were they so similar?

'Then it's settled,' he said, surprised at how easy it had been to win their agreement for something so potentially dangerous. He wondered vaguely how he was going to explain it all to Hayley when he saw her again. 'You talk to my brother and magic up whatever it is you need to do to get us —' He stopped abruptly as something moved around the corner of the hut.

'What's the matter?' Sorcha asked, her hand on the hilt of her sword, instantly alert.

'Nothing ...' Ren frowned. He squinted, trying to decide if he'd seen something real or just imagined it. 'I thought I saw something, that's all.'

'What did you see?' Ciarán asked, his knife already in his hand, looking around just as Sorcha was.

Ren shrugged, feeling a little foolish. 'Really, it was nothing ... just my imagination running away with me.'

'Let us be the judge of that,' Sorcha said. 'What did you see?'

'You're going to think I'm crazy.'

'We'll probably think that anyway,' Sorcha snapped. 'What do you imagine you saw, *Leath tiarna*?'

355

Ren sighed, bracing himself for their derisive laughter. 'I thought I saw a *Leipreachán*.'

Without a word Ciarán and Sorcha closed in on Ren like bodyguards on assassination watch. Alert, tense and facing outwards with Ren protectively between them.

'Where?' Sorcha demanded.

Ren was stunned. 'Seriously?'

Brógán was looking around now, too, with a worried expression. 'Where did you see the *Leipreachán*?'

'Over by the hut,' Ren said, staring at the Druids as if they were mad. 'I thought I saw him ducking behind the wall ...'

'See what you can find, Brógán,' Ciarán ordered.

Brógán hurried up the slope to the hut, holding a silver dagger at the ready.

'Can you describe him?' Sorcha asked.

'Yeah ... he looked like a *Leipreachán*.'

'How did you know it was a *Leipreachán*? Have you ever seen one?' Ciarán asked, glancing over his shoulder at Ren. Brógán had disappeared around the side of the hut. There was no other sound but for the soft rustle of a faint breeze in the trees.

'Friend of mine had a toy one,' Ren told them. 'He looked just like —'

'There's nothing there,' Brógán announced, appearing from the other side of the hut. 'If it was a *Leipreachán*,' the Druid added, walking toward them, 'he would have vanished the moment he realised Rónán spotted him.'

Sorcha and Ciarán relaxed a little and turned to each other.

'What do you think, *an Bhantiarna*?' Ciarán asked Sorcha, calling her 'my lady'. 'Can we risk it?'

Sorcha shook her head. 'Breaga's a known haunt for *Leipreachán*. In fact, I can't think of a worse place to use as a safe haven, if you're trying to avoid any of the lesser *sídhe*. Those wretched weremen should have proven that last night.'

Ciarán nodded, apparently in agreement with the warrior, and then he turned to Ren. 'You said the *sídhe* looked like something you knew. What was it?'

'You're gonna think I'm crazy.'

'If he says that one more time,' Sorcha complained, 'I'll run him through myself.'

Ren took a step back, a little alarmed by Sorcha's vehemence.

'I have a friend,' he explained. 'Back in my reality. Her name is Trása and she has this creepy *Leipreachán* doll called Plunkett ...' His voice trailed off as he noticed their incredulous expressions. 'Now what?'

'Trása?' Ciarán asked in a strangled voice. 'You have a friend named Trása?'

He nodded. 'So?'

'Describe her,' Sorcha ordered.

'Um ... about yay-high, pretty, really long blonde hair.'

'How long have you known her, Rónán?' Brógán asked, looking positively nauseous.

'A few days.' He studied the three of them. 'Do you guys know her, or something? You're all staring at me like I've started spewing pea soup and I'm about to do a three-sixty with my head.'

None of them understood what he was talking about and they didn't seem interested. Sorcha turned to Ciarán. 'Darragh needs to know this. And we need to move Rónán.'

'The little *sídhe* bastard is probably reporting to Marcroy as we speak.' Ciarán nodded in agreement and then turned to Brógán. 'Why didn't you tell us about this?'

'I didn't know, Ciarán,' he said, clearly worried about something. 'I swear, we saw no sign of any *sídhe* in the other realm. They're not supposed to be able to survive there.'

'Fullbloods couldn't,' Sorcha agreed. 'But Trása's a mongrel. And there might be enough magic left in the other realm to sustain a *Leipreachán.*'

'Trása's a *Faerie*?' Ren asked.

Ciarán turned on Ren angrily, towering over him. 'Trása Ni'Amergin is the mongrel get of the *leanan sídhe,* Elimyer and the bard, Amergin, the worst traitor the Druids have ever spawned. If you have befriended her, *Leath tiarna*, and if you should wish to keep that friendship over allegiance to your own kind, then it would be quicker and easier if I give you my sword so you may fall on it now, and save us the trouble of executing you for treason.'

CHAPTER 40

Darragh glanced around at the gathered Druids, the rest of whom were still masked. He caught sight of Marcroy out of the corner of his eye, standing to the left of the dais where Farawyl had led the ceremony thus far, next to Álmhath and Torcán. Marcroy seemed impressed that Darragh was uncowed. He wondered if the *Tuatha* envoy thought him brave, or too naïve to be intimidated.

He fixed his gaze on the high priestess. 'I have been busy, *a Mháistreás*.'

It wasn't the response Farawyl was expecting. She frowned. 'You do not honour your position, *Leath tiarna*, by being glib.'

'I speak the truth, my lady, nothing more. Why have you convened the Council of Druids?'

Farawyl hesitated. She was probably composing a verse in her head, so the Council would be recorded for posterity. As high priestess, it was her duty to maintain the oral record of Druid history, just as it was Colmán's job to ensure every important moment in the lives of the Undivided were captured and preserved in verse. Although Darragh couldn't see Colmán, Darragh knew that behind him somewhere on the edge of the circle, the Vate would be taking it all in too, and probably trying to find a way to make it rhyme.

'It has been suggested, *Leath tiarna*,' she said after a long silence, 'that your brother, the lost twin of the Undivided, is truly lost and can never be returned to us.'

'Suggested by whom?' Darragh asked. He was tempted to look directly at Marcroy, but that would be revealing too much of what he was thinking.

Farawyl didn't like having to explain herself. Not even to one of the Undivided. 'That is not really the point, *Leath tiarna*.'

'Am I not permitted to face my accusers?'

'You are not being accused, my lord. It is merely a suggestion. At this stage.'

Darragh glanced around the circle. It was hard to tell which Druid was which under their animal masks. 'And at what point does the stage change, my lady?' he asked. 'You're hardly suggesting I be removed. There are no heirs to take the place of my brother and I. He may not be here, but you cannot deny he lives, or the magic would not flow and I would be dead.'

Farawyl paused, took a deep breath, and gestured toward the Celtic queen. 'Our guest, Queen Álmhath, has some news in that regard, which she wishes to share with us.'

For the first time, Darragh felt unsure of himself. The real reason for the queen's visit with Marcroy would now be revealed. But why had she chosen the Council of Druids to reveal it? He glanced at the queen and then fixed his eyes on Marcroy. It was Marcroy and not the queen pulling the strings in this particular puppet show. 'Is her majesty planning to take on the role of the Undivided herself?'

Álmhath stepped forward and raised her chin, the better to be heard. 'I bring you tidings of great joy, princes of the Druid,' she began loudly, holding her arms out wide. 'Like you, our people have grieved the lost twin of the Undivided these past fifteen years. I am happy to reveal that the pain his absence has caused us will soon be a thing of the past.'

Darragh fought to keep his expression neutral. *They've found Rónán*, his mind was screaming. *How? This Council was organised days ago. How could she know Rónán is back? How does Marcroy know he's back? How would he have known Rónán would be back in time for this?*

Darragh fixed his gaze on the queen and spoke as calmly as he could manage. 'Your words fill me with anticipation, *an Bhantiarna*. Are you telling me you have found my brother?'

Álmhath smiled at him, shaking her head. 'Alas, no, *Leath tiarna*. I wish I brought such happy tidings for you.' She looked up and addressed the rest of the Druids. 'I do, however, have happy tidings for the rest of us. We no longer *need* to find the lost twin. The Faerie have found new heirs!'

Darragh's relief that Rónán's return remained a secret was so intense that, for a moment, he didn't fully appreciate the ramifications of Álmhath's announcement.

'Not wishing to burden you with false hope,' the queen continued, 'Lord Tarth did not bring this news to me until he was certain these *are* the heirs we've all been searching for. Lord Marcroy has examined the twins and confirmed they are,

361

indeed, psychically linked and capable of fulfilling our part of the Treaty of *Tír Na nÓg*.'

This was the last thing they were expecting. It was the last thing Darragh was expecting, too. Why hadn't he seen this coming? His dreams were filled with dark images of murdered babies and an argument with his brother. While disturbing, the visions had sustained him, because they meant that one day Rónán would come home. They might fall out over those unnamed baby girls in the future, but it didn't matter, so long as Rónán was found.

But he had had no warning of this particular revelation, and it rattled him to the core.

'What can you tell us about these precious heirs, *an Bhantiarna*?' he asked, trying to figure out how this was going to change his own plans. 'Where are they? When can we meet them? When can they be brought to *Sí an Bhrú*?'

'Their names are Broc and Cairbré,' Álmhath said. 'They are currently under Lord Tarth's protection at *Tír Na nÓg*, and will remain there until arrangements have been made to brand them.'

'Where did you find them?' a voice from the circle called out.

'They hail from a remote village in southern Limerick.'

'When were they born?' another Druid wanted to know.

'They are seven years old.'

That news sent another buzz of concern through the ranks of the gathered Druids.

'How is it these boys remained undetected until now?' Farawyl asked the queen, her voice full of concern. The *Matrarchaí* were supposed to check every set of twins born in the realm to find the next Undivided. It was hard to believe there were seven-year-old twins anywhere that had slipped past them.

'They came from a small, insular community, and their mother was unable or unwilling to name the father,' Álmhath explained. 'Their grandfather kept them hidden, in the hopes of making a marriage alliance with a neighbouring farmer, by convincing him his daughter was pure.' She glanced at Marcroy, who nodded in agreement.

Darragh didn't doubt the story for a moment. Nor did he doubt Álmhath was speaking the truth about having found new heirs. There was no way to fake something like that. But why hadn't she mentioned they were girls?

'And when do you propose to bring these remarkable children to *Sí an Bhrú*?' he asked. This unexpected turn of events was going to change everything for him and Rónán.

Álmhath glanced at Marcroy before she answered. 'It has been suggested that *Lughnasadh* would be an appropriate time to transfer the power.'

'The Autumn equinox?' Darragh asked. A month was plenty of time to figure out what to do. And then he realised what she'd said. 'Wait ... did you say, *transfer* the power?' he asked incredulously. It was one thing to brand new heirs in anticipation of them one day assuming the role of the Undivided. But it was quite another to transfer the power while the current Undivided were alive and well.

Álmhath turned to Farawyl, who nodded slowly. 'The queen of the Celts is right. We must consider what action we can take, within the confines of the treaty, to restore the power of the Undivided.'

'I wasn't aware the power of the Undivided was compromised,' Darragh shot back.

Farawyl's lips narrowed. She was unused to people talking back, and certainly not in front of the full Council.

'Clearly, wherever he is, your brother lives, *Leath tiarna*,' she conceded. 'Even you have acknowledged it is unlikely he will ever be found. Surely your Sight would have told you otherwise, if that were not the case?'

'I have never said anything of the kind.'

'You gave up your brother's place at table,' Farawyl reminded him.

'I have not given up hope, however,' Darragh said. 'Nor have I shared my visions, so there is nobody present who can say whether they are reliable or not.' Darragh was in no mood to get involved in a discussion about the reliability of his Sight. Besides, he had a more immediate problem. He held up his tattooed palm for all of them to see. 'I survived receiving the power, an investiture I shared with my missing brother. I'll not survive having it taken away. And wherever he is, neither will he.'

'That is the nature of the treaty, *Leath tiarna*,' Farawyl agreed, clasping her hands together in the sleeves of her robe. 'Your predecessors, LonHarian, surrendered their power willingly for the good of their people.'

'LonHarian were grown men with full lives behind them. I'm in excellent health. You are passing a death sentence on me and my brother if you transfer the power now,' Darragh said. 'What is the point of shoving me aside to invest the power in a couple of seven-year-olds?' He glanced around the circle, wishing he could read the faces behind the masks. 'Is that what you want? Another ten years of Regency? Do you not recall how the last one turned out?'

Should I tell them Rónán is back? he wondered as he waited for someone to answer. *Could I end this now, by telling them the Undivided have been restored?*

But the announcement of these new heirs had blindsided him. For the first time, Darragh was uncertain about his future. He'd seen his brother in his visions, but there had been no hint in *that* future of the one confronting him now.

Was his vision flawed? What did he know of his brother, anyway? He'd met Rónán for a few hours, he didn't know him yet. There hadn't been time to perform the *Comhroinn*, and to complete it. He needed his brother's total trust and co-operation and he didn't even know if Rónán would agree to stay in this realm.

'I suggest we decide what to do once we've seen these boys,' a voice called out from somewhere behind Darragh. '*Lughnasadh* is not that far away. We can decide then whether to make the transfer or whether we need to give the young lads time to adjust.'

A general murmur of agreement rippled around the circle. Darragh remained silent about his brother. He needed time to figure this out. He needed time to look into his future.

Perhaps he was destined to die a month from now and his recurring dream hadn't been a vision, but simply … a dream.

'Aye,' another voice called out. 'We are missing one of the Undivided, but we've been missing him for the past fifteen years. Another month won't matter, one way or another.'

That comment was also met with a general murmur of agreement. Farawyl nodded and turned to Álmhath. 'Then it is decided, *an Bhantiarna*.' She turned to Marcroy and added, 'Will you bring them to us for the *Lughnasadh* and inform your queen that we have new heirs to be invested?'

'A duty I will perform on her behalf with great pleasure,' Marcroy said, looking pointedly at Darragh. There seemed to be some sort of silent warning in the look, but then Marcroy looked away, as if something had distracted him, leaving Darragh to face the high priestess.

'Then we are done,' she announced. '*Danú* has spoken. May the blessings of *Danú* and her kin stay with you in your endeavours. We thank the powers of the sun.'

'We thank the powers of the sun,' the Druids echoed.

'We thank the powers of the moon.'

'We thank the powers of the moon ...'

And on it went, as Darragh stood in the centre of the circle in the hot sun, Farawyl droning on, counting the moments until he could get back to Breaga and speak to Rónán.

Hopefully, his brother would be ready to embrace his destiny.

If he wasn't, then they were both as good as dead.

CHAPTER 41

As the high priestess began the long ceremony to wind up the Council of Druids, Marcroy watched Darragh. He felt a moment's pity for the lad. It was clear Darragh hadn't seen this coming. Interesting. The lad had the gift of Sight, which was one of the first things they looked for in a twin, when one was seeking a new set of heirs. And yet the young man looked stunned when Álmhath announced they'd found Broc and Cairbré. Clearly, Darragh had not had any hint that his future was about to be cut short.

Their eyes met for a moment as Marcroy tried to decide if Darragh's Sight had failed him, or if the young man had seen a future that extended beyond *Lughnasadh*. If he had, then perhaps the fault lay with Marcroy's plans and not Darragh's prescient abilities. Marcroy would have to discuss this possibility with Jamaspa when he returned, pleased beyond words he'd thought to give Brydie the brooch inhabited by the djinni. Jamaspa would have some interesting tales to tell about Darragh, Marcroy thought, having spent so long in the young man's chamber while he romanced Álmhath's court maiden.

'*Psssst!*'

Marcroy realised someone was hailing him, and looked down to find Plunkett O'Bannon crouched on the hem of his cloak. Marcroy glanced around, but the Druids, the Celtic queen and her son were engrossed in the closing ceremony.

'By *Danú*, you'd better have a good reason for seeking me out here,' Marcroy hissed, lifting his foot and bringing it down sharply so the *Leipreachán* was pinned by his neck to the stone paving of the Druid circle.

The little man nodded, his eyes wide with fear.

Marcroy cursed softly, and turned his attention back to the Council. He wasn't pleased by the outcome. Doing nothing until *Lughnasadh* was not what Marcroy had hoped for, and it was not enough to hold Jamaspa and the Brethren at bay. They wanted Darragh — and, by default, his missing brother in the other realm — disposed of as soon as possible.

Still, the Autumn equinox wasn't that far away. They could wait, he supposed, until then.

The ceremony was likely to go on for some time yet. Marcroy took the opportunity to drop his kerchief and then squat down in the pretence of retrieving it — his foot still on Plunkett's throat — to look the little *Leipreachán* in the eye.

'If you're back here in this realm,' he whispered, 'I can assume your companion returned with you safely?'

Plunkett nodded silently.

'Your mission is accomplished?'

Plunkett squirmed uncomfortably, his face turning an interesting and not unpleasant shade of blue. The *Leipreachán* managed a strangled reply: 'Of course, *tiarna*.'

'Then why are you here?' Marcroy hissed. He straightened, stepping a little harder on the *Leipreachán*'s throat. He looked around. The Druids were still giving thanks for everything from last night's dinner to the very air they breathed. Only Torcán seemed to notice the *Leipreachán* under Marcroy's boot, and he found it amusing, rather than cause for concern. At a nudge from his mother, he turned back to repeating the prayers Farawyl was reciting.

Marcroy glanced down at Plunkett then joined in the prayers, ensuring all the deities were thanked. When the thanks were done, the circle full of Druids, led by Darragh, filed out of the stone circle and headed down the grassy slope toward the huge quartz-covered *Ráith* with its turf-covered roof that was *Sí an Bhrú*.

Marcroy waited until he was alone with his minion. He bent down, grabbed Plunkett by the throat and picked him up, holding the wriggling creature at arm's length. 'Why are you here bothering me, Plunkett? Is it because you failed me, and you wish to confess your ineptitude in the hopes of clemency?'

'No, no!' Plunkett gasped. 'We did exactly what ye asked! I swear we did! We put him in a place he canna ever escape from, *tiarna*, I promise ye!'

There was an edge of panic in the *Leipreachán*'s voice that worried Marcroy. This was not the report of an underling proud of what he had achieved. This was the panicked whining of failure and repentance. 'What happened?' he demanded.

'I did what ye said,' Plunkett was desperate to point out. 'Exactly as ye asked. We found him. It took months, but we found him. And I came up with a plan. I found a way for the mongrel to put the lad away and, when we got back, I went straight back home to Breaga. Just like ye ordered me to.'

'Then what's the problem?' The irritating creature wasn't sweating undiluted fear because he'd done exactly as ordered. Something had gone wrong and Marcroy was in no mood for a drawn-out narrative.

'Ye told me to report anythin' unusual, once I be home.'

'And ...' Marcroy prompted.

'I saw him. In Breaga.'

'Saw who?'

'Darragh,' Plunkett said. 'I saw him meeting with Ciarán and Sorcha. They be meeting in a shepherd's hut outside the village. I figured that was unusual enough that ye need to know about.'

Marcroy frowned. What was Sorcha doing in Breaga? She was a complication he didn't need. For that matter, what business did Ciarán have in the remote coastal town? Or Darragh? 'When did you see them?'

'No more'n a few hours ago.'

Marcroy shook the *Leipreachán*. Hard. 'That's not possible. Darragh is here.'

'I swear, *tiarna*, it's as true as me hangin' here,' Plunkett insisted.

Marcroy wanted to disbelieve him. But he knew Plunkett well enough to know that only fear of his master's wrath, should this sighting *not* be reported, would bring Plunkett O'Bannon willingly within Marcroy's reach now his debt was paid.

Had Darragh sneaked out? Was that why the boy seemed so smug at the start of the Council? He had supposedly spent the last few nights with Brydie.

'Breaga, you say?' Marcroy asked. It was an insignificant little coastal hamlet. What were two powerful warriors doing there, meeting with Darragh?

Plunkett nodded.

Marcroy eased his hold around the *Leipreachán*'s neck. 'Show me,' he said. 'Show me what you saw in Breaga.'

CHAPTER 42

Trása's summons to visit her uncle, Marcroy Tarth, arrived via *Leipreachán*. Although he could have called her using any one of the numerous shallow pools that collected moisture among the branches, he sent Plunkett O'Bannon, that irritating little *sídhe* Trása had been so glad to see the end of when she returned to her own reality.

The *Leipreachán* appeared on the wide branch outside her mother's dwelling, and began knocking with his *shillelagh*. Trása emerged, poking her head out to see what the racket was about. She'd thought it might be Éamonn, her mother's pet artist, who was prone to artistic tantrums when he feared his inspiration was fading.

Her heart skipped a beat when she saw Plunkett. 'Is my uncle back?' she asked, tying an iridescent, finely woven spider-silk shawl around her body. Although it was common, here in *Tír Na nÓg*, to shed her human inhibitions and the need to cover her body, she'd not spent so long back home that nakedness came easily to her in front of strangers.

'Aye,' the little man grumbled unhappily. 'And he wants to see ye.'

Trása couldn't hide her smile. 'I can't wait to tell him what we did.'

'Aye,' the *Leipreachán* agreed, in a tone that was anything but enthusiastic. 'It's going to be a thing to behold, I can promise ye that.'

Trása looked at him oddly. Plunkett seemed flustered. His coat was rumpled, his hat awry and he was definitely out of sorts.

'Where is he?'

'Where's who?'

'My uncle, of course.'

'Oh ... ye're to come with me.'

'To where?' she asked. 'Is he here? In *Tír Na nÓg*?'

Plunkett shrugged. 'He's waiting for ye. Somewhere else.'

It was not unusual for Marcroy Tarth to be cagey about his movements, partly to avoid his own kind from bothering him, and partly because he liked to seem mysterious. Trása smiled in anticipation of their meeting. Her achievement had no parallel in her world. She had been to another realm — one where she had only her wits to rely on — and she had found the missing Undivided twin. More importantly, she had made certain he could never come home.

After a lifetime of not quite fitting anywhere — neither in the human world of her father nor among the magical beings of her mother's people — Trása was looking forward to a reward that would elevate her in the eyes of the *Tuatha Dé Danann*. Once word of her feat got about, she would be revered — she was certain — rather than looked upon with pity and disdain as the unfortunate consequence of the union between a dismal human and a careless Faerie muse.

Despite her mongrel heritage, Trása was a child of relative wealth and privilege in both the human and Faerie worlds. But she hungered to be accepted by either her mother's or her father's people — and she didn't care which — with an ache that sometimes made her feel hollow inside.

'Is it far?' she asked, unable to dampen her enthusiasm, even in front of a *Leipreachán*. Trása glanced around the surrounding trees. Above her, other *sídhe* went about their business without sparing her a glance. Beneath them, in the branches housing less well-connected *sídhe*, they knew better than to look up or give the impression they were spying on, or judging, their betters.

'I told you, already. He's not here in *Tír Na nÓg*, if that's what ye're not-so-subtly asking,' Plunkett told her grumpily, leaning on his *shillelagh*. 'I'm to take ye to him. Ye'll need a cloak.'

So Marcroy was somewhere in the human world, Trása concluded. Some place where the vagaries of wind and weather ruled. Somewhere unlike the pleasant, warm confines of *Tír Na nÓg*. Somewhere cold.

'Mother thought Marcroy was at *Sí an Bhrú*,' Trása remarked, turning into the hollowed-out part of the trunk that made up the only room of her mother's residence. She bent down and threw open the trunk where she kept the few material possessions she owned. *Had Plunkett heard the catch in her voice?* she wondered, as she rifled through the trunk. Could he tell how desperately she wanted to go to *Sí an Bhrú*? How much she wanted to see Darragh again?

'Aye, Marcroy was there,' Plunkett agreed, looking about nervously.

It wasn't the height of the branches that frightened him, Trása guessed, as she found what she was looking for. She stepped back out onto the branch and shook out the dark woollen cloak embroidered around the hem with gold knot-work that had been folded at the bottom of the trunk. Plunkett's nervousness was probably fear of running into one of the queen's cousins: *sídhe* like her mother, who were notoriously intolerant of the lesser *sídhe* and who weren't averse to kicking them off their branches, if they thought the smaller creatures had outstayed their welcome.

Not that the fall would kill the little *Leipreachán*, of course, but the sudden stop when he hit the ground a hundred feet below them would undoubtedly be very unpleasant.

'But he's not at *Sí an Bhrú* now?' Trása asked.

'He's in Breaga,' the *Leipreachán* said.

'What's he doing there?' Trása didn't really expect an answer. She was compelled to obey her uncle. He wasn't compelled to explain anything to her. But she had been to Breaga a number of times, and she couldn't imagine what Marcroy was doing there. The rude village had little to commend it, although it was rumoured that the stone circle there could open a reality rift with relative ease due to its proximity to the ocean.

'Ye can ask him yourself when we get there,' Plunkett said.

'Ask who what, dear?'

Trása looked up in time to see her mother floating down from the branches above. Naked and elegant, Elimyer seemed to glow and the lightness of her descent meant she had fed recently and well.

'Marcroy wants to see me,' Trása explained. She glanced around looking for Éamonn.

'Say hello to my brother for me, won't you, dearest?' Elimyer said, as she gently touched down beside her daughter. She fondly cupped Trása's cheek, the magic tingling on her skin at her mother's touch.

'I will. You look well sated,' Trása remarked with a frown. It was unusual to see her mother like this. Had she been human, Trása would have thought her drunk. In a way, she was. But she was drunk on magic, and it was so much magic Trása could feel it in Elimyer's touch. Rarely, unless they were out working a battlefield, had Trása seen her mother like this.

They'd visited quite a few battles since she'd been sent to live in *Tír Na nÓg*. With Trása's *Beansídhe* senses able to identify who was about to die, she could point out the vulnerable lives to the *leanan sídhe*. Her mother, and sometimes her similarly gifted aunts, were able to suck dying soldiers' life force from them in such a way that the man passed away in bliss and the *leanan sídhe* were able to feed without seeking out a commitment from a human which might — if one was not careful — result in a mongrel child. Like Trása.

It had been a while, though. Not since that border skirmish last year between the O'Flahertys and the O'Malleys had she seen her mother so intoxicated.

Elimyer smiled. 'I am sated, daughter. I am filled with life.'

Oh shit, Trása thought. 'Whose life, mother?'

'The boy's … what was his name?'

'Éamonn?'

'Yes,' she said, with a wistful smile. 'He was so pretty. So talented.'

'Then why did you kill him?'

'He was much too demanding, darling,' Elimyer said with a shrug. 'Much too clingy.'

'You made him that way,' Trása pointed out, wishing now that she'd said something to the young man. Perhaps she should have warned him he was about to die.

And perhaps he wouldn't have believed her. He certainly wouldn't have expected his doom to come from the hand of the muse he imagined he was in love with.

'It's of no matter,' Elimyer said. 'He's gone now.' Her smile faded as she noticed Plunkett. 'What are *you* staring at, creature?'

Plunkett dropped to his knees, threw his *shillelagh* down and bowed his head. 'I bring a message for the mongrel, *an Banphrionsa*.'

Trása frowned, but her mother didn't seem bothered by Plunkett's description. She was more concerned that her tree was being invaded by a lesser *sídhe*.

'And you dare deliver it here?'

'The message is from your brother, *an Banphrionsa*.'

Elimyer was so full of Éamonn's life force that she couldn't maintain her irritation very long. 'Ah, well, if the message is from Marcroy …' She turned and floated across to a nearby tree, where one of her sisters lived.

'And they reckon the *Leipreachán* can't hold their magic,' she heard Plunkett mutter, as he picked up his *shillelagh* and climbed to his feet.

'You watch your tongue, Plunkett O'Bannon,' Trása warned. 'I could easily tell my uncle of your disrespect, you know.'

'Ye tell him anything ye want, Trása,' the little man responded. 'Assuming he'll listen to ye.'

'Why wouldn't he listen to me?' Trása asked. There was something far too smug and insolent in the *Leipreachán*'s manner.

'Wait 'til ye get to Breaga,' the *Leipreachán* said, 'then ye'll see.'

With that Plunkett vanished into thin air, reappearing a few moments later on the lower branches of a neighbouring tree, and a few moments after that, even further away and almost out of sight. Cursing, Trása dropped her embroidered cloak, changed into the white owl shape she favoured, snatched up the cloak in her beak and followed Plunkett through the branches before she lost sight of him again, leaving only the spider-silk wrap lying puddled on the branch behind her, to let her mother know she was leaving.

CHAPTER 43

'My lord Ciarán! You're back!' Colmán exclaimed.

Darragh looked up at the Vate's exclamation, just as surprised to see Ciarán striding into the hall as Colmán. Darragh was both grateful for the interruption and bothered by it. He was grateful, because in addition to bringing Ciarán up-to-date on what had happened this morning at the Druid Council, Colmán was driving him mad with his latest epic detailing the momentous and historical events of the meeting. The bard was having particular difficulty finding words to rhyme with Cairbré, and wanted Darragh's opinion on each verse as he composed it.

He had never missed the eloquent Amergin more.

Darragh hadn't yet had the time to figure out what he was going to do about the Council's decision to kill him and his brother as soon as it was deemed convenient. Nor had he been able to reconcile the events that were happening around him with what he knew to be his vision of the future. Ciarán's arrival meant the opportunity to share his uncertainty with the one person he trusted to give him sage advice.

He was bothered, however, because only the most dire news would have taken Ciarán away from his charge to protect Rónán at all costs.

'I'm not officially back, Lord Vate,' Ciarán said, forcing a smile that Darragh could tell was false. He pushed past the servants who were carrying out the extra tables that had been set up for the Celtic queen and the visitors from *Tír Na nÓg*. Marcroy Tarth was nowhere to be seen, and Álmhath had left *Sí an Bhrú* after the meeting, taking her annoying son, Torcán, and his fiancée with her.

Darragh didn't know if Brydie had left with them, or was still waiting for him in his rooms.

'I … er … just had some … weapons I wanted to pick up,' Ciarán muttered.

Darragh cringed. Could Ciarán not have thought up a more imaginative excuse? But Colmán didn't seem to find the pretext at all strange. It was probably because he didn't understand warrior Druids as a caste. To him, Druids and fighters were mutually exclusive professions. He considered Ciarán — who was both a gifted magician and a fabled warrior — to be a paradox. He was never certain how to deal with him.

The Vate stroked his forked beard, his brow furrowed. 'Whatever the reason, I am glad you're here, Ciarán. You must talk some sense into Lord Darragh.'

'Is he doing something foolish?'

'He is being unreasonable.'

Ciarán glanced at Darragh. 'How so?'

'The Vate fears I am not accepting my death sentence with sufficient equanimity, I fear,' Darragh told him in a voice laden with irony. A couple of passing servants glanced at him, looking a little worried. Darragh realised he probably shouldn't make comments like that in public, but then ... a bard dogged his every step in order to chronicle his life. Nothing he said in *Sí an Bhrú* was ever truly private.

The warrior's eyes widened. 'Death sentence?' he asked.

'Marcroy Tarth has found our Undivided heirs,' Colmán explained, wringing his hands. 'Lord Darragh, rather than see this as a positive event, thinks there is a plot afoot to murder him.'

'I've missed much while I've been away,' Ciarán remarked, looking at Darragh curiously. 'Might I have a word in private with you, *Leath tiarna*?'

'If you have matters to discuss of import with the Undivided,' Colmán said, 'then I should be there.'

'This is a personal matter,' Ciarán said. Darragh understood immediately that Ciarán wanted to discuss Rónán. The hall was not the place for any such discussion. It was always possible the *Tuatha* had spies among the servants at *Sí an Bhrú*. For most of Darragh's life, the Vate of All Eire, the most trusted Druid in the whole world, had been Marcroy Tarth's agent.

But to go outdoors was arguably more dangerous, because one never knew if a vole or a fieldmouse was in fact a *sídhe* sent to listen in on mortal conversations. 'A problem involving my affairs, not the *Leath tiarna*'s.'

Colmán frowned, afraid he might miss something important.

'It's fine,' Darragh assured him. 'You need to work on your epic, anyway. You can be sure Álmhath's bard will be itching to present his version of the Council at the next feast we share with them. We cannot be outdone, now, can we?'

The Vate nodded, suddenly more concerned about being overshadowed by a rival than he was about Darragh. 'If you're sure you don't mind, *Leath tiarna*?'

'Go with my blessing,' Darragh said. 'Do us proud, Vate.'

Colmán hurried from the hall, his footsteps shuffling on the flagstones as he tucked his hands into his sleeves and began muttering to himself, probably still trying to find a word that rhymed with Cairbré.

'Nothing like a bit of professional rivalry to get the creative juices flowing,' Darragh remarked as the Vate walked away. He turned to Ciarán. 'Let's talk in my rooms.'

They said nothing as they made their way through the labyrinthine halls of *Sí an Bhrú* toward Darragh's private chamber. People stood back as they passed, some bowing or nodding a greeting. Many just looked away, aware that here was a young man with a life span that might be measured in days.

As soon as they were behind the closed doors of his bedchamber, Darragh magically lit the lamps and cast his senses around the room to ensure there were no *Daoine sídhe* eavesdroppers disguised as mice or cockroaches. There was no sign of Brydie. She was gone for now, along with her clothes. Perhaps to find some lunch, or maybe to report to her queen. Another thing to worry about. Once he'd spoken to Ciarán, Darragh needed to find her. Darragh had unfinished business with Brydie Ni'Seanan.

'What's wrong?' he asked. 'Has something happened? Is Rónán all right?'

'He's fine,' Ciarán said. 'What in the name of *Danú* has been going on here?'

'Colmán tells it true,' Darragh said. 'They've found another set of twins. It was proposed at a special Council today that the boys be branded at *Lughnasadh* and the transfer of power take place immediately.'

Ciarán didn't answer. He didn't need to. The Druid warrior knew what that meant.

'I am a victim of my own cleverness, I fear,' Darragh added with a sigh, taking a seat on the edge of his bed. The faintest hint of Brydie's scent lingered on the furs. 'I was so busy setting things up for the dramatic return of my brother, I didn't see what was coming.'

Ciarán shook his head impatiently. 'Didn't you tell them Rónán is back? They wouldn't even consider transferring the power if they realised the Undivided are whole once more.'

'I said nothing.'

'Why not?'

Darragh shrugged. 'I can't say. I was going to. I thought the same as you. But then I caught the look on Marcroy's face and knew I mustn't.'

'That's a ridiculous excuse,' the warrior said. 'You go out there right now, you fool, demand they reconvene the Council and tell them we've found Rónán, that he's back and the Undivided are restored. I'll bring him here. Today. We'll put this nonsense about transferring the power to these new heirs to bed, once and for all.'

Darragh shook his head. 'There's no need, Ciarán. I'll be fine. They're not going to kill me.

But Rónán is at far too much risk if we bring him here unprepared. We stick to the original plan. I have to trust my Sight.'

Ciarán snorted derisively. 'If your Sight is so damned reliable, *Leath tiarna*, how come you didn't see *this* coming?'

Darragh still didn't have an answer for that. He knew his visions though, and knew what they portended. 'I have a recurring dream, Ciarán,' he explained. 'Actually, it's more like a nightmare but in it, Rónán and I are grown men. We are arguing over the fate of two children — baby girls, although I don't know their names. One of us thinks they have to die, the other wants to spare them.'

'Which is which?'

'I've never been really sure. And I have no idea who the babies are. I used to think perhaps they might be our heirs, but the heirs Álmhath is bringing here are boys, and they're already seven years old.'

'Then the vision is wrong.'

'I don't think so,' Darragh said, frowning. 'And I'm pretty sure Rónán has had the same dream, although I won't know for certain until we share the *Comhroinn*.'

'Which will be fine consolation, I'm sure,' the warrior said, 'as they take your power and you and your brother die an agonising death from the withdrawal.'

'You're missing the point, Ciarán,' Darragh said, rising to his feet a little impatiently. 'In my vision, Rónán and I are grown men. The dream takes place here, in *Sí an Bhrú*. We will not die on *Lughnasadh*. We will live long enough to fight over the fate of those children.'

Ciarán shook his head, unsure of Darragh's logic. He folded his arms across his chest, looking grim. 'I think you're a fool. I think you need to bring Rónán to *Sí an Bhrú*, let them know the Undivided are restored and let these newly discovered heirs be trained and allowed to grow to manhood in peace.'

'And I would do it, Ciarán,' Darragh said. 'In a heartbeat ... if I didn't know there were already power hungry Druids lining up to take on the Regency of the new Undivided. There are too many people out there who would benefit from these new heirs being invested as children. Look what happened with me and Rónán. Look what they did to Sybille.'

'You don't know for certain they killed her, Darragh.'

'Yes,' Darragh replied. 'I do.'

Ciarán sighed unhappily.

'Rónán is unprepared for this life as yet,' Darragh added. 'He knows nothing about us. We've already had to bring Sorcha in on this to protect him, and we haven't even brought him here yet. We don't even know for certain that he wants to stay.'

'I wasn't aware we were giving him a choice.'

Darragh smiled thinly. 'I'm hoping once we've shared the *Comhroinn*, he'll decide to stay. But what if he doesn't want to? Do we know anything about the life he had in the other realm? Are we so certain he wants to give up everything he had there for what he will have here?'

'Actually, that brings me to the reason I'm here,' Ciarán said. 'We have a problem.'

'Only one?' Darragh sighed. 'That's an improvement.'

'We're going to have to move him.'

'To where?'

'Somewhere safe,' Ciarán said cagily. He, too, lived in fear of Marcroy's spies. 'I have a few ideas.'

'I thought he *was* somewhere safe,' Darragh said.

'He might have been,' Ciarán said, wincing. He took a seat on the bed where Darragh had been sitting a few moments before. Darragh wondered if the warrior had been in a fight recently. If he had, it wasn't a good sign. He'd thought an out-of-the-way village like Breaga would have been perfectly safe. 'If your little friend hadn't found him first.'

'What are you talking about? My little *friend*?'

'Seems Rónán made a new friend in the other realm, just before he joined us here. A young lady, to be precise. Said her name was Trása. She even had a *Leipreachán* with her.'

Darragh's heart skipped a beat. He hadn't seen Trása for almost three years. He still missed her. Still wished they hadn't sent her away. He knew why they had, of course, and they were right, but all the same …

'Trása crossed a rift to find Rónán?' he asked, trying to sound more interested in the mechanics of the problem rather than the subject. 'But she's *Beansídhe*. Surely she would perish in a world without magic.'

'She's only half-*Beansídhe*,' Ciarán reminded him. 'She's human enough to survive there, apparently. And to survive long enough to find your brother. Thank *Danú* that Brógán and Niamh found him when they did, or who knows what might have happened.'

Darragh put aside his confused feelings for his childhood friend in order to consider the ramifications of that piece of news. Trása had crossed the rift into Rónán's world and somehow managed to find him first. Had she spoken to him?

Of course she had ... that's how Rónán knew her name.

But what did she want with him? She hadn't harmed him. She hadn't even revealed who she was or where she came from. If she had, Darragh's existence would not have registered as such a shock with his brother.

'Did he say what she was after?' Darragh asked.

'He says she asked nothing of him. She just appeared a few days before we found him, claiming to be the granddaughter of a neighbour. They were just getting to know each other when there was some sort of accident. He did try to explain what happened but it made no sense to me, although Brógán seemed to understand it. Perhaps that's because he told most of it in the language of the other realm. Anyway, a friend or cousin was badly injured. In an effort to bring the person responsible to account, Rónán ran afoul of the authorities and finished up in gaol, which is where Brógán and Niamh found him.' Ciarán shook his head with a sigh. 'At least, that's how Brógán explained it.'

For a moment Darragh was envious of Rónán and the life he led in the other realm. It was a world where one could speak to a half-*Beansídhe* without earning the wrath of two entire species. He wondered what else Rónán had seen and heard and done. He tried to imagine the liberty his brother would have enjoyed there. To be free, to have none of the burden of being the Undivided, a burden Darragh had carried alone all his life. The idea was so enticing, it was hard not to feel envy.

But he didn't have time to dwell on it. Right now, they had to deal with their enemies in this world.

'Rónán is still safe, is he not?'

'For now.'

'There is a "but" in that comment I can hear clearly, Ciarán, even if you're not saying it aloud.'

The big man leaned forward and lowered his voice. 'Rónán thinks he saw Plunkett O'Bannon in Breaga, this morning.'

Plunkett O'Bannon? What is that irritating little troublemaker up to?

'Is he sure?'

'No,' Ciarán said. 'Given your brother's limited experience with the little folk, it's possible he mistook one *Leipreachán* for another. The problem is, he saw a *Leipreachán*. If the little folk know Rónán is back, you can bet they're telling Marcroy Tarth about it, even as we speak.'

Darragh frowned. He'd seen the look on Marcroy's face at the Council. The *Daoine sídhe* lord had been itching for the power transfer to take place. He had stood at Álmhath's side in a show of unprecedented solidarity with the human queen. So anxious was he that the power be transferred, that he was prepared to risk the life of these young twins — not to mention take the life of Darragh and Rónán — in order to see it happen. Why?

'You said we had a problem with Rónán,' Darragh reminded Ciarán.

'He wants to do a deal with you.'

'What sort of deal?'

'He wants to return to the other realm, and bring a friend back to this one.'

Darragh smiled. 'Is it a girl?'

'How did you know that?'

'He's my other half, Ciarán. How could I not know?'

CHAPTER 44

It was uncomfortable, being a mouse. One was always being distracted by food. Mice, being scavengers, were frequently sidetracked from their purpose by the whiff of a fragrant midden, the aromatic temptation of a discarded crust or the mellow bouquet of a mouldy piece of fruit. Out here in the countryside, away from such distractions, it was a little easier, but Marcroy still had to concentrate.

Good thing, too. Otherwise he would have missed everything.

He'd followed Plunkett to this out-of-the-way shepherd's hut, mostly because he was certain the *Leipreachán* was leading him on a merry chase. He thought he was giving Plunkett enough rope with which to hang himself and was looking forward to the moment when the little man realised he'd run out of slack.

Instead, Marcroy ran straight into the very thing he feared most.

Rónán of the Undivided. Alive and well and here in the realm Marcroy had taken such pains to remove him from.

Once the Brethren found out about this, there

would be hell to pay. Thank *Danú* that Jamaspa was still locked inside Brydie Ni'Seanan's brooch back at *Sí an Bhrú*.

Rónán hadn't stayed in Breaga long. Plunkett had been careless — naturally — and Rónán had caught sight of him. By the time Marcroy and the *Leipreachán* returned, Sorcha and Brógán were getting ready to move him to a more secure location. Somewhere the *Tuatha* would have difficulty finding him. There were not many places where he couldn't be found by the *Tuatha*, but there were enough of them for Marcroy to be worried he'd lose Rónán if he let him out of his sight.

Marcroy was angry. Trása had promised she'd taken care of the boy. Rónán was supposed to be trapped somewhere in another realm. Certainly not returned to be reunited with his brother.

No wonder Darragh had seemed so smug at the Council of Druids. Darragh had stood there and not said a word. He had not given the slightest hint that at *Lughnasadh*, when they intended to transfer the power of the Undivided to the new heirs, he intended to march into the circle of Druids with his Undivided twin by his side.

Marcroy wasn't used to underestimating humans so badly.

The serendipity of the *Leipreachán*'s discovery was not lost on Marcroy. He was so thankful for it, in fact, that he had sent Plunkett to fetch his niece, rather than turn him into a worm for having the temerity to turn up at a Council, tugging on the edge of his master's cloak.

In his guise of a fieldmouse, Marcroy was now able to get close enough to the hut to hear Rónán and the others talking. Close enough to see Sorcha, Ciarán and a young Druid Marcroy recognised from *Sí an Bhrú* but couldn't name.

The younger man Marcroy dismissed as insignificant. He wasn't surprised to find Ciarán here, though. Darragh trusted nobody more. If Darragh of the Undivided had cooked up a plan to find and retrieve his brother from another realm, it could not have been executed without the Druid warrior's help.

Sorcha's presence worried the *sídhe* lord more. He'd not seen her in some time, and knew her to be unsympathetic to the *Tuatha Dé Danann*, whom she blamed — along with Marcroy Tarth — for being trapped in *Tír Na nÓg* for so many years.

It was Sorcha's quest to become a Druid magician that had sent her to *Tír Na nÓg*. She had no magic to speak of, so she would never achieve the status of a man like Ciarán, who was both magically gifted and a mighty warrior. She'd thought travelling to *Tír Na nÓg* would change that.

Marcroy, when he was feeling generous, could admit to being in some way responsible for her misapprehension. She was a beauty, and he'd been quite enchanted with her at the time. As a Druid novice, however, she would never entertain the idea of a casual affair with a *sídhe*. She was much too focussed on her desire to be the greatest Druid warrior that ever lived.

So Marcroy had let her believe that if she came to *Tír Na nÓg* her wish would be granted. He hinted that he could arrange for her to be branded with the magical tattoo that would allow her to channel *sídhe* magic, if she came to his land, where magic sweated out of the skin of every *sídhe*.

Sorcha, who had been sixteen, foolish and blinded by an impossible ambition, had swallowed his hollow promises. Several attempts in the human world to tattoo her left breast over the heart had failed. Like others who wished to wield magic but couldn't, she'd been tattooed twice, but within days the magical ink faded, leaving her a simple warrior, and a slip of a girl warrior at that.

So she entered the magical lands of the *Tuatha* believing Marcroy would grant her the ability to wield magic. Once under the spell of his world, he'd wooed her and loved her, indulging her desire to be a great warrior by allowing her to be taught by the greatest warriors of the *Tuatha Dé Danann*.

She learned everything she could from them, mastered every technique they showed her. But the magical tattoo remained nothing more than a hopeful dream.

One of Marcroy's sisters had let slip the news that Sorcha could never be marked for magic. It may have even been Elimyer who gave the game away. By then, Marcroy had already lost interest in Sorcha and moved on to other, less challenging, conquests.

Sorcha, by now a formidable fighter, finally left *Tír Na nÓg* to discover a horrid truth. The Druids had warned her about travelling to the land of the *Tuatha Dé Danann*. Warned her that *sídhe* magic distorted time and that the world she left behind travelled at a different pace. She'd known of the danger, of course, and believed she'd kept track of the time. In fact, in her mind, she'd been in *Tír Na nÓg* no more than six months. In the real world, however, as Sorcha discovered when she returned home, sixty years had passed. Sorcha came back to a world she didn't know; a family long dead, a home lost, a world destroyed. She'd come home to nothing.

Marcroy felt a little sorry for her. But mostly he felt sorry for the fact that he had created an enemy in the heart of a woman who had once been a lover.

That she was here now, helping protect Rónán of the Undivided, was proof enough of that.

'... take him to ...' Ciarán was ordering Sorcha as Brógán kicked over the fire and began to remove traces of their makeshift camp. Marcroy cursed. He wasn't close enough to hear the details. Perhaps it was his rodent hearing. But to change into anything larger — like the wolf shape he favoured when taking animal form — would alert the humans to his presence.

'Where's that?' Rónán asked. Marcroy crept a little closer, in the hopes of discovering what village 'that' might be. He studied Rónán from beneath a small tussock of grass growing by the hut wall. It was cold hiding here, shaded as it was by the hut's western wall, but it gave him an excellent vantage point and he was now close enough to hear what they were saying.

Marcroy marvelled at how much like his brother Rónán was. He really was identical to Darragh, except he had shorter hair, a more slender frame, and the triskalion tattoo marked his left hand, rather than his right. Marcroy had sent him through the rift to a world of no magic, which meant technology and a lifestyle that didn't require proficiency with weapons. He studied the young man with his rodent senses, battling the temptation to scuttle under the uneven boards of the hut's walls and rummage for crumbs. Whiskers twitching, he watched and waited as they made their plans, but he still had no idea where they were planning to take the lad.

Rónán was complaining: '... but you promised.' His shoulders were set in the same, intransigent pose Darragh adopted when he was being stubborn.

'Ciarán promised nothing of the kind, *Leath tiarna*,' Sorcha said, as she buckled on her sword. 'He said your brother might agree to it. He certainly never offered to champion your insane bargain.'

'But you can help Hayley! If we've got to make ourselves scarce for a while, why don't we just go back to my reality and get her? It would be better than holing up in some fortress in the middle of nowhere, constantly looking over our shoulders for fear the cockroaches are listening in.'

Marcroy would have frowned, had his mousy features permitted it. *What was Rónán talking about? Fortress in the middle of nowhere? Going back to his reality? To get whom?*

'We can kill two birds with one stone,' Rónán said, imploring the others for help.

Marcroy wished he knew what the lad was trying to convince them to do. The key to managing humans was knowing what they wanted, and this boy clearly wanted something very badly.

'It's so simple, it's perfect!' Rónán insisted. 'We vanish through the rift until the Autumn thingy, we find my friend, and then we come back and kick butt.'

Sorcha smiled. 'I appreciate your fervour, *Leath tiarna*. It's truly a pity the course of action you want to apply your fervour to is so preposterous.'

'Did you ask Darragh if it's preposterous?'

Ciarán shrugged. 'He said he would consider your request.'

'It wasn't a request, dude,' Rónán replied in the same tone with which Marcroy had heard Darragh issue a thousand orders. Until that moment, Marcroy had always thought Darragh merely good at parroting the instructions given to him by Amergin and, lately, the fool Colmán. Seeing Rónán using the same tone of voice, the same stance, the same mannerisms, forced him to reassess his opinion of both boys.

'Darragh knows of your desire, and will discuss your offer as soon as he can get away from *Sí an Bhrú*,' Ciarán said, placing a fatherly hand on the young man's shoulder. 'There are other things afoot in the land, *Leath tiarna*, that he must deal with, before he can consider it.'

Rónán didn't look happy, but he seemed to accept Ciarán's assurance. Within a few minutes, they'd packed up the camp and turned for Breaga and the stone circle. They would spirit Rónán away until it was time for him to make his triumphant return at the *Lughnasadh* festivities, throwing all of Marcroy's plans into disarray.

Marcroy watched them leave, waiting until their voices faded. He forced himself to be still, fighting both his rodent and his *sídhe* instincts to move before he was sure he was completely alone. His nose twitched with the overwhelming smells of the earth, while his stomach rumbled, demanding he do something about the remains of the roast, not to mention the bonfire still smouldering a little further down the hill.

It was only once he was satisfied that it was safe to return to his true form that Marcroy changed from a mouse back into the tall *sídhe* lord. Naked, but no longer bothered by the chill air now he was back in his own form, Marcroy entered the hut and fetched a small, three-legged stool. He placed it near the door in the sunlight and sat down to wait for Plunkett O'Bannon and his niece to make an appearance. He intended to give them both a piece of his mind.

CHAPTER 45

Trása circled the shepherd's hut near Breaga once to be sure she had the right place. When she spotted Marcroy sunning himself on a stool, she dropped the cloak she was carrying and came in to land.

Marcroy saw the cloak floating down to earth and stood up, snatched it from the air and wrapped it around himself before Trása reached the ground. There was no sign of Plunkett.

As soon as she landed, Trása resumed her true form, smiling in anticipation of her welcome. The air was cool, but it didn't bother her much, and although she was naked, she was less self-conscious this time. Besides, Marcroy was also naked, which meant he'd recently taken on an animal form, too, and had been caught out here in the human world without human clothes in which to disguise his spectacular *sídhe* physique.

'If I'd known the cloak was meant for you, *Uncail*, I'd have brought one of yours.'

'Did you think to ask?' Marcroy said, fastening the cloak under his chin before brushing an imaginary fleck of dust from his shoulder.

Trása was a little worried by his tone. She

had not been expecting icy disdain. 'No ... I just assumed ...'

'Ah,' Marcroy said. 'You assumed. Just as you assumed that Rónán of the Undivided was trapped in the other realm, I suppose?'

Trása nodded, relieved she could reassure her uncle on that matter, at least. 'The Druids will never find him. He'll be imprisoned for life. It's what they do to people who kill other people in that realm.'

'And you arranged for him to kill someone?'

'I arranged for him to be blamed for another's death,' she explained, expecting a reward for her cleverness. 'It was Plunkett who started the fire, but Rónán who was arrested for it.'

'And you *assume* they'll simply blame him and lock him up for the crime?'

His tone was decidedly unfriendly. It started to bother Trása a great deal. Did he not fully appreciate the scope of her achievement?

'They did lock him up, *Uncail*,' she said. 'I waited until they took him away to be certain of it.'

'Did you not worry that he might not be detained?'

Trása shook her head. 'It was on TV that night. It was all over the news that he'd been arrested and was facing life in prison.'

'Tee ... *vee* ...?'

'It's a ... a thing they have there. People appear in a glowing box ...' Her voice trailed off as she saw the expression on Marcroy's face. She didn't understand how television worked herself. She had no hope of explaining it to her *sídhe* uncle who could not even imagine electricity. 'The town criers confirmed his fate,' she amended.

'So, if I told you he was here,' Marcroy said, taking a seat on the stool as he painstakingly spread the cloak around him, 'and that I have seen Rónán of the Undivided in this very place, on this very day, I would be mistaken?'

Trása laughed, a little nervously. 'Of course ... well, I mean, you would not be mistaken, just ...'

'Yes?'

'It's not possible,' Trása said flatly. And then she smiled. 'You are teasing me, aren't you, *Uncail*?'

'Trása, my pet, you have known me all your life. Have you ever known me to make a joke?'

'Well ... no ...'

'Then why do you suppose I would start now?'

Trása's stomach sank as she realised he was right. Marcroy had no sense of humour. Humour was a human trait. One he didn't understand and didn't appreciate. If Marcroy claimed Rónán was here in this realm, then Marcroy truly believed he was.

'Have you considered the possibility that it is Darragh playing a prank on us, *Uncail*?' Trása suggested cautiously. 'He knows we seek to keep his brother hidden from him. Perhaps he has conceived some complicated scheme to make us think Rónán has returned, in the hope of tricking the *Daoine sídhe* into revealing his location in the other realm?'

'Perhaps,' Marcroy conceded.

'Did you see them together?' she asked.

'No.'

That was a relief. 'Then if you thought you saw Rónán, it's more than possible that it was Darragh posing as his brother, is it not?'

'A likely scenario, Trása,' Marcroy agreed, with

a warmer expression. 'Except for one tiny little detail.'

'What's that?'

'Darragh bears the triskalion seal on his right hand. The boy I saw — the one protected so diligently by Ciarán and Sorcha, who were panicking at the idea that a *Leipreachán* may have revealed their presence to me — that boy bore the tattoo on his *left* hand.' Marcroy stood up, towering over Trása. 'Now, who do you suppose that might have been?'

Trása stumbled backward, overwhelmed by fear and confusion. She'd been so sure Rónán was safely out of harm's way. How could he be in this realm? And so quickly? She'd seen no sign of Druids around him in the other world. Admittedly, his face had been all over the news for days. But for the Druids to have found him, and brought him back through the rift so quickly ... 'It can't be him,' she gasped.

Marcroy raised a brow. 'Are you suggesting I am *wrong*?'

'No!' she babbled. 'Of course not! It's just ...'

'That you think I'm mistaken?'

Trása was trembling. She was in a dilemma and there was no way out. Either she'd failed and let her uncle down, and Rónán had indeed returned to this realm, or she hadn't failed, and would have to prove to Marcroy that he was mistaken about what he'd seen. Both involved angering a *sídhe* lord.

'*Uncail*, I swear. I left Rónán in the other realm facing life imprisonment.'

'Facing it is not the same as being certain of it.' Marcroy gripped Trása by the shoulders with his long, slender fingers and his cat-like eyes bored into her. 'Of course, I might have misread the situation.'

Held in her uncle's vice-like grip, Trása knew Marcroy's seeming change of heart was something to be wary of. 'You might?'

'We need to ascertain the truth,' he told her. 'Put the matter to rest, once and for all.'

Trása nodded warily.

'Ciarán spoke of taking the boy to a fortress in the middle of nowhere,' he said. 'Why don't you take to the air and see what you can discover?'

Trása nodded again, relieved that the task he'd set her could be so easily accomplished. There were a few places that might fit that description. There was a *Ráith* at Drombeg where Ciarán had grown up. The people there would shelter the warrior and any who were under his protection.

'I'll do it right now,' she promised, 'and be back before you know it.'

Marcroy let go of her shoulder and held out his arm like a hunter offering a perch to his hawk. Trása immediately changed into her owl form and flew up to perch on his forearm.

Marcroy scratched her fondly under the beak, muttered something under his breath, and then he smiled. 'There you go, precious. Fly away, find your would-be lover and his twin. I have no further use for you.'

The comment seemed at odds with his smile. Trása launched herself from his arm, circled the hut once, and then landed near the cold fire pit. She didn't want to go anywhere until she found out what he meant by not having any further use for her. Was she banished from *Tír Na nÓg* forever, or was he simply sending her away until she could confirm Rónán had not returned to this reality?

Trása's claws dug into the soft earth as she landed and she willed herself to return to her true form.

Nothing happened.

She tried again, but although she could picture her true shape in her mind, it would not form. Her tiny heart pounding, Trása realised she had lost the power to break out of her bird form.

Panicking, she squawked and flapped as she tried to force the change, but the magic simply dissipated as if it was being absorbed by an invisible sponge.

Trása was trapped.

Marcroy wandered across the grass toward her until he was standing over her.

'It's no use, my dear,' he informed her. 'You are an owl and you will stay that way until I decide otherwise.'

No! Trása flapped and squawked in protest, but could not speak.

'I've left you a loophole, though. That's the law, you see, when turning someone into something else. There always has to be a way out of it. In your case — because what I lack in humour, I make up for with a truly devastating sense of irony — you may be free of the trapping spell if you can convince one or the other of the Undivided to release you.' He folded his arms across his chest and admired his handiwork. 'Of course, you're going to have to make one of them realise who you are first, and then one or the other of them will have to figure out if they have the power to release you, but that's your problem. For the moment, you need to find Rónán for me, and you need to tell me where he is, and when he and his brother are going to be together again. And you're going to have to do it before *Lughnasadh*. If you can't bring me the information I need before then, *a Stóirín*, you truly are of no further use to me.'

Even in her bird form, Trása understood the threat. She beat her wings in protest, but Marcroy remained unmoved. After a few more moments of helpless flapping, she knew that if she kept this up, she would have no energy to fly, so she launched herself into the air, wishing birds could weep so she could give voice to the hurt and fear that threatened to overwhelm her.

With a final plaintive screech, she turned and headed west, to find out if Rónán of the Undivided had somehow found his way back to this realm and with no notion of how she could do anything about it if he had.

PART THREE

CHAPTER 46

It was weeks before Darragh saw Rónán again. It was weeks before he managed to achieve something he'd never thought possible.

Darragh finally managed to be alone with his twin brother.

Rónán was much more comfortable with the language now. His Druid gift for mastering tongues held true — even in the other reality — and he'd been taught a version of Gaelige at school. Weeks of speaking little else and it was already hard to detect any hint of an accent.

They climbed to the battlements of the small *Ráith* where they could talk in private. The moon was full and the skies were clear, so clear that the chilly night was lit brighter than the main hall of *Sí an Bhrú*. The sigh of waves breaking against the cliffs a few miles away provided a soothing background to their first real and meaningful conversation.

'Does it seem any less strange to you, brother,' Darragh asked, as he glanced over the edge of the weathered, mossy stones of the tower to the ground eighty feet below, 'now you've been here a while?'

'Not as strange as having someone who looks just like me calling me brother.' Rónán turned his gaze to the sea where the moonlight turned the occasional breaking wave into a luminescent foam that lasted a few fleeting moments, before being swallowed by the black waters of the straits between the coast and a small island just offshore.

It was impossible for Darragh to tell what Rónán was thinking — yet.

'You'll have to forgive me.' Darragh smiled. 'I don't seem to be able to help myself.'

Rónán shrugged. 'Not a lot of this makes any sense to me.'

The comment puzzled Darragh. With Rónán returned, the world had never made better sense in his eyes. 'What do you mean?'

Rónán leaned against the stonework, his expression grave. 'Okay. Let's start with the magical power thing. If I have this awesome ability to channel magic, how come this is the first I've heard of it? How come I haven't been turning people into toads all my life?'

'Didn't Ciarán explain that to you?'

Rónán shook his head. 'Ciarán's been mostly concerned with finding ever new and creative ways of running me through with his sword. So has Sorcha. She has an interesting interpretation of *protection*, I have to say.'

Darragh smiled. 'They are under orders to teach you how to protect yourself.'

Rónán raised a brow at Darragh. 'So how come nobody's been instructing me how to zap my foes into oblivion with magic instead of risking life and limb trying to teach me how to use a sword?'

'Well, for one, it's not possible to turn a human into an animal. Only the *Tuatha* can do that, because they are shapeshifters by nature. And not all threats in this world are magical. Besides, the Treaty of *Tír Na nÓg* forbids us from using *Daoine sídhe* magic to kill.'

Rónán threw his hands up. 'Oh, well that helps.'

Darragh smiled even wider. He couldn't help it. Rónán was so like him. 'It must be very hard for you, brother,' he said, 'to come to terms with all this. You've spent most of your life in a reality where there is barely enough magic to sustain a lesser *sídhe*.'

'What about the dreams?' Rónán asked, his eyes narrowing.

'Did you have a particular dream in mind?'

'Ciarán says you … we … have the gift of Sight. That we can dream the future.'

Darragh nodded slowly. 'That's true.'

'Do you ever dream about me? About us? In the future?'

There was something in Rónán's tone that warned Darragh to tread carefully. 'Sometimes,' he said.

Rónán was silent for a time and then shook his head. '*There's* a reason for me to go back to my reality and stay put, right there.'

So he's had the same dream, Darragh thought. He'd suspected as much.

'The future is a fluid thing, Rónán. The dreams don't always come true.'

'I don't know that I can stay, Darragh,' Rónán said.

'I know,' Darragh said, holding up his hand to forestall the conversation. 'And we'll discuss your return to the other realm in a moment. I just want you to know what you might be giving up, if you decide to go back.'

'So far, all I think I'll be giving up is body lice, crappy food, and people who want to kill me,' Rónán said, frowning.

Darragh sighed. He understood his twin's frustration but knew that once Rónán had shared the *Comhroinn*, he would understand. 'You have so much more than that awaiting you here, Rónán. You just don't know how to access the power yet.'

'And how long is it going to take me to *learn* how to access it?'

'Not long at all,' Darragh assured him. 'I'll share the information with you and you can share what you know with me.'

'That could take forever.'

Darragh realised Rónán had no idea what he was talking about. 'We're more than twins, brother. We are psychically linked, which is why we manifest each other's injuries.'

'Yeah …' Rónán said. 'About that. I get the cuts. I've had enough lessons with Ciarán to learn he's not very forgiving, so I get how they happened. But dude, back home, they had to pump my stomach a couple of times. What was that about?'

Darragh's smile faded. 'There are those who resent the power of the Undivided and who would give much to see us destroyed.'

Rónán rolled his eyes. 'You mean somebody tried to *assassinate* you? You know, you might want to think about coming back to my reality and staying there with me. This place is frigging dangerous.'

'Being in a different realm doesn't alter the nature of the link between us, Rónán. If one of us dies, the other will suffer the same fate, usually within a day.'

Rónán was silent for a time, and then he asked, 'I thought it was only Faerie silver that could harm us both? What did they poison you with?'

'We are the Undivided, Rónán,' Darragh reminded him. 'Normal poison doesn't affect us.'

Rónán nodded in understanding. 'Because Druids can do that magic healing thing?'

'Exactly.'

'So these guys who tried to poison you ... us ... they used what? A magic potion?'

'In a manner of speaking. They were somewhat put out, by all accounts, when it didn't work.'

'And it didn't work,' Rónán said, as he began to grasp their situation, 'because in my reality, there wasn't any magic, it was just a poison they were able to counteract with twenty-first-century medicine.'

Darragh looked at him oddly. 'They only have *twenty-one* centuries in the other realm?'

'We count the years from the birth of Christ. What year is it here?'

'It is the year four-thousand-thirty-five. We count our calendar from the construction of *Choir Gaure*.'

Rónán looked at him in surprise. 'Stonehenge? Really? We were always taught at school that it predated the rise of the Druids by a good fifteen hundred years.'

'I didn't say we *built* it, brother. Just that we count our calendar from its completion.' He shook his head in wonder. 'By *Danú*, there is so much you and I have to tell each other. I cannot begin to

comprehend the world where you were raised —
although once we've performed the *Comhroinn*
things will be much clearer for both of us.'

'*Comhroinn?*'

'It is how Druids share what we know. It is
what preserves our oral history. It allows us to
teach, to impart vast amounts of information, to
know each other completely.'

Rónán pushed off the battlements, looking
worried. 'You mean you do the *Comhroinn* and
you get to see everything going on in my head?'

Darragh nodded. 'I will know what you know,
Rónán. More importantly, you will know what
I know.' He smiled and offered his outstretched
hand. 'At the very least, it means you'll be able
to give Ciarán a run for his money in your next
training bout.'

Rónán took a step backward in alarm. 'Whoa!
You wanna do it *now*?'

'It's imperative we share the *Comhroinn* as
soon as possible,' Darragh said, uncertain as to
why Rónán was resisting. 'You are one half of
the Undivided, Rónán. Without the knowledge to
access your latent power, we are both at perilous
risk.' Darragh realised this was going to take
something more than a hollow reassurance to
convince Rónán to participate, and without his
co-operation, there was no point in trying. The
Comhroinn only worked if both parties wanted it
to. The slightest resistance and it would fail.

'Without it,' Darragh added carefully, watching
for his brother's reaction, 'we cannot risk returning
to the other realm to help your friend. If you want
to strike a deal to heal your friend, that is the cost
of my co-operation.'

Rónán fixed his gaze on his brother, his eyes narrowing. 'Are you telling me that if I let you do this ... sharing thing ... you'll open a rift back to my reality —'

'*This* is your realm, Rónán.'

'Yeah ... whatever. But you'll do it? You'll take me back so we can help Hayley?'

'Does she need your help?'

Rónán seemed a little confused by the question. 'What do you mean?'

'You've been gone from the other reality for weeks, Rónán. In your world, she may have recovered already and may need no help from you at all. Or she may be dead, in which case she definitely doesn't need your help. Are you prepared to risk everything here to find that out?'

Rónán was silent for a moment and then looked straight at Darragh. 'If you were me, what would you do?'

Darragh didn't hesitate. 'Whatever I felt was my duty.'

'Yeah ... well that's fine for you, brother. You have a lifetime of duty indoctrinated into you. The people I care about the most are back in another reality, and when I left, one of them was on life-support. My sense of duty isn't telling me I ought to be here, it's telling me I need to help Hayley.'

Darragh understood exactly what Rónán was feeling. But he was concerned his brother still didn't appreciate the magnitude of what he was asking. 'You do realise, don't you, that it's not as simple as stepping through the rift, finding your friend and healing her, Rónán? You do understand that we'd have to bring her back here?'

'Why … oh, because magic doesn't work in my reality.'

Darragh nodded. 'And there is a strong possibility the cure will only *last* while she's in this realm,' he warned. 'If we heal her magically and then send her back before her own body has accepted the imposition of a magical cure, the healing will not hold without *sídhe* magic to sustain it.'

Rónán pondered that possibility for a moment, and leaned again on the cold granite blocks that made up the *Ráith*'s single tower. In the sky, silhouetted against the moon, a lone white owl swooped and dived, probably spotting a fieldmouse for its dinner. 'So, what you're saying,' Rónán said after a moment, 'is if we bring Hayley to this reality, she might be stuck here for a while?'

'She may well be stuck here forever, brother. Of course,' Darragh added reassuringly, 'given that in our world she will be whole again, it may not be a difficult choice for her to make.'

Rónán pulled a face. 'Funny how *she* gets a choice, but I don't.'

Darragh felt sorry for his brother, but found himself growing a little impatient. If Rónán would only allow the *Comhroinn* there would be no need for such a discussion. All of this, he would instinctively understand. 'You were not given a choice when you were thrown through the rift, Rónán. Bringing you home is redressing an injustice, not perpetrating one.'

'From where you stand, maybe.'

'Was the world you left behind so wonderful?' Darragh asked. 'Do you have such a bright life awaiting you there? What *did* your immediate future hold?'

Rónán suddenly grinned and turned to look at Darragh. 'Not much more than mung beans and dog shite, actually, when you get down to it.'

'Then what are you afraid of?'

Rónán shrugged. 'I don't know. You'd have to see my reality to understand, I suppose. Do we have a deal?'

Darragh nodded. He didn't want to risk losing Rónán again, but realised that without some sort of reassurance, Rónán would never allow the *Comhroinn*, which needed his full co-operation to work. Once they had shared everything about each other, Darragh figured Rónán would be much more amenable to reason. Hayley's fate might not seem so important when Rónán truly understood what was at stake.

'This sharing thing,' Rónán asked. 'You're not going to tell anybody else what goes on in my head, are you? I mean ... at times ... it's a pretty messed up place.'

Darragh shook his head. 'You will know me as well as I know you, Rónán. I will trust you with the same sort of secrets with which you trust me.'

'So we'll be what? Telepaths?'

'Unfortunately, no. But we will have an understanding, a sympathy.'

'Will it hurt?'

'No.'

'Will I be a Druid after it's done?'

'You are a Druid now. But you'll have the knowledge of how to tap into your power,' Darragh told him. 'Competence comes with time and practice, I'm afraid.'

In the distance, an owl hooted, a plaintive cry that sent an unaccustomed shiver down Darragh's spine.

'Let's do it, then,' Rónán said, clapping his hands together and rubbing them, as if he still needed to convince himself. 'How do we do it?'

'Give me your hand,' Darragh told him.

Rónán didn't have to ask which one. He held up his tattooed palm. Darragh took a step closer and then placed his own tattooed palm against his brother's hand.

There was a moment of intense pain, like a bolt of lightning shooting between them, and then a whirlpool opened before them and the brothers plunged into darkness.

The only sound Darragh registered as he fell was the strange, plaintive hooting of a lone white owl that had come to perch on the battlements.

CHAPTER 47

When Ren recovered consciousness, it was to find Sorcha leaning over him. His head was pounding, filled with a chaotic collage of images and thoughts, many of which he was certain weren't his. He turned his head slightly and saw Ciarán helping Darragh into a sitting position. Brógán was standing behind Darragh, his back to them, as if searching the moonlit sky for something.

'I can't see it,' he was saying. 'It might be flying in the shadows.'

'Which almost guarantees it was *sídhe*,' Sorcha said. She stared intently at Ren. 'Are you all right?'

'Jeezus …' Ren groaned, turning his head to look at Darragh. 'I thought you said it wouldn't hurt?'

'You performed the *Comhroinn*, didn't you?' Ciarán asked Darragh. He didn't look happy about it.

'It had to be done, Ciarán,' his brother said, shaking his head as if to clear it. 'And the sooner the better. How long were we out?'

'Not long, as far as we can tell,' Sorcha said, taking Ren's hand and pulling him to his feet.

He staggered a little before gaining his balance. The tattoo on his palm still burned, but aside from that — and a head full of thoughts that weren't there before the *Comhroinn* — he felt okay.

'But long enough for the *Tuatha* to find you, that's for certain,' Brógán said.

'Find us? What is she talking about?' Ren asked his brother.

'There was an owl sitting on the battlements when we got up here,' Ciarán explained, as he helped Darragh to stand.

'And the *Tuatha* are shapeshifters,' Ren said, a little surprised he knew instantly what Ciarán meant. 'You fear it was one of them.'

'It took off as soon as it saw us,' Brógán added, scanning the horizon for any sign of it. 'It's still out there somewhere. We don't have much time.'

'Aye, it'll be reporting to Marcroy Tarth as soon as it is able,' Sorcha agreed. 'Can you stand on your own?'

Ren nodded. 'I think so. What do we do now?'

Darragh was silent for a moment, and then he looked at Ren. 'I keep my end of the deal.'

Ren nodded, needing no further explanation. 'We go back to my reality.'

Sorcha shook her head in disgust. 'You can't be serious, *Leath tiarna*.'

'That was our deal, Sorcha. Are you coming with us?'

'Whoa! That's a very bad idea, Darragh,' Ren said, trying to imagine Sorcha negotiating the intricacies of his world without running someone through. 'She doesn't speak the language for one thing. And neither do you, come to think of it.'

'I do now,' Darragh said, and Ren realised it was true. What he knew, Darragh knew. 'I can imprint Sorcha with your English language before we go. What about you, Ciarán, are you coming with us?'

'You're not suggesting you go with him, are you, Darragh?' the warrior asked in alarm.

Ren realised the *Comhroinn* had backfired on Darragh. His brother had been certain that once they knew the same things, Ren would abandon the idea of going home. But Darragh now had Ren's memories, too, and suddenly the idea of Ren's realm entranced Darragh. But as the other half of the Undivided, although he could open rifts at will, Darragh was forbidden to travel to another realm, for fear of being trapped there. This was likely to be his only chance to see another realm. Once he made his appearance at the *Lughnasadh* festival with Rónán by his side, there would be no hope of either of them ever being free. Darragh had only one chance, and Ren didn't intend to let it go to waste.

'He'll be fine,' Ren said. 'For the next couple of weeks, if he's gone from *Sí an Bhrú*, nobody will question it. They'll put his absence down to his desire to ready himself for the Council of Druids and the power transfer.'

'It would take both of them out of Marcroy's reach until *Lughnasadh*,' Sorcha said, surprising Ren with her support. Was she anxious to see another realm, or just anxious to do anything that might foil the plans of the *Daoine sídhe* envoy? 'And I will see they come to no harm.'

Darragh suddenly grinned. 'Come with us, Ciarán. You open rifts for others all the time. Take the chance to be a rift runner, just this once.'

The big warrior shook his head, not so much disagreeing with Ren's assessment of the danger, or with Sorcha's offer to protect them, but more expressing his objection to the entire enterprise. Ren realised he knew Ciarán much better now, with the benefit of knowing his brother's mind.

'If you insist on this insanity,' Ciarán said, 'I'll need to stay here to open the rift so you can return, *Leath tiarna*. Believe me, I would be of no use to you in the realm Brógán and Niamh described.'

'You'll need Amergin's jewel,' Ren said. He had a feeling he was stating the blindingly obvious to the Druids but the information was all so new to him, he felt the need to give it voice, just to be certain he understood the knowledge he'd suddenly acquired.

He glanced at Darragh, wondering how he was coping. Ren suddenly knew much more about the world Darragh lived in. He wondered how Darragh was dealing with the knowledge that filled Ren's head, such as the PIN to the security gates at home or the easiest way to defeat an orc in *World of Warcraft*.

Darragh gave him a wan smile. It told Ren a great deal. Ren, at least, had the advantage of a rudimentary grasp of history. Darragh's world was foreign to him, but not completely unfamiliar. The reverse could not be said for his brother. The unfamiliar images crowding Darragh's mind were probably, for the most part, incomprehensible. It didn't surprise him that Darragh suddenly felt the need to see Ren's realm. Without some sort of context for the memories he now owned, he might go mad.

'You do need his jewel to open the rift, right?'

Ciarán nodded. 'You understand that now?'

Ren closed his eyes for a moment, as if to sort the chaos in his head. Then he opened them and nodded. 'The jewels are engraved with symbols the Druids and the *Tuatha* can use to open rifts to other realities. Is that right?'

'Near enough,' the older man agreed, and then glanced up at the moon with a frown. 'Do you have the jewel?'

Darragh nodded. 'We need to get moving.'

'You want to do this *now*?' Ren asked. He had expected they'd try to stall him some more, but Darragh seemed anxious to act on his decision before he changed his mind.

'If that was a *sídhe* spying for Marcroy, then Marcroy may be on his way here already,' Sorcha said. 'I agree. I think this idea is insane, but if we're going to do it, we need to do it tonight.'

'So ... how come you don't do it all the time?' Ren asked as Ciarán started to herd them down the worn stone steps to the *Ráith*'s courtyard.

Darragh was just ahead of him. He glanced back over his shoulder. 'What do you mean?'

'Look,' he said and waved at the yard, which smelled of dung, wood smoke and cooked cabbage. Sorcha grabbed his arm, and indicated he should pull up the hood of his cloak before they went any further. They'd been here for some time, but nobody had been allowed to see his face, even though Sorcha and Brógán assured him the people of Drombeg were completely trustworthy. He lowered his voice. 'You can jump across realities for fun. Why are you sitting here, living in stone huts and eating gruel? You could be out there jumping around the universe.'

Nobody answered him, which was to be expected, Ren supposed.

They waited for a moment in the shadows of the moonlit yard, while Ciarán went ahead to arrange for them to have the gate opened. This was something the occupants of the *Ráith* would not normally do after moonrise on the night of a full moon. It had been a full moon the night he arrived, Ren realised.

God ... I've been here nearly a month already ...

'We don't jump across realms for fun, Rónán,' Darragh explained softly, while they waited. 'We do it to find scarce resources, not the least of which are the jewels that make rift running possible.'

'What about the *sídhe*? Do they do it for fun?'

Sorcha answered him before Darragh could. 'The *Daoine sídhe* need magic to survive. They can open rifts but can only jump to realms where there is magic, otherwise they perish. Quickest way to kill one, actually, is to shove him through a rift into a realm with no magic.'

'But Trása was walking around my reality like she owned the place,' Ren said. 'And she had that wretched *Leipreachán* with her.' Ren looked sharply at Darragh. At the mention of Trása's name, he felt something from his brother and it felt suspiciously like anguish. He wasn't sure why his brother would have that reaction. He thought it was odd, given he was now supposed to know everything his brother knew. When Ren quickly scanned Darragh's memories for thoughts of lovers, it wasn't Trása who appeared, but a drop-dead gorgeous brunette named Brydie. Maybe

Darragh had locked some memories away so they couldn't be accessed, or put them out of mind to protect himself from pain.

For the first time, Ren really noticed the vague but constant link between himself and Darragh. He could sense his brother's presence and was aware of his emotions. It was a bizarre feeling and Ren wasn't sure he liked it. He wished he could spend a bit more time searching his brother's memories.

'Trása's a halfblood,' Sorcha explained in a low voice, unaware of Ren and Darragh's inner turmoil. 'She's human enough to survive in a magicless world.'

'And we don't have time to stand around here discussing it, either,' Darragh pointed out, in a fairly unsubtle attempt to change the subject. 'We have a few hours of darkness left. I'd like to make the jump before sunrise. Look, they're opening the gate. Keep your face in the shadows,' he added to Ren. 'It's bad enough they know I'm here. We don't want to give the good people of Drombeg anything else to talk about.'

Ciarán signalled them and they ran toward the gate, Ren with his face shadowed by the deep cowl he wore. Once they were through, Ciarán thanked the gatekeeper and they turned for the open road. Drombeg's stone circle was about half a mile from the *ráith*. It would only take a few minutes to get there, but they would be in the open and under the scrutiny of Marcroy's shape-shifting spies the whole time.

Sorcha led them down the road at a run. Ren hoisted the rough cloak up to allow himself a longer stride, and drew level with his twin, who was running like he trained for this, three or four times a week.

'I was thinking,' Ren said, panting a little as he ran, 'when we get to my reality ... it would be useful ... if we open the rift in a circle that'll bring us as close as possible to home.'

'And where is home?' Sorcha asked, as she ran with an easy, ground-eating pace that seemed to take no effort at all.

'Dublin,' Ren told them, not so much for Darragh's benefit — he already knew it — but for Sorcha's.

'Where is that?' the warrior asked.

'*Eblana*,' Brógán told her, panting even more heavily than Ren. Perhaps all those months in Ren's reality had softened him. 'And Rónán ... has a good point. You'll need to get ... as close as possible ... to the city.'

'Aren't you coming with us?'

Brógán shook his head. 'You don't need me to show you the way around your own realm, Rónán.'

'The owl's back!' Ciarán warned from behind them.

They picked up speed, although Ren thought five humans on foot had little chance of escaping a bird in flight. And there was no proof this owl was a *Daoine sídhe* spy, just a suspicion. It wasn't as if owls didn't fly at night.

Ren heard the bird hooting. He began to think the others might be right. He didn't think owls hooted so insistently on the wing. They hunted without making a sound. No hunting bird was going to betray its approach with a shriek.

The creature screeched at them again. Ren was certain it was hooting *at* them. The white owl flew

424

in low over their heads as they ran and then circled and came back for another run, like a fighter plane making a strafing pass.

The circle was only a few hundred yards away. Ren's thighs burned as they scrambled up the slope. Darragh was already reaching inside his shirt for the engraved jewel that would allow them to open a rift to another world.

'If it's a *sídhe*, why isn't it going back to report to Marcroy?' Sorcha shouted. She beat at the swooping creature with her sword just as they entered the stone circle. Darragh tossed the ruby to Ciarán who ran to the stone platform in the centre, jumped onto it and closed his eyes, the jewel grasped firmly in his fist.

The Druid warrior held his fist toward the sky. Ren felt the magic surging around them, felt the rift opening even though he couldn't see it yet, and then the circle filled with red lightning, arcing between the symbols carved into the standing stones. The owl came around for another swoop as the rift opened. The hair on Ren's body stood upright. Ren found himself staring at a vast expanse of greenery on the other side of the rift, through an opening bordered in red lightning.

'Go!' Ciarán yelled at him.

Ren was about to jump, when he remembered that Sorcha couldn't speak modern English. In his reality she'd be lost and probably dangerous, as well. Once they were through the rift, the magic would be gone.

He turned to Darragh who was right on his heels. 'Sorcha!'

With the link they now shared, no further explanation was necessary. Darragh grabbed the warrior by the arm, swung her around to face him and slapped her forehead with his tattooed palm, holding it there for a few seconds, until she collapsed in his arms.

'She'll be fine,' he shouted at Ren. 'Go!'

Ren did as his brother ordered and jumped through the rift, and right behind him came Darragh with the unconscious Sorcha in his arms — who hopefully now spoke English. Darragh shouted the all clear to Ciarán who gave them a short wave and lowered his hand. The lightning-touched edges of the rift began to shrink. In the distance, the owl screeched as if in fury at being left behind.

Ren could see the bird diving for another pass. The rift closed, growing smaller and smaller as the spell collapsed. Brógán was standing in front of the rift on the other side. Ren held his breath, waiting for the owl to disappear.

At the last moment, when the rift was almost gone, the owl burst through.

He ducked instinctively then looked up, half expecting it would come back for another attack. But the sky was empty. The owl was gone. Vanished, as if it had never been there.

Ren wondered if that meant the creature was magical and had perished in this reality where no magic existed. Then he heard a groan behind him.

On the ground a few feet away, rolling to a stop on the grass in the ruins of a stone circle, was a naked girl with long, wavy, blonde hair.

She scrambled to her feet, checking for injuries caused by her rough landing, and then turned to stare at them.

'Jesus Christ,' Ren said, shaking his head in disbelief.

Darragh lowered the unconscious Sorcha to the ground. He studied their unexpected companion for a moment, and turned to his brother.

'If I'm not mistaken, Rónán,' he said, 'this is not the first time you've met Trása.'

CHAPTER 48

Hayley hated sitting in her armchair by the window, like a little old lady in a retirement home. They moved her there each morning when it came time to change the bed. She'd sit in the chair as the sun streamed through her east-facing window, listening to her Discman, trying to lose herself in the occasional audio-book and songs that all too often went on and on about losing someone, breaking up with boyfriends and other generally depressing topics that did nothing to elevate her mood.

Sometimes it was better to just concentrate on the music and not think too hard about the lyrics.

Hayley had no escape into music this morning unfortunately. The batteries in her Discman were flat. Neil had promised to bring new ones in when he came to visit, but that wouldn't be until later this afternoon, after school was out. In the distance, she could hear the nurses making their morning rounds, talking in that chirpy, professional way they had about them, checking meds, changing bandages and asking stupid questions like 'how are we today?' to which most patients invariably replied 'fine' which was nonsense. If they were fine, they wouldn't still be in hospital.

Hayley turned her face to the window. The sun did take the chill off the air-conditioning, but no sounds leaked in from the outside world. The double-glazed windows saw to that. She remained cocooned in a world made of hospital noises and the bandages that still encased her eyes.

Soaking up the caress of the warm rays, she sat still for a time with the sun on her face as she imagined being outside. She tried to picture what it looked like, storing the memories away against a future that would include no new visual images to add to her mental archive.

Nobody had said it aloud, but Hayley knew. She was going to be blind. Forever. They just hadn't figured out how to break it to her yet. Hayley was hoping they'd leave it for a while longer. She wasn't sure how she was supposed to react; didn't know what to say. She didn't even know if she was angry or just heartbroken over the things she'd never get to do, never get to see …

And she wasn't sure she believed it, anyway. Her eyes were fine, according to the doctors. She was suffering, the doctors had tried to explain to her, from cortical blindness. Her eyes received sensory information just fine, but her brain couldn't process it correctly, so although she had vision, she couldn't *see*.

The damage in her brain was to part of the visual cortex, Hayley now understood, thanks to the well-meaning specialists who'd been poking and prodding and scanning her brain these past few weeks, and who seemed to delight in bombarding her with eight-syllable words. The damage to Hayley's visual cortex was impressive they told her, as if she'd achieved something clever. Bilateral.

In layman's terms — she couldn't see a damned thing.

It was awkward every time the family gathered in her room with the doctors for an update. Hayley was always afraid somebody would say something final; afraid they'd make some horrid absolute announcement that would make her blindness real.

Right now, she was in hospital with bandages over her eyes. That meant that there was still a possibility that one day she *wouldn't* be in hospital and when the bandages came off, everything would be fine. Nothing was permanent, yet. Nothing was carved in stone.

It was strange, suffering from blindsight, which is what one of the nurses called it. Hayley could see nothing, but she was knew what was happening about her. She could turn in the direction of sounds, discriminate simple shapes and she could shape her hands in a way appropriate to grasping the object she couldn't see. She could almost tell one colour from another and her pupils reacted to light, like any normal, sighted person. That was what made it so frustrating. If she'd lost her eyes, or if they'd been damaged beyond repair, it might be a little easier to accept her blindness. This diagnosis of 'your eyes are fine, they're just not talking to your brain' was much harder to deal with.

Murray Symes had been to visit once, offering his apologies and the name of a colleague for her parents to contact, once she was out of hospital.

Hayley was going to need counselling, he told them softly, assuming she couldn't hear his guilt-ridden voice. She wondered if he was going to foot the bill for all this first-class treatment. Kiva had taken care of her medical expenses so far. Hayley knew that because her father had told her about it, impressed the actress would do something so generous. Strictly speaking, Hayley wasn't family. She was five when her divorced father, Patrick Boyle, married Kerry Kavanaugh, and although she knew no other mother, Kerry was only Hayley's stepmother. That meant Kiva was her step-cousin a couple of times removed and under no obligation, when it got down to it, to do anything for her chauffeur's daughter.

Murray Symes should bear some of the cost, Hayley thought, with a flare of anger that always seemed to accompany any thought of the psychiatrist.

He was, after all, the one who had run her down.

The accident and its aftermath remained a complete mystery to Hayley. She remembered seeing Ren across the road with that blonde girl. The next thing she knew, she was waking up in hospital. Everything that had happened in the intervening time was a blank — a hole punched in her memory that had left nothing but a big black fissure in its wake.

The doctors told her it was unlikely she would ever remember what had happened that day. *The mind has a way of blocking things like that out*, they said. And not seeing things too, apparently.

The gap in her memory annoyed Hayley. She had a better recollection of the weird dreams she had experienced while she was in the coma than she did of that pivotal moment in her life. She hadn't shared her dreams with anyone, however, because a lot of them involved Ren — or a somewhat romanticised version of him with longer hair and a more muscular physique. Besides, these days, Ren's name was only something one uttered around Kiva if one wanted to trigger a fit of weeping.

Ren was still missing. Once they'd finally let her have the remote control for the TV, Hayley was able to find that out for herself. The story was no longer front-page news, but it still rated a mention now and then. There were occasional sightings of young men who looked like him, but they had all come to nothing. Ren had vanished into thin air. He'd not used a credit card in a month, not used his name, not been seen anywhere since he'd stepped into a lift at the city watch-house with a man and woman wearing suits. They also remained unidentified.

Kiva feared the worst. She was egged on by her publicist, Emma Pimms, who was convinced Ren had deliberately fallen foul of the law to disrupt Kiva's chances at next year's Oscars. The cynical publicist fully expected Ren to resurface any day, probably stoned and naked, in front of every paparazzo he could find. She was already writing 'damage control' press releases, apparently, for every imaginable contingency from Ren being kidnapped by drug lords, up to and including him turning up dead.

Kerry and Patrick, who probably knew Ren better than his own mother, were quietly worried for him. Like the Gardaí, nobody had any idea who the man and the woman in the grainy surveillance recording were. And Ren seemed to go with them willingly, according to her father, who the police had shown the recording to, in the hope Kiva's chauffeur might have seen the couple before. Patrick knew no more than anybody else did, but he shared what he knew with Hayley. He didn't think keeping information about Ren secret served any useful purpose, even if Kiva and Kerry did.

Hayley couldn't watch the recording, which frustrated her. She was Ren's best friend and if there was any chance the man and the woman — who'd somehow knocked out every cop in the watch-house — were people Ren knew, then Hayley was quite certain she'd have seen them before, too.

Hayley heard footsteps in the corridor. Someone wearing heels. She turned toward the door, bracing herself. It was the only thing to do when Kiva and her entourage came to visit.

Hayley listened carefully for a moment, judging how far away her visitor was. She pushed herself up out of the armchair.

Four steps to the bed. Three to the foot of it. Five to the bathroom by the door. If she could make it there and lock the door before her visitors arrived, maybe they'd go away. She was in no mood for Kiva, mostly because she didn't know what to say to her. She didn't know where Ren was and there was nothing she could say to his mother that might ease her mind.

Reaching her hand out in front of her, Hayley stepped to the bed, felt the soft weave of the hospital bedspread. In the distance, the clack-clack of high heels on hospital-grade linoleum warned her she didn't have much time. Kiva didn't visit her that often now that Hayley was off the critical list. Since Ren's disappearance, Kiva preferred to stay in the house, rather than face the inevitable barrage of the paparazzi.

Hayley took the five steps to the bathroom and was almost inside when the door opened and Kiva stepped into the room. She wasn't alone. Emma Pimms was with her, and so was someone else.

'Hayley, pet! What are you doing? Should you be out of bed?'

'I'm not crippled, Kiva,' Hayley pointed out with a sigh. There would be no hiding in the bathroom now. She turned to the publicist. 'Hi, Emma. Nice outfit.'

There was a moment of tense silence before Emma laughed nervously. 'Oh ... you're just pretending you can see me. I get it. Very funny.' Then she stopped laughing and asked, in a concerned voice, 'How did you know it was me?'

Because I can smell your horrid perfume from the car park, Hayley was tempted to reply, but thought better of it. Let Emma think she'd traded her sight for a sixth sense. It made Hayley seem more mysterious, and it unsettled Emma. Hayley was bored in hospital and unsettling Emma Pimms seemed as entertaining as anything else on offer. 'Who's your friend?'

'God,' she heard Emma mutter softly to Kiva. 'It's creepy the way she does that.'

Hayley bit back a smile.

'We've brought Gavin to see you, darling,' Kiva said, taking her by the hand and leading her the five short steps back to the bed.

'Hey, Hayley,' a male voice called out. Presumably, that was Gavin.

'Who's Gavin?' she asked, sitting on the edge of the bed. There was no escaping this visit now. All she could do was pray it would be a short one.

'Gavin's a photographer, dear,' Kiva explained. 'He's doing a feature on you for *OK! Magazine*.'

'No,' Hayley corrected, 'he's doing a feature on *you*, Kiva. Nobody gives a rat's arse about me.'

There was another moment's awkward silence, and then the actress sighed. 'Thing is, we don't have much choice, sweetie. This business with Ren has done us no end of harm. Emma says we need some positive publicity.'

'*We?*'

'You're family, Hayley,' Kiva said, hugging her warmly. 'What affects one, affects us all.'

'Do Mum and Dad know you're planning to exploit me like this?' Hayley asked cheerfully.

'Oh, now, that's not —' Kiva was cut off by her phone ringing. She answered it and then said to Hayley, 'I'm sorry, sweetie, I have to take this. I'll be back in a minute.' The promise was followed by the clack of heels on linoleum and the door closing as Kiva left the room.

'You ungrateful little bitch.'

'*Excuse* me?'

Hayley felt Emma plant herself, hands on hips, in front of her. She couldn't see her hands, of course, but she could tell that's where they were, just by her tone of voice.

'Do you have any idea how much Kiva has done for you?'

'I'm sure you're about to tell me,' Hayley said. She didn't like Emma. Never had. Hayley was pretty sure this woman was the one who had wanted Ren sent off to Utah.

Well, she had her wish. Ren was gone. And now, here she was, trying to use Hayley like a movie prop for good publicity, just as she always had with Ren.

'Kiva has done *everything* for you,' Emma told her in a low voice full of restrained anger. 'You've had the best medical care money can buy, you're being moved to the best rehabilitation facility in the country —'

'Whoa!' Hayley cut in. 'I'm *what*?'

'You're being moved,' Emma told her impatiently. 'That's why we have to get the shot today. By tomorrow, according to your father, you'll be too preoccupied with living-skills classes, or whatever they call them, for Gavin to do the shoot. And we can't do it any other time because Kiva is leaving soon for the States. She's booked to appear on *Oprah* next week. We need to give her something other than that missing fugitive kid of hers to talk about.'

Gripping the edge of the mattress, Hayley didn't really hear the last bit. All she heard was that she was being moved. Released from hospital. Finally.

But she wasn't going home. The thought panicked her.

'Why am I being sent to a rehab facility?' she managed in a surprisingly steady voice. 'I don't have a drug problem.'

'It's not that sort of rehab,' Emma snapped. 'It's some place in the city where they work with disabled kids. You'll be fine. There'll be plenty of other cute little blind kids there for you to bond with. In the meantime, we need a shot of you and Kiva together.

You don't need to do anything except look pathetic and a little bit grateful to her. The bandages say it all, really. After that, we'll leave you alone and you can go back to listening to "Lady Marmalade", or whatever it is you've got in that thing,' she added with — presumably — a wave in the general direction of the Discman.

Hayley wasn't listening. *Don't send me to a place for blind kids!* she was screaming inside. *I'm not blind! My eyes are fine. I've just got to wait until my brain heals and can work out what it's seeing. I don't need to learn how to cope with a disability! I don't have one! I'm going to get better!*

She felt the tears welling up in her eyes, and was grateful for the bandages. She didn't want Emma to see her crying. She wanted to scream, to sob uncontrollably. She'd known they were going to tell her she was blind, but she'd wanted someone to hold her while they said it. She wanted her father to reassure her and tell her it was only a temporary thing ... that it would be all right. That the blindness would go away. She cracked her skull, that's all. Once it was mended ...

'Fine,' she said tightly, forcing back her tears. There would be no getting rid of Emma or Gavin and Kiva until this was done and, more than anything at this moment, Hayley wanted to be alone. She wanted to weep. She wanted to feel sorry for herself, even for a short while, because later, when Patrick and Neil and Kerry came to visit and break the news that when she left here, she wasn't going home, she'd have to pretend she was taking it on the chin.

She wanted her father to be proud of her and her little brother not to worry too much.

'Get Kiva in here and let's do this. I'm tired. I want to go back to bed.'

'Good girl,' Emma said brightly, as if nothing was amiss. 'I'll fetch Kiva. Gavin, can you check the light in here? It's all wrong. You may have to pull the blind down a bit. That sunlight is far too harsh for Kiva at this hour of the morning.' Hayley heard Emma heading for the door as she rattled off her orders, the faint squeak of the hinges as it opened and the publicist calling Kiva back into the room.

I'm not blind, Hayley repeated to herself like a mantra, in the hope of keeping her tears at bay long enough to suffer through a photo shoot. *I don't need to learn how to cope with a disability. I don't have one.*

CHAPTER 49

Jamaspa managed to break out of *Sí an Bhrú* late one night a couple of weeks after Marcroy left, escaping the confines of Brydie's brooch while she lay sleeping alone in Darragh the Undivided's bed, pretending he was with her.

She'd done it twice now, the djinni had spluttered furiously, when he finally caught up with Marcroy in *Tír Na nÓg*, waking him as he slept in his tree house. Marcroy emerged, wrapping a spider-silk cloak around his shoulder to find the djinni standing on the bough, hands on his hips, turning dark blue with fury. A month ago Darragh had slipped in and out of his room unseen, the djinni ranted, and that shameless hussy Álmhath had thrown into his bed was covering for him, by pretending he was still there.

It took a bit to calm Jamaspa down. More than a few curious *sídhe* poked their heads through the branches of their trees to see what all the fuss was about. Marcroy shooed them away, hoping the ruckus would not disturb Orlagh. The last thing he needed was the queen wanting to know why a djinni was disturbing the peace of her kingdom.

Once he'd convinced Jamaspa to calm down, he had time to ponder the intelligence the djinni brought. The news about Darragh puzzled Marcroy for a number of reasons. The first was why the girl Álmhath had planted in *Sí an Bhrú* to spy for her was now actively aiding Darragh. The second was to wonder what Darragh was doing, when he disappeared from his room in the dead of night. And the last, and most bothersome, question was *how* Darragh was doing it.

Marcroy was afraid he knew, and that meant the Brethren's fears about the danger of these Undivided twins were well founded. They may have even underestimated them.

'What else did you learn?' Marcroy asked the djinni.

Jamaspa had taken an almost solid form. He paced up and down the long bough outside Marcroy's tree house. 'I learned I can learn nothing when I'm being smothered,' the djinni complained, wringing his blue hands. 'The human girl sleeping with Darragh is an untidy creature. She never hangs anything. She would toss her cloak to the floor — and me with it — as soon as Darragh looked at her sideways ... the shameless slut ... leaving me buried under mounds of fabric. More often than not, I heard only the sounds they made as they rutted like creatures of the forest — and even then, I'm not sure how often they were genuine cries of pleasure, and how often it was simply the woman pretending he was still in the room when he was long gone.'

'But how was he getting out of the bedchamber?' Marcroy asked. 'Every rodent in *Sí an Bhrú* belongs to me. Nobody reported him leaving. And they were watching for it.'

'He must be able to transport himself,' Jamaspa concluded. 'Like a *sídhe*.'

The idea that a human had acquired such a skill was too horrible to contemplate. Marcroy felt like wringing his hands, too. 'It's not possible. *Only* the *sídhe* have that ability. Darragh is human.'

'Are you *sure* there's no Faerie blood in the Undivided line?' Jamaspa asked. His pacing was making the leaves quiver. 'That would explain a lot.'

Marcroy shook his head. 'We'd have seen physical signs of it before now. The vertical pupils, pointed ears, pointed teeth … There's never been a hint of it. No. The boys are human. The line is human. For that matter, it's not even a line. RónánDarragh share no familial ties with LonHarrian. Their mother was a Gaul. And the new twins come from another line with no discernible link to Sybille.'

'We must find Darragh,' Jamaspa announced. 'Find out where he is and how he's been getting there.'

'Of course,' Marcroy agreed, wondering if there was a way to send Jamaspa back to *Sí an Bhrú*. Or anywhere else, really. Back to Persia would suit Marcroy best. Trása — still trapped in her owl form — had brought him news, finally, of Rónán's location. He was at Ciarán's home *Ráith* at Drombeg. That was undoubtedly where Darragh had gone.

It had taken Trása a couple of weeks to track down Rónán. If he'd thought about it, Marcroy should have looked there himself, but it was such an obvious place for the warrior to seek sanctuary that Marcroy had dismissed the notion as ridiculous. Having since learned that was exactly where Ciarán had taken Rónán to hide, he was unable to decide if it meant Ciarán was a brilliant tactician or the greatest fool that ever lived.

Either way, the ruse had worked. The last place they expected Ciarán to take Rónán proved to be the last place they looked.

He couldn't tell Jamaspa that, however, without confessing to his greater failure — the Undivided were now both in this realm, and if he didn't find a way to remove one or the other of them, come *Lughnasadh*, there would be no transfer of power to the less dangerous heirs they'd discovered. RónánDarragh would step forth to take their place as the reunited Undivided and every fearful consequence of that arrangement would come to pass.

'Is it worth questioning the girl?' Marcroy asked, thinking that would be a way to distract Jamaspa.

The djinni's eyes lit up. 'That would mean revealing myself to her.'

'Then perhaps you should,' Marcroy said. It would be easy to blame the djinni for anything that went wrong, should the humans discover there was a djinni among them. 'If you returned to *Sí an Bhrú*, you could trap Brydie in the brooch with you before Darragh returns. Then you could interrogate her at your leisure and nobody would be any the wiser. Darragh would simply assume she'd left of her own accord, and when you're done with her, you could simply glamour away her memory of the interlude.'

Jamaspa stopped pacing. Almost as soon as he did, the lower half of his body faded into a wisp of blue smoke, and his upper body swelled significantly, a sure sign he was no longer worried about what to do. Marcroy smiled. The Djinn, for all their power, were simple creatures when it got down to it.

'You are clever, Marcroy Tarth,' Jamaspa said. 'I will do as you suggest. The girl will tell me what we need to know.'

'Then you should return immediately to *Sí an Bhrú*,' Marcroy advised. 'So you can capture her before the Druids awaken and discover a djinni in their midst.'

The djinni vanished in a puff of blue smoke without saying goodbye. Marcroy breathed a sigh of relief and turned to look out over the magnificent trees of *Tír Na nÓg* without really seeing them. 'Plunkett!' he called.

The *Leipreachán* appeared at his feet almost immediately.

'My lord?'

'Where did Trása go?'

'She left for Drombeg already, *tiarna*.'

'Then we should follow,' Marcroy announced, shedding his spider-silk cloak so he could change form. 'We need to rid ourselves of the Undivided problem, Plunkett, before that wretched djinni returns.'

CHAPTER 50

Trása's rough landing hurt. A lot. She'd not expected to change back into human form in mid-air. She wasn't even sure what had made her dive through the closing rift. In her own realm, she'd been trying to warn Darragh that Marcroy knew about his brother. Her anger at being trapped in bird form these past weeks had all but smothered any lingering loyalty she might have had for the *Tuatha Dé Danann*. Marcroy had betrayed her and she was quite happy to betray him in return. She would warn the Undivided Marcroy knew Rónán had returned.

It was not, she told herself, as she staggered to her feet to confront the Undivided twins, in any way connected to the fact that in her own reality, only one of these young men could free her from the curse put upon her by her uncle.

Rónán hurriedly removed his cloak and offered it to her, as if embarrassed by her nakedness. She snatched it from him to cover herself, refusing to look Darragh in the eye. Rónán she could bear to look at, finding him much less intimidating than her childhood friend.

'The owl,' Darragh said, staring at her. 'It was you.'

'Why didn't you just land on the road outside Drombeg and tell us it was you?' Rónán asked.

Sorcha groaned softly. Trása wasn't pleased she had come through the rift with the Undivided. Sorcha might be a great warrior in her own realm, but in this one she would cause nothing but trouble.

'I couldn't,' she said, pulling the cloak around her tightly. 'Marcroy cursed me when he discovered Rónán was back. What did you do to Sorcha? Is she going to be all right?'

'I imprinted her with the language of this realm,' Darragh said. 'But I had to do it in a hurry. I'm afraid I wasn't very gentle.'

'You shouldn't have brought her here, Darragh,' Trása said. 'She'll never be able to cope with this world.'

'Why don't you let me worry about that?' Darragh replied in a frosty tone that caused even Rónán to look at him strangely.

'Why would Marcroy curse you for my return?' Rónán asked. 'What has it got to do with you?'

Trása didn't respond, not sure how to answer without making both Darragh and Rónán angry.

'Because her job in this realm was to see you didn't return,' Darragh concluded with a frown when she didn't answer. 'That's why you were in gaol. She thought it would contain you in this realm and you wouldn't be able to escape to get home. She didn't realise Brógán and Niamh had also found you.'

Rónán stared at her in shock. 'You set me up?'

Trása remained silent, unable to deny the charge.

'You nasty little bitch! You killed an innocent man! And they were going to charge *me* with his murder!'

'Technically, it was Plunkett who set you up, Rónán, not me,' she told him, daring the faintest hint of a smile. It was wasted on him. Rónán was furious.

'You killed someone!' he repeated.

'It was Plunkett who —'

'That's just playing with words,' Rónán cut in, angrier than she'd ever seen him. Angry in the way Darragh could get angry. 'You killed some poor homeless guy, just so I could never find my way back to your reality? You really are a piece of work, aren't you?'

He turned away, squatting down to check on Sorcha, who seemed to be slowly coming around. Trása wasn't sure if Rónán cared about the warrior or was just looking for an excuse to not engage in any further conversation.

Darragh relinquished Sorcha's care to his brother and stood up to confront Trása. 'If Marcroy cursed you,' he asked, clearly not believing a word she'd said, 'why are you now in human form?'

Trása shrugged. She'd been wondering the same thing. 'I guess there isn't enough magic in this realm to sustain the curse. Why are you here?'

Rónán glanced up from taking Sorcha's pulse. 'Does that mean the curse is broken, or will she turn back into an owl as soon as we get back to the other reality?'

'She'll turn back,' Darragh said. 'Curses like that are not easily undone.'

'This one is,' Trása said, determined not to let this moment pass. She needed Darragh — or Rónán, although that seemed unlikely at the moment — to rescue her, once they got home. 'This curse can easily be undone by one of the Undivided.'

'You expect us to *help* you?' Rónán asked, looking at her with a complete lack of compassion. Sorcha was struggling to sit up, still groaning. She probably had a headache from Darragh's hasty *Comhroinn*. Rónán helped her up, steadying her with his arm.

'That's what friends do, Rónán,' Trása said.

'Really? And here I was thinking they just murdered random strangers so their *friends* could do twenty-five to life.'

'Shall I dispose of her for you, *Leath tiarna*?' Sorcha asked, as she gained her feet, her hand already on her sword hilt. 'It will be my pleasure. Believe me.'

'No!' Rónán exclaimed, slapping her hand away from the weapon. 'We won't be killing anybody. There's been enough of that already.'

'Rónán is right,' Darragh said. 'In this realm, it would be unwise to use a blade to resolve a dispute. Even less wise to carry it, *Mháistreás*.'

'Darragh has a point,' Trása said. Her safety in this group — and any chance she had of returning home and being restored to her true form — lay with allying herself with the Undivided, not making enemies of them. And she had a lot of fences to mend. It seemed unlikely that she could re-establish her familiar relationship with Darragh, or her new friendship with Rónán. Not while the brothers blamed her for doing things like framing one of them for murder.

But she had been to this realm before. She'd spent the better part of the last six months here.

Darragh and Sorcha needed her simply in order to survive.

And then it occurred to Trása that she had no idea *why* they were here.

She glanced around, wondering where they were exactly. Ciarán obviously hadn't sent them to the same circle in Drombeg from where they'd left. There were no cities near Drombeg, even in this realm. They'd landed in another stone circle, but this one appeared to be hidden in the rough on a golf course. She could see a moonlit sand bunker surrounded by perfect lawn just beyond the tree line.

Beyond the golf course lay a sea of lights. Trása wondered which city it was and then she turned to the others and treated them to her best smile. It was time to act like one of the gang. Hopefully, if she did, they'd treat her like one. 'Does anybody have any idea where we are?'

'Ciarán was trying to send us to *Eblana*,' Darragh said stiffly, not responding to her cheerful manner. He turned to Rónán, apparently not trusting Trása's opinion. 'Did he succeed?'

'Hard to tell,' Rónán said, turning to stare out over the city. 'From here, it could be any city in the world.'

'Not any city,' Trása said. 'Only a city built in a place where Druids have been in the past.'

Rónán looked confused. 'How do you figure that?'

'Look around you,' she said. They were standing in the middle of an ancient stone circle. It was all but hidden in the undergrowth, weathered down to a few small stones worn almost smooth by the passage of time and a few thousand years of neglect.

'I guess that means we're somewhere in Eire,' Darragh agreed, glancing around.

'Or England,' Rónán added, frowning. 'Or Wales, or Scotland. Or France. Or Germany. Or any one of a hundred other places in Europe you can find ruins like this.'

'I think you vastly overestimate Ciarán's powers if you think we're not still in Eire,' Sorcha suggested. 'Let's assume he threw us through to the nearest circle to *Eblana* he could connect with in this realm. What do we do first?'

Rónán glanced around at their group, his eyes lingering longest on Trása. 'Find a phone,' he said. 'And you're going to have to ditch the weapons, Sorcha.'

Sorcha bristled at the very suggestion. 'I don't think so.'

'The *Leath tiarna* speaks wisely, *Mháistreás*,' Trása assured her, in as respectful a tone as she could manage, reasoning if she could get Sorcha on side, she might have some hope of softening the twins' anger toward her. 'In this realm, your current mode of dress — and your weaponry — will get you arrested, which would draw unnecessary attention to our group.'

'And we don't want that,' Rónán added, in a voice laden with irony, 'because thanks to our *friend* here, some of us are wanted for murder.'

'They probably want you for escaping, too,' Trása reminded him, which might not have been a wise move, given the glare he treated her to. 'We really must do whatever we can to avoid the authorities in this realm.'

Darragh seemed to find that amusing. 'And to think, Ciarán told me your life in this world had been uninteresting and dull, brother,' he said, grinning at Rónán.

'It was,' Rónán said, glaring at Trása. 'Until she showed up.'

'So why *did* we come back here?' Trása asked. Why would Rónán and Darragh risk so much to come here? It wasn't just the problems confronting them here in this realm they had to deal with. The fallout when they returned to their own realm and the Druids learned that the Undivided had been rift running, would dwarf anything the authorities in this reality could dish out.

'We came back to help Hayley,' Rónán told her. 'Did you have anything to do with her accident?'

'It wasn't me,' Trása repeated, truthfully enough. It was Plunkett, after all, who'd made the car go faster, and she hadn't known about it until afterward so, strictly speaking, she was innocent of that charge. 'But how can you help her? You can't heal her here. The magic won't work.'

'If she needs our help, we'll take her back with us,' Sorcha explained. 'A task that could be accomplished much more easily, *Leath tiarnas*, if you would allow me to remove the problem of this mongrel halfblood *Beansídhe*, so we can get on with the job.'

'Tempting as that is, Sorcha,' Rónán said, his gaze fixing unsympathetically on Trása, 'we have more important things to worry about.' He turned to Darragh. 'Before we do anything, we're going to need transport, a phone, and probably money.'

'What about our clothing?' Darragh asked. 'We're not going to blend in anywhere in this realm dressed as we are.' He glanced at Trása and added, 'Or *not* dressed, as the case may be.'

Rónán glanced at them and frowned. 'Yeah ... that could be a problem.' He thought for a moment and then said, 'Okay, if anybody asks, we're on our way home from a fancy dress party.'

'A what?' Sorcha asked.

'Fancy dress. It's a cliché, I know, but it should work. You're Xena, the Warrior Princess. You're a Jedi, Darragh, and you,' he said, turning to Trása, 'can be ... Lady Godiva. Just keep the cloak closed. I'm pretty sure we don't want to put your costume to the test. I'll be ... your escort.'

'I've been here before, you know,' Trása reminded Rónán, tugging the cloak tighter. She was a little concerned with the way he was taking charge. She was the one who needed to be needed. If she wasn't, they might abandon her in this realm. Right now, that seemed a fearfully real possibility. Neither Darragh nor Rónán seemed keen for her company and Sorcha was cheerfully frank about wanting to kill her.

'Yeah, I remember you being here before,' Rónán said as he turned and headed down the small slope toward the green. 'That's how come I came to be the lead story on *Garda Patrol*.'

CHAPTER 51

Although he knew things about this realm, thanks to the *Comhroinn*, Darragh discovered that knowing and understanding were two entirely different things. When Rónán said they needed a phone, he immediately knew what a phone was and where they might find one, but the how and why completely eluded him. He would know a phone if he saw one, but was quite certain he would have no hope of using it successfully, despite what he'd learned from his brother.

He hurried after the others across the perfectly manicured lawn of the golf course, amazed at the lush perfection of the fairways. Once again, he knew they were on a golf course, understood that this flawless swathe of lawn was a part of the game, but why anybody might want to indulge in such a pastime remained a mystery.

Once they left the shelter of the tress, Darragh realised what else unsettled him about this place. There was no magic. He could feel its lack. It was as if the air was missing some indefinable quality to which he was so attuned that he didn't notice it until it was gone. The air in this world smelt different too. Darragh wasn't sure, however, if the strange smell was because the world lacked any usable magic or if it had something to do with the technological progress that destroyed it.

He wasn't sure what time it was. In his realm, it was near midnight when they dived through the rift with Trása in pursuit. He glanced sideways at her, trying to decide how he felt about her presence here. He'd missed her terribly, after they sent her away from *Sí an Bhrú*, and he'd never truly believed she'd callously tried to seduce him in order to make him void the Treaty of *Tír Na nÓg*. But even her own father hadn't been certain that wasn't something Marcroy hadn't coaxed her into doing, even unwittingly. So Amergin had sent Trása away. It confirmed what everybody knew about him. Amergin had been a loyal and trustworthy Vate, willing to sacrifice even his own family in order to protect the Undivided.

It wasn't until his deathbed confession about his part in the plan to separate the Undivided twins that the true depth of Amergin's betrayal was revealed. His sacrifice in sending Trása away — in light of his confession — had seemed less like heroism and more like a craven attempt to cover up his own treason. It also made Trása a suspect. Darragh had grown up with Trása thinking of her as a trusted friend, and the only child of an equally trusted friend. She proved to be the daughter of a heinous traitor and, now, if he believed Rónán — and he had no reason not to, with access to his brother's memories confirming every detail — Trása had compounded her crime by trying to trap Rónán in this realm by framing him for murder.

And yet, Darragh realised he still missed her. Feeling his gaze upon her, she turned to glance

453

at him. He quickly looked away. Despite her treachery, despite everything he knew she'd done, Darragh was secretly thrilled to be back in her company, even if they were enemies. He couldn't trust Trása, he knew that, but the knowledge meant she couldn't betray him again unless he allowed her to.

That thought set him thinking about Brydie. Another complication he didn't want or need at the moment, albeit a delightfully distracting one. She was back at *Sí an Bhrú* even now, waiting for him to return.

As Darragh pondered the complicated mess his life was becoming, they walked through the moonlight across the golf course, groped by the chill fingers of a brisk westerly. By the time they reached the last tree-filled border to confront a huge white two-storey building lit by artificial lights, the moon was almost set. Darragh hurried to catch up with Rónán.

'I know this place,' Rónán said. He stopped and pointed to the building, surrounded by a large car park.

'Ciarán sent us to *Eblana*?' Darragh asked, glancing over his shoulder to ensure the others were keeping up.

'Get used to calling it Dublin,' Rónán advised. 'And speak English. The language you guys speak won't get you far at all in this reality.'

'Okay, let us speak English,' Darragh said, trying it out, the words feeling odd as they formed on his tongue. Just as he knew what a phone, a golf course and a car park were, he knew English from his *Comhroinn* with Rónán. But the intricacies of the language that came only with speaking it every day, were things he would have to pick up on his own. 'Where are we?'

'The Castle Golf Club, I think.'

'Is that the castle?' Sorcha asked, staring at the clubhouse. As soon as Rónán had named the place, the memory burbled to the forefront of Darragh's mind. This was not a castle, but a meeting place for an exclusive club whose members liked to play the game of golf. The windows were brightly lit in some places, others were dark, but it was obvious there were people about, even though none could be seen from where the group stood among the trees on the other side of the car park.

'You competed in a tournament here,' Darragh said to Rónán.

Sorcha was impressed. 'You joust, *Leath tiarna*?'

Rónán smiled. 'Not that sort of tournament. It was a school thing. We had a choice of extracurricular sports. Golf got me out of the rowing squad.'

'Why did you not want to row?' Trása asked, placing herself beside Rónán, as if to put as much space as possible between herself and Darragh. 'It seems a far more useful skill than golf.'

'Well, for a start, rowers have to get up at the crack of dawn to train,' Rónán said. 'I wonder what time it is.'

'After midnight, I would think,' Darragh suggested, glancing up at the moon.

'What day is it, do you suppose?' Rónán asked. 'It was August, 2001 when I left. I wonder if it's a Saturday or a Sunday.'

'Does it matter?' Darragh asked, pleased to realise he knew what days of the week were called here.

'Kinda,' Rónán said thoughtfully. 'If it was the weekend, I'd expect to see more cars in the car park.'

'What's a car?' Sorcha asked.

'A … um … horseless carriage,' Rónán told her. 'Like that.'

He pointed to one of the vehicles in the car park. They sat there squat, cold, and unimpressive, although Darragh knew they could be fast and rather dangerous, based on Rónán's impression of them.

'Will one of these horseless carriages solve our transportation problem?' Sorcha asked.

'Sure. Right up until we get arrested for stealing it,' Rónán said.

'I'll get us a car,' Trása volunteered.

'How?'

She pointed to the clubhouse in the distance. The faintest strains of music wafted to them on the gusty breeze. 'From him.'

The clubhouse door was opening as she spoke, and a man stumbled out. He wore a tweed jacket and knee-length pants with matching chequered socks and was wending his way rather unsteadily in their direction. Over his shoulder, he carried a large golf bag full of clubs with covers shaped like small furry animals. He seemed more than a little intoxicated, struggling to maintain his stability with the clubs, which were throwing him off balance. He fiddled with something as he walked. Then he dropped it and stooped to pick it up. The clubs slid out of his bag and spilled out onto the ground.

Rónán looked at her askance. 'You're just going to walk up to that guy and ask for his car, I suppose?'

'Watch me,' she said, dropping Rónán's cloak.

'Oh, my God,' Rónán muttered, as Trása left them standing in the rough and made her way across the car park, naked as a newborn. The drunk was still trying to stuff his golf clubs back into the bag. 'What is she doing?'

From the shadow of the tree line, they watched Trása stop in front of the man, watched her bend down to help him gather up his clubs. The man's gaze was glued to the naked young woman who had come so unexpectedly to his assistance. She spoke to him for a few moments and he handed her something. Trása turned to face them, holding up a set of keys and jiggling them with a broad, and rather self-satisfied, grin.

'A naked Faerie just approached him,' Sorcha remarked disapprovingly. 'If she's not fulfilling all his wildest fantasies, I'll warrant she's giving him a few new ones.'

Rónán muttered a curse and hurried after Trása.

Darragh glanced at Sorcha. 'Well? Shall we?'

'This won't end happily,' Sorcha predicted, her hand flexing on the hilt of her sheathed sword. 'Not for any of us. You really do need to let me kill her, Darragh.'

'No killing, *Mháistreás*,' he ordered. 'At least not until we get home. Then we will deal with Trása Ni'Amergin, and her bastard uncle Marcroy Tarth in the appropriate manner.'

Sorcha frowned, but nodded in agreement and picked up the cloak Trása had discarded. 'It is about time somebody did something about that treacherous *sídhe*,' she said.

'And we will,' Darragh assured her.

'How?' she asked.

'The only way you can do something to discipline one of the *Daoine sídhe*,' he told her as they walked across the bitumen. 'By reporting him to the queen of the *Tuatha* and letting her deal with him.'

'This is Warren,' Trása announced, as they piled into the man's car. 'His wife's away, visiting her mother in Limerick. He said we can stay at his place.'

Warren was a man of early middle age, Darragh guessed, with an impressive combover, a paunch and the bleary eyes of a man who drank too much, too often. As Rónán loaded Warren's golf clubs into the boot of his car for him, Warren scowled at them with alarm, and turned to Trása.

'You shaid a *few* friends ...'

'Oh, I have many more friends than this,' she told him cheerily. 'Trust me, this is only a few of them.'

'Put this on,' Sorcha ordered, thrusting the cloak at Trása. She pulled the cloak over her shoulders, much to the disappointment of Warren, and then opened the front passenger door for him.

Darragh opened the back door. Sorcha eyed the car with a frown and then climbed into the back seat. Darragh piled in after her, followed by Trása, who had tossed the keys to Rónán.

It was tight in the back seat, pushed so close together, but there wasn't much choice. The front of the vehicle only allowed for two. They had to shuffle around a bit to fit, and Sorcha had to remove her sword but, finally, they were able to close the door, although that meant Darragh had Trása's body pressed against his in a very unsettling way.

Rónán turned his attention to the ignition and started the car. The engine roared to life. Sorcha let out a small squeal of fright. Then they moved off smoothly, Darragh trying to pretend he understood how this vehicle was propelled, reminding himself that despite seeming to be self-propelled, the vehicle was the result of technology and not magic.

'Where are we going?' Trása asked, as Rónán turned the car out of the car park and onto the main road. The other cars on the road had painfully bright lights and so did the road itself. Darragh stared out the window, entranced and appalled, all at once. The speed they were travelling was frightening, but not so bad if one kept one's gaze fixed forward. When he turned his head sideways and saw the rate at which the world was rushing past, Darragh felt quite nauseous.

'Good question,' Rónán said, and then turned to Warren. 'Where do you live, Warren?'

'Castleshide Drive,' Warren mumbled, craning to look at Trása in the back seat. 'I'll show you the way.'

'Do you live alone?'

The drunk nodded and then shook his head as if he'd changed his mind. 'Yesh ... no ... I mean ... the mishus ish vishiting her mother. Took the kidsh with her.' He fixed his gaze on Trása. 'Are you really a fairy prinshesh?'

'In the flesh,' she promised him with a smile. 'You can have your three wishes as soon as we get to your house.'

'You can't grant him three wishes!' Sorcha hissed at her in a low voice, leaning forward to see past Darragh. 'Only the Djinn can do that, and

459

even they couldn't grant wishes here because we're in the wrong realm for them to survive!'

'He doesn't know that,' Trása pointed out with a shrug.

Sorcha was appalled. 'I can't believe you told him you were a Faerie princess.'

'Well, I am. Sort of.'

Sorcha was the only one who seemed to have a problem with Trása's ruse. Even Darragh acknowledged it was clever. Thanks to Trása's shameless audacity, they had access to a vehicle, shelter, clothing, and probably a chance for Rónán to find Hayley without raising the alarm. Darragh had enough of Rónán's awareness to know that in this realm, it was very easy to be traced if one left a 'paper trail', whatever that might be.

If a little white lie was all it took to keep a middle-aged drunk happy and the rest of them safe until they could find Hayley Boyle and take her to a magical realm where she could be saved, then so be it.

CHAPTER 52

Warren's home proved to be an upmarket detached suburban house that backed onto the golf course. If Warren had been sober and in the mood for a bit of a hike, he could have walked home across the greens. As it was, Ren had to take a far more circuitous route, past Rathfarnham Castle, which sat at the western end of the golf course, then double back and turn east again, back toward the houses bordering the greens.

Ren parked in the driveway and glanced at Warren, who'd already started to nod off. He shook the man gently. 'Hey! Warren! Wake up! We're home!'

The man eventually stirred and stared at Ren myopically. 'Wha ... Who are you?'

'I'm one of the Faerie's friends, remember?'

Warren saw Trása in the back seat and smiled drowsily. 'Oh ... yeah ...'

'Your house keys are on here, yeah?' he asked, holding up the keys for the Audi and shaking them to get his attention.

'Mmmm ...'

'Do you have an alarm?'

'What?'

'Is your house alarmed?' Ren asked. One glance at the houses in this street, and Ren was certain it was the kind of neighbourhood where people installed alarms. If you could afford to live in a city like Dublin with a golf course in your back yard, you had things you wanted to protect. It would defeat the purpose of hiding out in Warren's house if the first thing they did was trip a silent alarm and have the security company around, banging on the door.

'Yeah.'

'What's the code?'

'Oh-four-oh-eight,' Warren said. 'It'sh my annivershary …' He glanced back at Trása with a smile. 'Wife shet the number sho I wouldn't forget.'

'Okay.' Ren turned to Darragh. He was the only one he trusted not to do something silly. Trása was not to be trusted. Despite the *Comhroinn*, Darragh was still trying to get his head around this realm, but Ren knew instinctively that he would do what he must to keep them safe. Sorcha would make an awesome bodyguard if he ever needed one, but when it came to the day-to-day practicalities of life in the twenty-first century, she was next to useless. 'Can you give Warren a hand to get inside?' Ren said to Darragh.

'Of course.'

'You girls,' he said to the others, 'follow me. Don't touch anything, don't do anything and don't talk to anyone. Got it?'

'I have been here before, you know,' Trása reminded him.

'We had that discussion already,' Ren replied sourly. 'It might help a bit if you stopped reminding me.'

He climbed out of the car and headed for the front door. The lights came on automatically as he approached. The front of the house was neat and well kept, mostly given over to a gravelled drive where two cars could comfortably park. The front door was wooden, with two glass panels inset into the wood and a brass deadlock. He studied the lock for a moment, found the most likely key on the ring, and inserted it, whispering a silent prayer that Warren's alarm system wouldn't be triggered by him opening the door. The key turned without resistance. He glanced up. The blue light mounted under the eaves would start flashing if he tripped the silent alarm. It remained off. He let out his breath and turned to the others who were gathered outside, Sorcha staring up at the automated lights with a suspicious glare. Trása and Darragh were supporting Warren between them, his arms slung over their shoulders.

'Gimme a minute to disarm the security system,' he whispered.

A few feet inside the hall, Ren found the alarm panel. He punched in the code and was relieved to see the red arming light turn to green. He motioned to the others and ordered Trása to lock the door and then led them inside, turning on the lights as he went.

'Trása, check all the blinds are down,' he ordered. She looked like she might object to his command, but nodded and headed back into the living room, to make sure nobody could see inside. Ren turned to Darragh. 'Can you get him upstairs? Find a bed for him and lie him down. He's on the verge of passing out as it is.'

463

Darragh did as he asked, leaving Ren alone with Sorcha. She was looking around the room, open-mouthed. They were in the kitchen-cum-breakfast room. The gleaming white cabinets and countertops, the shiny appliances and general cleanliness left her gaping.

Ren smiled. 'Welcome to my world.'

'This palace is … unbelievable.'

'I guess it must seem that way, but can you do me a favour?'

'What's that?'

He pulled out one of the stools by the breakfast counter and pointed to it. 'Sit here and don't touch anything.'

She nodded and did what he asked without complaint, which Ren found a little odd, but it was one less thing to worry about. Ren headed through the kitchen into the formal dining room, noting the flower arrangement on the table. Either they had a housekeeper or the wife and kids hadn't been away that long. Warren didn't seem the type to care about fresh flowers.

He walked into the living room pleased to find the blinds drawn. The sofas were comfy brown leather and covered with cushions, a fire laid out in the fireplace that was obviously gas-fired — the logs only for show. He walked on through to the hall and glanced up the stairs. Darragh was heading down.

'How's Warren?'

'Out before his head hit the pillow,' Darragh said. 'I don't envy him the hangover he's likely to have in the morning.'

'Or his surprise to discover that the naked Faerie he met in the car park of the golf club was

464

real,' Ren added. 'Speaking of our fairy princess, where is she?'

'She found a bedroom upstairs that had some clothes she thought might fit her,' his brother told him. 'I suggested she find something appropriate to wear.'

That seemed like a good idea. 'We should probably send Sorcha up to get changed too,' Ren said.

Darragh shook his head. 'Not unless you want bloodshed. Let Trása get dressed first, and then we'll send Sorcha up. We need to find something for us to wear, too.'

'We can check the cupboards,' Ren agreed, 'but I don't like our chances. Warren's shorter than us, and considerably wider. Maybe we can send Trása out in the morning to buy us something to wear that doesn't make us look like we've escaped from a comic book convention.'

Darragh frowned. 'Do you trust her to do that?'

'Do we have a choice?'

'I suppose not.'

'Okay, then,' Ren said, wishing his thoughts would clear for a moment so he could get his head around everything that had happened in the last couple of hours. It was hard to credit, standing in this suburban hallway, that a few hours earlier he'd been standing on the battlements of a fortress hundreds of miles — and an entire reality — away from here, having his brain magically slam-dunked by the twin brother he didn't even know he had until a few weeks ago. 'We should get some sleep. It's nearly three am and I don't know about you, but I'm exhausted. In the morning, we'll sort out clothes, and I'll find out where Hayley is.'

'Will she not be in the place you left her?' Darragh asked.

A terrible thought occurred to Ren. If Hayley was still in the ICU, and still in a coma, how was he going to get her to the nearest reality rift so he could have her magically healed in another reality, if she didn't survive the journey through?

The first thing Ren did on waking the following morning was take a shower. It felt so unbelievably good, he almost ran the hot water out, letting the grime and the confusion of the past few weeks wash away with the water.

The only sour note to the morning was that he'd dreamed the dream again. It wasn't as vivid as it used to be, but that might have been because Darragh was here with him. Or perhaps their recent actions had changed the possible future they both saw, and the dream was no longer relevant. Did that mean staying in the other realm would alter that future? If he only had the dream when he was in this reality, perhaps it was staying here that would make it come true.

He let the water cascade over him, trying to decide what would be better. Stay here and suffer nightmares for the rest of his life, or return with Darragh to an uncertain world where he might have some hope, perhaps, of controlling his fate?

Ren wasn't sure what day it was. In Darragh's reality, all the days seemed the same. Because of the moon, he knew he had been away for a month or so. By now, all his friends were back at school. Life would have gone on without him ...

It was a disconcerting thought.

Once he was out of the shower, Ren borrowed

Warren's razor, something far easier to use and far safer than the thin cut-throat razors on offer in Drombeg. He then went looking for some clothes and had a stroke of luck. Warren owned nothing likely to fit Ren or Darragh, but the 'kids' Warren referred to were obviously teenagers. The first bedroom door he opened was painted pink, filled with posters of Britney Spears, and an alarming number of stuffed animals. Darragh was stretched out across the frilly floral bedspread on his back, snoring softly.

The second bedroom revealed a shrine to all things heavy metal. There were posters of Megadeth on the wall over the bed, a Guns 'n' Roses towel draped over the window to cut out the light, and a Metallica poster on the other wall beside the built-in closet, and when he flipped the light switch, it proved to be wired up to a UV light over the dresser. Ren grinned and went to the closet. Sure enough, in addition to a number of school uniform shirts and a blazer bearing the crest of the nearby Terenure College, the wardrobe was full of blue jeans and black T-shirts.

He pulled out a pair of jeans and was relieved to find they were of a size that might fit him and Darragh if they wore a belt. When it came to shoes, he wasn't quite as fortunate, but he figured that wasn't such a big deal. Their boots from Darragh's reality would pass casual scrutiny, concealed under jeans.

Ren gathered up the clothes and walked back into the hall, wondering where the others were. Darragh was asleep in what was clearly the room of Warren's teenage daughter, Warren was passed out on the sofa in the upstairs study, which was where Darragh had left him last night. He assumed Sorcha and Trása had crashed in the lounge.

Ren headed down the stairs carrying the clothes. He heard the television. It wasn't coming from the lounge, but from a wall-mounted set in the kitchen. Trása was sitting cross-legged on the counter, dressed in black jeans and pink T-shirt proclaiming 'Boys are cute, every girl should own one' in glittery writing on the front. She was eating a bowl of fruit puffs, and was engrossed in what appeared to be a program on the E! Channel.

She ignored Ren until he picked up the remote and started flicking through the channels, looking for the news. That was the fastest way to work out what day it was.

'Hey! I was watching that!'

'I need to find out what day it is.'

'Thursday, 6 September 2001,' she told him, through a mouthful of fruit puffs. She snatched the remote and switched back to the E! Channel.

Ren decided not to argue about it. He headed for the fridge, hoping the absence of Warren's wife didn't mean the absence of anything edible. 'I don't know why you watch that crap,' he said, as he jerked the fridge door open.

'Don't knock it,' she said. 'It's how I found you. Where's Warren?'

'Still sleeping it off in the study upstairs. Have you seen Sorcha?'

'Last I saw of Sorcha, she was patrolling the grounds.'

'Shit,' Ren muttered, slamming the fridge shut. The last thing they needed was one of the neighbours spotting Xena the Warrior Princess in the yard, armed to the teeth, ready to fight off … well, whatever it was she thought she was protecting them against. 'Why did you let her go outside?'

'Interesting. You say that like I had any say in the matter.'

Ren looked out the kitchen window. He couldn't see Sorcha, but that just made it worse. She might be halfway across the golf course by now. 'I'd better go find her. Can you show Darragh how to put these on? How to work the zip,' he asked, pointing to the clothes he'd dropped on the counter beside her.

She nodded and kept eating her fruit puffs. He was at the back door before she stopped him. 'Rónán.'

He turned to look at her. 'What?'

'I'm sorry I got you into trouble,' Trása said, sounding genuinely contrite. 'I thought I was helping Marcroy.'

'You *were* helping Marcroy,' Ren said.

'I didn't mean for anyone to get hurt.'

He wished he could be certain her apology was real but she had framed him for murder. And thanks to the *Comhroinn*, he had enough of Darragh's lingering mistrust of her, to doubt Trása's sincerity. 'I'm sure the homeless guy you killed would be thrilled to know that, Trása.'

She sighed, as if his anger was exactly the response she expected. 'I won't let you down again, Rónán,' she promised. 'You or Darragh.'

'Damn right, you won't,' Ren said, as he jerked open the back door. ''Cause believe me, Trása, you won't get the opportunity.'

CHAPTER 53

The air in this realm was wrong.

Sorcha didn't feel the loss of magic. She had no magical ability to speak of, so she was no more handicapped here by her lack than she had been in her own realm. But the air smelled wrong, and because of it, she felt uneasy.

From her perch in the trees, she could see the back of the house, and plenty of other houses besides. They all seemed too big and too close together, a mishmash of styles that didn't look right. On her right, the golf course — whatever that was exactly — stretched out before her. Defensively, it was a nightmare. The large open swathes of clipped grass were broken up by lines of trees and undergrowth that might have some useful purpose, but offered too much cover for an advancing foe.

She heard a door opening and turned to survey the building. Rónán was coming out of the house, dressed — she presumed — in clothing appropriate to this world. He cut a much leaner figure than his brother, and lacked Darragh's athleticism, but that was something they could address once they got back home. A few months of training should fill him out and put some meat on his bones.

Rónán looked around, his expression worried.

He's looking for me, Sorcha realised.

'Psst!'

Rónán turned his head in the direction of her hiss. 'Sorcha?'

She grabbed the branch she was squatting on, tucked in her head and rolled forward until she was hanging by her arms a few feet off the ground, and then she dropped, landing on the soft lawn with bent knees. 'If you yell my name a little louder, *Leath tiarna*,' she remarked as she straightened, 'perhaps the people in the next village will know I'm here, too.'

Rónán regarded her for a moment. 'You do realise we're not in a village, don't you?' he asked. 'We're not even in what you would call a town. This is Dublin. There are a couple of million people living around here.'

'Well, that would account for why the magic is gone from this world,' she said. 'What happened in this realm to make *Eblana* the centre of the world?'

Rónán seemed puzzled by the question. 'The centre of the world? Dublin? You're kidding, right?'

Sorcha shook her head. 'Not at all. Why else would all these people gather here, if it were not the centre of learning and government for this realm?'

'You think Dublin's the largest city in this reality?' Apparently amused by her question, Rónán turned and headed back to the house, obviously expecting her to follow. With a final glance around to assure herself they were safe, she followed him to the porch. He opened the back door and stood back to let her enter.

'Isn't it?'

He shook his head. 'It's not even close. Do you suppose you could come inside and get changed? I don't want the neighbours ringing Warren to ask why Conan the Barbarian is patrolling his back garden.'

Sorcha gathered he was referring to her clothing. Maybe even her weapons. And the back garden was overlooked by the upstairs windows of several neighbouring houses. Although she'd been hidden from view in the tree, on the ground, she was vulnerable.

She wasn't happy about having to change, however. 'Are you going to make me wear clothes like the mongrel *sídhe* is now wearing?'

'You mean like Trása?' He shook his head. 'There should be some jeans in Warren's daughter's room that fit you, but if you're not a fan of pink sparkles, Warren Junior seems to be a metal-head. There should be something in his room with enough studs and chains to keep you happy ...' He paused, and then gave her an odd look. 'What?'

Sorcha shook her head. 'I am discovering, *Leath tiarna*, there is a great deal of difference between understanding your words and understanding their meaning.'

'Yeah, well —' His words were cut off by a panicked cry from the half-*Beansídhe* traitor who'd followed them through the rift.

'Rónán!' The call came from somewhere deep in the house. The *Beansídhe* was no longer in the kitchen.

'What?' Rónán called back. He shut the door behind Sorcha and locked it.

'You'd better come here!'

'Jesus Christ, what now?' Rónán muttered.

Sorcha followed him through the dining room — with its long table polished to a mirror shine and plush chairs fit for a council of kings — and into the front room. The *Beansídhe* was standing in the middle of the room. Next to her was Darragh, dressed in a similar fashion to Rónán. They were staring at a small box on one of the side tables by the far wall, which sat next to another small rectangular box resting in a cradle. There were blinking lights on both.

'Could we keep the yelling to a minimum?' Rónán said, as he stalked into the room. 'Warren's still asleep. What's wrong?'

'I heard the box talking,' Darragh said, pointing at the blinking red light.

'The answering machine?' Rónán walked to the oddly shaped silver box in question and started pressing buttons.

Sorcha sidled up to Darragh and asked, 'Why do they have machines here to answer questions?'

Before he could explain Rónán pressed another button and a woman's voice emerged from the box.

'*It's me,*' the voice said. '*Pick up the phone.*' There was a pause, and then an exasperated sigh. '*Okay then, I was just ringing to let you know we're on our way home. I've had a gutful of my mother. I can't do anything right, according to her. I'm a heartless monster, our kids are a lost cause and you're a hopeless loser. I swear, the next time I'll listen to you and just send the miserable old bitch a card and a bunch of flowers for her birthday.*' There was another sigh, and the woman added: *'We should be home around dinner time, so if you've been having wild parties while we were away, honey, you've got until then to clean up the mess.'* She chuckled and added, *'Although knowing you, you've probably eaten at the club every night since I left ... anyway, we'll see you later today. Don't forget to put the garbage out.'*

The woman's voice was replaced by a horrible beeping noise that Rónán shut off with the press of another button. Then he turned and looked at them. 'Anybody care to hazard a guess as what *later today* means?'

'If Warren's wife is in Limerick,' Sorcha pointed out, wondering why he looked so worried, 'then we have a day or more, surely? If this city is *Eblana* as you claim, then Limerick is more than a hundred and twenty miles from here and they have no ability to travel magically via the stone circles.'

'Yeah, but the magic of the internal combustion engine could have them here in a couple of hours if the traffic's with them,' Rónán said, looking very concerned. 'Shit! I was hoping we'd have more time.'

'More time for what?' Darragh asked. Trása flopped into one of the big armchairs, picked up a magazine from the table beside the chair and began flipping through the pages. It was enough to make Sorcha want to slap her. Trása shouldn't have been here, but now that she was, the least the mongrel *Beansídhe* could do was act as if she cared what was happening.

'I need time to find out Hayley's condition,' Rónán said. 'Time to figure out how we're going to get her from the hospital to wherever we need to

474

go, to get her back to your reality. Time to figure out where that is, by the way. Jesus! Just time!'

'Who the fuck are you lot?'

Warren was standing at the living room door, staring at them in shock. He was rumpled and unshaven, still dressed in his golf clothes from the night before, bleary-eyed and obviously confused. Sorcha, who was standing closest to him, summed up the situation in a heartbeat. They needed time, Rónán said. At worst, they had only two hours before Warren's family got home. Warren's appearance was robbing them of precious minutes.

Without a word, she stepped up behind the man, put her arm around his neck so her forearm was pressing against his Adam's apple, and then she pushed his head forward with her other hand, squeezing hard. Five seconds later, Warren slumped in her arms. She let him go and he dropped to the floor like a sack of potatoes.

'What the fuck!' Rónán exclaimed in shock. 'What did you do?'

'You said we needed time,' she reminded him, a little offended at his tone. 'He was wasting it.' Sorcha rolled her eyes. 'What were you expecting me to do? Give him a fighting chance by letting him land the first few blows?'

'But you knocked him out cold!'

'It's not that difficult, Rónán,' Darragh said. He too seemed a little puzzled by his brother's attitude. 'If the blood vessels that feed the brain are robbed of blood, it induces almost instant unconsciousness. You didn't want her to kill him, did you?'

'Enough!' Rónán exclaimed. 'Christ! What was I thinking bringing you lot back here?'

'Strictly speaking, *you* didn't bring them here,' Trása said, looking up from her brightly coloured magazine. 'They brought you. It was Ciarán who opened the rift.'

'Shut up,' Rónán snapped. He turned to Darragh. 'Can you check if Warren's okay?' he asked, pointing to the unconscious man. 'We'll need to lay him out somewhere until he comes around. And make sure you put him on his side. We don't want him suffocating on his own tongue. We have enough problems as it is.'

'What about me?' Sorcha asked as Darragh manhandled their host into the hall. 'Do you have any orders for *me*, *Leath tiarna*?' Her tone left Rónán in no doubt about what she thought of his orders, but he ignored it, and took her question at face value.

'Yes, I do. Get out of those clothes and into something that isn't going to get us arrested the moment you step out of the house. And stop hitting people.'

'Yes, Sorcha, do as the *Leath tiarna* says,' Trása added cheerily. 'Stop hitting people.'

Rónán turned on the *Beansídhe*, no more appreciative of her interjection than Sorcha was. 'Will you shut *up*?'

'I could render the halfling unconscious just as easily as I did the man,' Sorcha offered, fairly certain that Rónán wanted to kill the mongrel *sídhe* even more than she did.

'Don't tempt me,' Rónán muttered, glaring at Trása.

'Pity,' the *sídhe* said. 'Because then you'd never learn what I know about Hayley.'

'You don't know anything about Hayley.'

476

'I do,' Trása said. 'And if you promise on your brother's life to release me from my curse as soon as we get back to our reality, I'll tell you what it is.'

Sorcha took a step closer, her hand on the hilt of her sword. 'Please, *Leath tiarna*, let me kill her. It will make things easier for us all.'

Rónán held up his hand to forestall her and studied Trása for a moment. 'What do you know?'

'Promise me first.'

'Okay, I promise. What do you know about Hayley?'

'She's not in hospital any longer.'

Sorcha let out an exasperated sigh. 'Please, Rónán. Don't let her waste any more of our time. She can't possibly know that.'

'Sorcha has a point. How do you know where Hayley is?'

Trása tossed the glossy magazine to Rónán, who caught it in one hand. He looked at her.

'Page twelve,' Trása said, pulling a face at Sorcha before adding, '*Kiva's Mission of Mercy* is the headline. There's a lovely article in there about how she's paying all the bills for her chauffeur's daughter's treatment after her terrible accident caused by the paparazzi outside her house. There are even pictures of your mother and your little friend, who is alive and well, you'll be glad to know. Oh, except that apparently, she's blind.'

Rónán tore open the pages until he came to the story Trása was gloating over. He scanned it quickly, his expression hard to read. Sorcha glared at the halfling *sídhe* and wondered if Rónán might eventually forgive her if she ran the little bitch through right now, and rid him of her, once and for all.

Before she could act on the impulse, however, Darragh returned. 'What's the matter?' he asked.

Sorcha didn't know if it was the psychic link between the boys that warned him something was amiss, or simply the look on Rónán's face. She wasn't even sure if the link still worked, here in this realm without magic.

'Hayley's been moved,' Rónán told his brother, frowning.

'To where?'

Rónán shrugged. 'I dunno. I need to get on the net. Don't suppose any of you noticed if Warren had a computer in the study?' Sorcha assumed he wasn't including her in the question. She still didn't understand the answering machine. She wouldn't know a computer if it jumped up and bit her on the face.

'I know you don't mean fishing, brother,' Darragh said with a thin smile. 'But that's about all I'm sure of.'

'The internet,' Rónán explained. 'I need to find where they've taken Hayley.'

'And this ... internet ... will tell you where she is?' Sorcha asked.

'Not specifically,' Rónán said, folding the pages of the magazine back to show his brother. 'But how many *exclusive rehabilitation facilities for the blind* can there be in Dublin? She's gotta be in one of them.'

'And once you find her, how will we get there?' Darragh asked, studying the pictures in the magazine with interest.

'We drive,' Trása said with the confidence of someone who believed she had proven her worth. 'We'll take Warren's car.'

Rónán shook his head. 'We can't. Even if he doesn't report it as stolen, his wife will. And if it's fitted with a LoJack, they'll be onto us before we can blink.' His statement evoked nothing but blank expressions from the others, even Trása and Darragh. Rónán threw his hands up in exasperation. 'Just trust me on this. We need to find a way to stop Warren reporting his car stolen, or we find another car.'

'Why don't we just take him with us?' Sorcha asked. 'If Warren is not here and neither is his vehicle, will not his wife just assume the two are together? If we drop him off somewhere along the way ... somewhere it will be difficult for him to raise the alarm, that will give us time, will it not?'

'But how do we get him in the car?' Trása asked. 'You knocked him out.'

'He won't be unconscious for long,' said Sorcha.

Darragh and Rónán exchanged a glance as a world of unspoken communication passed between them.

'Fine,' Rónán said. 'We locate the rehab place where Hayley is staying, load Warren into the car and get the hell outta Dodge before his wife gets back. Best guess is we have about an hour and forty-five minutes to be gone from here.'

'Time enough for our warrior princess here to get changed into something more feminine,' Trása reminded them, with a smile designed to needle Sorcha.

'And I *will* need to change,' Sorcha agreed pleasantly, unsheathing her blade as she stepped toward the *sídhe*. 'These clothes are going to be covered in blood, shortly.'

'Hey!' Darragh and Rónán shouted in unison, stepping between Sorcha and Trása.

'Enough!' Darragh exclaimed. 'I won't stand for this! Trása, mind your tongue! Sorcha, remember who you are!'

It irked Sorcha to have Darragh reprimand her, but he was right. She was a Druid warrior. It was unbecoming to allow a halfling mongrel *Beansídhe* to incite her to rage. She was better than that.

And there would be plenty of time, later on, when they returned to their own realm, to deal with the problem of Trása Ni'Amergin.

CHAPTER 54

Ren drove carefully, acutely aware that time was not on his side. He scanned the road constantly for Gardaí cars, obeyed all the traffic rules so as not to draw attention, and wished he could think of somewhere safe to hole up while he found Hayley. Warren, still hungover and semi-conscious, was locked in the trunk of the car.

The article in *OK! Magazine* said that Hayley was blind. He tried to imagine what that must be like for her, but couldn't. Hayley was such an active, sporty person. She played soccer in winter, camogie in the off-season, skated, and danced. She could whip his arse in *World of Warcraft*. It seemed a cruel blow to rob her of her sight. He owed Hayley the chance to be whole again, if not in this reality, then certainly in Darragh's.

Ren felt a sudden wave of guilt. Darragh was going to be in serious trouble for coming to this realm, Ren realised that now. It was one thing to be thrown into another reality against one's will, as Ren had been. But it was quite another to do it deliberately, when the rules of Darragh's world were very clear about the consequences for the Undivided endangering the Treaty of *Tír Na nÓg* by leaving the world where he belonged to go adventuring. This was an ill-conceived idea at best, Ren knew, and he was sure — knowing what he did of his brother now thanks to the *Comhroinn* — that had Darragh thought this through, they would not be here. They would still be in Darragh's reality, toeing the line like good Druids.

He still didn't think of the other reality as home. This world of motorways and traffic lights and long hot showers was his home, and now he was back in it, Ren wasn't sure he should be considering leaving it behind.

But it was a decision he didn't have to make yet. First, he had to find Hayley.

'Do you think you can read English, or just speak it?' Ren asked his twin. The others were in the back seat.

Darragh turned from staring, open-mouthed in wonder, at the city. 'I see some things and they make sense. Others mean nothing to me. I suspect if the words are words you use a lot, then I'm more likely to understand them.'

'Cool. Can you look out for an internet cafe?'

'Internet cafe,' Darragh repeated, as if testing the words. 'That is a place with many computers, is it not? Where one can access the "net"?'

Ren smiled. 'You've got it, dude.'

Darragh returned his smile ruefully. 'I know what to look for, Rónán, but I really have no idea what a computer does.'

'Well, just so long as we find one. Warren's computer had passwords. We'd still be trying to get online if we'd stayed at his place. A cafe should have better speed. And it'll be harder to trace us.'

'Then I will try to find one for you,' Darragh promised. 'Even if you do sound as if you're speaking in tongues.'

'I know what an internet cafe is,' Trása announced from the back seat behind Darragh. 'If you let me sit up front, I could be looking for you.'

'Yeah … well you didn't call *shotgun*,' Ren told her.

She let that pass, perhaps because she didn't know what he meant, and turned to the others. 'Am I the only one who's hungry?'

'Can we risk stopping for food?' Darragh asked.

'So we're just going to starve, then?' said Trása.

'We need to keep moving,' Ren said.

'The *sídhe* has a point though,' Sorcha remarked, albeit a little reluctantly. 'We must eat.'

'And nobody really knows where we're going, if I'm not mistaken. Hence the need for an internet cafe.'

'We're not stopping,' Ren told them, slowing the car as the lights turned amber. Admittedly, other than cereal, there had been slim pickings in Warren's house. His wife's suspicion that he had eaten at the club every night was well founded. But they should have eaten something before they left the house.

'There's a McDonald's up the road with a drive-thru,' Trása pointed out.

'What are we going to use for money?'

She held up a black leather wallet and leaned forward to show it to Ren. 'Warren's paying.'

'Perhaps someone there will know where the nearest internet cafe is located,' Darragh suggested.

Ren glanced at his brother. 'What do you think?'

Darragh shrugged. 'I think this is your world, Rónán. Only you know if we can risk it.'

Ren glanced around. It was a Thursday morning and the traffic was heavy with commuters heading into the city. The traffic lights were about to change, which meant he had only seconds to decide if they were going to turn into the McDonald's car park. Then a loud thump from the trunk rocked the vehicle, followed by a muffled yell.

'Warren's awake,' Trása said, quite unnecessarily.

That decided him. As soon as the light turned green, Ren slammed his foot down, surging ahead of the traffic, and dived across three lanes to swerve into the McDonald's entrance. He swung the car sharply as he entered the parking lot. Rather than heading into the queue lined up at the drive-thru, he parked the car at the end of the lot, as far from the restaurant as possible.

He turned the engine off, and twisted in his seat to face the others. 'You two can go fetch us food. I don't care what it is, just pay cash for it, so whatever Warren has in his wallet, that's all you can afford.'

'What about you and Darragh?' Sorcha asked, not at all pleased to be sent off with Trása. She obviously considered it her job to protect the Undivided.

The car rocked with another thump and more muffled shouts.

'Darragh and I are going to have a chat with Warren.'

With some reluctance, Sorcha followed Trása to the restaurant. Ren watched them leave and then turned to his brother. 'Can you check the glove box?'

Darragh looked at him blankly. 'The what?'

'In here,' he explained, leaning across in front of his brother to open it. As Ren hoped it would be, the glove compartment was filled with the vehicle's logbooks and the general clutter that seemed to collect in every car, including, Ren was delighted to discover, an unopened roll of duct tape.

'Bingo,' he said, snatching up the tape and slapping the glove box shut. Another thump and shout came from the trunk. 'Time to explain the situation to our friend in the trunk, don't you think?'

'What are you going to do?'

'Shut him up, for starters,' said Ren, climbing out of the car.

He glanced around as they made their way to the rear of the car. Nobody seemed to be taking any notice of them. There were cars parked closer to the building, and a steady line in the drive-thru and, of course, the road was packed with the last of the morning's peak hour.

Ren grabbed Darragh and made him stand beside him facing the back of the car, which blocked the view of the car's trunk from the restaurant. 'Stay right there,' he told him.

'Why?'

'There might be security cameras.' He popped the trunk with the remote control, and quickly grabbed Warren by the throat as he tried to sit up, pushing him back down as hard as he could. 'Not a word!' he hissed. 'Or you're gonna regret it!'

Warren must have believed him. He went limp under Ren's choking grip, staring up at the twins with fear-filled eyes.

'That's better,' Ren said, relieved he hadn't had to back up his threat. He didn't have the faintest idea how to knock somebody out by squeezing their arteries, so he wasn't sure how he was supposed to make Warren regret anything. 'Here's the deal, Warren. We don't want to hurt you. We're not *going* to hurt you. We just need your car for a bit and then we'll let you go and you can call the cops and scream all about us to the high heavens, and we won't care because we'll be long gone.'

'I ... I ... won't say a thing ...' Warren stammered. 'You can let me go. Take the car ... it's insured ... just don't hurt me ... please ... I have a family.'

'I know you do,' Ren told him sympathetically. 'Unfortunately, I don't trust you not to run straight to the nearest phone if I let you go.'

'I give you my word ...'

'And you probably mean it. Right up until we drive off.' Ren tore a strip off the roll of tape long enough to cover Warren's mouth. 'Sorry, dude. We'll let you go when it's safe. For us. In the meantime, think of what a hero you're gonna be at the golf club when you're telling them all about this a couple of days from now. Shit, you'll dine out on this for years.'

He plastered Warren's mouth shut and then secured his hands and feet, taping them together enough to restrain him, but not enough to cut off the circulation. Another of the many tricks he'd picked up while getting under the feet of the stunt crew on one movie set or another. Once he was satisfied that Warren was contained for the time being, he closed the boot and glanced back at the restaurant. All seemed well. At least there was nobody standing in the window, pointing at them or yelling for help.

'Let's wait in the car,' he suggested, acutely aware that there might be cameras and that his face was among the most wanted in Europe. Darragh's face too, come to think of it.

I wonder what they'll think if a camera picks us up somewhere and they see two of us.

Darragh climbed into the front passenger seat of the car and slammed the door. He turned to his brother as Ren secured his seat-belt. He had no intention of being pulled over by the cops and getting himself arrested, over something as minor as a traffic infringement.

'This is a very strange realm, Rónán.'

Ren smiled. 'You know, I can remember thinking that when I woke up in your world.'

'I miss the magic. I feel lost without it.'

'Yeah, well, you can't miss what you've never known,' Ren pointed out, wondering if he would ever be able to discuss using magic and not have to stifle a grin at the absurdity of the notion. He glanced in the rear-view mirror, but there was still no sign of the girls. Warren was also silent, thankfully. 'You know, at some point, you and I are going to have to sit down while you explain a whole lot of shit to me, brother.'

'We have shared the *Comhroinn*, Rónán. You know what I know.'

'Yeah ... but it doesn't make sense to me. Just like you *know* what an internet cafe is now, but you've no idea why or how it works. I suddenly have all this knowledge in my head, but it doesn't have any context. I know how to open a rift. If I think of it, I really do. But that's not the same as being able to do it.'

'It will come with time, Rónán,' Darragh assured him.

'Which is something we don't have a lot of. Damn, I wish I knew where they'd taken Hayley.'

'If the pictures in the magazine are accurate, except for the blindness, she appears to be otherwise well.'

'Which is way easier than sneaking her out of an ICU, I'll grant you, but ...' Ren stopped and looked at Darragh curiously. 'Dude, how *are* we getting back?'

'To our realm? Ciarán will open a rift for us.'

'When?'

'As soon as I let him know we're ready.'

'You can contact him?'

'Not easily, but —' He stopped abruptly as he spied Trása and Sorcha hurrying across the car park, clutching several brown paper bags. Trása was balancing a tray of drinks. 'They're back.'

A moment later the girls piled into the car. Ren turned the key in the ignition and shifted the vehicle into reverse. He turned to look out the back window, but was stopped by Trása who handed him a cell phone.

He slammed his foot on the brake, evoking a muffled grunt from the trunk. 'Where did you get that?'

'The man in front of us left it on the counter.'

'You *stole* it?'

'Of course I stole it,' she said.

'Why?'

'You said we couldn't use Warren's cell phone last night because the Gardaí might be able to ... what did you call it? Triangle our position?'

'Triangulate,' he corrected.

'Well, they don't know who owns this phone, do they?' she said. 'You can use it to find Hayley.'

He appreciated the gesture, but it was pointless. He took the phone from her. 'Sure, Trása, I'll just ring Kerry ... or better yet, my mother, and ask her where Hayley is, shall I? There's a plan.'

'Not your mother, silly,' she said, rolling her eyes. 'Ring old Jack. He'll know where they've taken her. And if I'm not mistaken, he's unlikely to report your call to the Gardaí.'

Ren stared at her for a moment. 'You know ... that's actually a good idea.'

Trása leaned back in her seat and smiled at Sorcha. The car was filled with the smell of hot French fries and burgers, that made Ren faintly nauseous.

'Told you so,' she said.

'You still stole something in broad daylight,' Sorcha reminded her.

'Good point,' Ren said, taking his foot off the brake. 'So let's get out of here and find somewhere quiet to stop for a bit.' He reversed the car, straightened the wheel, and slipped it into drive. 'I have a call to make.'

CHAPTER 55

Jack O'Righin had an abiding mistrust of the law and anybody involved in keeping it. He was unilateral in his hatred of the judicial system. He didn't particularly care who was running the show, what their political or religious views were — he hated them all. So when young Ren Kavanaugh rang him and asked to meet, Jack didn't think twice about agreeing to help him, or not betraying his location. It would have been more out of character for him had he refused to help the boy.

He glanced in his rear-view mirror, but the road was clear. Jack remained unconvinced he was free of surveillance, so he turned away from the park he was headed toward, and took a route in the opposite direction. The blue Honda behind him turned as well.

Now, isn't that interesting. Are you following me or was that just a coincidence?

The fallout from Ren's arrest and disappearance was still settling, and Jack found himself caught up in it along with everyone else who knew the lad, much to the consternation of his publicist. There was a story that Jack's granddaughter had been mixed up in the alleged arson, the death of some old homeless bloke, and Ren's escape from gaol.

Jack had thought them all insane, and told everybody — including the media — that he'd had nothing to do with any of it. Anybody who'd so much as glanced at the dustcover of his book would know his wife and daughters died more than thirty years ago. He had no family. He had nobody. He certainly had no granddaughter and no idea who they were talking about when they accused him of being involved in the fiasco that had resulted in one dead homeless man, one missing teenager, one extremely pissed off drug lord and a smoking ruin that used to be a warehouse in downtown Dublin.

Jack turned right again, leaving the turn until the last minute. The Honda sailed past the intersection, the driver not so much as glancing in Jack's direction. He breathed a sigh of relief and turned right a second time, so he could resume his earlier course. He turned his thoughts back to his imaginary granddaughter.

Murray Symes claimed to have seen her. Even Hayley said Ren had been with a girl matching Murray's description of Jack's 'granddaughter' the day she was hit by his car in the mêlée outside Kiva Kavanaugh's house. Under interrogation, Ren had insisted that the girl was with him at the warehouse, the Gardaí told Jack. Ren had even asked his lawyer, Eunice Ravenel, to find out what had happened to the girl. Worse, there were photos of a slender blonde holding Ren's hand, taken by the paparazzi at the scene of the accident.

But even though everyone had grilled Jack relentlessly on his connection to the girl, he stared at her picture and drew a complete blank. He didn't know who she was or remember ever seeing her before.

There were other reasons he felt guilty about Ren's troubles; guilty enough that he thought he owed it to the lad to help him out. The day after Ren's arrest Jack had received a very angry call from one Paddy McGrath, an old cellmate from The Maze, who accused him of dumping him in all sorts of strife with the currently incarcerated — and very irate — Dominic O'Hara. Jack listened in stunned disbelief as Paddy ranted at him. He didn't know what the man was on about. Even Paddy's furious accusation that *'I told you about that deal in confidence and y'threw me in the shite!'* made no sense to the old man. What he was able to glean, however — besides the loss of Paddy's dubious friendship — was that Ren had received the information about Dominic O'Hara's warehouse drug deal from Jack.

Jack couldn't say how, and he couldn't imagine what had possessed him to involve a nice kid like Ren in anything so shady but, apparently, he'd been the lynchpin around which the ensuing trouble revolved.

The least he could do was help Ren get out of it.

He turned again, after glancing in the rearview mirror, and once he was satisfied the road was clear, turned toward the park where Ren had asked him to meet. He spied Ren across the empty lot, near a few scattered picnic tables, one of which was occupied by a few kids Ren's age, and an older man. The remains of a takeaway meal sat on the table in front of them. Ren was leaning on the trunk of a late-model silver Audi.

Ren waved. Jack drove diagonally across the parking lot's painted lines and pulled up beside the boy. The group sitting at the table watched him warily, and now he was closer, he could see the older man had his mouth taped shut.

'Jayzus H Christ!' he said, climbing stiffly out of his car. 'What the fuck have you gone and got yourself mixed up in, laddie?'

'Thanks for coming, Jack.'

'Don't thank me,' Jack warned. He stared at the man with the tape over his mouth. The man's hands and feet were taped, too. 'You adding kidnapping to your repertoire, now, you stupid git?'

'It was kinda unavoidable,' Ren said, a little defensively. 'We haven't hurt him.'

'No, but you've let him see you. All of you,' he added, turning to look at the other kids. One of them, the dark-haired woman with the dangerous look about her, he didn't know, but on closer inspection, she seemed to have a few years on her companions.

'Jayzus H Christ!' he muttered again. The pretty girl with the long blonde hair he recognised from the paparazzi photos as his alleged granddaughter, and the other lad ... Jack stared at him in disbelief. 'What the fuck ...?'

Ren smiled briefly. 'Funny. That's exactly what I said.'

Jack stared at Ren's twin, shaking his head. 'Who ... how ...?'

'It's not going to be easy to explain.'

'Aye,' Jack agreed, 'but if you want my help, Rennie, my boy, you're gonna have to give it one hellava good try.'

Jack listened to Ren's story, growing more and more incredulous by the minute. Except that sitting opposite him was the proof of Ren's wild tale. Not only was Trása there — he still didn't recall ever seeing her before — but sitting next to Ren was Ren's identical twin brother. Yet the crazy story Ren was peddling — involving Druids and alternate realities — seemed ludicrous, even after Ren and Darragh showed him identical tattoos on their palms, each on the opposite hand to that of his brother.

The mysterious wounds Ren suffered; the wounds Jack had observed himself — caused by Faerie silver, if you believed their tale — were the result of the psychic link across realities between the brothers. The whole story was insane, except that it answered so many questions about Ren, it actually made a strange sort of sense.

'Hold on a minute,' Jack said, trying to keep the story straight. He jerked his head in the direction of the man with the duct tape across his mouth. 'Who is this?'

'That's Warren,' Trása told him, smiling brightly.

'We found him in a car park at the Castle Golf Club,' Ren explained. 'We needed a car and didn't want him reporting the Audi stolen …'

'So you stole him instead?' Jack looked at the frazzled, terrified man. He looked like an accountant or something equally dull. 'I'll be bound you're wishing you'd stayed home from the club last night.' He turned to Darragh who was sitting closest to Warren. 'Take the tape off his mouth.'

Darragh glanced up at Ren, who nodded. He peeled the duct tape off and tossed it on the table next to the remains of their takeaway meal. Warren stared at Jack, as if trying to figure out how he knew him. Then he nodded as it came to him. 'I know you. You're that terrorist who wrote the book.'

'Yeah ... thought you might figure that out. Not very bright of you to admit, though. You'd be better off pretending you have no idea who I am. Given my history'n all.'

Warren shrank back from Jack.

Then Jack turned to Ren and the others. 'What are you going to do with him?'

'I was hoping you'd have a suggestion,' Ren said.

'We have to silence him,' Darragh said. Jack regarded Ren's brother silently. Reading the subtext of Darragh's words, if he needed proof that this boy had been raised a whole world away from Ren, it was in the matter-of-fact sort of tone with which Darragh pronounced a death sentence on this hapless accountant. Darragh may not come from another reality, Jack thought — still not sure he believed that part of their tale either — but he certainly didn't come from Ren's world of red carpets, personal trainers and private music lessons.

'Silence him how, exactly?' Ren asked.

'You know how,' the dark-haired, dangerous-looking woman said. 'We'll have to kill him.'

Warren stared at them all, one at a time, through bleary, disbelieving eyes. 'Kill me? Are you fucking kidding me? You're gonna *kill* me?'

'You don't have to kill him,' Jack said. He had a feeling both Darragh and the woman — Sorcha, she said her name was — were perfectly capable of carrying out the threat. He'd not seen that sort of pitilessness since he was a lad planning to blow up a bus in downtown Belfast. He recognised it for what it was now. At the time, when he was young and had a cause to die for, he'd mistaken such disregard for life as heroism. Now he knew better. It wasn't heroism, or loyalty to the cause. It was the inevitable result of growing up seeing too much injustice, death and violence and being numbed by it.

'If you let him go,' Darragh pointed out, 'he's going to tell everyone about us. Rónán says the Gardaí are looking for him.' He looked pointedly at Trása but she couldn't meet his gaze. 'We can't risk him being arrested. We have to get back to my realm.'

'I said I was sorry,' Trása mumbled.

'Let him tell anybody he wants,' Jack suggested. 'What's he going to say? "I was accosted by a naked fairy from an alternate reality who took me home, spent the night, and then shoved me in the boot of my car and drove me around Dublin for the morning?" I mean, that's all you've done with him, isn't it? You haven't robbed a bank, or tried to kill anybody, have you?'

'Not yet,' Sorcha said in a rather ominous tone.

'I can tell them about *you*,' Warren threatened, glaring at Jack.

'You're not helping your cause, mate,' Jack told him. He glanced at Ren, who was standing at the end of the picnic table with his arms folded, looking apprehensive. 'Don't worry about me, lad. I'm an old hand at this. My tracks are covered. As far as the rest of the world knows I'm having a massage, and the lass who's giving it to me will go to her grave insisting I was at the Happy Moon

496

Therapeutic Massage Parlour all morning. Warren can tell people he's met me. I'll deny it, and I've got witnesses who'll back me up.'

'The cops will know you're lying, O'Righin,' Warren said.

'Are you sure? I won't be the one telling the naked fairy story.'

Ren was still not convinced. 'I don't know ...'

'In my realm, he would be dead already,' Sorcha remarked.

'We're not in our realm,' Trása reminded her.

'Enough, already,' Ren snapped impatiently at the girl who claimed to be half-Faerie. Jack tried to recall her, tried to remember her in his house, but she remained a blank hole in his memory.

Ren turned to his brother. 'What do you think?'

'I think Sorcha is right. In our world, this would not be a discussion. But Trása is also right. This is not our world. You know better than I how to proceed.'

Jack decided he liked Darragh. The lad had a head on his shoulders, for all he had probably seen too much death and violence for one so young.

'Then we don't kill Warren,' Ren announced.

'What are you going to do with him?'

Ren grinned suddenly and glanced at his brother, who smiled too. Jack wasn't sure if it was because the boys really were psychically linked, or they'd just had the same thought at the same time. Turning to look at Warren, Ren smiled even wider. 'How do you feel about massages, Warren?'

The balding accountant looked at them blankly. '*What?*'

'A massage,' Ren said. 'That should keep you occupied for the next few hours.'

Warren turned to look at Jack. 'Is he serious?'

'I think so.'

'Then we have a happy ending,' Trása said brightly.

Jack shook his head. 'Only if I pay extra, lassie,' he said with a sigh. 'Ying Su's happy endings don't come cheap.'

CHAPTER 56

It took some time to get the truth out of Brógán, but Marcroy Tarth eventually learned what he needed to know. The news left him stunned and somewhat at a loss.

He knew the boys had entered a rift. What he hadn't known, until he'd tortured Ciarán to make Brógán talk, was that both Darragh and Rónán had jumped to another realm, the one where Rónán had grown up.

That was a mixed blessing for Marcroy. It solved his short-term problem about what to do with the Undivided, but it didn't do much to fix his longer term problem — how to explain to Jamaspa and the Brethren where Darragh had gone without admitting that Rónán had been found, and that the boys had been reunited — even in another reality. Not to mention his failure to stop it happening.

Brógán had not yet revealed the reason for Darragh's jump to the other realm to Marcroy. But he'd already betrayed the Undivided once. Marcroy was confident he could make the Druid healer do it again.

'Is he conscious yet?'

Plunkett poked at the bloodied body on the floor of the roundhouse with the toe of his boot.

'I think ye may have killed him.'

'No. I can feel the life in him,' Marcroy said. 'Throw some water on him.'

Plunkett muttered something under his breath that Marcroy didn't catch, but did as his master bid, waddling outside to find a bucket. Marcroy sighed and turned to Brógán, who was seated behind him, restrained by invisible magic bonds that caused him no physical harm, although one would never guess, given the tears streaming silently down his cheeks. The brindled light seeping through the rough twig walls made it hard to read his expression, but Marcroy didn't need to see Brógán's face to know the man was consumed by guilt, remorse and fear.

'For pity's sake, can you not let him be?' Brógán begged in a low, defeated voice that made Marcroy smile. It was the voice of abject surrender.

'Only you have the power to free him, *Liaig*,' Marcroy said, squatting down to look Brógán in the eye. 'If you wish to halt Ciarán's suffering, all you have to do is tell me why Darragh went back to the other realm with Rónán.' He reached forward and gently wiped a tear from the young man's cheek with his thumb. 'Ciarán would want you to. While he still has all his fingers.'

'May *Arawn* strike you down,' Brógán spat, in a bold attempt to appear uncowed. 'May the King of Hell consume you, may the God of *Annwn* feast on your liver. May the —'

'Yes, yes,' Marcroy cut in impatiently, rising to his feet. 'I get the idea. Although it's a bit late for a show of defiance, don't you think? You've already told me most of what I want to know. And while Ciarán was still conscious to hear your betrayal, what's more. I think that's not going to reflect well on you at the next Druid Council.'

'I will confess my betrayal to the Council myself,' Brógán announced. 'I will tell them how you captured us, how you tortured Ciarán to make me talk ...'

'You'll tell them how I captured you?' Marcroy laughed, genuinely amused. 'You'll sully the reputation of the fearsome Ciarán mac Connacht to save your own neck? How do you think that will go down in Council? What are you? A lowly healer? And you think they'll believe you when you tell them the mighty protector of the Undivided was tricked by a *Leipreachán*, a mouse and a handful of *Brionglóid Gorm*?'

Brógán averted his eyes, aware Marcroy spoke the truth.

The two Druids had made a fatal error in assuming that — once the rift had closed — Marcroy's spies were gone. But Marcroy was not nearly so complacent as they imagined. He didn't trust Trása any more than he trusted Plunkett.

Disguised as a wolf, running by night, sleeping by day, immersed in his animal form, Marcroy had arrived in time to see the lone white owl flying into the rift. He wasn't really surprised Trása had followed them. Once he'd told her only the Undivided could release her from his curse, he knew she'd not rest until she found them, looking for their help.

He hadn't expected her to jump through a rift after them. Nor was he sure what might have happened to her on the other side. She was trapped by a magical curse that couldn't be sustained in the other realm. There was a good chance, he'd realised as he changed back into mouse form, that she was dead.

That would be ... inconvenient. He'd had further plans for his mongrel *Beansídhe* niece.

Still, her dramatic flight through the closing rift had given Plunkett the opportunity to get close to Ciarán. It was not possible to glamour a Druid, but it was possible to knock them out cold with *Brionglóid Gorm*.

Marcroy had watched as Trása swooped and dived at the Undivided and their Druid escort, heading at a run for the stone circle. In his favoured wolf form, he had loped along beside the road, hidden in the shadows, curious as to what the Undivided were up to. He knew they were heading somewhere ... it had shocked him when Ciarán raised his red jewel and opened a rift to another realm, rather than a link to another stone circle in this realm.

He'd watched as first Rónán, and then Darragh carrying the unconscious Sorcha, dived through the rift, followed at the last minute by the owl that was his cursed niece. Marcroy had resumed his *sídhe* form while Ciarán and Brógán were still standing there wondering what the owl's disappearance into the rift meant.

That had been the time to strike.

'Plunkett!' he hissed.

The *Leipreachán* appeared, and dropped to his knees, bowing obsequiously. 'I be here, *tiarna*. As ye told me to be. Waiting for yer call.'

Marcroy was unconvinced by Plunkett's grovelling subservience, but it suited him to let the lesser *sídhe* think he was. He pointed toward the stone circle in the moonlight, where Ciarán and Brógán were. 'Go and tell Ciarán you have news for him. About the Undivided.'

Plunkett was puzzled. 'Are ye certain, *tiarna*? He hates me.'

'Then you'd better talk fast, so you can get the words out before he runs you through,' Marcroy told him unsympathetically. 'Did you bring what I asked?'

The disadvantage of travelling in wolf form meant Marcroy couldn't carry anything he couldn't hold in his mouth. Making the *Leipreachán* follow him was almost as convenient as having pockets. Plunkett nodded and reached into his own pocket, pulling out a handful of blue powder.

Marcroy nodded. 'When he grabs you by the throat, as I'm sure he will the moment you get within reach, blow it in his face. I'll take care of the other one. He's not armed.'

It had been as easy as that. All it had taken to capture the two Druids was Plunkett allowing himself to get close enough to Ciarán to be caught. Neither man had thought to check the *Leipreachán*'s pockets for *Brionglóid Gorm*. Or field mice.

Brógán was sweating, despite the chill in the air. 'When the Council sees what you've done to Ciarán ...'

'Sees what?' Marcroy asked, looking down at the unmoving warrior. *Where is that wretched* Leipreachán *with the water?* 'We'll heal him up and he'll be as good as new, as soon as we're finished here. Unless ...' He let the sentence hang, and turned to look at Brógán. 'Well, if he dies because you won't talk, the Druids will be able to draw their own conclusions when they see his body.'

'They'll know Ciarán was murdered.'

'How?'

'I'll make sure they know who is responsible.'

'You most certainly will not,' Marcroy told him, marvelling at the young Druid's naïveté. 'If Ciarán dies, my lad, you'll die with him. Or perhaps not,' he said, changing his mind as a better plan came to him. 'Perhaps I'll just send you to *Tír Na nÓg*. And let it be known among the Druids that you're enjoying the full delights of my magical homeland. I'll arrange for you to have your very own *Daoine sídhe* lover. Trása's mother is particularly fond of young Druids ...' He smiled sympathetically. 'The conclusion the Council will draw from that news will be that Ciarán was betrayed by one of his own. Good thing being trapped in *Tír Na nÓg* will mean a time shift for you, isn't it? Perhaps, by the time you convince somebody in my land to show you the way out, everyone in this land will have forgotten your treachery.'

Brógán shook his head. 'Nobody will believe a Druid would betray his own kind.'

'Ah, what delightfully short memories humans have. Has the name Amergin already faded from your thoughts?'

The young man looked away, unable to meet Marcroy's eye. 'Of course not.'

'So, the Council will believe you betrayed Ciarán.' He turned his back on the young man, adding, 'In fact, by now they're probably expecting it. Hardly surprising, I suppose, that the Undivided — the supposed pinnacle of Druid wisdom and prudence — have gone whoring around another realm for a bit of a lark.'

'They're not whoring around another realm!' Brógán objected before he could stop himself.

'Then enlighten me, young Brógán,' Marcroy said, still with his back to the bound Druid. 'What *are* they doing there, if not having a lark? Refining their magical skills? I doubt it, given they've jumped to a world without magic. Or perhaps they've gone there to fetch technology. Is that it? Are the Undivided now so corrupted by the one-half of them raised in a world filled with poisonous technology, that they have gone to that world to bring back the tools to destroy us?' Marcroy didn't really believe that, but as he was saying it, it occurred to him the argument would sound very compelling when he delivered it at the *Lughnasadh* Council.

In fact, with this foolish act, the Undivided had handed him the very weapon he needed to remove them. With the return of Rónán, his plan to remove them had seemed doomed, but now there was real hope.

Even if Darragh returned with Rónán in time for the *Lughnasadh*, all Marcroy had to do was reveal where they'd been. He was quite certain, in light of such news, the idea of transferring the power to the new heirs, even with the Undivided alive and well — and restored — would seem prudent, rather than premature.

Before Brógán could answer his question, however, the *Leipreachán* returned with a pitcher of water, which he unceremoniously tossed over Ciarán. The warrior groaned, but didn't regain consciousness as the water pooled on the dirt floor around his head.

Marcroy didn't mind. He could have healed the warrior and restored him completely. Even Brógán, had Marcroy left him unbound, had the power to undo all the damage done to Ciarán thus far. That was part of what made this method of extracting information so effective. It wasn't that Brógán *couldn't* stop what was happening to Ciarán. It was knowing he *could* ease the warrior's pain, heal his wounds, take away the hurt ... if only he were free.

Or if he betrayed the Undivided.

One option was in front of him, visibly suffering. The other in another reality with no guarantee — Marcroy had been at pains to point out — they might ever return.

It had never occurred to Marcroy to do the reverse — torture Brógán to make Ciarán talk. The warrior Druid would have stood there and watched him pull Brógán apart, limb from limb, and not offered so much as a comment on the weather, if that comment meant betraying the Undivided.

Having observed Ciarán's fanatical devotion to the boys since they were babies, Marcroy often wondered if it was Ciarán himself who'd fathered them. It wasn't an unreasonable assumption. The boys were conceived during a Druid festival, after all, in which both the warrior and their mother would have taken part. Even Marcroy had been there, tasting the pleasures of human flesh, masked and anonymous as any Druid. If Ciarán wasn't their father, he might well believe he was, which would have the same effect and could account for his loyalty to them. Whatever the reason, Marcroy knew there was no point trying to torture Ciarán.

'Ye may have to wake him up the hard way,' Plunkett remarked, frowning at the lack of response his pitcher of water had evoked from the Druid warrior.

'Perhaps you should nip outside and see if the sun has fallen from the sky and been replaced by a pudding,' Marcroy said.

'Eh?' Plunkett responded with a puzzled look.

'That's probably the only circumstance under which I'm likely to take the advice of lesser *sídhe*, Plunkett. I just thought it would be useful to know if we're there yet.'

Plunkett's shoulders slumped as he mumbled an apology.

'I should think so,' Marcroy said. 'Now leave us. Brógán and I have much to discuss.'

Plunkett didn't need to be asked twice. He blinked out of sight, the clay pitcher shattering into several pieces as it fell from his vanished hand. Marcroy turned back to Brógán and took the stool opposite him, pulling it closer so he could look the young Druid in the eye. 'Do you know the danger, my hopeless young friend, that you court by protecting RónánDarragh?'

'I'm not afraid of anything you do to me,' Brógán announced. It was so obviously a lie that Marcroy couldn't imagine why he bothered to waste his breath.

'I'm not speaking of physical discomfort. Clearly, you're not going to succumb to anything so crass.' Marcroy let the compliment sink in. 'I speak of the danger to our whole world.'

'What danger?'

Ah, you puny humans are so easy to lead in a merry dance. 'Rónán has spent his life in a realm that has no respect for magic. No respect for our traditions. And worse, no understanding of the danger he brings with him into our world.'

'And whose fault is that?' Brógán asked. 'You sent him there.'

'And if you'd not interfered, that's where he would have stayed. Do you not see, my young friend? You all condemn Amergin for his part in the plan to remove the Undivided, but he was a greater patriot than any who has come before. He sacrificed everything because he could see it.'

Brógán was looking confused. 'See what?'

'The danger of those boys.' He held up his hand to stop Brógán interrupting him, even though he was quite sure the Druid hadn't been going to say a thing. 'I know. You're going to tell me there's been bad Undivided before and you've managed just fine. But these boys ... Amergin would never admit it, but he thought the boys responsible for the deaths of LonHarian.'

'That's absurd,' Brógán said. 'They died when the boys were not yet three. Lon fell from his horse.'

'Think about that,' Marcroy said. 'What are the chances one of the Undivided would break his neck in a riding accident and be without a guardian or a *Liaig* to aid him? Think about the absurdity of Lon falling from his horse at all. Not only was he a master horseman, he was a Druid. He spoke to the animal directly. It would not have thrown him unless compelled to do so, by forces beyond Lon's ken. And, when you think about it, who other than a Druid with the power of the Undivided could wield those forces?'

'The *Daoine sídhe*,' Ciarán answered from the floor. 'Don't listen to his Faerie tales, Brógán. He's spinning you a yarn made of lies and spider webs.'

'Am I?' Marcroy asked, looking over his shoulder at Ciarán. The warrior was too injured to do anything other than argue. 'What would you know, you magically gifted thug? You wield magic with all the finesse with which you wield a sword in battle. Amergin knew the danger these boys represented. He also knew the only way to save the Treaty of *Tír Na nÓg*, preserve the power of the Druids and their relationship with the *Tuatha*, was to ensure the unbroken line of the Undivided remained intact. He found a way to do that, and instead of hailing him a hero, you all condemn him for it.'

'He aided you in tossing one of the Undivided through a rift,' Ciarán reminded him, attempting to sit up — no mean feat with two dislocated shoulders. 'How is that … helping to preserve the unbroken line of the Undivided?'

'He kept Rónán and Darragh apart,' Marcroy said. 'But the magic stayed intact. All you had to do was find the new heirs and transfer the power to them, and everything would have been fine. Darragh and his missing twin would have faded into history as a quirk, soon replaced by heirs who were worthy of the mantle of the Undivided, and not just waiting for an opportunity to destroy everything.'

Marcroy turned back to Brógán. Arguing with Ciarán was a foolish idea, but if Ciarán was going to be a part of the conversation, Marcroy needed the Druids to hear a few unfortunate truths. Truths were not normally something he would contemplate sharing, but in this case, truth was probably the only thing that would sway either man to his way of thinking.

'You lie, Marcroy,' Ciarán said, lowering his head back on the muddy floor. He was in too much pain to do anything but lie there. Still, the man's courage was the stuff of legend. He might eventually find a way through the pain. Marcroy waved a hand over the warrior's broken body, tying him to the floor with the same invisible bonds he used to secure Brógán to his stool.

'I've no need for deception,' he informed them, rising to his feet. With an audience of two, he needed to be in a position to read both their faces. 'I wish only to mitigate the damage you two have done by letting the Undivided go rift running.'

'Ignore him, lad,' Ciarán said. 'Ignore him and his silver-tongued stories. They're all lies and trickeries.'

Brógán nodded, Ciarán's courage bolstering the lad's resolve.

No matter. He turned to Brógán. 'Tell Ciarán of the technology-ridden reality where you found Rónán of the Undivided, lad,' Marcroy said.

Confused, Brógán looked up at him. 'Tell him *what* about it, exactly?'

'Nothing,' Ciarán insisted from the floor, gritting his teeth against the pain. 'Don't … listen to him. Tell me nothing.'

'Tell him of the man you found Rónán with,' Marcroy said, pacing between his two captives. 'About his father.'

Brógán was looking very confused. For a moment, Marcroy wondered if he'd been mistaken. Perhaps he should have interrogated Trása a bit more closely about Rónán's familial arrangements in the other realm before condemning her to avian form. 'Was the boy not in the company of a dark-haired man of middling height? A man who saved him from drowning as a child, and then raised the boy as his own?'

The young Druid shook his head. 'He was adopted by a woman. A famous woman, in her realm ...'

'Who was the man?' Ciarán asked despite himself.

'The only man Amergin trusted in the other realm to take care of Rónán,' Marcroy told him, squatting down to regard Ciarán's swollen, battered face. 'Himself.'

CHAPTER 57

'She's an in-patient at St Christopher's Visual Rehabilitation Centre,' Jack told them, when he rang later that morning. 'Room four-three-two.'

'You managed to get her *room* number?' Ren was impressed.

'I rang Kerry and told her I wanted to send Hayley some chocolates to cheer her up.'

'And she believed you?'

'Why wouldn't she?' There was a pause on the line, before Jack asked, 'You gonna be okay, lad?'

'Yeah, Jack, I'll be fine. Thanks for this.'

'Least I can do.'

'That, and taking care of Warren,' Ren reminded him, glad the Audi's owner was no longer their problem. Jack had promised to keep him occupied for the next few hours, which hopefully was all they would need to find Hayley and get her back to the stone circle at the Castle Golf Club. Warren had made a few token protests, but Ren suspected it was for show. Since informing Warren that his captivity for the next few hours would be taking place in a massage parlour, he had become remarkably co-operative. He'd left with Jack and they'd not had to spare him a thought since. 'Is he behaving himself?'

'Taking his punishment like a man,' Jack chuckled. 'You toss that cell phone you're on as soon as you're in the clear, won't you?'

'Sure. I owe you one, Jack.'

'Laddie, you owe me more than one. I hope we both live long enough for me to collect some day.'

Ren ended the call and leaned forward in the driver's seat, studying the entrance to the small antique shop where Trása and Darragh were currently hunting for a crystal bowl.

'Any sign of them yet?' asked Sorcha.

When Darragh told Ren he needed to contact Brógán to let him know when Ciarán should open the rift again, Trása announced they'd only be able to make the call using a scrying bowl. They couldn't use a plastic bowl, she'd said. It needed to be crystal. Something with a trace of lead in it.

Worried a shopping centre might have cameras and security, Ren had spied this cluttered little store on the side of the road as they drove past. It was the kind of place likely to have an inexpensive crystal bowl, and they had enough cash left over from Warren's wallet not to have to use his credit card.

But they seemed to be taking an inordinately long time.

'What's taking them so long?' Sorcha asked.

'Maybe they can't find the right sort of bowl,' he suggested.

'Or the half-*Beansídhe* bitch has run off with the money.'

Ren looked at Sorcha with a frown.

'She is nothing but trouble, *Leath tiarna*,' she said. 'You would do well to remember that.'

'I haven't forgotten. She's the reason I'm wanted by the cops.'

'A plan her monstrous uncle put her up to,' Sorcha said with complete certainty, and a surprising amount of venom. Sorcha had something of a history with Trása's 'monstrous uncle', Ren guessed.

'That's Marcroy Tarth, right?' he asked, rifling through the muddied memories he'd acquired from his brother. 'What's his problem?'

'What do you mean?'

'I mean, why's he trying to mess with the Undivided?'

'*Mess* with?'

'This is the guy who chucked me through the rift, right? Isn't there some sort of treaty you guys have that's supposed to prevent stuff like that?'

'You speak of the Treaty of *Tír Na nÓg*,' Sorcha said. 'It was drawn up nearly two thousand years ago, to turn back the Roman invasion of Britain. It bestows power on the Druids through you and your brother, but I doubt there's anything specific in it preventing Marcroy from trying to sunder the Undivided, although I believe there are specific clauses preventing the *Tuatha* from killing you.'

'What a comfort,' Ren said, turning to look at her. 'So the Druids and the Faerie did a deal and kicked Caesar's arse —'

'Claudius,' she corrected. 'Julius Caesar tried and failed to invade Albion years before Claudius sent his army across the *Oceanus Britannicus*.'

'So how come you needed Faerie help? I thought

514

the Celts were big hairy dudes who could fight like demons.' Then he added, 'Not unlike Ciarán, now I come to think of it.'

Sorcha apparently didn't think that was funny. 'It's obvious why we needed help,' she said. 'In this realm — without it — the Druids lost.'

'Fair point,' Ren said, the conversation bringing more and more of Darragh's knowledge to the fore. 'So, what happens next? The Romans are coming, you're all shitting yourselves, and the *Tuatha* offer to help?'

'The *Tuatha* were at even more risk than the Druids,' Sorcha explained. 'The Romans are fond of innovation and technology. Allowing them to expand their empire would eventually lead to a realm like this — full of machines and empty of magic.'

'They couldn't have *known* that.'

Sorcha looked at Ren oddly. 'Of course we could *know* it. You think rift running is a recent thing? The *Tuatha* have been aware of the consequences of allowing technology to flourish for thousands of years.'

Ren hadn't considered that.

'In the Druids,' Sorcha said, sounding much more like the eighty-five-year-old she was than the young woman she looked like, 'the *Tuatha* found a human civilisation that shared many of their beliefs and worshipped the same gods.'

'But the trouble was, humans who could wield *sídhe* magic weren't exactly common,' Ren said. The knowledge was in his mind, once he knew to look for it. 'And they needed an army of magicians to defeat the Romans. Hence the tattoos.' He held up his hand to examine the triskalion.

'Psychic twins proved the most susceptible to the magic,' Sorcha told him, although Ren already knew it. 'The Undivided are the gateway for the magic. The Druids all have the same triskalion mark tattooed in magically infused ink, usually above their hearts. It enables those who have the ... predisposition ... to tap into the *sídhe* magic. The tattoos allow the flow of the magic.'

'So what happens while we're gone?'

'What do you mean?'

'I mean Darragh and me are both here in this reality. Does that mean the Druids are screwed until we get back? Actually,' he added with a frown, 'if the magic isn't flowing, can we even *get* back?'

'The magic still works,' Sorcha assured him.

'Are you sure?'

She nodded. 'Were you not harmed by *airgead sídhe* any number of times in this realm, even with the rift closed?'

'I guess,' he said, frowning, a little worried now that they would try calling up the other reality, only to find they were stuck here forever. Ren might not have minded, under normal circumstances, but now the cops were after him, and staying here in this reality wasn't likely to be much fun if they found him.

Trása and Darragh appeared in the entrance of the antique shop. Darragh was carrying a plastic supermarket bag with a Superquinn logo that had obviously been recycled by the store's owner.

'Finally!' Ren exclaimed.

He gunned the engine to life as Trása and Darragh got into the car, pulling away from the kerb before Trása had fully closed the back door.

Ren glanced at the bag in Darragh's lap. 'Did you get what you needed?'

'I hope so.'

'Now we need rainwater and somewhere private,' Trása said, buckling up her seatbelt.

'Why?' Sorcha asked.

'The scrying bowl won't work otherwise,' she said.

Sorcha scoffed. 'Why should we believe anything you tell us, *Beansídhe*?'

'I don't think she's lying, Sorcha,' Ren said. He remembered the first time he'd seen Trása on Jack's terrace, astride the marble garden seat, stark naked and talking into a bowl.

'I'm not lying,' Trása said, giving him a grateful look. 'It's something to do with the chemicals that permeate everything in this world. I was here for nearly six months. It took me four of them to find a way to contact home, and I only managed it then because —' She abruptly stopped talking.

'Because why?' Ren asked.

Trása was biting her bottom lip, as if she was afraid. She hesitated and then let out a heavy sigh. 'I had a triskalion pendant with me. I brought it from our realm. It had enough magic in it to enable me to link with home.'

'And, of course, you don't have one with you now,' Sorcha said, glaring at her.

'I *flew* here,' Trása reminded the warrior. 'Remember?'

'So we can't phone home and get them to open the door? Is that what you're saying?' Ren asked.

'Not without a triskalion,' Trása said, folding her arms and slumping into her seat.

'Okay. No problem. You can buy Celtic jewellery everywhere around here,' Ren pointed out. 'The souvenir shops are full of it.'

'It would have to be a triskalion infused with trace magic from our realm,' Darragh said, frowning.

'How did Brógán and Niamh contact you then?' Ren asked, wracking his brain for a solution. 'They must have had a way of calling home to let you know they'd found me?'

Darragh shook his head. 'We set a schedule of openings,' he said. 'Every full moon for the better part of a year, Ciarán took a fishing boat out from Breaga with a stone circle concealed in the hold, opened the rift and waited.'

Ren almost missed a red light. He slammed the brakes on, wishing someone had mentioned this *before* they left the other reality. He glanced at the clock on the dash. It was almost five and the traffic was bumper to bumper again.

At this rate, they'd never get to Hayley. Every time Ren thought of her, blinded and alone, his heart lurched, mostly with guilt. He couldn't shake the belief it was his fault she'd been injured. Murray Symes might have run her down, but the only reason she'd been trying to cross the road was because he was on the other side of it. With Trása. The half-*Beansídhe* who had been sent here to keep him from his true reality by framing him for murder.

There was so much traffic at the intersection, there was no point moving forward. Filled with frustration, he slammed his open palms onto the Audi's steering wheel. It hurt more than he expected it to. He glanced down at his stinging palms for a moment then held up his left hand.

'Is *this* triskalion still infused with trace magic from your realm?'

Darragh stared at Ren's tattoo and then opened his own hand. He nodded slowly. 'It might be. Our link survived crossing the rift. There might be enough there ... perhaps if we both —'

'You'll have to do it naked,' Trása cut in.

'What?' Ren asked, turning to stare at her.

'You'll have to take your clothes off,' she said. 'There're too many artificial fibres in the clothes of this realm. They interfere with the link. The light's green.'

Ren discovered Trása was correct. He eased the car forward and glanced at Darragh. 'Is she right?'

He shrugged. 'Probably.'

'Great,' Ren sighed. 'We'd better find somewhere secluded, then. They have laws in this reality, about getting your kit off in public.'

'The more trees the better, too,' Trása added from the back seat.

'Of course,' Ren said, rolling his eyes. Why was nothing ever easy? *What's the point of magic, if it's going to be so frigging complicated?* 'Anything else?'

'No,' Trása said, either ignoring his tone or not getting it. 'That should do it.'

Ren looked at the clock again. It was 5:13. He figured they had until about eight o'clock before they could no longer just walk into St Christopher's Visual Rehabilitation Centre pretending to be visitors. After that, they'd either have to break in to the facility or abandon their rescue attempt until tomorrow.

The trouble was, any minute now, Warren would arrive home. Whatever happened between him and his wife, whatever she believed or didn't believe about his wild tale, the fact was, his car was missing.

One way or another, at some point in the next few hours, the Audi they were driving was probably going to be reported stolen.

CHAPTER 58

'You speak nonsense, Marcroy Tarth.'

Marcroy was losing patience with Ciarán. His tiresome insistence on interjecting every time Marcroy drew breath was starting to irk the *sídhe* lord.

'It's only nonsense because you don't like what I'm telling you,' Marcroy said, standing over the prone warrior, still bound to the floor by magic.

'Every word you utter is a lie!' Brógán said, no doubt in an attempt to appear defiant. The young Druid healer had been much more forthcoming when Ciarán was unconscious.

Marcroy was tempted to send Ciarán back into unconsciousness now, except it might be useful to have him hear what Marcroy was about to reveal. It might even make an ally of him.

After all, Marcroy had once managed to turn the Vate of All Eire into a spy. Ciarán mac Connacht was hardly even a challenge after that feat.

'Despite the self-serving deathbed confession Amergin made, it was Amergin himself who chose where to send Rónán,' Marcroy said, ignoring Brógán's protests. It wasn't strictly the truth, of course, but it was close enough to fit with what these Druids knew to be true. 'And to where does one abandon a child one is sworn to protect, without breaking one's oath?'

The two Druids didn't answer immediately. Marcroy wasn't sure if it was because they could not work out what he was telling them, or whether they were too appalled by it.

Eventually, Brógán spoke up. He shook his head in wonder. 'Amergin sent the child to the other realm's version of himself.'

'Don't listen to him, Brógán,' Ciarán insisted. 'What he says is not possible. There is no magic in the world where they sent Rónán. You know that. You've been there.'

'Of course there is no magic,' Marcroy agreed. 'But the Druid line Amergin was descended from remains true. Amergin sent Rónán to the man he would have been, had the treaty of *Tír Na nÓg* never been forged. His *eiléféin* in the other realm.'

'Patrick Boyle,' Brógán said.

Marcroy turned to Brógán. 'Is that his name? Patrick Boyle?'

'It's the name of the man who rescued Rónán from the loch.' Brógán was starting to accept the possibility even in the face of Ciarán's objections. Marcroy supposed it was inevitable that Brógán be the one see the connection first. After all, he'd spent months in the other realm tracking Rónán down, and every waking moment with the boy in this realm since their return.

'You actually met Rónán's father in the other realm?'

Brógán shook his head. 'No. And he wasn't Rónán's father, as such. But he was certainly around while he was growing up. I believe he married the housekeeper employed by Rónán's adopted mother.'

Marcroy nodded. It made perfect sense. 'Keeping an eye on the child he was sworn to protect with no understanding of why he felt compelled to do so,' he said. 'So you see the danger. If Rónán tries to bring this Boyle character back to this realm —'

'Amergin is dead,' Ciarán pointed out from the floor. 'It makes no difference now.'

'But that would make Hayley Boyle the alternate reality version of Trása,' Brógán added thoughtfully, following his own train of thought.

That news caught Marcroy completely off guard. 'He has a *daughter*?'

'It's why they've gone back,' Brógán said absently. 'She was injured and Rónán wanted to help her. But she can only be healed magically by bringing her back here and —' Brógán abruptly shut his mouth.

Marcroy was flabbergasted.

'*That's* why the Undivided have gone rift running? To bring back Trása Ni'Amergin's *eiléféin*?'

'Do not say another word, you fool,' Ciarán ordered, with a remarkable amount of authority despite being bound and helpless on the floor. 'You've said too much already.'

Marcroy was too entranced by the idea of Trása's *eiléféin* to bother chastising the warrior. What was she like, this human version of his niece? Did they look alike? Was her mother of *sídhe* stock like Elimyer, or was she the result of some random coupling that rendered any latent power she might possess completely useless?

And what would happen when they brought her back here?

In a heartbeat, Marcroy's plans had again changed. This unexpected bonus, brought on by the foolishness of two boys with an overdeveloped sense of chivalry, was a gift from *Danú* herself.

Everything he'd done he could now explain to the Brethren. The Undivided would break the treaty themselves, and the *sídhe* would be free of its obligations. He couldn't hide his smile. 'By the goddess, do they not realise what they've risked by doing this?'

To knowingly bring back someone's *eileféin* ...

That wasn't just foolish, it was criminal; a breach of *Tuatha* law that defied belief. That in itself was enough to breach the Treaty of *Tír Na nÓg*.

Marcroy turned on Ciarán. 'You permitted this?' he asked. 'Worse, you actively encouraged it by opening the rift for them?'

'No law has been broken,' Ciarán said. Interesting that he had stopped accusing Marcroy of lying.

'Not yet,' Marcroy said. 'But the moment those boys step through the rift with both Trása and this girl ... what did you say her name was?'

'Hayley Boyle.'

'Hayley Boyle,' Marcroy repeated, savouring the taste of his victory. 'The moment she sets foot in this realm, the treaty is broken.'

'There is nothing in the treaty about the Undivided going rift running,' Ciarán reminded him.

'I'll grant you that, but the clause regarding human respect for *Tuatha* law is very specific,' he said. 'You know this, Ciarán, better than most. You've been gifted with the power to open rifts into other realms. Do you not remember the responsibilities that go with that power? The oath you swore when it was given to you?'

Ciarán couldn't meet his eye, which was encouraging. 'I remember.'

'And yet here you stand ... or rather ... lie,' Marcroy said, 'complicit in the very act that will destroy the Treaty of *Tír Na nÓg* and the Druids along with it.'

Brógán stared at Ciarán in alarm. 'Is that true? Have we broken the treaty?'

'Of course not,' Ciarán said, but he sounded less certain than he had a moment ago. 'There is no *Tuatha* law that prevents both the Undivided leaving this realm. It's a Druid law, and unlike the laws of the *Daoine sídhe*, we can break those as often as we please without fatally incurring the wrath of our queen. As for this girl ... there's no guarantee they'll even find her. Or that they'll bring her back. And even if they do, you heard the *Leipreachán*. Trása flew through the rift into the other realm in bird form. Assuming she even survived the crossing, she would have to come back to this realm with Rónán and Darragh *and* the other girl for the *eileféin* law to be breached.' Ciarán looked up at Marcroy, his eyes furious. 'It'll take more than you twisting the facts to bring down the Druids, Tarth.'

'Bring down the Druids?' Marcroy gasped, his hand on his heart, offended by the very suggestion. 'Bring down the Druids? Can you not see, my old friend? I'm doing my utmost here to preserve them, something you're sworn to do too, are you not? I'm trying to save these foolish boys from themselves, not destroy them. Or your silly little order of Druids.' He turned to Brógán. '*You* understand I'm trying to help, don't you?'

'If you're trying to help, why did you capture us the way you did? Why torture Ciarán? Why not just come to us and explain?'

Ah, Marcroy thought. *He has a point there.*

'Because there is no other way to make you listen,' he said, hoping the young man was too befuddled to notice the flaw in his logic. 'You know what Ciarán is like. I had no choice but to restrain him. He'd run me through if I ever got close enough and you weren't going to talk to me because he'd poisoned your opinion of me before we'd even met. How else was I meant to warn you of the danger in which these foolish boys have placed your entire order in?'

Brógán shook his head. Ciarán wasn't helping much, either. Perhaps it was time to kill him.

For a moment, Marcroy pondered the ramifications of killing a Druid lord as powerful and well connected as Ciarán mac Connacht. The Treaty of *Tír Na nÓg* wasn't clear on that point. Although killing using magic was strictly forbidden, it wasn't exactly forbidden to kill a Druid using mundane means — or for a Druid to kill one of the *Tuatha* for that matter. Those who had drafted the original treaty had been wise enough not to fill it with conditions that could not easily be kept, so the past deaths had never actually caused a treaty breach.

Orlagh — when she bothered to take notice of what was happening outside the *sídhe* kingdom — claimed it was because practical women and not men had written the agreement. Orlagh and Boadicea had hammered out the terms in plenty of time to defeat the Romans, while Claudius was gathering his forces in Gaul. By the time he arrived in Albion, ready to take the islands, Boadicea had an army of gifted Druids at her back. A good thing, too, Marcroy thought. In other realms, where Boadicea ignored or refused an alliance with the *Tuatha* — so Marcroy had heard from half-human rift runners who had visited other worlds — things had gone rather badly for her and rather much better for the Romans.

Before Marcroy could make up his mind whether Ciarán mac Connacht would live or die, Brógán suddenly sat straighter in his chair, and his eyes rolled back in his head.

Recognising what it meant, Marcroy hurried over to the young Druid and squatted down to listen.

'They're trying to contact you from the other realm, aren't they?'

Brógán shook his head, but there was no denying it.

'Warn them!' Ciarán called out from the floor. 'Warn RónánDarragh they'll be coming home to a trap!'

Marcroy waved his hand in Ciarán's direction, extending his bonds to cover his mouth, and turned his attention to Brógán.

'Ignore Ciarán,' he said, as Brógán fought the magical link. He needed water to make it complete, but that was easily fixed. It was raining outside. Marcroy just needed to be sure Brógán told whoever was trying to contact him only what Marcroy wanted them to know.

'It's a trap!' was high on the list of things he'd prefer Brógán keep to himself.

'Your duty is to make sure RónánDarragh are returned to this realm in safety,' Marcroy said carefully.

Brógán nodded, straining against his bonds.

'If you alarm them,' said Marcroy, 'that won't happen, you understand that, don't you?'

The young Druid nodded again, his eyes desperate.

'Then I'm going to let you go outside and find some clear water, and you're going to speak to whoever is seeking to contact you from the other realm. You will assure them everything is fine here, then find out when and where they want Ciarán to open the rift, and nothing more.'

Brógán glanced at Ciarán, but the warrior couldn't move at all.

Marcroy moved, blocking Brógán's view of the Druid lord. 'If you don't, my brave young friend, I will kill Lord mac Connacht, and then you. Then the Undivided will never come home.'

Ciarán would know that preventing a rift runner from coming home violated the treaty so comprehensively that Marcroy could never carry out such a threat, but Brógán still had much to learn.

Brógán nodded, and Marcroy released his magical bonds. He offered Brógán a hand to steady him, satisfied that the Undivided would have no inkling of what waited for them on their return from the other world.

CHAPTER 59

'You're not going in there alone,' Sorcha announced.

Ren turned to stare at her in the back seat. Her expression was set.

'And what do you think you're going to do to help?' Ren asked. 'Scream with terror when we get in a lift? Pull a knife on the first orderly who asks you why you're there?'

'He has a point, Sorcha,' Darragh said, a little more sympathetically than Ren. 'This is not your realm. Or mine. Trása is a better choice to accompany Rónán.'

They were sitting outside the St Christopher's Visual Rehabilitation Centre as far from the main entrance as they could get and still be able to see it. Although it wasn't quite seven in the evening, it was dark, the street lit by glistening puddles of light. A misty rain was falling, obscuring their clear view of the six-storey building — a square, ugly, concrete-and-glass monstrosity squatting on a street of more elegant older buildings.

Ren had parked the car in the shadows while they decided their next move. If there were cameras at the entrance, Ren didn't want them to capture more than a fleeting glimpse of any of them. Once Hayley vanished from her room, he figured there'd be some hard questions asked at St Christopher's about how the centre lost one of their patients.

There was also the question about whether or not Hayley would even agree to come with him. Ren had no idea what she'd been told about his disappearance. For all he knew, she thought he was dead and would scream the house down when he appeared. He didn't think that likely — Hayley was a level-headed sort of girl — but it wasn't impossible. Then there was the problem of how he would explain what was going on. How was he going to convince her he had come to help? Or even that he could help her? '*Hi, Hayley, did you want to come with me to an alternate reality so we can heal your blindness with magic?*' It didn't seem like a very promising opening.

And even if she believed him, would she consider leaving this world for another, with the possibility she might never come back?

Ren had the advantage there. He'd grown up knowing he was adopted — that somewhere out there he might have another family. As a small child, he'd fantasised his real family would find him one day. When they were finally reunited, his long-lost mother would hug him and kiss him and tell him the fabulous story of how he'd been kidnapped by evil faeries and spirited away, and how she hadn't slept since that moment.

Ren smiled briefly. He may not get his moment with his long dead mother, but he really had — as it turned out — been kidnapped by evil Faeries.

Still, he wished Hayley had some other sort of

injury. One that didn't obstruct her vision. Then he could have just appeared in her room with Darragh at his side, told her about the whole psychic twin business with his brother there to prove it, and everything would be so much more believable.

He didn't share his fears about Hayley's reaction with the others. They were already worried about their conversation a short while ago, with Brógan.

The puddle-phone had worked, eventually. It had taken forever to get through to Brógan, and by the time Brógan's face appeared in the water bowl, Ren was freezing. Not only was the rainwater icy, but they were sitting in the rain without a stitch of clothing on, their hands soaking in the chilly bowl, concealed in a small thicket in a suburban park as the sun went down, while Sorcha and Trása kept watch.

It had taken the combined magic of both tattoos to reach the other realm. And when they did make contact, it wasn't what they were expecting. Ren wanted to know why they were even bothering with Brógan. Not that he didn't like the young Druid, but it seemed far more efficient to contact Ciarán directly, seeing as he was the one who had to open the rift.

Both Darragh and Sorcha had scoffed at the idea. Brógan was, in the general scheme of things, fairly unimportant. He was not likely to be noticed if his eyes suddenly rolled back in his head, a sure sign that someone was trying to contact you by puddle-phone, apparently. Ciarán would have had many more questions to answer if he was caught in such a compromising act. It was better not to make things more awkward for him than they already were, by advertising that he had opened an unauthorised doorway to an alternate reality so the Undivided could go rift running.

Brógán seemed nervous and evasive when Darragh spoke to him, particularly on the subject of where Ciarán was. But the call had been necessarily brief. It had ended with Brógán promising to have Ciarán open the rift at moonrise.

That might have been useful information if Ren had some idea of when moonrise was going to happen.

Still, at least they had a timetable now. Ren put aside the bizarre notion that they'd called up someone from another reality using a bowl of water and a tattoo, and instead worked on the more immediate problem of finding Hayley. He figured they had a couple of hours to get into St Christopher's, locate Hayley, convince her to come with them, get her out of the building, drive back to the Castle Golf Course, find the stone circle again and jump through the rift.

After that ... well, he'd deal with that when they got there.

'Let's go, then,' Trása said, her hand on the door latch. 'Time's awasting.'

'Wait!'

'For what!'

Rónán pointed to the entrance of St Christopher's. A Gardaí car had pulled up in the 'no parking' zone at the entrance. Two officers climbed out of the vehicle and entered the building.

'Shit,' Ren muttered.

Darragh looked at him curiously. 'Is there a problem?'

'The cops are here.'

'That may not have anything to do with us,' Trása said, leaning forward to stare over Ren's shoulder through the rain-spattered windscreen. 'I mean, they didn't arrive in a blaze of light and sirens. If the Gardaí realised you were here, Rónán, wouldn't all the police in Dublin be converging on us?'

Trása had a point. Chelan Aquarius Kavanaugh was an escaped fugitive on the run from a murder charge. If they thought he was here, they'd be descending on the place like a swarm of locusts. And probably armed. The Gardaí didn't carry guns as a rule, but if they thought they were in pursuit of an escaped murderer, someone was sure to have brought out the sidearms and started handing them around.

'How would they even know we are here?' Sorcha asked.

'Warren might have blabbed,' Ren said, not entirely happy with the way they'd dealt with their hapless captive.

'I thought you said Jack was going to take care of Warren.'

'Yeah, but even if he doesn't tell anybody about us, an anonymous tip-off might be his way of getting revenge. I mean, he heard us talking enough.'

'Not about this place,' Darragh said.

'No, but he heard us mention Hayley. Maybe he phoned in a tip, and the cops are just checking if everything's okay with her.'

'Then it's a good thing we waited,' Sorcha said. 'When they return to their vehicle, it will be safe to proceed, yes?'

Ren shrugged. 'I suppose.'

It took a nerve-wracking half-hour before the Gardaí returned and climbed back in their car. As it pulled away from the kerb, Ren turned to Darragh.

'Did you pick up enough during the *Comhroinn* to learn how to drive?'

Darragh looked around the car a little dubiously. 'I certainly know the *principles* involved, but I'm not sure if that's the same as knowing how to control this thing.'

Ren shrugged. It would have to do. 'If we're not back in thirty minutes, make your way back to the golf course, wait for Ciarán to open the rift and then go home.'

'I won't leave you here,' Darragh objected.

'Sure you will,' Ren told him, glancing at the clock on the dashboard. They were running out of time and really didn't need to have this discussion. At least, not here. Not now. 'You can come back and get me when it's safe. It's not like you won't have done it before.'

'No.'

'Dude, we really don't have time to argue about this. If I'm caught here — in this place, in this reality — I am royally screwed. There is no reason on this earth — or any earth for that matter — for you to go down with me.'

'Your brother displays wisdom worthy of the Undivided,' Sorcha told Darragh approvingly.

'Wisdom?' Trása asked with a short, sceptical laugh.

'Nobody asked for your opinion, *sídhe*.'

'Good thing, too,' Trása said, leaning back in her seat with a scowl. 'Because if they had, I might have been compelled to point out that the

Undivided both jumping into a magic-depleted realm where one of them is wanted for murder so they can kidnap some girl who might not even want their help, hardly qualifies as *wisdom*.'

'And what was your reason for jumping through the rift after us into this magic-depleted realm where one of them is wanted for murder because of something *you* did?' Sorcha asked. When Trása just looked away and didn't answer, Sorcha turned to Ren. 'Don't worry, *Leath tiarna*,' she assured him. 'I'll make certain Darragh gets home safely.'

'But how will we even find the golf course and the stone circle without you?' Darragh asked.

'I remember the way,' the warrior assured him. 'I have an excellent sense of direction, even in this realm.' She turned to his brother. 'Go, Rónán. We're losing time.'

He nodded. 'Come on, Trása. Let's go.'

Trása showed no inclination to move. 'Oh, so my *opinion* isn't wanted,' she said sulkily, 'but you need me to hold your hand on your little adventure?'

'I need you to keep watch while I explain things to Hayley.'

'Give me one good reason why I should help?'

'Because if you don't,' Darragh informed her flatly, 'when we get back to our realm, rather than release you from Marcroy's curse, I'll add another one to it and you'll never be free.'

Ren wasn't sure if Darragh could do that, but Trása seemed to believe it. 'Fine,' she snapped, opening the door. 'Let's go find your friend and get out of here. I'm sick of this realm. I want to go home.'

CHAPTER 60

Dinner was served before five every evening in St Christopher's Visual Rehabilitation Centre. Like the hospital from which she'd so recently been discharged, the meal schedule had more to do with the time the cooks finished work and the nurses changed shift, than the time people might want to eat. Hayley ate in the dining room with the other inpatients, an eclectic mix of people, who, like Hayley, had been recently blinded — either by accident or degenerative eye disease. They were all learning how to deal with it.

By seven thirty she was usually hungry again, but by then the dining room was closed, and although there were scheduled activities for the residents of the facility, they didn't involve anything more than a cup of tea and biscuits. Fortunately, Kerry had brought her a plastic container full of homemade shortbread earlier in the day. Now Hayley was out of actual hospital — although she had a visit every day from either her father or her stepmother — the whole family only visited as a group on weekends. Neil had school, and homework, and football practice and her parents both had jobs.

Kiva Kavanaugh still required her entourage, regardless of Hayley's problems.

Hayley munched on Kerry's deliciously buttery shortbread and leaned her head against the cool glass of the window, wishing she could see the city lights. She still hadn't accepted she was going to be blind. She didn't want to master blind chess. She didn't care if she could take up archery with a spotter, or sailing, or skeet shooting, or one of a score of sports the chirpy counsellors here kept trying to interest her in. She wanted to go back to school. She wanted to hang with her friends at Frascati Mall, not have them visit her one at a time in this determinedly cheerful place where they sat with her in painful, drawn-out silences, because they didn't know what to say.

The idea that her life could have changed so dramatically just because she ran out onto a suburban street, was incomprehensible to Hayley. And even if she *could* believe it, she didn't want to.

Ren's mother had been to visit her again, without the publicist, thank God, leaving Hayley with a set of crystals that Kiva's homoeopath had assured her would aid her recovery. Thus far, Hayley hadn't noticed a difference, but Kiva's blindness-curing crystals certainly gave the rehabilitation therapist and the counsellors something to smile about.

Hayley hated her 'independent living' lessons, too. Learning what they were trying to teach her about sewing safely and using an iron — a pointless lesson, she thought, when the obvious solution was simply to buy stuff that didn't need ironing — meant admitting she *needed* to learn it. That meant accepting her sight was irrevocably gone.

Her first day at St Christopher's, they'd shown her around and told her all about the things she needed to relearn, like cleaning her teeth and applying make-up, doing her own laundry, cutting her toenails and managing money, now that she couldn't tell one note from another. Rather than cheer her up, the list depressed her — a perfectly normal reaction, they promised her cheerfully, and something they'd help her work through.

She wasn't blind, they said, she was *challenged*. 'Visually impaired' was the politically correct term. *Up the creek without a paddle* was the expression Hayley considered more appropriate.

Deep down, Hayley knew the counsellors were right. She would have to accept her disability eventually. She really didn't have a choice, and she'd been lucky. With the head injury she'd sustained, she could have been injured much worse, suffered brain damage or even been killed.

Admitting that, however, felt like giving in.

Hayley didn't want to nobly accept her fate and go forward like a little trooper. As petulant and unrealistic as she knew it was, Hayley wanted her life back the way it was before.

'Damn you, Ren Kavanaugh.'

Hayley said it aloud, because blaming Ren out loud helped to mask her own woes. Her predicament was his fault. She'd never have been standing in the path of Murray Symes's car if it hadn't been for Ren. And as if her injury wasn't bad enough, he'd compounded his mistake by being mixed up with that girl and some drug dealer.

People had been cagey about what they thought Ren's disappearance meant, but Hayley could read between the lines. Even though they hadn't discussed it with her, everybody considered Ren dead, killed by Dominic O'Hara's henchmen, who'd busted him out of gaol to keep him quiet.

It was plausible, she supposed, except she knew Ren better than anybody. He was no drug dealer's lookout, although she was finding it increasingly difficult to convince herself Ren was still alive and well out there somewhere and staying away by choice.

The Ren she knew would have moved heaven and earth to reach her, if he'd thought she was in trouble. That he hadn't so much as tried to call her was enough to make Hayley think the cops might be right about Ren being dead and lying in a shallow grave somewhere.

She heard the door open, but didn't react. It was probably her roommate, Carrie, back from another thrilling evening of listening to the TV. Carrie was twenty-five and losing her sight to diabetic retinopathy. Far from being pissed about it, Carrie was facing her future with equanimity, which might have been why they'd roomed her with the cranky seventeen-year-old who didn't want to accept the truth.

Despite that, Hayley liked Carrie. She figured there wasn't much to be gained by burdening her roommate with her bad mood.

'Did you want some of my mum's shortbread?' Hayley asked. She could make out a shadow roughly the size of a person coming toward her. When the shadow didn't answer, she realised it wasn't Carrie. For one thing, her roommate was in the throes of a passionate love affair with Elizabeth Taylor's new White Diamonds perfume, which

Carrie's fiancé had given her for her birthday a couple of weeks before Hayley arrived. On a good day, you could smell her coming down the hall.

'Love some,' her visitor said.

'*Ren?*' she squealed.

'Yell it out a bit louder,' he said with a smile in his voice. 'I don't think they heard you in Antarctica.'

Hayley dropped the box of shortbread onto the floor in a shower of buttery crumbs and threw herself at him. Ren hugged her tightly as she burst into tears, not sure if she was crying from relief, happiness, shock or fear.

'Christ *almighty*, Ren,' she gasped, tears running down her cheeks. She sniffed inelegantly and wiped them away. 'Where the hell have you been? Have you called your mother? Do the cops know you're back? Why didn't you tell someone —'

'Hey!' he said, placing his finger on her lips to silence her. 'Enough with the questions. I'll explain everything, but we can't talk here.'

'We could go to the common room,' she suggested. 'There's a phone in there, too, if you want to call Kiva. She's been sick with worry, you know. We all have. God, Ren, she cancelled an opening.'

'Wow,' Ren said. He sounded genuinely touched. 'Kiva missed a red carpet because of me? That's epic.'

'You have to call her, Ren. Everybody thinks you're dead.'

'And I will be, if we don't get out of here soon,' he promised her in a tone that made her realise he wasn't joking. 'Can you just walk out of this place or do we have to sign you out?'

'I can leave.' She sounded a little worried by the question. 'It's a rehab facility, not a hospital. They don't close the place to the public until after nine. Where are we going?'

'Somewhere we can talk,' he said. 'I've got so much to tell you, Hay, and some of it's going to be really hard to swallow. But ...' He hesitated. She could feel his nervousness. 'Look, just trust me, okay?'

Before she could answer, the door opened again. 'You done saying hello to your girlfriend yet?' an unfamiliar female voice asked impatiently. 'I'm getting funny looks from people out here, and I'm guessing they're staff because the patients can't, well, you know ... look.'

'Who's that, Ren?'

'It's Trása,' he explained, taking Hayley's hand. 'She's ... a friend.'

Hayley was instantly suspicious. She knew all Ren's friends. There wasn't a Trása among them. In fact, the only one she'd ever heard of was ... 'Is that the girl you were with the day of the accident?'

Ren was silent for a long time before he said, 'Yeah ... that's her.'

She stepped back from Ren and folded her arms, wishing she could read his expression. 'The girl claiming to be Jack O'Righin's granddaughter?'

'Yeah, sure ... look, can we talk about this later? We need to go.'

'Go where?'

'I want to take you someplace that'll ... explain things.'

'Explain what, exactly?'

'Explain ...' Ren was floundering. He couldn't find the words he needed to convince her.

Ironically, he probably wouldn't have needed to convince her of anything, had she not realised he was still hanging around with that blonde cow. 'I know some people who can help you, Hayley. People who can fix what's wrong with your eyes.'

'And what exactly is wrong with my eyes, Ren?' she asked, filled with a contrary urge to be difficult. How dare he think he can just waltz in here after disappearing for weeks, and expect her to just go along with whatever he had planned? And with that girl, too.

God, what if someone saw him coming in here? What if someone's called the cops?

'Your occipital lobe is damaged,' he said, his voice filled with impatience.

'How do you know?'

'The whole frigging world knows, Hayley. You're a feature in *OK! Magazine*.'

She'd forgotten that. She hadn't realised the latest edition had hit the stands yet.

'And when have you had time in your busy schedule of breaking out of gaol, being on the run and not calling anybody who cares about you, to book me in with a specialist who can fix my damaged brain?'

Ren let out an exasperated sigh. 'I have a twin brother.'

If Ren was hoping to distract her with shock tactics, that was a doozey. '*What?*'

'I have a twin brother,' he repeated. 'He ... knows people who can help you. Trása's a friend of his.'

She was still trying to get her head around his first revelation. 'You have a twin brother?'

'Matching tatts and all.' She could hear Ren

moving about the room as if he was checking out the street below and the bathroom to ensure they were alone. 'His name is Darragh. He's waiting outside to meet you, something I'd *really* like him to do before the cops get here.'

Hayley didn't know what to say. Suddenly everything she thought she knew about Ren, that girl, her accident … it all seemed pointless now. 'My coat's on the hook behind the door.'

She heard Ren grab the coat and let him help her into it. Then he took her hand and squeezed. 'It's gonna be okay, Hayley,' he said. 'Trust me.'

'I should probably call Dad and let him know I'm going.'

She could feel, rather than see, Ren shaking his head. 'I'd rather you didn't. If you tell Patrick you've seen me, he'll be obliged to call the cops.'

Hayley wasn't so sure. Her father, deep down, was something of a closet anarchist. At least that's how Kerry fondly described him. When it came to Ren, the child he'd saved from drowning, Hayley suspected he'd happily break any number of laws to protect him. But Ren was right. It was pointless endangering either her father or her stepmother unnecessarily. 'My dad wouldn't betray you, Ren. You're like a son to him.'

'Yeah … but let's not take the chance, eh?' he suggested. 'Besides, if it ever came out that Patrick knew where I was and didn't let the cops know, he'd be in a whole mountain of trouble. Let's not make it harder for him.'

Hayley nodded in reluctant agreement. 'Don't let go of my hand,' she ordered, unable to think of anything else more profound to say.

She heard the door open and sensed Trása waiting for them.

'Hayley, Trása. Trása, Hayley,' Ren said as he led her into the hall, introducing them almost as an afterthought. 'Are we still good?'

'I think so,' Trása said. 'But someone's coming. I just heard the lift.'

'Maybe we should go back inside before … Crap,' Ren muttered under his breath.

'What's wrong?' Hayley asked, hating that she was so reliant on everybody else to tell her what was happening.

'Trása,' Ren said urgently in a low voice. 'Get Hayley to the car. I'll meet you down there.'

Something was wrong, Hayley knew, but she couldn't tell what it was. Ren had suddenly tensed and she could hear footsteps coming toward them.

'Ren!' she hissed. 'Who is it?'

'Detective Pete.'

CHAPTER 61

There was a moment ... a split second of suspended time as Ren recognised the cop and the cop recognised him ...

Then Pete let out a shout and Ren bolted.

Although his first instinct was to head down, Ren went for the fire escape, and took the stairs, two at a time, toward the upper floors. He had to buy Trása time to help Hayley, and if that meant leading every cop in the building all over the St Christopher's Visual Rehabilitation Centre, so be it.

He had something of a head start on Pete, who must have stopped long enough to call in Ren's sighting. Ren heard the fire escape door opening below him as he hit the fifth floor landing. He jerked the door open and bolted down the hall, then realised that by running he was drawing attention to himself. He slowed to a walk, took several deep breaths to calm his racing heart, and tried to look like he belonged. It wasn't easy. He'd come out of the fire escape into a medical ward and it certainly wasn't visiting hours.

Trying to look as if he belonged, he stepped out of the ward, turned right, and spied another fire escape at the very end of the corridor.

'Are you right there, mate?' a man asked as he passed the nurses' station. The man who questioned him wore a set of scrubs, plain blue pants and a pale shirt covered in fluffy white bunnies, with a stethoscope around his neck. Ren wasn't close enough to see his ID, but he figured — fluffy bunnies notwithstanding — he wasn't someone to be trifled with.

'Yeah ... um ... I'm looking for my parents. They came in last night with my little sister ... they said she'd be up here.' Ren tried to sound calm, hoping his constant checking of the hallway behind him didn't look suspicious.

'What's your sister's name?' the nurse asked.

'Hayley,' Ren replied. 'Hayley Boyle.'

'She's not in Medical,' the man told him, turning for the computer. 'I can check where she is for you, though, if you just want to wait there a min ...'

Ren never heard the rest of it. Down the hall, the fire escape door opened and Pete, with two security guards on his tail, spied their quarry and took off in pursuit. With the nurse yelling at them to stop, and something about this not being a football stadium, Ren bolted down the hall toward the second fire escape.

'Kavanaugh! Stop!' Pete yelled.

Oh, yeah ... like that's gonna happen.

Ren didn't waste his breath responding.

'You're cornered, Kavanaugh!' Pete bellowed. 'There's nowhere to run!'

Shows how much you know, Pete, Ren replied silently as he spied the door to the next stairwell, the sound of pounding footsteps behind growing closer. Without taking the time to look, he grabbed at a cleaner's trolley parked by a utility room near the stairs and shoved it into the path of his pursuers. They went down with a clatter as Ren jerked open the fire escape door and bolted down the bare concrete stairs to the next floor.

This time, Ren didn't wait for them to find him. He let himself out on the third floor, bolted straight past the service lifts, and made for the main elevators further along the hall, near the entrance to the closed Physio department. Gasping for breath, he pressed the button and waited. He was rewarded a few achingly long moments later with a ding advising him the lift had arrived. Ren tapped his foot impatiently until the door opened. He smiled at the young woman in the lift, unable to hide his grin of relief at the shout of frustration from Pete and the security guards as the doors closed on them.

'Are we going up or down?' Ren asked.

She turned to him, holding her cane in front of her. 'Down. Are you all right? You sound a little ... breathless.'

'Asthma,' Ren said, as the elevator rocked to a halt on the first floor. He stood back and let the woman and her cane exit first, and then, with his head down and shoulders hunched, he stepped out of the lift, took a sharp right into the next corridor and opened the first door he came to.

It turned out to be the chapel.

The silence rang in Ren's ears as he lowered himself to the carpeted floor, breathing hard, his pulse racing. He wasn't sure how long it would take them to find him. He figured they'd have to work out what floor he'd got out on, and then — assuming there were cameras and he was lucky enough that nobody was watching the monitors — maybe go back through the surveillance tapes to discover where he'd vanished to, after he emerged from the lift.

Ren looked up, wondering if there were cameras in the chapel, but the ceiling boasted no obvious surveillance equipment or any telltale tinted glass domes that might hide cameras. The crucifix on the altar seemed to be glaring at him, accusing him of something. With his arms resting on his knees, he closed his eyes, leaning his head back against the panelled wall. It was a risk, trusting Trása to get Hayley clear. Trása was good at eluding the authorities, but she was only on their side by default. With luck, her desire to be released from Marcroy's curse when they got back to their own reality was enough to keep her motivated. There was always a chance she'd ditch Hayley to save herself. If she did that, Ren decided he'd add his own curse to Darragh's threat — and he realised he knew how, thanks to the *Comhroinn*.

He just hoped Darragh and Sorcha wouldn't panic and try to rescue him. He could get out of this on his own. Their help would merely complicate matters.

Ren forced his breathing to slow and opened his eyes.

The chapel door swung open. There was nothing he could do. Nowhere he could run.

The cop who found him was in uniform. Detective Pete must have called in reinforcements. And she was armed. She drew her weapon and pointed it at Ren.

'Don't move.'

Ren raised his hands. He'd been right about them arming the cops once they suspected he was in the building. He could only hope Trása was already outside with Hayley. Maybe they'd been distracted by their search for him long enough for her to get Hayley to the car with Darragh and Sorcha.

Hayley's fate was now in the dubious hands of his brother and his first attempt to drive.

But Ren's fate was in the hands of this cop. *Will she really shoot if I make a break for it?* He was taller than her and quite a few pounds heavier. If she hesitated, he might be able to get past her, and back into the hall — a grand plan provided he did it in the next five seconds, before the hall filled with more cops.

'Found him,' the cop announced into her shoulder-mounted radio. 'He's in the chapel.'

So much for *the next five seconds* plan.

'Aren't you gonna be the hero?' Ren said with a sigh. There was no point fighting someone pointing a loaded gun in his face, and the longer they were focussed on him, the longer Trása and Hayley had to get clear. Darragh could come back for him some other time. Brógán and Niamh had broken him out of gaol once. They could do it again.

'We're on our way,' someone crackled in reply. It sounded like Detective Pete, but the radio distorted the voice too much to be certain.

The officer took a step backward. 'On the floor, Kavanaugh. Face down.'

Ren sighed. 'It's okay. I know the drill.'

He did as she ordered, wincing but not resisting, as she slapped the cuffs on him and then helped him to his feet, a lot more gently than the ERU guys had done. By the time Detective Pete arrived, panting heavily from the pursuit, she was pushing Ren out of the chapel and into the hall, which was — as he'd feared it would be — teeming with police.

'Looking a bit unfit there, Pete,' Ren remarked, as the detective bent double for a moment while he caught his breath.

Pete didn't rise to the bait. He straightened up, said, 'Come on, Kavanaugh,' then grabbed Ren by the shoulder and pushed him down the corridor, through the main foyer, past the curious stares of staff and visitors, and out into the bitter, rainy evening.

There was an unmarked Gardaí car parked in front of the facility. Pete opened the back door, pushed Ren into the back seat with his hand on the top of Ren's head, slammed the door, and turned to issue orders to the other Gardaí who'd followed them.

Ren sat forward, finding it too awkward to lean back against the seat with his hands cuffed behind his back. The driver was sitting hunched over the wheel as if he was freezing, bundled into a Gardaí standard-issue duffle coat with the collar pulled up, his hat down over his eyes.

'Stay calm, brother,' the driver advised. 'We'll be gone from here soon enough.'

'*Jesus Christ!*' Ren's jaw dropped. Darragh was driving the Gardaí car.

His brother turned and grinned at him over the collar of his stolen coat. 'Turns out I know how to drive, after all. Sort of.'

'What the fuck are *you* doing here?' Ren turned to see where Pete was. The detective was still talking to the other cops. But he was barely three feet from the car. They only had seconds before he was in the car with them. 'How did you get here?'

'You underestimate both Sorcha's skill and her desire to ensure the Undivided safely return to our rightful realm,' Darragh said, grinning like an idiot. 'Should we leave now?'

'No! God, no!' Ren had visions of Darragh careening out into the traffic, alerting every cop in the vicinity there was another escape underway. 'Wait ...'

'Wait for *what*?'

Ren glanced at the cops outside the car. 'Wait until Pete gets in and then *ease* away from the curb.'

'Why do we want him to come with us?'

'We don't. We can drop him off somewhere once we've lost the rest of the cavalry. We just don't want to make a scene. Where's Hayley?'

'In the other car. With Trása. They're already heading for the rift. Your friend is very pretty.'

Ren glared at Darragh. 'You found time to notice *that*?' Then another thought occurred to him, which swamped his surge of jealousy. 'Hang on ... they've left already? How? Who's driving?'

'Trása.'

'She doesn't know how to drive!'

Darragh shrugged, apparently unconcerned. 'She assured me she understood the fundamentals.'

'Oh my God ...' Ren was suddenly nauseous. *Great plan you've got going here, Kavanaugh: save Hayley from injuries sustained in one car accident, so you can get her killed in another.*

The back door of the car jerked open. Darragh quickly turned his face forward. Between the turned-up coat collar, the hat and the poor light, his face was hidden. There was no telling, however, how long they had before this paper-thin ruse was discovered. If Sorcha hadn't already killed the cop who'd been driving the car before Darragh got behind the wheel, he might stumble out any moment, to raise the alarm.

If she had killed him ... well, that didn't bear thinking about.

'Let's get out of here,' Pete ordered, leaning back in his seat.

Darragh took his foot off the brake and the car rolled forward. So far so good.

'What? No seatbelt?' Ren asked, hoping to keep the detective's attention on him and not on who was driving the car. Pete hadn't yet noticed that his driver was not the same driver he'd arrived with.

Pete looked at Ren askance. 'Oh, so *now* you're worried about breaking the law? That's rich.'

'I'm reformed,' Ren assured Pete, bracing himself. He had a feeling he knew what was about to happen. Sure enough, Darragh spotted a gap in the traffic and the Gardaí car surged forward, darting into the oncoming traffic. There was a squeal of brakes, blaring horns and curses.

'Bloody hell, Andy!' Detective Pete exclaimed, as they careened into the traffic. 'Who taught you to drive?'

Darragh turned to look at them over his shoulder. He was grinning like a fool. 'Nobody. I don't actually drive. Are you all right, Rónán?' The car began drifting into the next lane.

'I'm fine. Watch the freakin' road!'

'Sorry!' Darragh turned his attention back to the

traffic. The car was all over the place. He really had no idea what he was doing.

But Pete had seen Darragh's face. He stared at Ren for a moment. 'What the hell is going on here?' he said and reached into his jacket for his weapon.

'He'll drive even worse if you shoot him,' Ren said.

The traffic carried them forward — miraculously without hitting any other vehicles. Pete pulled out his gun and pushed it against Ren's leg.

'Pull over, or I'll shoot your friend's kneecap out.'

Darragh glanced in the rear-view mirror, assessed the situation in an instant, and jerked the steering wheel, oblivious to the other traffic on the road, trusting them to get out of his way. The unmarked Gardaí car hit the curb with a thud in front of a car dealership. It crashed over the curb and came to a stop against the chain-link fence. Darragh shut down the engine and glanced back at Ren. 'I am sorry, brother. My heroic rescue attempt appears to have failed.'

'It's okay. I appreciate the gesture.'

'Put your hands on the steering wheel where I can see them and don't move,' Pete ordered Darragh and Darragh did as he was told without complaint. With the gun still pressed into Ren's knee, the cop stared at Darragh for a long moment, then at Ren and then at Darragh again.

'Jesus wept. There are two of you.' He pulled a long plastic cable tie from another pocket and handed it to Darragh. 'Cuff yourself to the wheel.'

It was now or never, Ren realised. If Pete called this in, they'd both be arrested and it was unlikely they'd get away a second time. Even with Brógán and Niamh on the case and an endless supply of *Brionglóid Gorm* — God, if only they'd had time to bring a bag of that magic blue dust through the rift with them — it would take a major effort to spring both of them out of gaol, and that was surely where they were headed. And even if they could be rescued by people from another reality, the problems back in their own reality caused by their absence were mounting every moment they were away.

It suddenly occurred to Ren how selfish his plan to rescue Hayley really was. Not only had he drawn Trása and Darragh into his folly, he wondered if Hayley even *needed* rescuing?

All he knew about her condition he'd read in *OK! Magazine*.

There was no way he could allow Darragh to be caught here. Whatever the future held for Ren, he needed to end this so Darragh, at least, could get away.

Before he could do anything heroic, however, Sorcha's head appeared over the front passenger seat. Ren hadn't realised she was crouched down in the front with Darragh, although it made sense. She would never let Darragh rescue him without her help. Pete barely had time to register she was there before her fist flew at his face. She knocked the detective out cold with a single short sharp jab.

'Should I finish him off?' she asked, looking at Ren questioningly.

'Christ no! Get these cuffs off me.'

It took a few seconds for Sorcha to climb into the back seat, rifle through Pete's pockets to find the keys, unlock Ren, and pull the unconscious cop out of the car onto the footpath. Traffic whizzed past, and the occasional car slowed down so the occupants could stare at them. As soon as he was no longer shackled, Ren jumped out of the back seat and jerked the driver's door open.

'I'm driving,' he said. Darragh nodded and climbed sideways into the passenger seat without protest. Pete was already starting to moan as he came to. Ren climbed in behind the wheel and turned to Sorcha. 'Get his radio.'

The warrior looked at him blankly. 'His what?'

Ren could try to explain what he meant or do it himself. Cursing, he jumped out of the car again, ran around to Pete, rolled him onto his back, grabbed his radio, tossed it on the ground and crushed it with his heel. Then he ran back to the car, climbed in, started the engine, slammed the transmission into reverse, and backed it out into the traffic with all the finesse of his brother.

A glance in the rear-view mirror as they sped away showed him Pete starting to pull himself upright. At least Pete wasn't dead. A pissed-off cop was one thing. A dead cop would bring the entire Gardaí down on them and they'd not get another mile, let alone back to the golf course.

Ren turned his attention back to the car and spied a switch on the dash with an external wire leading under the front console. Guessing it was the car's concealed police lights, he flicked it on and was rewarded with a piercing squeal as a siren howled to life. Almost immediately, the traffic began to part ahead of them.

'All right!' he said, grinning. 'Now we're in business.'

He pushed the accelerator down, running the next red light as cars pulled over for them.

Glancing in the rear-view mirror again and seeing no sign of pursuit, Ren allowed himself a little hope. At this speed, provided it took Pete a few more minutes to flag someone down and alert the rest of the cops of their escape, they might actually get away.

CHAPTER 62

Driving turned out to be trickier than it looked.

Trása managed to keep the car on the road and not hit anybody or anything, but driving a real vehicle wasn't anything like driving those pretend cars in the video arcades that Plunkett used to hang around, looking for victims with ready cash or credit cards.

After pubs and bookies, video arcades had been his third favourite place for finding fools easily parted from their wealth, he had once told Trása.

Having a blind passenger didn't help matters much. Although Hayley couldn't see where they were going, she had a disconcerting habit of squealing whenever Trása hit a curb, swerved to miss another car or leaned on the horn to clear other vehicles out of her path.

It was very off-putting and made Trása want to slap her, but she couldn't take her eyes off the road long enough to deliver the blow.

Hayley Boyle turned out to be prettier than Trása was expecting, the same height as she was, with dark hair and blue eyes and something about her that seemed hauntingly familiar. Although Rónán had gone on and on about her since they arrived in this realm, Trása had only seen Hayley in the flesh once before, on the day of the accident. She didn't remember much about the girl, just how devastated Rónán had been by her injuries. Everything else she knew about Hayley she had learned via Rónán, who seemed inordinately attached to his not-quite-cousin, although she gathered he thought of Hayley more as a sister than a girlfriend.

This girl was, apparently, the stepdaughter of his adopted mother's cousin. Trása didn't think there was a word in either realm to label that relationship.

Even so, she was a little jealous of Hayley. She had true friends. Loyal friends. Friends who'd risk anything for her. Rónán cared enough about Hayley to rescue her from another realm. He'd risked everything to come back here and find her, in the hopes of taking his friend through the rift to the place where she could be magically healed.

Darragh, on the other hand, had let the Druids banish Trása to *Tír Na nÓg* and barely raised his voice in protest.

'Hang on!' Trása called, as she swung the steering wheel sharply to the left. She recognised the camera shop on the corner as one they'd passed on the way from the golf course when they still had Warren in the trunk of the car. Trása had learned the advantage of noting landmarks like that the last time she had been in this realm. She was confident she could find the Castle Golf Club again and with it, the rift Ciarán was going to open for them at moonrise. Trása leaned forward and looked up, trying to gauge the time to moonrise, but couldn't see anything for the streetlights and the low, dark rain clouds that blanketed the twilight sky.

'Damn!'

'Damn *what*?' Hayley asked, sounding more than a little panicked. 'What do you mean by that? Why are you saying it? What's happening?'

'It's starting to rain again. I can't see a damned thing through this window.'

'Turn the wipers on then,' Hayley said in exasperation.

Trása glanced at Hayley uncertainly. 'How?'

'Are you *kidding* me?'

'No.'

'They'll be on the steering column,' the human girl told her. She reached up and felt around for the handle mounted on the roof near the passenger side door and gripped it as if her life depended on it.

'The steering *what*?' Trása asked, looking around the front of the car urgently. The rain was getting heavier by the minute. Were it not for the blur of red tail-lights in front of them, she'd have no idea where the road was.

'It's the thing holding the steering wheel on. It'll be a lever on the side and the end will probably turn. I'm not sure where; depends on the model of the car.' Hayley checked her seatbelt was secure and closed her eyes. 'Bloody hell, we'd be safer if I was driving.'

Trása found the wipers, which swished back and forth as the windscreen cleared. The road ahead was straight. Relieved, Trása took a deep breath.

She had time, for a moment, to converse with her passenger, and she discovered she had a few things to say. 'You could thank me, you know,' she said.

559

'Thank you for *what* exactly?' Hayley asked. 'Trying to kill me? Where's Ren?'

'I don't know.'

'What happened to him?'

'He was arrested. That's why Darragh and Sorcha went after him.'

Hayley was silent for a moment, and then she turned her unseeing eyes toward Trása. 'Is Darragh really Ren's twin brother?'

'He told you about that, did he? What else did he say?' Rónán couldn't have told her much, Trása reasoned. He was only alone with her at St Christopher's for a few moments.

'Not very much at all. Just that he had a twin brother and that he'd been with him these past weeks. Are you related to him, too?'

Trása shook her head and then realised what a useless gesture that was. 'No. I'm kind of ... a friend of the family.' She glanced sideways at Hayley as a disturbing thought occurred to her. 'You're not a Druid, are you?'

'Excuse me?'

Trása bit her bottom lip for a moment, trying to figure out how to ask the question she needed an answer to. 'Are you a Druid?'

'Are you insane?'

'I just meant ...' Trása had no idea how to explain what she meant. Bringing someone from one reality to another was always a risk, because of the *Tuatha* prohibition about bringing *eileféin* through the rifts. Having extracted a promise from Rónán to undo Marcroy's curse once she got back to her own reality, it would be very unfortunate to discover she'd inadvertently brought someone's *eileféin* back and end up dead because of it. She studied Hayley for a moment, wondering. *What are the chances of there being another Hayley Boyle in my reality?*

'Who are these people Ren says can help me?'

'Is that what he told you?'

Hayley turned to her with a suspicious frown. 'Are you telling me that's not where we're going?'

'No ... it's just ...'

'Pull over,' Hayley ordered. 'Let me out.'

'Hang on, turn coming up!'

Hayley squealed in fright again as Trása wrenched the wheel hard right and skidded across an intersection, slipping in front of a car that slammed its brakes on so hard to avoid her, it slid sideways on the slick bitumen and crashed into a parked car on the other side of the street. Trása managed to right the Audi without losing control, and was gratified to see a road sign ahead advising the approach of the Castle Golf Club turnoff.

She smiled. This driving thing wasn't so hard. 'Sorry ... did you say something?'

'I said *let me out*,' Hayley repeated, with an edge of panic in her voice.

'Why?' Trása asked, a little wounded by this girl's ingratitude. Didn't she realise Trása had mastered driving for her? She leaned forward, peering through the rain, looking for the entrance to the golf course. On the right, she could see the course through the wire-mesh fence, bordered by trees. The entrance must be coming up soon.

'If you're an example of the people Ren has lined up to help me, I think I'm better off blind.' Hayley felt around for the door latch. 'Stop the car!'

'Don't be an idiot.'

'If you don't let me out, I'll jump.'

'Fine,' Trása said with a shrug, too focussed on her driving to look at Hayley. 'Jump. This wasn't my idea, you know, and Darragh is risking a lot, letting Rónán take you back to our realm. You want to jump and remove the problem by killing yourself? Be my guest.'

Clearly, Hayley wasn't expecting to have her bluff called. She slumped back in the seat just as Trása spotted the entrance to the golf course.

'Who the hell are you people?'

'Rónán ... Ren can explain when he gets here,' Trása said, slowing the car gradually, now she'd figured out where the brake was and that it worked much better if one stepped on it gently rather than stomping on it like you were squishing a large hairy spider. She glanced in the rear-view mirror. There was no sign of the others yet. '*Assuming* he gets here.'

'Where is *here*?' Hayley asked unhappily.

'Castle Golf Club,' Trása told her, seeing no reason to keep their destination a secret.

'Ren's friends who can help me are waiting at a *golf* club?' Hayley sounded sceptical. Trása supposed that was to be expected. This must seem very strange to her. She wondered why Hayley had agreed to come at all. If their situations were reversed, she'd want a much better assurance all was well than a hasty hug, a few moments of frantic catching up, and an unsubstantiated promise of a cure.

Hayley must trust Rónán a great deal to leave the safety of St Christopher's for the dubious company of a felon on the run.

'Not exactly at the club itself,' she explained as the large white clubhouse came into view. She managed to park the car, although it wasn't very straight and took up several spaces. Trása turned off the engine, wondering what to do next. Should she take Hayley and head for the stone circle? Wait here for the others? Go through without them?

She turned to her passenger. 'You up for a bit of a walk?'

'I want to know where Ren is,' Hayley insisted stubbornly.

Trása sighed. 'He's either back in gaol and you'll never see him again, or he's on his way here. Either way, it's almost moonrise or, worse, it's past it already, and I want to go home. You can come with me or not.'

Although Hayley didn't realise it, Trása would never have left Hayley here alone. Trása needed to be in Rónán's good graces when they returned. If she abandoned Hayley to save her own skin, he'd leave her flapping about as an owl until Marcroy decided she'd been punished enough. Assuming Marcroy ever actually decided she'd been punished enough, of course. Her *Daoine sídhe* uncle could hold a grudge for a very long time.

'Okay, then. Where are we going?'

'Across the greens,' Trása explained. 'But don't worry, I'll hold your hand. You won't get lost or fall over, or anything.'

Hayley hesitated and then seemed to give in. She unbuckled her seatbelt and felt around for the door catch. Relieved her companion wasn't going to be any further trouble, Trása climbed out of the car and hurried around to the passenger side in the rain. She opened the door for Hayley and took her hand. Hayley accepted the help, a little begrudgingly, and stepped out of the car.

Trása looked around. They seemed to have made it here undetected. The clubhouse across the rain-slick car park was brightly lit, and although the car park was filled with cars closer to the main building, at this end it was fairly deserted. In the distance, she could hear the traffic on the wet roads, and the faint wail of a siren approaching. She sincerely hoped it wasn't coming for them.

'You ready?'

'Don't you have an umbrella?' Hayley asked, turning her collar up against the rain.

Trása shrugged. 'It's only water.'

'We'll probably end up catching pneumonia,' Hayley complained, as Trása took her by the hand.

'Don't worry about that,' she assured Hayley, tugging the young woman forward in the direction of the course and — if Brógán was as good as his word — the gateway back to the realm where she belonged. 'Where we're going, they can fix that too.'

CHAPTER 63

The Audi was parked at the far end of the Castle Golf Club car park. The headlights were still on, the keys still in the ignition and there was no sign of Trása or Hayley Boyle. Sorcha studied the car, walking around it in the rain, looking for some hint as to what might have befallen the two young women. She turned to Darragh and Rónán.

'Well, they appear to have made it here in one piece,' she remarked, shivering a little in the cold rain that was seeping down the back of her collar. Sorcha was not comfortable in the clothes of this realm. She was looking forward to getting home and back into clothes that felt right.

'But where are they now?' Rónán asked, glancing in the direction of the road. They hadn't exactly been subtle with their getaway. Sorcha didn't think it would be long before the place was swarming with every Gardaí officer in the city. Sorcha wasn't worried about taking a few of them out, but there were probably more than she could comfortably handle and Rónán seemed squeamish about killing.

'They've probably gone toward the rift,' Darragh said, squinting into the darkness toward the stone circle. It was starting to rain even harder. His dark hair was plastered to his head, flopping into his eyes, a problem Rónán didn't have because of his shorter hair.

Rónán looked around uncertainly and then glanced up at the sky. 'Is it moonrise yet, do you think?'

'Well past it, I'd say,' Darragh said. 'Ciarán may well have opened the rift already.'

'Guess there's one way to find … oh shit …'

Sorcha turned in the direction Rónán was looking. Through the chain-link fence in the distance, she could make out several sets of flashing blue lights, accompanied by the frantic wail of sirens. She made a quick calculation and turned to the Undivided. 'If they know we're here, we won't make it to the rift before they reach us.'

'The hell we won't,' Rónán said, running back to their stolen Gardaí car. 'Get in!'

Darragh didn't hesitate. Sorcha glanced at the approaching cars and then the golf course they would have to negotiate to reach the rift and wasn't so sure. Still, she had no choice but to trust Rónán.

He was already behind the wheel, gunning the engine. At the entrance to the club, a Gardaí car was turning in, lights ablaze and sirens screaming. There was no time left to debate the merits of Rónán's plan. It was the only one left to them.

Sorcha ran to the car, jerked open the door and dived into the back. Rónán took off before the door was closed, throwing Sorcha back against the seat.

'Hang on!' he called as he crashed through the barrier separating the paved parking lot from the shrubbery and trees on the edge of the course.

Sorcha scrambled upright and turned to look through the back window. The Gardaí car had spotted them, and several more had joined the chase. Their car bounced over the rough shoulder, scraping a tree as they passed it, and then dropped onto the smoother surface of the fairway. Rónán turned the wheel sharply. The car skidded on the slick grass, but eventually straightened as he accelerated, leaving long dark scars on the pristine lawn.

'The other vehicles are getting closer!' Sorcha warned, as their pursuers' headlights turned on them. The following cars also seemed to have trouble gaining traction on the wet grass. Sorcha looked forward again and gasped. Even through the rain, she could make out the tree line approaching at an alarming rate, and Rónán seemed to be going faster, rather than slowing down.

'Look out!' Sorcha was certain they were going to slam into the trees. Rónán wrenched the wheel to the left at the last minute, making a sharp turn at the end of the strip of grass. They knocked down a flag standing in the middle of a neat circle of lawn, carving it up with their wheels as they dug a deep furrow across the green. Their wheels spun futilely for a moment, and then seemed to grab the earth again and the car lurched forward and onto the next long narrow strip of grass.

The cars behind them were gaining. Rónán glanced in the rear-view mirror. He swore, and jerked the wheel again, heading straight into the trees. Darragh, who was bracing himself against the dash with one hand while he scanned the rainy golf course for any sign of the rift, let out a yelp of fright. Rónán just made the car go faster, aiming it at a gap in the trees Sorcha was sure they would never fit through. She closed her eyes as they raced toward it, wincing at the screech of torn metal as the car's side mirrors tore off, as the vehicle squeezed through a gap no car was ever meant to go through.

'There!' Darragh called out. 'The rift!'

Sure enough, through the rain and another approaching line of trees, Sorcha could just make out the jagged red lightning of the rift. 'There are Trása and your friend,' she said, pointing to the two dark figures running toward the lightning, one leading the other. 'Don't run them over.'

'Thanks for the tip,' Rónán said. 'You reckon we can outrun the cops?'

'Do we have a choice?' Darragh asked, looking back, as Rónán was, at the Gardaí bearing down on them.

Rónán began to slow the vehicle. He unclipped his seatbelt and glanced in the rear-view mirror again. 'How do you guys feel about jumping out of moving cars?'

'The ground is wet and soft,' Sorcha said, surveying the rain-drenched terrain with a warrior's eye. 'We should be able to disembark without serious injury. Can you make this thing go on without us?'

Rónán nodded. Now they were slowing down, the Gardaí behind them were much closer. They didn't have long. 'Darragh, get in the back with Sorcha,' he said. 'When I tell you, jump out and roll. They'll be watching the car, so you should be able to get clear, once they've gone past you. Then I'll point the car up the fairway and I'll bail, too. It won't take them long to catch the car, but by the time they realise we're not in it, we should be through the rift.' As he spoke, Darragh was already climbing through the gap between the front seats. Sorcha moved closer to the door to make room for him. As soon as he was in the back, Rónán slowed the car even more. 'You ready?'

'When you are,' Darragh assured him.

Rónán glanced in the mirror at his brother. 'See you on the other side, Bro.'

'Count on it,' Darragh replied with a grin. Then he punched Rónán's shoulder and added, 'Bro.'

Sorcha opened the door, and glanced down, alarmed at how fast the ground was moving beneath them. She didn't hesitate, however. Taking a deep breath, she dived forward, tucking her shoulder under as she hit the ground, rolling over on the cold wet grass, before she slid to a stop on the tree line. Darragh was right behind her, his landing heavier and less elegant than hers, but he appeared to have made it in one piece.

'Are you injured, *Leath tiarna*?'

'I don't think so,' he said, lying on his belly beside her. As Rónán predicted they would, the Gardaí cars sailed straight past them, intent on pursuing the car ahead. Rónán swerved his car sharply to slam the back door shut, and kept on driving.

Sorcha glanced to her right. She could see the red lightning of the rift much more clearly from here. They had only a narrow stretch of grass, perhaps fifty paces wide, and then a short distance through the rough to the old stone circle ruin. With the Gardaí focussed on Rónán's vehicle, they should be able to make it easily. Until the cars turned back toward them at the end of the fairway, the Gardaí were driving away from the rift. 'Let's go.'

Muddy and drenched to the skin, Sorcha rose to a crouch and checked they were still clear. Then she sprinted across the grass toward the rift, where she could see Trása and Hayley waiting, their figures dark silhouettes against the red lightning. Trása was holding Hayley by the hand, a grip from which the blind girl seemed to be trying to break free.

'Agh!'

Sorcha stopped when she realised it was Darragh crying out in pain behind her. He wasn't following her, but was still on the ground, clutching his ankle. She ran back and squatted down beside him. He was drenched, shivering, and grimacing with pain.

'You're injured.' It was a statement, not a question. Had Darragh been whole they would have been through the rift by now.

'My ankle,' he said, wincing.

'Is it broken?'

'I don't think so. But I can't put any weight on it.'

Sorcha glanced toward the rift. They were caught in the rough separating the two fairways. The stone circle sat in the rough of another dividing strip of carefully cultivated wilderness. Sorcha could have screamed with frustration. A mere fifty paces away was the doorway to safety and a magical cure for Darragh's relatively minor, but crippling, injury. She needed Rónán. Darragh was far too big for her to carry, and with him hobbling beside her, they would never make it over the open ground of the fairway before the Gardaí found them.

Over at the rift, Trása had spied them and was beckoning them, urging them to hurry. If she was calling out to them, Sorcha couldn't hear her over the rain and the sirens.

As she summed up their predicament, her thoughts were interrupted by a noise so loud it seemed the very ground shuddered with it. She looked up. At the far end of the fairway, the car Rónán was driving crashed into a tree followed by another crash as the closest Gardaí car behind it, unable to find purchase on the slick ground, collided with the Audi's rear end. Figuring Rónán must be out of the car and on his way back to the rift by now, Sorcha scanned the rainy darkness, but she couldn't see him. He was either still in the car and trapped, or he was better at concealment than she imagined. Perhaps some of Darragh's warrior training had passed to his brother during the *Comhroinn*.

'Wait here,' she said urgently, figuring she had no other choice. 'Stay low. I'll get help.'

If Trása and Rónán helped her carry him, she might be able to get Darragh to the rift before they were discovered. With Ciarán waiting with his sword for them on the other side, it would be a foolish man who would follow the fugitives through the lightning. It would certainly be a one-way trip.

'There's Rónán,' Darragh said, pointing past Sorcha.

Rónán's crouched and running profile was now also silhouetted by the red lightning of the open rift. When he reached the stone circle, he took Hayley by the hand, trying to coax her into the rift. Sorcha wasn't surprised. She was more surprised Rónán had managed to convince the girl to leave the safety of the rehabilitation facility to embark on this perilous journey in the first place.

Sorcha couldn't see into the rift, but she assumed Ciarán was waiting for them on the other side. *How much longer can the rift stay open?* she wondered. Although there was no theoretical limit to how long a rift between worlds could be maintained, it took a lot of effort. Even though it had been only a few minutes since it opened, Ciarán would begin to tire before long. The *Tuatha* who channelled the magic directly might be able to sustain a rift for long periods, but a mere Druid — the Undivided excepted — couldn't maintain one for very long at all.

'I'll be back in a moment, *Leath tiarna,*' she promised, and ran across the open ground toward the rift.

As she sprinted across the wet grass, she glanced up the fairway at the scene of the crash. With the rain, the lights, and the confusion, the Gardaí still hadn't noticed the rift in the rough on the next fairway. Ahead of her, outlined by the red lightning, Hayley was stepping through — albeit reluctantly — to the other realm. Trása turned and spotted Sorcha running toward the rift and shouted at her to hurry. Having seen Hayley safely through the rift, Rónán turned too, and realised Darragh wasn't with Sorcha. He started toward her at a run but had only taken a couple of steps when a sharp crack rang out across the golf course.

Rónán dived to the ground.

For an instant, Sorcha froze. She had no idea what the sound was, but given Rónán's reaction to it, she figured it wasn't a good omen. Glancing up the fairway, she realised the Gardaí had finally noticed them. Or at least they'd spotted Rónán and the rift.

Another sharp crack rang out. The Gardaí were running toward them shouting something about stopping and threatening to shoot again. Suddenly a dazzling light coming from the roof of one of the Gardaí cars pierced the darkness. It lit the rift like daylight, but threw the open ground where Sorcha was trapped into comparative darkness.

We're not going to make it. Sorcha made the decision in a heartbeat.

'Come back for us!' she yelled, and then she turned and ran back toward Darragh. The Gardaí had found Rónán, but he could still escape through the rift. Darragh's only hope for eluding capture now was Sorcha.

She reached him a few seconds later and glanced up. The overhanging branches looked sturdy enough to carry their weight, the vegetation thick enough to conceal them and they were low enough for Darragh to lift himself up without having to put pressure on his ankle. Darragh saw the direction of her gaze. He pushed himself onto his one good leg, and stared at the rift. 'He'll come back for us, won't he?' he asked.

'You came for him,' Sorcha pointed out.

Darragh nodded and reached up, grabbed the branch and pulled himself over it. He then reached down and offered Sorcha his hand. She took it and he all but lifted her slight frame into the tree beside him.

'Higher,' Sorcha ordered.

Darragh repeated the move, pulling himself higher into the thick wet foliage, using his upper-body strength, rather than his legs. Once safely concealed in the branches, Sorcha opened a small gap in the leaves. Another shot rang out. Rónán seemed to be hesitating on the edge of the rift, but Trása grabbed his hand and dragged him toward the opening.

Trása pulled Rónán into the rift almost at exactly the same time as another sharp crack rent the rainy night. With a blinding burst of magical energy Sorcha had never witnessed previously, the rift flared and then disappeared, leaving the Gardaí running toward nothing but a smoking circle of stones where their quarry had been only a moment before.

'What was that light?' Darragh asked in a whisper, blinking painfully as his eyes reacted to the explosion.

'I have no idea,' Sorcha told him in a low voice, white spots dancing in front of her own eyes. 'I've never seen a rift close like that before.'

'Do you suppose they got through safely?'

'We'll find out soon enough,' she said. 'You'll have to arrange another time for Ciarán to open the rift, perhaps even another place. Do you think you can make the connection to our realm without the residual magic of Rónán's tattoo to aid you?'

Darragh smiled briefly. 'Using the puddle-phone?'

'That's a stupid name for it,' she said, annoyed he had adopted Rónán's infantile term for the magical link between realms.

'Accurate, though.'

'Can you do it?'

'I don't know,' Darragh said, settling back against the trunk of the tree. 'And we're not going to find out tonight, I suspect.' He rubbed his upper arms against the chill and moved his leg so it was stretched out along the branch. Even in the dark Sorcha could see how swollen his ankle was. Darragh was bedraggled, in pain, and in danger but he seemed in good spirits. 'How long do you think the cops will be down there poking about?'

'All night, I would imagine,' Sorcha said, glancing down at the milling Gardaí. 'Do you think you can stay up here that long?'

Darragh smiled. 'Ciarán taught me to hunt, Sorcha.'

She nodded in approval. If Ciarán had taught Darragh, he had been well instructed on how to remain in a blind, quiet and still, for days if necessary.

'Then we wait,' she said, squirming around to get as comfortable as she could on her perch. There really wasn't anything else they could do.

CHAPTER 64

Pushed through a crackling curtain of light so bright even Hayley could sense it, she landed hard on her hands and knees, surprised to find the ground bone dry. Grunting with the pain of the impact, she turned in confusion, calling out to Ren, not sure what was happening. Until the explosion of light that blew her to the ground, Trása was yelling, Ren was urging her to go through ... whatever it was she was supposed to go through, and there had been gunshots. Several of them.

Hayley had a bad feeling they were shooting at her. Or at least shooting at Ren — who had been right beside her — which was, essentially, the same thing.

Angry rather than frightened, the abrupt silence worried Hayley almost as much as the vanished rain. She pushed herself up, wincing at her skinned knees, wondering where she was. She was still in the open — the cool gentle breeze on her face warned her of that much — but there were no sirens, no shouting, no voices other than someone softly groaning in pain nearby.

'Ren? Ren, where are you?' She turned in a circle, her arms outstretched, but there was nothing within reach. 'Where am *I*?'

'*Trása?*'

She turned in the direction of the voice. It was a male voice, and it wasn't the one who was groaning. Nor was it Ren. Or his brother whom she'd met briefly before they shoved her in the car with that maniac, Trása, because Darragh had sounded exactly like Ren. 'My name is Hayley Boyle,' she said. 'I'm not Trása. Why would you think I was Trása?'

The man who spoke was silent for a time, and then he brushed past her and said something she didn't understand, although if she had to guess, it sounded something like the Gaeilge she learned at school.

'What?' she said.

'You only speak English?'

'Obviously.'

'I said come here. We have to help Marcroy.'

Hayley turned, following the voice. 'Marcroy? Who the hell is Marcroy? What happened to Ren? And Trása? And his brother? And the cops? And the rain, come to think of it?'

'I don't know,' the man said. 'Please come over here.'

'Come where?' she asked. 'I can't see you. I'm blind.'

'Oh.' A moment later, she felt a cool hand on her forehead and a sharp spear of pain behind her eyes. Hayley jerked back from the sting, blinking furiously.

'There. Now come and help me. Please. Something is seriously wrong with Marcroy. He seems to be dying and I'm not sure if I have the power to heal one of the *Tuatha Dé Danann*.'

Hayley opened her eyes. Before her lay a moonlit vista of gently rolling hills dotted with hedgerows under a clear, starry sky. She was standing on a rise inside a stone circle that looked as if it had been constructed a few days ago, not thousands of years in the past. There was no sign of Ren, his brother, the cops, or anybody else ... nor the city of Dublin.

But more importantly, Hayley could *see*. 'What the *hell* ...?'

'Please, I need your help.'

Still trying to come to grips with the sudden return of her sight, Hayley turned to find a young man dressed in a brown robe kneeling over another young man wearing a cloak so fine it looked spun from spider webs. He was the one moaning. His skin was deathly pale, his chest covered in blood.

'Oh my God!' she said, hurrying over to them. 'Have you called an ambulance?'

'I've tried to stem the blood flow,' said the young man who had so casually cured her blindness. 'But I think his heart is wounded. Although I'm not even sure if *sídhe* have hearts, and that's certainly a valid question in Marcroy's case. But still, he shouldn't be like this. He should be able to heal himself. I don't understand why ...'

'He's been shot, that's why ... what's your name?'

'Brógán.'

'Then, Brógán, you need a phone,' she told the distraught young man. 'This boy needs paramedics and an ambulance and major surgery, right now. Do you have a phone? I'll call them if you want, but you need to stop that bleeding. Put some pressure on it.' Even with nothing more than her rudimentary Girl Guide first-aid training, she could see this was beyond the scope of anything she could do. And probably beyond the scope of anything this young man could do, either.

He looked up at her in confusion. 'What do you mean "shot"?'

'I mean *shot*,' she said, looking at him oddly. 'You know … bang, bang, you're dead.' When Brógán continued to stare at her blankly, she formed her hand into a gun with her thumb and forefinger and repeated the words.

'Oh, you mean he has a bullet in him?'

'Well … *duh* …'

Brógán slapped his forehead as if he'd just had an epiphany. 'Of course! The bullet comes from the other realm. It'll be sucking the magic out of him! That's why he's dying.'

'Yeah,' she agreed. '*That's* the reason.'

'We need to get it out!'

'Hence the aforementioned paramedics, ambulance and major surgery,' Hayley said, squatting down beside him. 'Are you sure you don't have a phone?' She was beginning to wonder if she'd fallen back into her coma. This bizarre scene had all the hallmarks of an insane dream world brought about by a blow to the head.

'How deep would it be?' Brógán asked, tearing open the wounded young man's shirt to expose the bloody hole in his chest. He was so pale it seemed all his blood had been drained from his body already. Hayley had no idea who he was but his pointed features were inhumanly pretty, even when contorted in pain. He had impossibly long, straight blond hair and oddly pointed ears. He reminded her, inexplicably, of Trása, and looked to be not much older.

'Excuse me?'

'The bullet?' Brógán asked, gingerly feeling around the edges of the bullet wound. 'How deeply would it have penetrated, do you think?'

'I don't know ... Oh God ... oh no!' Hayley exclaimed, jumping to her feet and taking a step back. 'You're not seriously going to ...'

But he did. Without so much as stopping to think about it, Brógán plunged the fingers of his right hand into the hole in Marcroy's chest and began fishing around for the bullet. Hayley backed away from them, gasping in horror, fearing she was going to vomit, as the wounded youth's back arched with the pain. Brógán — bloody to the wrist — felt about for the lead pellet that had torn Marcroy's chest asunder.

'Stop it! You're killing him!' she cried, hoping this really *was* a nightmare. It had to be. On the face of it, there was no other reasonable conclusion.

'Not as fast as this bullet is killing him,' Brógán replied, closing his eyes to concentrate on feeling for it. 'I'll not be the one made to answer to Queen Orlagh when she asks how her envoy died.'

Hayley cast about for a weapon. Maybe there was a branch or a rock nearby she could use to disable this madman before he killed this poor dying boy and then probably her, straight afterward. Before she could find a weapon, however, Brógán let out a yelp of triumph and pulled his fingers out of Marcroy's chest, clutching the bloody bullet that had almost killed him —

and likely would kill him yet, given the brutal way Brógán had removed it.

'You're insane!' she cried, backing away from him even further.

The young man who'd been shot cried out in agony, and then, inexplicably, almost as soon as Brógán's fingers cleared his chest, the bleeding seemed to stop of its own accord. Hayley watched in astonishment as the jagged bullet hole began to shrink.

Within moments, it was completely gone.

'No freaking way.'

Marcroy blinked a few times, as if trying to remember where he was. He stared at Hayley. '*Trása?*'

'Why does everybody keep asking me that?' she said. 'My name is Hayley.'

The young man pushed himself up on his elbows and glanced around before looking at Brógán with a concerned expression. 'Where are they?'

He asked the question in the language that sounded like Gaelige, but this time, she understood it. Perhaps she really was in a coma. She'd heard of people who went into a coma speaking one language and came out speaking another. It was the only explanation that made sense. Unlike Ren, who had been known to speak a language like a native after only a couple of weeks of hearing it spoken consistently, Hayley struggled with them. But she understood every word of what Marcroy was saying, as though it was her native tongue.

Brógán was shaking his head, looking very worried. 'I don't know, *tiarna*,' he said in his own language. 'There was a great deal of confusion. This girl came through the rift first. Rónán and

Trása were stepping through when you were wounded by one of the weapons from the other realm.' He opened his palm to show Marcroy the bloody bullet he'd just pulled from his chest. Marcroy reached for it but snatched his hand back when Brógán added, 'Be careful. It's of the magicless realm.'

'Did the Undivided make it back?'

Brógán shrugged uncertainly. 'When you collapsed, the rift imploded. I don't know what happened to them. Or your niece.'

The young man was silent for a moment, pondering the news. Hayley had a million questions, but couldn't figure out which one to ask first.

'You are Rónán's friend?' Marcroy asked her, climbing to his feet as if nothing was wrong with him. Were it not for his bloodied shirt, and the fact that Hayley had witnessed his injury for herself, she would never have believed that this young man with the strangely pointed ears had lain dying on the ground only minutes ago. 'You are the one he and Darragh returned to the other realm to find?'

Hayley nodded, a little apprehensively, trying to process what her eyes were telling her. Nowhere could she find an explanation for his disconcerting eyes or his small, sharply pointed teeth.

'Where is Ren?' She asked it in English and then realised she knew the words in his language, so she repeated them. '*Cá bhfuil* Ren?'

'That's an interesting question,' Marcroy said, cocking his head to one side. 'You are the daughter of one Patrick Boyle, are you not?'

Hayley wasn't expecting that. 'You *know* my

father?' she asked, replying in the same language, a part of her fascinated by the fact that she could.

'I know of him,' Marcroy said with a shrug. He studied her curiously for a moment and then smiled. 'Trása's *eiléfein*. How fascinating. You certainly bear a resemblance to her, although one has to be looking for it. Perhaps it's the hair.'

'I'm sure it is,' Hayley said, feeling uncomfortable with the way he was staring at her. 'What happened to Ren and his brother?'

'They're still alive,' Brógán assured her.

'How can you be sure about that?'

'I healed you,' he told her. 'If the Undivided were dead, the magic would stop flowing to the Druids and you would still be blind and unable to comprehend us.'

Although she understood his words, for Hayley, not a single thing about that sentence made sense. She glanced at Brógán, trying to get her head around everything she'd witnessed in the past few moments. 'How did you do that, by the way? Some of the best specialists in Europe said my brain damage was likely to be permanent. You slapped me on the forehead like some crazy TV evangelist and I was cured.'

Marcroy smiled at her, stepping a little closer. 'You have no idea where you are, do you?'

'Stuck in a bizarre hallucination brought on by falling back into a coma, I suspect.' Even as she said it, Hayley knew if this was a coma, she probably wouldn't be dreaming she was in it. This place was real. Improbable, but real.

'You have crossed into another realm,' Marcroy explained. 'Realities, you might call them. Here you are in the realm of the *Tuatha Dé Danann*.'

Hayley smiled at that, certain she must be delusional. 'The land of the Faerie?'

'You don't believe it?' he asked. 'How curious. Look about you, Hayley Boyle. The world you know has vanished in an instant, replaced by this world, where nothing is as it was. You stand here after stepping through a veil in the very fabric of the universe itself, having witnessed several miracles in as many minutes and yet you deny the evidence of your own eyes? Eyes that can now see as a result of one of those miracles.' He stepped so close to her she could see his alien eyes with their vertical, cat-like irises. 'Tell me, Trása's *eileféin*. Do I look human to you?'

Hayley shook her head mutely.

'Do you see anything of your world here?'

Again, Hayley shook her head, mesmerised by his hypnotic gaze.

'Do you believe in magic?'

'No ... maybe ...'

Marcroy smiled, and took Hayley's hands in his. His touch was electric.

'Then you have a treat in store, my sweet. Let me take you to *Tír Na nÓg*. I will show you magic, the likes of which you cannot imagine. And given you are Trása's *eileféin*, who knows? Perhaps you have the same ability to wield it.'

'My lord?' Brógán said nervously.

Marcroy glanced over his shoulder at the young man. 'You dare question me?'

'No ... I mean ... it's just ... well ... I agreed to help you because you said that if we aided the Undivided in bringing Trása's *eileféin* back, then the treaty would be destroyed.'

'And I was right.'

'You said you could help stop a catastrophe.' He sounded very upset.

'And I have stopped it,' Marcroy said, smiling at Hayley. 'Trása's *eileféin* is only Trása's *eileféin* if Trása is here with her. She has not returned, so we have no conflict.'

'But you gave me your word!' Brógán cried. 'I betrayed the Druids for you! I betrayed Ciarán! You said you would preserve the treaty.'

'And have I not done exactly that? The Treaty of *Tír Na nÓg* remains intact. The Undivided live on and the Druids still have their power. How have I not kept my word?'

Brógán looked on the verge of tears. 'But they're missing! The rift collapsed. We have to find them. We have to get the Undivided back!'

'Well why don't you speak to Ciarán about that?' Marcroy suggested, raising Hayley's hand to his lips. Her fears, her doubts, even her inhibitions fell away at the touch of his magical lips on her fingers. She found herself utterly enchanted by the *Tuatha* lord; so enchanted the unsettling conversation he was having with Brógán faded to a minor irritation.

Still holding her hand, Marcroy glanced over his shoulder at the Druid. 'If you get back to him in time, Ciarán may still be alive. He'll open another rift for you ... assuming he doesn't run you through the moment you heal his wounds. And if he doesn't live ... well, I'm sure if you go to the Druid Council and explain that you, a lowly *Liaig*, and their great hero, Ciarán mac Connacht, facilitated the Undivided jumping through a rift into a world without magic so they could break the *Tuatha* law against bringing an *eileféin* back to this world, they'll understand.' Marcroy turned back to Hayley and smiled at her with devastating charm. 'Did you want to see the magic of *Tír Na nÓg*, my lady?'

Hayley nodded, not trusting herself to speak.

Marcroy put his arm around her waist. 'Then hold on, sweet Hayley Boyle, and let me show you the wonders of *my* world.'

Putting her arms around the *sídhe*, Hayley closed her eyes, and a moment later, the stone circle disappeared with the fading echo of Brógán's cry of protest.

Hayley didn't care any longer. If this was a dream, she just hoped that this time she wouldn't wake from it for a long, long time.

CHAPTER 65

By dawn, Darragh was in agony. He was chilled to the bone, his ankle throbbed mercilessly, and he was cramped by the awkward position he'd maintained all night. He didn't think Sorcha had fared much better, but she was stoic by nature — or perhaps just pigheaded. If she was suffering, she did not intend to complain about it.

They had waited in vain for the crowd around the stone circle to dissipate. There seemed to be a great deal of confusion down there about what had happened to Rónán and Hayley. When Darragh accessed Rónán's memories of her, they left him feeling just as protective of her, just as anxious to see her safe.

What he hadn't bargained on was that the Gardaí were now treating a large part of the golf course as a crime scene. The authorities of this realm had no explanation for the disappearance of Rónán, Hayley and Trása and it seemed they weren't going to leave without one. All through the night, working under portable lights bright enough to blind anybody foolish enough to look directly at them, the Gardaí had scoured the area around the crash site and the old stone circle with its inexplicable burn marks, trying to figure out the answer to the mystery.

The strip of rough separating the fairways where Darragh and Sorcha were concealed was just outside the perimeter of the area cordoned off by the Gardaí. Unless Darragh and Sorcha drew attention to themselves, they were safe for the time being. Unfortunately, they couldn't go anywhere. They might — if the Gardaí were distracted — be able to get down out of the branches. They were a good fifty paces from the other strip of rough where the old stone circle lay. But with Darragh barely able to walk, it didn't matter. They couldn't go anywhere until the Gardaí and all their equipment and assorted hangers-on had left.

Despite the drizzling rain, which hadn't let up all night, the Gardaí looked like they were settling in for a good long stay.

Still, it had been entertaining to watch the shenanigans going on below them, which was useful, because if either of them fell asleep, they risked falling out of the tree. Although they'd only caught fleeting snatches of conversations, Darragh soon concluded the Gardaí were at a loss to explain what had happened. That amused him. All this so-called technology and they didn't have the first clue about rift running.

He was bothered by the tone of their conversations, however. They seemed convinced that Rónán, with Trása as his accomplice, had kidnapped Hayley and had some nefarious purpose in mind for her. Their discussions often repeated the fear that the first forty-eight hours were critical if they hoped to find Hayley alive.

As daylight crept over the city, increasing their

risk of discovery, the full extent of the carnage they'd wrought over the golf course became apparent. The fairways were scoured with deep tyre ruts, the greens gouged out by spinning wheels, the damage compounded further by the many other vehicles driving on to the course bringing Gardaí, search teams and the media, who'd set up a veritable war camp in the car park, waiting for news.

Just on dawn, a newcomer arrived. He climbed out of a Gardaí car that pulled up a few paces away from their tree. As soon as the woman who seemed to be directing the other Gardaí spied him, she waved, finished her conversation with another Gardaí officer wearing white overalls, and came toward them. She walked across the rough, almost directly under Darragh's feet, and stopped just inside the tree line and the meagre shelter it offered from the patchy rain.

'What are you doing out of hospital?' she asked the man. Darragh recognised him immediately. It was the Gardaí detective Rónán had called 'Detective Pete'.

'I'm fine, Inspector Duggan,' he said. 'It's just a concussion.'

She frowned at him. 'Then come back to work when you're not concussed,' she suggested, a little impatiently. The Gardaí inspector turned to walk away.

'There were two of them!' Pete said.

She stopped and looked at Pete. 'We know. We caught him on CCTV at St Christopher's. He had that girl with him. The one claiming to be Jack O'Righin's granddaughter.' The older woman frowned. 'Now go home, Pete. You're no good to me in your current condition and we're going to need all hands on deck to save Hayley Boyle from these lunatics.'

'I'm not talking about the girl. There were two Ren Kavanaughs.'

The inspector walked back beneath the trees to where Pete was standing and put a motherly hand on his shoulder. 'Pete,' she said, 'it's been a long night, and it's not your fault he got away again. Go home, lad. Get some rest. We'll keep you posted.'

'I wasn't seeing things, Inspector Duggan. Ren has a brother. An identical twin brother.'

'You saw this alleged identical twin brother?'

Pete nodded. 'Of course I saw him! He was driving the car they stole from me!'

'Is he the one who knocked you out?'

'No. That was the little bitch who popped up out of nowhere in the front seat and knocked me for six. But I swear, Inspector, I'm not delusional. There're two of them out there. We have to find them.'

The inspector nodded in agreement and then raised her hand and beckoned another Gardaí officer to her — the driver who had brought Pete to the golf course. When he hurried forward to see what she wanted, she turned to address him. 'Take Detective Doherty home, please.'

'But ma'am!' Pete objected. 'I'm not seeing things. You have to believe me! There *are* two of them!'

Inspector Duggan kept walking across the fairway to the stone circle, where she resumed giving orders to the Gardaí. Beneath the trees, Pete cursed angrily, but allowed his driver to escort him back to the car.

Darragh glanced at Sorcha, who'd watched the exchange with interest. 'They don't believe I exist,' he whispered, smiling.

'Excellent!' Sorcha whispered back grumpily. 'Then we can just jump down from here and walk away. They won't see you if you don't exist.'

Darragh understood Sorcha's frustration. They would be here for a long while yet. He closed his eyes for a moment and tried to push away the pain. He could ignore the cold and the cramping, but his ankle was pounding. What a terrible world this was where one could suffer so, and not have the ability to heal or be healed, by magic.

Not long after Pete was driven off, another car bounced across the fairway. This wasn't a Gardaí car. Darragh recognised it from Rónán's memories.

It was Kiva Kavanaugh's Bentley.

Darragh signalled silently to Sorcha, who shifted slightly to get a better look. The appearance of the Bentley caused a frenzy among the waiting press, but the Gardaí charged with holding them back kept things under control. The car pulled up directly beneath the tree, as Pete's car had. A uniformed man hurried out from the driver's side of the car and opened the passenger door. A moment later a slight woman wearing a tailored pants suit and wrapped in a luscious white fur coat emerged.

'Who is that?' Sorcha mouthed silently at Darragh.

'Rónán's adopted mother,' he whispered back.

The woman turned to the uniformed man before they left the car, and hugged him briefly.

'You wait here, Patrick,' she ordered, clutching the man's shoulder comfortingly. 'I'll speak to them. They'll just stonewall you and tell you everything is fine.'

The chauffeur nodded and closed the door as Kiva marched across the wet ground. Darragh watched the woman with interest, his own observations overlaid by Rónán's confused emotions.

Rónán's feelings were a mishmash of affection and frustration, fondness and irritation for this woman. Kiva Kavanaugh was a generous and giving woman, but easily distracted, easily influenced, self-centred and she spent far too much of her time worrying about what the gossip magazines were writing about her.

Their real mother was nothing more than a vague memory, even for Darragh, so he was fascinated by this pseudo-mother he now shared with Rónán through their memories. *Is she the way out of this mess?* he wondered. He watched her gesticulate as she demanded answers from Inspector Duggan, who seemed rather put out that the actress had been allowed through the police barricades and onto the golf course.

'Mother of God!' a voice hissed below them. 'Ren? Is that you?'

Alarmed, Darragh glanced down to find the man who'd been driving the Bentley staring up at them. Patrick, he recalled the man's name was, a name accompanied by a warm feeling of trust and affection that rivalled, if not exceeded, Rónán's affection for his mother.

But was this a man they could trust?

Darragh would know soon enough.

'Don't look up!' Sorcha hissed at him angrily. 'Someone might be watching!'

Patrick immediately looked away, which gave Darragh hope. If the man was planning to betray their presence, he could already have shouted out for the nearby Gardaí and they'd be swarming the tree as they spoke.

'What have you done with my Hayley?' Patrick called up to them in a loud whisper.

The question was critical, Darragh realised. This was Hayley's father.

'Nothing,' he whispered loudly, scanning the people on the fairway for any indication their conversation had been noticed. 'She's fine.'

'Then where the fuck is she, lad? And don't give me any bullshit.'

Ah ... that was the problem. *We sent her through a rift to another realm so her blindness could be healed by magic*, wasn't going to get him very far.

'I can explain,' Darragh told him in a low voice. 'But not here. Can you help us?'

Patrick risked a glance up at them. 'Who's yer one?'

'A friend.'

'She the one pretending to be old Jack's kin?'

'No.'

Patrick hesitated, thrusting his hands into his pockets, as he turned to look at Kiva. She was wagging her finger at Inspector Duggan, loudly demanding to know what the Gardaí had done to find her son and rescue her cousin's daughter, because clearly this mystery girl nobody could identify was pulling all the strings and her poor Ren was just a dupe in her evil plan. Apparently, Kiva didn't accept for a moment that Ren was responsible for Hayley's disappearance, even

593

though by the sound of it, she'd seen the CCTV tapes from St Christopher's already and was in no doubt as to the identity of the young woman's kidnappers.

'You promise me my girl's not been hurt?' Patrick asked after a time.

Darragh nodded. 'I swear.'

Patrick looked around for a moment. 'Can you get to the car park?'

'We'd never make it,' Sorcha said. 'Darragh is injured.'

Patrick glanced up at her uncertainly. 'Who?'

Darragh nearly fell out of the tree in shock when he clearly saw the chauffeur's face for the first time. 'I've sprained my ankle,' he explained quickly. And then he turned to Sorcha and mouthed *Call me Ren*. There would be time later to explain who he really was.

Patrick debated the issue for a long, tense moment and then, with an air of studied nonchalance, walked casually to the back of the car, which was parked directly beneath the overhanging branch where they were concealed. He popped the trunk with the remote control and bent over the large empty compartment, pretending to fix something inside.

'You reckon you can jump into the trunk?' Patrick asked, glancing toward the car park. The media were desperately trying to get a shot of Kiva. The raised trunk offered a small and not very effective shield against their long, curious lenses. The trunk of the tree shielded them from the Gardaí around the stone circle.

'What if someone sees us?' Sorcha asked.

'Then we're all screwed, lassie.'

They didn't have any time to quibble about it, in any case. Patrick was offering them a way out, although once they were in the trunk of the car — a trunk considerably larger than the one they'd confined Warren in — they would be at Patrick Boyle's mercy.

Darragh had no choice but to trust Rónán's feelings, and his own, about the dependability of this man. 'Move back.'

Patrick did as he asked and Darragh turned to Sorcha. 'You go first.'

She nodded and with a lithe grace that belied the cold night they'd spent cramped in the branches, she lowered herself down, landing in the Bentley's trunk with hardly a sound.

They waited, holding their breath to see if anybody had noticed, but nobody raised the alarm. Kiva was still telling off Inspector Duggan. The press were still trying to get a shot of it, and the rest of the police were too intent on searching the ground for clues.

'Okay, now your turn!' Patrick hissed.

Darragh didn't land nearly so silently or elegantly as Sorcha. As soon as he landed, however, Patrick started to close the trunk. Darragh managed to move around a little until he and Sorcha somehow managed to fit. It was then that Sorcha gasped as she spied Patrick's face clearly for the first time.

'Don't know how long it's gonna be before I can let you out, laddie,' Patrick told them softly, as Darragh elbowed Sorcha sharply to warn her to remain silent. 'Try not to make any noise.'

'Thanks for this, Patrick.'

'You can thank me, lad,' Patrick Boyle told him with a frown, 'by bringing back my girl.' And then he slammed the trunk shut, and they were plunged into darkness.

Sorcha wiggled uncomfortably behind Darragh. It was cramped but blessedly dry and surprisingly warm.

'Wonderful plan, *Leath tiarna*,' she said softly. 'We are now locked in the darkness at the mercy of the man who thinks you kidnapped his daughter.'

'He won't betray us,' Darragh whispered back.

'Why?' He could hear the scepticism in her voice. 'Because he looks like Amergin?'

He knew she'd seen it. That's why she gasped. 'Amergin took a magical oath to protect the Undivided. I believe that oath holds true for his *eileféin*.'

'Amergin stole your brother from you and threw him through a rift with the express intention of sundering the Undivided at the behest of a *sídhe*,' she reminded him, her body pressed against his like a sleeping lover.

'But don't you see?' he asked softly, wishing there was room to turn and face her so he could explain what was suddenly so clear to him. And hoping there was nobody outside listening to them. 'Amergin sent Rónán to his *eileféin*. Why would he do that?'

'Because he was a vain, self-centred fool as well as a traitor?'

'He knew his oath would transcend realms,' Darragh whispered, certain of the truth of it. He knew Amergin better than Sorcha.

'Then you might want to consider something else,' Sorcha told him, clearly unhappy with him. 'If the man who just locked us in this pitch black box, with a vague promise of release, is the *eileféin* of your good friend and loyal traitor, Amergin, then his daughter — the girl you and your brother just sent through the rift — is Trása's *eileféin*.'

Darragh hadn't thought of that. 'I suppose you're right. Why?'

'Because if she is, and the *Tuatha* ever discover what you've done, *Leath tiarna*,' she informed him, 'then the Treaty of *Tír Na nÓg* is dead and you and your brother, with your foolish notions of heroism and chivalry — for the sake of a traitor's daughter, I might add — may have destroyed the Druids in our realm forever.'

CHAPTER 66

'God ... what happened?'

Ren had landed hard on his shoulder in the explosion. His ears were still ringing, his eyes blinded by dancing lights.

'I ... I don't know.'

He pushed himself up unto his hands and knees, surprised it was Trása who'd answered him. 'Trása? Where's Hayley?'

'She's not here.'

Worried by the realisation, Ren rubbed his eyes and looked around. They were in a stone circle, but it was nothing like the one in Dublin. That had been weathered away to almost nothing. This looked new and was engraved with characters he didn't recognise.

'Where are we?' he asked, pushing himself painfully to his feet. His palms and knees were raw, his shoulder aching and he could taste blood.

'I don't know, but we're not in my realm,' Trása announced with certainty as she sat up, rubbing the bump on her head. She was on the ground a few feet away, still wet and bedraggled from the rain of the other realm.

Ren scanned the moonlit circle, with no way

of telling where they were, other than that it was warmer here and was no longer raining. 'How can you tell?'

'I am still human,' she said, holding out her hands in front of her, as if checking to be sure she wasn't mistaken. She looked at him and shrugged. 'Unless you thoughtfully decided to lift the curse on me as we stepped into the rift, then I'm still bound by it. In my realm, I would turn instantly back into an owl the moment I stepped through the rift, and I'd have to stay in that form until you or Darragh chose to free me.' She closed her eyes for a moment and the bruise on her forehead slowly faded to nothing. 'But I can still heal myself,' she added. 'It's like we're home ... but not.'

Ren turned a full circle, trying to figure out where he was. This stone circle didn't look like the one in Dublin, nor the circle from which they'd left Darragh's realm, in Drombeg. 'I can feel the magic,' he said.

Ren could feel it in a way he'd never have expected to before the *Comhroinn*. He could feel the difference in the air, the difference in the way he perceived the world. It wasn't just the difference between a world of trees and hand-drawn ploughs and a city blanketed in petrochemical fumes. It was something that resonated in his bones. He'd felt the same thing when he woke up in the shepherd's hut in Darragh's reality, but back then, without the benefit of what his twin brother knew, he hadn't recognised it for what it was.

Ren closed his eyes for a moment, trying to find Darragh's memory of healing. It turned out not to be an instructive memory so much as a *knowing*. He just had to make it happen.

Concentrating on his scraped knees first, Ren willed the pain away and the skin to heal. He was rewarded with exactly that. Opening his eyes, he looked down at the clear pink flesh showing through the wet denim of his torn jeans and grinned like an idiot. 'Cool.'

'I'm so pleased you find it entertaining,' Trása said, climbing to her feet. 'What happened to the rift?'

'You're asking *me*?'

'That explosion ...' she said, looking around with a frown. 'I've never seen anything like that before.'

'Could something have happened to Ciarán?' he asked. He was the one who had supposedly been opening the rift. A sudden, awful thought occurred to him. 'There were bullets flying around back there. Suppose one of them got through the rift?'

Trása thought on that for a moment and then nodded. 'It's possible.'

'That might explain why the rift shut down like that,' Ren said. 'And why we're apparently not in Kansas anymore, Toto.'

'Are you saying we've been thrown into a completely different realm?' she asked, looking at him oddly.

'You tell me. You're the one who jumps through realities and messes up people's lives for a living.'

Trása didn't appear keen on committing to anything. 'Do you have any idea where we are?'

He looked at her askance. 'Can't *you* tell?'

'How am I supposed to know?'

'I can count the number of times Darragh and I have crossed realities on the fingers of one hand. You're a rift runner. Don't *you* have some way of knowing?'

'Of course not.'

'Then how do you know where you're going when you open a rift?' he asked. 'If there's a gazillion realities out there, how do you know you're jumping into the right one?'

'That's what the jewels are for,' Trása said, squatting down to study the symbols on the nearest standing stone. In the bright clear moonlight, Ren could see they were shorter than the ones in Dublin, and the standing stones in Darragh's realm. The circle itself was much larger, too.

As Trása spoke of the jewels, Darragh's memories filled in the details for Ren. The jewels were engraved with the symbol of each realm. He also realised now how Darragh had known where to look for him. His brother had received the information from the traitorous Vate, Amergin, on the old man's deathbed.

It all seemed to make sense now. From his own recollections, Ren remembered Darragh tossing something to Ciarán as they opened the rift one time.

Well, that proved a spectacularly unsuccessful endeavour, given I'm standing here in this lost place with Marcroy's spy, while my brother and the girl we'd hoped to rescue are missing ...

The jewel he had tossed to Ciarán was Amergin's jewel — the same jewel the traitor had used to open the rift to send Ren into another world as a child — where Patrick Boyle just happened to be on set that day.

Ren had a fleeting thought that there might have been something coincidental in that, but didn't dwell on it. He had other, more immediate concerns. Like where was Darragh? And Sorcha? And Hayley?

It was still dark, so he couldn't tell much about where they were, other than inside a large stone circle surrounded by trees.

'Darragh and Sorcha are still in my reality,' he said, recalling Sorcha's shouted instruction to come back for them. Why had she done that? Was Darragh injured when he jumped from the moving car? Ren wanted to go back right now and find out.

'Almost certainly they're still there,' Trása agreed.

'Shit.'

'That's helpful,' Trása remarked.

'What happens if they get caught?'

'Then we'll have to go back and rescue them, won't we?' she said, cocking her head as she examined the strange symbols on the stones. 'As worlds go, Rónán, yours isn't that bad. I mean, even if they catch him and think he's you, they're not going to kill him, are they?'

'No,' Ren agreed, a little uncertainly. If Darragh tried to run from the cops, he could be shot, but Darragh should know that. As Ren now carried his brother's knowledge of his reality, so Darragh carried knowledge of Ren's. 'Probably not ... but still ...'

Trása rose to her feet and turned to look at him. 'First we have to find out where we are, then we have to figure out how to get back to your reality, then we have to find your brother —'

'And Sorcha,' Ren reminded her.

'If we must,' she agreed with some reluctance. 'And once we've done that, we have to find a way from your old world back to the one where you both belong, preferably before *Lughnasadh*, because that's when the Druid Council is going to transfer the power to the new heirs.'

Trása had summed up their predicament concisely. It wasn't a very encouraging assessment.

'So how long have we got?'

She shrugged. 'I dunno. A couple of weeks, maybe.'

'No pressure, then.'

'Hey,' Trása said, frowning. 'It wasn't my bright idea to go rift running to save your little friend. I'm just trying to help.'

'Ah, that's right. You didn't have anything to do with the fact that if they catch Darragh in my realm and think he's me, they're going to throw him in the slammer for twenty-five to life for murdering someone you killed, did you?'

'And kidnapping someone *you* decided to kidnap,' she reminded him. 'This mess isn't my fault, Rónán. If you'd just left well enough alone, Hayley would still be fine — blind, perhaps, but still fine — and you and your crazy brother would be doing what you're supposed to do, which is being the Undivided and keeping the peace with the *Tuatha Dé Danann*. And for the record,' she added, 'Darragh isn't going to be stuck in gaol. He'll be dead. Just like you. *Lughnasadh* is only a couple of weeks away.'

Ren couldn't argue with that logic, so he turned from Trása and bent down to look at the strange symbols on the nearest stone. There was no sign of the triskalion or any other recognisable Celtic symbol.

He did recognise them, however. 'This looks Japanese,' he said pointing to the nearest stone.

Trása stared at it for a moment and then shook her head. 'It can't be.'

'Are you saying it's impossible?'

'Well ... no ... It's just the *Youkai* ... they don't have the ability to open rifts.'

'Apparently, in this world, they do. Who are the *Youkai*, anyway?'

Trása turned in a circle, studying the carved symbols with a very puzzled expression. 'I suppose you could call them the Japanese *Tuatha Dé Danann*.'

'Wonderful!' Ren said. 'Ninja Faeries. I wonder if they're as much fun to deal with as your lot?'

She turned on him angrily. 'For your information —'

Trása's words were cut short by an arrow slicing the space between them. It shattered on the stone behind them, leaving a black-fletched stub and a scattering of splinters on the ground at their feet.

'Bloody hell!' Ren exclaimed. He grabbed Trása and pushed her to the ground as another arrow speared through the space where his head had been only moments before, this time sailing over the stones to thunk solidly into a nearby tree. He landed almost on top of Trása.

'I guess that answers the question about ninja Faeries,' he hissed, daring a look around, but he could see nothing in the dark.

'You don't know it's the *Youkai* shooting at us,' Trása said in low voice. 'Can you tell where it's coming from?'

'Over there,' Ren whispered, pointing to the right. 'If I —'

'There are horses coming,' she warned, as she lay stretched out flat on the ground.

'How can you tell?'

'Feel the ground.'

Ren placed his ear against the singed dirt of the stone circle. Sure enough, he could feel the ground vibrating with the approach of oncoming horsemen. And they were moving fast. Even he could tell that.

'How many?' he asked softly.

'Who cares?' she snapped back in a whisper. '*One* is too many!'

'We have to get out of here.'

'And go where?' she asked.

'That way,' he said, for no other reason than there seemed to be slightly more trees in that direction, which meant slightly more cover. 'Come on!' He scrambled to his feet, wishing it were a cloudy night. The moon was shining like a stadium light.

Why couldn't it have been raining in this reality, too?

He ran low and crouched across the burned ground with Trása at his heels, diving past the perimeter of the circle as soon as they reached it. He scrambled to a duck behind the nearest stone with Trása taking cover behind the one next to him. The trees were another few yards away, but he and Trása were protected, temporarily, by the stones.

'Now what?' Trása asked, flinching as another arrow slammed into the stone behind which she was crouched.

'Can you fly?'

'*What?*'

'If you can change into a bird, you could fly over there and find out what we're dealing with,' he said, ducking lower as another arrow shattered a few inches from his head.

'And be stuck in bird form again the moment I change,' she replied. 'Sorry, but I'm human right now and I'm staying that way until we're back in my reality and you've officially broken Marcroy's curse.'

Aerial surveillance had been a nice idea, Ren thought, but he couldn't blame her for not wanting to be stuck as a bird. Annoying and untrustworthy as she was, he needed Trása whole and able to communicate in a language that consisted of more than tweets and whistles, if he was ever going to get home — wherever home might be. Darragh needed him, and God knows what had happened to Hayley.

And they only had a couple of weeks before they were dead, if they hadn't found a way home by then.

Was Ciarán or Brógán explaining the concept of alternate realities to Hayley back in the other world, even as Ren tried to avoid being somebody's target practice in this one?

Or had she also been thrown into some bizarre alternate reality by the same explosion that sent Trása and him to this strange place where unseen assassins took pot shots at strangers appearing in their stone circles.

'Fine,' he told Trása impatiently, trying to judge how many seconds they would be in the open before they reached the trees. They couldn't risk it for long. He could hear the horses clearly now.

'When I say go, run for the trees. But don't run in a straight line.'

She nodded, sparing him a smile that made him fear she thought this was fun. 'Ready when you are.'

Another arrow cracked against the standing stones.

'Go!' he hissed, guessing it would take the sniper a few seconds to reload his bow. He took off in the direction he'd figured was the safest, just as the horsemen burst out of the trees ahead of them. They carried flaming torches and the riders wore heavy samurai armour. They also brandished katanas that would slice them to pieces in seconds if they resisted. Trása ran straight into them.

'*Kosan! Kosan!*' Ren shouted, throwing his hands up to show he was unarmed as the soldiers bore down on them, grateful for the whim that had made him decide to study Japanese at school last year. 'Say *kosan!*' he shouted to Trása. 'It means you surrender!'

'*Kosan! Kosan!*' she cried as she was knocked to the ground.

One of the samurai must have heard them because someone yelled, '*Yamero! Yamero!*'

The samurai ceased their attack, but immediately dismounted and rushed to overwhelm them, grabbing both Ren and Trása and pulling them to their feet. The leader of the troop, the one who'd ordered the others to stop, approached them on horseback. He stared at Ren for a moment and then at Trása.

'*Onushirano shogunho namaewo mouse?*' he demanded.

'What did he say?' Trása asked, as they dragged her over to stand beside Ren.

'I think he wants to know the name of our lord.' Ren looked up at the samurai and bowed as well as he could manage given the way he was being held.

'*Warewareniha shogunha imasen,*' he said politely. '*Warewareha mayoteiru tabinomonodesu.*' In the schoolboy Japanese Ren spoke, he'd told the samurai they had no lord, but were lost travellers. He fervently hoped it meant roughly the same thing in this realm.

The man glared at Ren, but it was hard to tell if he believed him or not. For that matter, it was hard to tell if the man even understood him. Like the Gaelige Ren had learned in his reality, it was possible the Japanese he'd been awarded a certificate for only a few months earlier was only a poor relation to the language spoken in this realm.

'*Sonomonotachiwo tsuretekoi,*' the man ordered, after debating the matter silently for a moment. '*Sonomonotachino unmeiha hemeni kimete itadaku.*'

'What did he say?' Trása asked.

'Something about letting the princess ... their *lady*? ... decide our fate. I think we're being taken to their leader.'

'You *think*? Don't you *know*?'

Ren never got a chance to answer. The soldiers shoved him forward toward a riderless horse. One of them bound his hands and then tied the rope to the saddle, and swung up onto his mount with an ease that belied the heavy armour he was wearing. Ren glanced across to see Trása similarly bound.

Bet she's wishing she'd changed into a bird and flown away now, he thought.

'The Autumn equinox is twelve days away, Ren!' Trása called after him as the soldiers jerked them forward, forcing them to trot along behind the horses. 'If we haven't found a way home by then, the Druids will dethrone you and Darragh, and invest the Undivided heirs as the new Undivided.'

'I know.' He had Darragh's memories now. The date was burned into his brother's brain.

'If that happens, you and Darragh won't just lose your power,' she warned as she stumbled beside him along the leaf-strewn forest floor. They were heading back through the trees, toward a row of faint lights at the foot of the hill. They weren't being dragged along behind the horses exactly, but Ren wasn't sure the samurai would stop if one of them fell. 'You'll die.'

'I know. I'll think of something.'

'You'd better,' Trása warned. 'I want to go home.'

Ren wanted that, too, but right now, stuck in a realm he didn't know anything about — a realm where he wasn't sure he spoke the language and with no notion of how he was going to get home — it seemed too much to deal with.

It was too early to decide what he had to do. Too early to make plans to escape. He had a few things going for him, though: things his captors knew nothing about.

He had a lifetime of his brother's memories in his head. He had a shape-changing half-*Beansídhe* on his side to aid his escape.

And Ren could feel the magic.

EPILOGUE

Brydie woke to a world that was tinted purple. For a while she lay on the hard, cold floor, trying to recall what had happened to her.

The last thing Brydie remembered was standing in Darragh's room, looking at herself in the tall polished bronze mirror. She was examining herself, wondering if she was pregnant yet. After their faltering start — once she'd been able to get him to spend the whole night in his chamber — Darragh had proved an excellent lover, and in the weeks since she began sharing his bed, they'd made love plenty of times, in between him sneaking out and disappearing to who-knows-where. Brydie had learned not to ask. Darragh wasn't going to tell her anyway, and her mission was to make a baby with Darragh of the Undivided, not keep track of his movements.

Had they done enough, she was wondering, to conceive?

Álmhath was anxious for a report. She'd sent a message, asking if Brydie's *mìosach* had come, or if she was with child yet. Brydie wasn't sure. She thought she might be a little late, but it was too early to tell.

Brydie turned sideways, thrusting her belly out, trying to picture herself heavy with child. She was almost eighteen, so she knew she was ready. Now was the safest time to have a child. Women who left it longer often had trouble, and many of them died, if there was no Druid healer to help them through the perils of childbirth. She smiled as she realised that fate would not befall her. If she was carrying a child of the Undivided, no risk would be allowed to endanger this child or prevent the child's mother bringing it to term.

She remembered having that thought ... but then the memory faded. There had been a noise, she thought ... had she turned to see if she was alone.

Perhaps she'd been attacked in Darragh's room, although it seemed unlikely. Deep within *Sí an Bhrú* was perhaps among the safest places on Earth for a woman.

But her memories stopped as she turned to investigate the noise ...

And she woke here, in this hazy purple world.

Brydie climbed to her feet and looked around. She seemed to be caught in a glassy bubble: the walls were faceted and as she looked out of each small window, she could see odd shapes outside the bubble that she couldn't quite identify.

Raising her hands to the glassy walls, Brydie realised she was imprisoned. Swallowing back a sudden surge of panic, she felt out the limits of her confinement. She could touch the walls on both sides. They were cold, smooth, translucent and tinged with mauve.

She pushed her face against the faceted window and tried to see out. After a moment she made sense of the shapes, and realised she could see Darragh's bed, but it was huge … much larger than she remembered. As she identified the bed, other familiar shapes took form. There was the side table. The lantern burning softly, filling the chamber with yellow light. And off to her left stood the big bronze mirror she'd been looking into.

Brydie glanced down then, and discovered that beneath her, she could make out the fine filigree knot-work of the brooch Marcroy Tarth had given her in the wagon on the way to *Sí an Bhrú*.

'Oh, by sweet *Danú*! I'm inside the brooch.'

She said it aloud, caught somewhere between wonder and terror. Her words echoed back at her, bouncing off the faceted walls.

She looked around and realised the odd shapes were the everyday items scattered about Darragh's chamber, made strange and terrifying by her reduced stature. She pounded on the walls, and shouted, knowing as she did that it was useless. If she was trapped here, then the brooch had been enchanted. Nobody would expect it. When they discovered she was missing nobody would think to look for her here.

She slumped down to the bottom of the jewel and tucked her knees under her chin. Was she trapped forever? Had Marcroy given her the brooch intending to trap her, or was it enchanted for some other purpose?

Will I starve to death, or will the magic that sucked me into the amethyst preserve my life?

Was it an accident? And if it isn't an accident … why am I here?

'You are here,' a voice boomed from every direction at once, so loudly she had to cover her ears, 'because I want to talk to you, young Brydie Ni'Seanan.'

Brydie pushed herself to her feet and looked around, but the jewelled cell was empty.

'Who are you?' she called out, afraid she sounded like a frightened child. 'What do you want with me?'

'I want to talk to you,' the voice boomed.

'About what?' she asked, her hands still over her ears to protect them from the pain of the jewel's voice.

'About the only thing I have any interest in, little human,' the voice told her, as the stone's walls darkened to a deeper shade of purple, a shade so deep they turned almost black.

Brydie forced her fear away, reasoning if the jewel had wanted to kill her, she'd be dead already. It wanted to talk. She knew something it wanted to know. That meant she had leverage. She wasn't an expert on enchantments and curses, but she knew *sídhe* law required every enchantment to have a loophole. The victim had to be allowed a way to escape, however obscure or unlikely.

'What do you want to know?' she asked warily, as she realised something else. The jewel hadn't trapped her, something else was possessing it. A *sídhe* of some kind, although probably not one she was familiar with.

'I want to know,' the voice informed her, fading to a more tolerable level, as a blue figure began to materialise, filling the space in front of her, 'what you know about Darragh of the Undivided.'

Brydie stared at the *sídhe* in horror. It was one of the Djinn. She'd never seen a djinni before, but she'd heard about them. And knew enough to fear him.

'What do you want to know, exactly?' she asked, pressing herself against the faceted wall, although there was no escaping the creature in the confines of her amethyst prison.

'Everything,' the djinni said. 'I want to know everything.'

THE WORLD OF THE FAERIE AND THE UNDIVIDED:

Proper names are in bold type
Name (Pronunciation) Description

A Mháistir (a MAW ster) Master.

A Mháistreás (a MAW stress) Mistress.

a Stóirín (Ah stor-een) Term of endearment.
Roughly translates as 'My love'.

Abbán (OB awn) One of the *marra-warra* people.
Trása's cousin.

Aintín (Ann-teen) Faerie word for Aunt.

Airgead sídhe (AR-gat Shee) Faerie silver. Fatal to
humans.

Álmhath (AWL uh va) Queen of the Celts; mother
of Torcán; Head of the *Matrarchaí*.

Amergin (aw-VEER-een) Vate of All Ireland until
his death; Trása's father.

Anwen (AN wen) Betrothed to Torcán.

Atilis (a TIL is) Gaulish lord.

Banphrionsa (ban frinsah) Princess.

Bealtaine (Byawl tuh nuh) Summer equinox.

Beansídhe (Ban-shee) Faerie with long hair and
red eyes due to continuous weeping. Their
wailing is a warning of a death in the vicinity.

Brionglóid Gorm (Bring-load gurm) Roughly translates as 'Blue Dreams'. Magic powder used by the Druids to induce instant unconsciousness.

Broc (brok) Undivided heir.

Brógán (BRO gawn) Druid healer.

Brydie Ni'Seanan (BRY dee nee SHAR nan) Celtic princess; niece of Álmhath; cousin of Torcán.

Cainte (KIN-cha) Master of magical chants and incantations.

Cairbre (CAR bry eh) Undivided heir.

Ciarán (KEER awn) Ciarán mac Connacht Warrior Druid.

Cillian (KIL ee an) Half-Faerie/Half-human *sídhe*.

Colmán (KUL mawn) Vate of All Eire; Amergin's successor.

Comhroinn (KOH-rinn) Name of the sharing ceremony that transfers knowledge between Druids.

Danú (DA nu) The goddess worshipped by both Faerie and Druid alike.

Daoine sídhe (Deena Shee) 'People of the Mounds'; refers to the Faerie race as a whole; also known as the *Tuatha*.

Darragh (DA-ra) Druid prince; one half of the Undivided.

Éamonn (AY mun) Elimyer's latest lover.

Eblana (e BLAN a) Druid name for Dublin.

eileféin (Ella-phane) The alternate reality version of oneself.

Elimyer (Ellie-MY-ah) Trása's mother; *leanan sídhe* who becomes Amergin's muse.

Ethna (EN ya) court maiden of Queen Álmhath's court.

Farawyl (Farra-will) Druidess and High Priestess of *Sí an Bhrú*.

Hayley Boyle (Hay-lee Boil) Daughter of Patrick Boyle and his first wife, Jane, stepdaughter of Kerry Boyle.

Imbolc (Im-bolk) Spring equinox.

Jamaspa (j'MAS puh) *Djinni*. One of the lords of the Djinn.

Leanan sídhe (Lan-awn Shee) A Faerie muse of exquisite beauty who offers inspiration, fame and glory to an artist in exchange for his life force.

Leath tiarna (Lah teer na) Half-Lord.

Leipreachán (LEP-ra-cawn) One of the lesser faeries.

Liaig (LEE eye) Druid healer.

Lughnasadh (LOON-a-sah) Autumn equinox.

Malvina (mal VEE na) Druidess attached to Queen Álmhath's court; one of the *Matrarchaí*.

Marra-Warra (MA ra WOR ra) Sea-people also known as the Walrus People.

Marcroy (MARK-roy) Lord of the Tarth Mound. Elimyer's brother.

Máthair (Mahar) Faerie word for Mother.

Matrarchaí (MAT tra ky) The Matriarchs; secret society of Druidesses devoted to preserving the Undivided bloodline.

Merlin (MER lin) Head Druid in Britain; second only in power among the Druids to the Vate of All Eire.

Mogue Ni'Farrell (moag nee FARRELL) Mother of Brydie; one of the *Matrarchaí*.

Muir Éireann (myooer AIR an) The Irish Sea.

Niamh (Neeve) Druidess.

Oceanus Britannicus (O shee ARN us Bree TAN ee coos) Roman name of the English Channel.

Orlagh (OR-la) Queen of the Faerie.

Ossian (Ocean) Druid stationed in Brydie's father's *ráith*.

Prionsa (Frin-sah) Prince.

Ráith (rawth) Ring fort consisting of a circular area enclosed by a timber or stone wall with a ditch on the outside called a cashel.

Rónán ((French variant — Renan)) Druid prince; one half of the Undivided.

Samhain (Sow-en) Winter equinox.

Shillelagh (Shil-lay-lee) Short gnarled club, usually fashioned from a tree root. Commonly made with a knobbed head they often serve a dual purpose as a walking stick.

Sídhe (Shee) Common name for the Faerie race in general.

Siuil linn a (shool-leen ah) 'Walk with us …' Druid ceremonial chant invoking their gods and goddesses.

Sorcha (Shore-shah) Druid warrior.

Sybille (S'BILL) Mother of the Undivided; one of the *Matrarchaí*.

Tír Na nÓg (Tear na knowg (with a hard g)) Land of Perpetual Youth; the traditional home of the *Tuatha Dé Danann*.

Torcán (TURK awn) Prince of the Celts; son of Álmhath.

Trása (TRAY-sah) Trása Ni'Amergin; half-Faerie/half-Druid offspring of Amergin and Elimyer.

Tuatha Dé Danann (Tua Day Dhanna)
    Commonly known as the Fae, Faerie or Fairy;
    also known as: Children of the Goddess Danú,
    the True Race, or the *Daoine sidhe*.
Uncail (UN cayl) Faerie word for Uncle.
Vate (VART eh) Druid; second only in power
    to the Undivided. Acts as regent when the
    Undivided are not yet come of age at their
    ascension to power.

THE DARK DIVIDE
Rift Runners: Book Two

Journey through a Britain where the Druids are the most powerful magical force on Earth.

The Dark Divide is the second book in the Rift Runners trilogy, an exciting contemporary epic fantasy spanning different realities and alternate worlds.

THE TIDE LORDS

Praise for THE TIDE LORDS

'a multi-hued tapestry of myth, deceit and ambition'
Publishers Weekly

'exceptional storytelling' *Good Reading*

'a rollercoaster ride of mortal and immortal
machinations' *Nexus*

THE HYTHRUN CHRONICLES

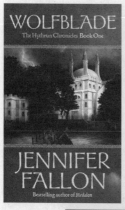
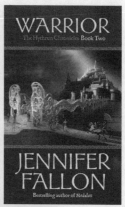

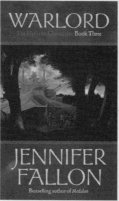

Praise for Jennifer Fallon

'[Jennifer Fallon] captures the reader from the opening paragraph and you can only break from her grasp when you reach the final page' *Altair*

'Intrigues, rivalries and romance provide an entertaining angle' *Publishers Weekly*

'intrigue and excitement by handfuls' *SF Review*

THE DEMON CHILD TRILOGY

'A la JRR Tolkien
[*Medalon* is] a story to
rival the grandest of
fantasy epics …
Like a tranquil woodland
pond in the heat of
summer, once readers are
immersed in the magical
realm of *Medalon* they
will find it extremely
difficult to leave.'
Barnes&Noble.com
Explorations

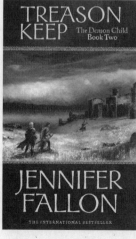

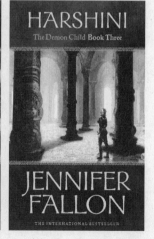

THE SECOND SONS TRILOGY

'one of those rare
hybrids, an SF plot
compounded with the
in-depth characterization
of a good fantasy tale'
Robin Hobb

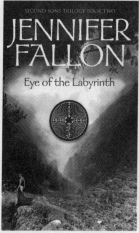